Amish

WOMEN OF LAWRENCE COUNTY

~TRILOGY~

Books 1-3

Tracy Fredrychowski

ISBN 979-8-9906105-6-9 (paperback)
ISBN 979-8-9906105-5-2 (digital)

Cover Design by Tracy Lynn Virtual, LLC

All Bible verses are taken from New Life Version Bible (NLV) and the New King James Version (NKJV)

Published in South Carolina by The Tracer Group, LLC
https://tracyfredrychowski.com

A NOTE ABOUT AMISH VOCABULARY

The language the Amish speak is Pennsylvania Dutch, usually spoken rather than written. The spelling of commonly used words varies from community to community throughout the United States and Canada. Even as I did research for this book, the spelling of some words changed within the same Amish community that inspired this story. In one case, spellings were debated between family members. Some of the words may have slightly different spellings, but all come from the interactions I've had with the people in the Amish settlement near where I was raised in northwestern Pennsylvania.

While this book was modeled upon a small Amish community in Lawrence County, this is a work of fiction. The names and characters are products of my imagination and do not resemble any person, living or dead, or actual events that took place in that community.

***

The Amish are a religious group that is typically referred to as Pennsylvania Dutch, Pennsylvania Germans or Pennsylvania Deutsch. They are descendants of early German immigrants to Pennsylvania and their beliefs center around living a conservative lifestyle. They arrived between the late 1600s and the early 1800s to escape religious persecution in Europe. They first settled in Pennsylvania with the promise of religious freedom by William Penn. Most Pennsylvania Dutch still speak a variation of their original German language and English.

GLOSSARY OF PENNSYLVANIA DUTCH "DEUTSCH" WORDS

Ausbund. Amish songbook.
boppli. Baby.
bruder. Brother
datt. Father or dad.
denki. "Thank You."
doddi. Grandfather.
doddi haus. A small house usually next to the main house.
fraa. Wife.
g'may. Community.
haus. House.
ja. "Yes."
kapp. Covering or prayer cap.
kinner. Children.
mamm. Mother or mom.
mei lieb. "My love."
mommi. Grandmother.
mun. Husband.
nee. "No."
Ordnung. Order or set of rules the Amish follow.
rumshpringa. "Running around" period.
schwester. Sister.
singeon. Singing/youth gathering.

CONTENTS

Emma's

Amish Faith Tested

THE AMISH WOMEN OF
LAWRENCE COUNTY SERIES - BOOK 1

PROLOGUE

October – Willow Springs, Pennsylvania

Emma Yoder snuggled in close to her husband, Samuel, and rested her hand on his arm. She took in the slow rise of his chest and thanked God for all the blessings He provided during their first year of marriage. Trying not to wake him, she listened as the winter wind whistled around the small doddi haus they called home. Samuel and her bruder, Daniel, were spending long hours building their new house in the field next to Samuel's parents. No heat and short days were making progress slow.

In the wee hours right before dawn, Emma treasured the few moments of her husband's warmth before the alarm jolted him from slumber. As she lifted her knee and laid it across his thigh, a small jolt from her protruding tummy woke him.

In a raspy voice next to her ear Samuel said, "I swear that boy will come out running."

She moved her cheek to his chest, "What makes you so sure it's a boy?"

He moved a wisp of her honey blonde hair from his chin and kissed the top of her head. "Wishful thinking, I guess."

Emma knew his heart was set on a baby boy, and she hoped and prayed if it was a girl, he'd love her the same.

Samuel turned on his side until their noses touched. He kissed the center of her forehead and squeezed her tight. "You've made me the happiest man." Reaching between them, he patted her stomach. "This child is one of many that will fill our new home."

She lifted her head and kissed his chin. "I hope you still say that when the restless nights and diapers pile up."

A nervous giggle emerged from him. "Deprived of sleep, no problem. Diapers? I might need to go to the barn if I'm called to change too many of those."

Emma lifted her hand and pushed his chest, making him fall to his back. "Oh no, we're in this together! Cries, diapers, teething, colic, and bad behavior ...the whole gamut. If I don't get to pick and choose, neither do you!"

She rolled off the bed and grabbed her robe to cover her white cotton nightdress, as he engulfed her in a hug from behind. He nuzzled her neck with warm kisses and muttered. "I think I'd like to stay right here for the day."

"Oh no, you don't; you have a house to work on and chores to do."

She stood to flip her robe around her shoulders as Samuel rolled from the bed. He slapped her bottom and said, "I'll start the coffee."

Emma reached for the hairbrush, sat down on the bed, and undid the long braid that fell over her shoulder. With each stroke through her waist-length hair, she said a prayer of gratefulness. Her life, as she saw it, was perfect. Samuel was the man of her dreams; a new house, her best friend and sister-in-law Katie Miller living across the street, and she was seven months pregnant with their first child. In her eyes, God had truly blessed her. With her hair still down, she pulled her robe closed and headed to the kitchen. The white porcelain pot on the stove had already started to gurgle as Samuel set two cups on the counter.

She filled a tiny pitcher with cream and sat it near his place at the head of the table, and asked, "What are your plans today?"

"Daniel and I are going to work on the kitchen. He's been a big help, and if we keep at it, we'll be able to move in by the time the baby comes. But first, we have to pick up the kitchen cupboards from your datt's shop. If all goes well, we'll get those hung today."

Emma pulled both hands up to her chin and clapped as a smile encased her face.

Samuel responded to her enthusiasm, "I guess by that little happy dance, you're excited."

"Now, understand, I love living here, but to have my own kitchen and one you built for me, for sure and certain is a woman's dream."

"I'll hang cupboards every day if it keeps that smile on your face."

She poured the hot brown liquid into his cup and set the kettle on a trivet in the middle of the table. He pulled her into his lap. "I still think I should stay home today."

"No, not that again!" She pushed herself back up.

"I have work to do, and so do you. Katie's coming over; we're working on a new baby quilt, and I want to make some gingersnaps before she gets here. Let me make you breakfast so you can get out of here, and I can get to work."

"So, Katie comes, and I'm out the door. I see how I rank!"

She slapped him with the towel. "Don't be silly. No one is more important than you."

***

Samuel whistled as he pulled on his boots and pushed his bangs back before covering them with his black felt hat. He winked at Emma and closed the door behind him. An early winter storm left the steps and sidewalk with six inches of fresh snow, covering up a thin layer of ice. He skimmed the porch for the snow shovel and bucket of salt but remembered he'd left it on the back stoop. He didn't take the time to shovel it and caught himself slipping on the icy steps before heading to the barn.

Samuel tipped his head to block the wind as he ducked inside the metal building. His new family buggy sat just inside the door amongst the implements used for strawberry season. Wishing he could take the enclosed carriage instead of the open wagon, he effortlessly lifted a shaft in each hand and backed the cart out the double doors. Before he had a chance to walk to the horse barn, Emma called his name from the front porch.

She held up a thermos. "Samuel, your coffee."

Before he had a chance to holler back, the steps were slippery, he saw a flash of white as her nightclothes, and wheat-colored hair spilled to the ground.

"Emma... nooooo!"

As if in slow motion, he ran to the crumpled form lying at the bottom of the steps. He knelt, placed his hand under the back of

Emma's head, and felt warmth penetrating his glove. His bellowing scream pierced the frozen air. "Heeeelp!"

CHAPTER 1

Mamm always said we have no control over the words that fill the pages of our book, and only God holds the pen. If I could re-write my story, I would erase the past thirty days for certain.

No matter how hard I try, the only comfort I find these days is when I sit at the foot of these two wooden crosses. Samuel doesn't seem to understand my need to spend time here, and he's afraid I'm not surrendering to God's will. There must be more to following the Lord than succumbing to His will.

Quite frankly, I'm sick of hearing about God's will. I've had more than one well-meaning neighbor tell me how and what I should be feeling. While I'm grateful for the outpouring of support they've shown, how can most know anything about losing a child? For seven months, I carried James inside of me as he grew in anticipation of life, but in a split-second, he was gone.

Even now, as the cold penetrates my wool stockings' I yearn to hold him. My only comfort comes from laying him to rest on top of *Mamm's* grave. When I close my eyes, I imagine her snuggling him and keeping him warm when I can't. When reality hits, I'm reminded his cold, lifeless body was left to decay in the earth, much like my hopes and dreams for his future.

Not even the sun that warmed the earth the day we put James to rest could melt the ice lodged around my heart. I still remember the look of pity etched on the faces of my family and friends on that October morning.

Samuel held me up, as I shook, and we watched the pint-size pine coffin being placed in the ground. I couldn't move and prayed I'd wake up from the horrible nightmare as Samuel whispered in my ear. "God willing, this will be the hardest day we'll ever have to face."

Placing a child in a pine box changes you. I don't know how it couldn't. Even the dirt hitting the wood reminded me of all the things we wouldn't experience.

Thud.

No first smiles.

Thud.

No first steps.

Thud.

No first words.

Thud.

In the days that followed, my family and friends surrounded me, and I felt their love. In reality, I knew I wasn't left alone to bear the weight of our loss, but I pushed them all away. Especially Katie. Now the mere sight of her protruding belly makes me cringe. Doesn't she realize what we once had will never be again? Just being around her is exhausting. It takes every ounce I have to pretend I enjoy her company. I wish she would stop coming by. I suppose with her being family and all, that won't happen.

Maybe Samuel is right. I need to stop coming here. Is it helping? Probably not since I haven't seen another person in this cemetery in the four weeks I've been making my daily visits. Am I the only one who can't let go? Or maybe I'm the only Amish woman in these parts going against all we've been taught, like hiding our pain under layers and layers of fake smiles and forced hellos. If one more person tells me God makes no mistakes, I'll scream. Because in this case, He did, and I'm not sure I'll ever get over it.

Look at me, sitting here alone on the cold ground talking to myself; Samuel thinks I'm losing my mind, and I have to agree. Nothing he says comforts me, and I can feel him pulling away. How do couples survive this? Nobody should bury their child; it's just not right. I don't care what they say, I'm not yielding to God's will, I won't do it!

***

Walking the twenty minutes down Mystic Mill Road and back toward home, I pulled my heavy brown bonnet tighter around my chin.

Snow from the dark clouds overhead started to cover the ground that reminded me of that fretful day just thirty days earlier. Alone with my grief, I screamed to the sky.

"What did you gain by taking him from me? You could have let him live. Why?"

***

Pittsburgh Memorial Hospital, 30 Days Earlier - October 15th

Caught somewhere between sleep and a dream, Emma tried to open her eyes to no avail. Voices in the room told her she wasn't alone, but she struggled to shake free from the hold unconsciousness had on her. An unfamiliar scent filled her nose, and the pounding in her head left her frozen in the strange surroundings. A constant beep replaced the murmur, and a gentle squeeze to her fingertips preceded a raspy whisper near her ear.

"Emma, please come back to me. Please, my love, wake up."

The urgency in Samuel's voice alarmed her, and she pushed through the last layer of darkness. Moving her thumb over the side of his finger, she turned her head toward his voice.

"Thank God, you're back."

Without opening her eyes, she asked, "Where am I?"

"At the hospital. Don't move; you have a nasty cut on the back of your head, and you have a concussion."

There was a heaviness in the room that told her all she needed to know long before she moved her hand to her sunken middle. She gave up the fight to open her eyes and drifted back to a place where only dreams would come true.

***

Samuel stood at the window in Emma's room overlooking the busy Pittsburgh highway. With each passing car, life went on, oblivious to his pain and the guilt he felt. The scene from four hours earlier played in his head. The pool of blood left in the snow from the gash on Emma's head wasn't half as bad as the puddle that seeped from her night dress when he picked her up. He was certain traces were still visible long after the ambulance had been summoned. With limited access to telephone and transportation, it took over an hour to get her help. The fall down the icy steps caused a placental abruption, and their baby died in the womb from a lack of oxygen. Even an emergency c-section didn't help in saving their first child's life. Because of his neglect, his son was gone, and he'd put his wife in danger. Collapsing in the brown leather chair, he buried his head in his hands and cried out.

"Please, Lord, help me make sense of all of this. If this is your will. Give me the wisdom to accept it gracefully no matter how hard it is, and please help Emma wake up in time to say goodbye to our son. Amen"

When he lifted his face from his hands, Emma's eyes fluttered open. She turned her hand over and wiggled her fingers for him to come closer. He scurried to her bedside, fell to his knees, and laid his head on her chest. Her warmth comforted him for just a minute before the door opened and a nurse entered carrying a small blue bundle.

"I have him ready and can give you about an hour."

Samuel stood and held out his arms as the older woman laid the lifeless body in the crook of his elbow.

"Your family just arrived. I told them to give you both a few minutes alone with him. Do you want me to hold them off longer?"

"No, Emma will want to see them."

The nurse hesitated and then whispered, "I know how hard it is, but you both need to say your goodbyes quickly."

Without responding, he turned to face his wife.

They had made so many plans about how they would welcome their first child into the world, but none of them included this. Now standing at her bedside, all he could do was offer her a glimpse of what could have been.

She turned her head and moved her arm, so he could tuck the tiny-wrapped figure under her chin.

In a rattled whisper, she cried, "Oh, my baby, I'm sorry I failed you."

A sob lodged in the back of Samuel's throat as his wife took his blame. No words would come as Emma ran her finger over the child's transparent skin and examined his tiny fingers. When he didn't think he could manage another moment, she kissed his forehead and cried. "See you soon, sweet boy."

Her hollow brown eyes told him he was free to take him from her arms. When he scooped him up, she closed her eyes and turned further into her pillow and wept.

As long as he lived, he'd never forget the look in her eyes. Seeing her suffer so desperately with no relief in sight was dreadful. All he could do was dig deep into his faith and remember what he'd been taught ...many things in life were not meant to be understood. It wasn't his job to question God's plan but to humbly submit to His timing, no matter the circumstances.

***

It had been well over a month since she held her son in her arms, and even though she never felt his warm skin against her own, she ached to hold him. The wind whistled as it ran through the leafless trees, wrapping itself with a vengeance around her shoulders. Her heart ran cold, much like Willow Creek and its icy banks. Taking shelter under the timbers of the old, covered bridge, she let her voice bounce off the trusses in an agonizing cry. "Lord, why did you take James from me? Tell me why."

When nothing but silence filled the air, she followed the sound of Samuel and Daniel's hammers home. It wouldn't be long before they could move from the small *doddi haus* into the spacious farmhouse Samuel had worked hard to complete. The excitement had long-lost its appeal, and it was all she could do to pull herself out of bed, let alone think about moving into their new home without a child to fill it.

Emma sighed when she saw Ruth, her mother-in-law, walking to the mailbox. If she could only find a way to melt into the landscape and go home unnoticed. Ruth meant well, and her concern was genuine, but she was the last person Emma wanted to deal with on days like today.

Ruth waved. "How are you?"

Emma smiled but didn't answer.

Ruth placed her hand on Emma's arm. "There comes a time when living in the past is worse than living in the present."

Emma didn't need to ask Ruth to explain; she knew exactly what she was referring to. Samuel had made it very clear he wasn't happy about her daily visits to the cemetery, and she was sure he shared his concern with his parents.

Ruth wrapped her arm around Emma's shoulders and guided her down the driveway. "Come inside. I have something I want to give you."

Emma's feet moved, and she tried not to let the heaviness in her shoulders melt Ruth's gentle touch. It was one thing to wallow in self-pity, but to let her darkened mood spill over to Ruth was another thing altogether. She followed Ruth up the steps and closed the door behind them. Warmth encircled her as she took off her wool coat and pushed the wrinkles out of her black cape dress. Slipping out of her boots, she placed them neatly on the mat beside the door before following Ruth to the kitchen.

Ruth pointed to the stove. "Put on the kettle for tea while I run upstairs. I'll be right back."

Emma carried the white porcelain pot to the sink and blew out a long breath. The last thing she wanted was to make small talk with Samuel's mother. Waiting for the water to fill, she glanced out the window to see Katie making her way around the house to the back door. Emma's stomach lurched when Katie's waddle reminded her that Katie would be celebrating her own new arrival soon.

Snow swirled in under Katie's feet as she struggled to close the door with the basket she was carrying.

Emma rushed to her side. "Let me help."

"Thank you. I didn't realize this was so heavy when I decided to cart it all the way here. But then everything feels heavier these days."

Emma forced a smile and turned her back toward the sink. "Your *mamm* and I were just about to have tea. Would you like some?"

Katie plopped down in the closest chair and continued taking off her bonnet and mittens. "I stopped over at your house this morning. I was hoping we could spend the day together sorting through some recipes."

Emma took three cups from the cupboard and the wooden box filled with tea and placed them on the table. "I went for a walk."

Katie blew into her cupped hands and looked at Emma. "I would have gone with you."

How could she explain to Katie that the very sight of her expanding middle sent her down a spiraling tunnel of despair? Before she had a chance to come up with a response, Ruth made her way back to the kitchen carrying a large white box.

"Katie, what a nice surprise. I didn't hear you come in."

Katie turned toward her mother's voice. "I brought over all my recipe books. I was hoping we could go through them to find some new recipes to try before the bakery opens back up." Katie ran small circles across her belly with the palm of her hand. "I'm a bit restless, and I'm trying to keep busy while we wait on this little one to arrive."

Without realizing it, Emma let out a small moan and covered her mouth with her hand as soon as it escaped her lips.

Katie reached her hand across the table and squeezed Emma's forearm. "I'm so sorry."

Emma pulled away. "You have nothing to be sorry about."

Ruth pulled the cover off the box in front of her. "I think trying a few new recipes is just what the doctor ordered for a day like today. But first, I have something I need to give to Emma."

She pushed the box across the table and pulled a chair up beside her. "I've been trying to find the right time to give this to you. The summer you were in Sugarcreek visiting your biological family, your mother crocheted three shawls. One for you, and one for both Rebecca and Anna. She knew there would come a time when each of you would need to feel her close. She knew then that her time on earth was short. I promised to give it to each of you when I felt you needed a piece of her the most."

Emma pulled the tightly weaved yarn from the box and held it to her cheek. The softness against her skin reminded her of her mothers' touch. Closing her eyes, she moved it to her nose, hoping a little piece of her lingered between the fibers. Deeply etched in the stitches, the faint sweetness of cherry and almonds tickled her nose. For sure and certain, it was the familiar scent of her *mamm's* hand lotion. Ruth slid a pink envelope across the table and motioned for Katie to follow her to the other room.

Tears clouded Emma's eyes as she recognized her *mamm's* delicate penmanship. Laying the cream-colored shawl across her lap, she reached for the letter.

Emma,

While I am not there to help you in this most challenging time, you need to know there is someone you can lean on. Someone who I did not get to know until just a short time ago. My heart aches that I will not be there to share the truth with you. Please know you are good enough, and you will see life without pain and turmoil in heaven, regardless of how obedient you were on earth. But first, you must let Jesus into your heart and rely on Him for your salvation.

This may confuse you for a short time. But regardless of the turmoil it may cause, search for the truth in Jesus.

My prayer is that you will wrap yourself in this shawl and remember my words as you search for a relationship with Jesus. He is there to help you every step of the way ...all you have to do is ask.

All my love,
Mamm

Emma placed the letter back in its holder, tucked it deep inside the box, folded the shawl, and secured it beneath the layers of tissue paper. She slipped her feet in her boots and tied her coat and bonnet before heading out the door. Without looking back, Emma held her *mamm's* gift in her gloved hands and walked home. A single tear rolled down her cheek as she whispered, *"I'm not sure how Jesus can help me through any of this. It's my fault. I must have done something to upset God for Him to take James from me. I don't understand and I have no energy to search for the truth you speak of. I just wish you were here to explain it all to me. Oh,* Mamm, *I miss you so!"*

CHAPTER 2

Katie stood at the window and sipped her tea as Emma walked down the driveway.

"I don't know what to do. I keep trying to reach out, but she keeps pushing me away. Even Daniel has tried, but we can't seem to make any headway with her."

Ruth moved a stack of fabric from the chair near the window so her daughter could sit. "You have to realize she may be having a hard time connecting with you right now. You shared the one thing that was taken from her. In her eyes, you are a constant reminder of all she lost. Give her some time; she'll come around."

Katie sat up straight and rubbed her lower back. "I miss her."

Ruth picked up a pair of scissors and cut around the paper pattern pinned to the black broadcloth fabric that would soon be a new pair of pants for her husband, Levi.

"It's hard to watch someone you care about go through something like this. All you can do is be there for her. I learned a long time ago that the one thing a person needs when something so traumatic happens is just time. Time to grieve. Time to heal. And time to accept the outcome."

"But it's been over a month, and I don't see her coming to terms with any of it."

Ruth sat in the chair behind the black treadle sewing machine. "You have to realize that losing a child is like losing a part of yourself. Your arms ache to hold the one thing that grew under your heart for so long. We might not always understand God's ways, but we must believe He has a plan, even when we can't see a way out of our grief. That's what Emma is going through right now. She can't figure out a way to escape her heartache, and she blames herself."

Katie shifted in the chair and rested her hand across her belly. "I thought talk of opening the bakery back up would help occupy her mind some. But I'm not even excited about that. I just don't know what to say. What do you say to a mother who came home childless?"

Ruth unpinned the brown paper from the fabric and slipped it under the sewing foot of the machine. Using her hands to guide the material, she pumped the treadle to put the needle in motion. "Not much you can say. All you can do is listen when she is ready to talk. Maybe the letter from Stella will help."

Katie stood back at the window that overlooked her parents' farm. From her mother's upstairs sewing room, she had views of both her and Daniel's house across the street, along with the tiny house next to the barn where Emma and Samuel were living.

"So much sadness in her eyes. I'm not sure any of us will get through to her. Even with Christmas being just a few weeks away, I find it hard to be excited for much of anything with Emma feeling so poorly."

Slowing the treadle machine down while she turned the fabric to sew the next seam, Ruth added, "Maybe I should write to Marie. A girl needs her mother at a time like this. With Stella being gone, maybe her biological mother can help pull her through this when we can't. Marie couldn't make it for the funeral with her husband's mother being so ill, but maybe she can come now."

"What a great idea. Emma loves Marie. A visit from her might be just what she needs. Maybe if she can't come here, Emma could go to Sugarcreek. A few days away from all the memories would help. It would give Daniel and Samuel a chance to put in some long hours on the house. They could have it done by the time she got back. That would cheer her up for sure."

Katie walked to her mother and placed a kiss on her cheek. "Thanks, *Mamm*, you always know the right thing to do."

"Now, don't get ahead of yourself. I'm not sure if Marie can come, or if she'd be up for a visit from Emma with her being so busy taking care of her mother-in-law. But I'll send a letter right off to her this afternoon."

Katie walked to the door and said, "I best go home to Daniel. He'll be coming in for lunch soon, and I want to tell him of your plans. I'll be praying all the way home it works out, and we see a smile on Emma's face again real soon."

***

Emma carried the box to the top of the stairs and stood in the hallway between the bedroom she shared with Samuel and the closed door of the child she never welcomed home. Pushing the slightly ajar door to her room open with her hip, she dropped the box on the bed and flipped the cover off. Her mother's note fell to the floor. Picking up the handmade item and draping it around her shoulders, she curled up in a ball at the foot of her bed. She couldn't even find the strength to cry again in the nightmare that wouldn't stop. Burying her head deeper in the crook of her arm, she murmured, *"I'm so confused. What are you trying to teach me, Mamm? Losing James is too much to bear. I'm too tired to figure your message out. My heart hurts so bad ...the pain is unbearable. I just want to be with you...and James."*

Sleep once again dulled the pain.

***

Like being dragged from the murky waters of a deep pond, Emma pulled herself to a sitting position when she heard Samuel's voice.

"Emma? Where are you?"

Without answering, she neatly folded the shawl and placed it back inside the box. Scooting it under the bed, she picked up the pink envelope and tucked it in her apron pocket before heading to the door. Willing herself to face the tension that had built up between her and Samuel, she filled her lungs with a deep breath and followed his call.

Avoiding his eyes, she brushed by him and moved to the stove. "I didn't give much thought to dinner. I hope tomato soup and toasted cheese is okay?"

The chair's wooden legs scraped across the polished pine floor as he pulled it away from the table and patted the chair next to him. "Come sit. We need to talk."

A heaviness in the air magnified his words to a point she had no choice but comply.

"Bishop Weaver paid me a visit today."

"And?"

"He asked about you and how you were feeling."

"That was nice of him, but I'm sure he had more to say."

"He did. He saw you revisiting the cemetery and is concerned I'm not leading my family in the ways of the *Ordnung*. He made it clear that the rules of our ways are to be followed, in both good and bad times."

She twisted the towel in her hands and waited for him to finish.

"He firmly but politely informed me that I must stop you from visiting James' graveside. He is afraid the community will take it as if you are not trusting in God's plan. Which will not be healthy for the members of the church."

In a soft whisper, she asked, "How is it anyone's business how I spend my days?"

"It is not our way, and the bishop won't tolerate your outward display. Just as we are to forgive our neighbors, he expects you to forgive God and accept whatever He places in front of us with grace and humility. Emma, He knows best, I'm sure of it."

Emma stood, pushed her chair in with more force than necessary, and walked to the sink, holding herself up by cupping the edge of the basin. "I refuse to push James so far from my mind I forget what his face looked like. How dare he think my pain is so shallow that I can move past it in a few short weeks?"

Samuel walked up behind her and wrapped his arms around her middle. "Your pain is real; I feel it too. But we must trust God makes no mistakes."

Rotating from his embrace, she snarled. "Not you too! How can you accept our son's death so easily? He was a living person for seven months; right here under my heart. We felt him kick, we talked to him, we made plans for his future. And in a moment, God took him from us, without even giving us a chance to hold his warm body. How can that be from God? And if it was, we must have done something to anger Him!"

Samuel tried to pull her in close, but she pushed him away and ran to the steps, only stopping to look his way for a moment. "You both can stifle my sorrow from the community, but you can't shield my heart from the pain I feel in these empty arms and full bosom. I'll never accept it. I won't. I promise you that!"

Her bare feet slapped against the cold wooden steps and didn't stop until the bedroom door rattled against its hinges.

Samuel laid his head on his folded arms on the edge of the table. How was he ever going to help Emma through this? Guilt magnified every time he saw the pain in her eyes. Maybe she was right. Perhaps, they had done something to upset God. Why else would he take their son from them?

His mind raced ...

If only he had worked harder.

If only he had followed the rules better.

If only he would have salted the steps.

If only he had remembered to pick up his thermos.

If only he would have ...what? Anything but be the one responsible?

The fear of not knowing what to do was exhausting, but the sound of Emma crying herself to sleep each night was heart-wrenching. It was almost more than he could handle. He knew he should go upstairs and comfort her, but instead, he grabbed his hat off the hook by the back door and went to work.

***

By the time Emma woke from her sleep-induced coma, the day had turned into night. A chill in the house reminded her she needed to add coal to the furnace, and a growl in her tummy prompted her to start supper. Brushing the sleep from her eyes, she focused on the windup clock on the nightstand. Ten o'clock? Turning toward Samuel's side of the bed, she felt his spot. The cold sheets told her he must have retreated to the daybed set up in the front room. After her earlier outburst, she couldn't blame him. But sleeping all afternoon and through supper was unacceptable, even if she had lost her desire to be a good wife.

There was an icy edge to the air, and she wondered why Samuel hadn't stoked the fire. Pulling the extra blanket from the foot of the bed and wrapping it around her shoulders, she headed downstairs. Not even the moon against the snow-covered ground filtered light into the pitch-black kitchen. She fumbled, lighting the lantern above the table, and knocked a jar of peanut butter across the table. By the looks of it, Samuel had fixed himself a sandwich before turning in. A sudden urge to find comfort in her husband's arms forced her to walk to the front room. His blanket and pillow were still neatly folded in the same spot they had been earlier. It was after ten, where could he be? She certainly couldn't blame him if he didn't want to come home. Half the time, she didn't want to be there herself.

***

Daniel had long left, and Samuel struggled to fasten the last cabinet to the wall by himself. After installing the furnace ducts two days ago, he could light a fire in the coal stove in the basement. If he couldn't help Emma, he could at least work hard to finish their new home before Christmas. He hoped the new house would avert her attention away from James and back to the present. There was no doubt in his mind he was working in survival mode, but it was the only thing he knew he could control.

His earlier conversation with Bishop Weaver left him feeling inadequate as a husband and leader of his family. Thoughts of how he failed Emma consumed every waking minute. Throwing himself into the house was all he knew how to do.

The back door swung open, and a burst of snow swirled around his father's feet.

"Boy, what are you doing still working? You should be home with Emma."

"I could turn it around. You should be home with *Mamm*."

"I saw the light on over here and wanted to check on you. Whatever you're working on can wait until tomorrow."

"I wanted to finish hanging this last cupboard, then I was going to call it a day."

Levi picked up the drill and tightened the last two screws while Samuel held it in place. He leaned into the battery-operated drill and asked, "Jacob did a great job. Has Emma seen them yet?"

"She has no interest in seeing what her father crafted for us."

"Your *Mamm* made her come in for tea this morning, but she left as soon as she opened Stella's gift."

Samuel checked the level one more time before stepping back. "A gift from her mother? She didn't mention it. But I suppose I didn't give her a chance before I told her about my visit with the bishop."

Levi picked up some tools off the floor and laid them on the counter. "I saw his buggy here this morning. I assumed he was checking on your progress."

"He did walk through the house, but he was more concerned about my control over my household."

Levi leaned back on the counter and crossed his arms over his chest. "What?"

"It doesn't look good to the community if Emma is still holding on to the past. He's afraid she hasn't succumbed to God's will. He was sympathetic to her pain but advised me to forbid her from making any more trips to the cemetery."

Levi furrowed his eyebrows. "That's why they encourage daily visits from the community. If she's struggling, she needs to accept the help from those checking in on her. No one should be alone in times like this. Has she let any of the women visit?"

"No, and they stopped coming. Emma let them in the first few days, but she refused to answer the door after that. She's even shut Katie out."

Samuel sat on the rung of the ladder. "I don't know what to do."

Levi stepped closer and placed a hand on Samuel's shoulder. "Son, none of us were born knowing exactly what it takes to be the head of a family. Some days are easier than others, but the key is to get out of God's way the best we can."

"Get out of God's way?"

"You know, like when your horse leads you one way when you want to go another? Most times he saw something in the road you didn't. It's the same with God. Many things in this life aren't meant to be understood. We simply aren't strong enough to bear knowing it all. Where there are gaps in our understanding, there is grace in knowing He carries all our burdens, no matter how big or small."

"How can I convince Emma to see that?"

Levi tugged on his beard. "I'm not sure. But in those times when I thought there was no way out, He showed me something greater than I could ever have imagined."

Samuel rested his elbows on his knees and clasped his hands together. "She has closed herself off from me and our marriage."

"I don't have an answer, but He will. Take it to the Lord and then wait. It takes great patience and faith to go through each day expecting to hear from Him."

"I've been doing that over and over again; nothing but crickets. When something does come to mind, I can't be sure if it's God reaching out or my own thoughts."

Levi propped his foot upon a turned-over bucket and leaned on his knee. "Not too long-ago Bishop Weaver preached on hearing from God. Do you remember that?"

"*Jah*, but I couldn't tell you specifically what he said."

"If we are unsure of what we are hearing is from God, we need to ask ourselves these few things. One, does what you hear line up with Scripture? Two, does it line up with messages you hear from church? And lastly, would it please God?"

Samuel stood and took off his tool belt and put on his jacket. "I'd forgotten about those three questions."

Levi headed to the door. "Look, I believe the Lord orchestrates all things for good. And even though losing James seems too big for Emma right now, I guarantee you at some point, you'll look back and realize the good that came from his death."

Samuel reached for the doorknob but hesitated. "*Datt* do you believe God punishes us?"

Levi studied Samuel. "Why do you ask?"

"No reason, just wondering."

Levi rested his hand on his shoulder. "Lord willing, we will do all He asks of us, and we'll stand before Him one day, and it won't matter."

Samuel stood in the doorway and waved goodnight to his father. Before turning down the kerosene light, he uncovered the book on the counter he and Daniel had been reading together and tucked it in a drawer out of sight. He pondered Emma's statement about them angering God on the short walk back home. He promised to protect her and his family, and he failed both so far. His stomach lurched as he kicked the snow off his boots before stepping in out of the cold.

CHAPTER 3

Emma hadn't left home in the two weeks since Bishop Weaver's visit. No visits with Katie, no walks, not even a trip to town. Samuel had all but given up on pulling her outside. The last few days, he made a point to be long gone before she wandered downstairs and didn't come home until she had gone to bed. It was all she could do to fix an evening meal and leave it on the stove. She was sure his mother was feeding him the forenoon meal since he gave up coming in for dinner.

Hammers and saws echoed in the air long into the night. Resentment filled those dark hours as she found herself lying alone. Samuel's lack of emotion was frustrating, and she couldn't fathom how he could be so callous about all they had lost. Her heart was breaking while he hammered away, building a future she couldn't imagine. She was certain he was burying his grief the only way he knew how. But all she could count on was that he wasn't lying beside her, holding her close or reassuring her they'd get through it. How was it he could deal with it so much better than she? Or maybe he was just better at hiding it. Whatever the case, she built a wall around herself, even true love couldn't break through.

***

Sun filtered through the blue-pleated curtain, forcing Emma to open her eyes. Illuminated dust danced in the beam of light, and for a moment, the heaviness in her chest disappeared.

The smell of coffee and bacon woke her stomach with a loud growl. She closed her eyes and tried to remember what day it was. Friday? No, Saturday? The clang of pans startled her to a sitting position while she rubbed the sleep from her eyes. Samuel's voice bounced up to her from below. "OUCH!"

Grabbing her robe from the end of the bed, she slipped it over her shoulders as she ran downstairs. Smoke forced her to open the window above the sink. "Are you trying to burn the house down?"

"I was mixing up the eggs, and the bacon burned. I only had my back to it for a minute."

Emma twisted her hair in a long coil and tucked it in the back of her housecoat before grabbing the towel from Samuel's hand. "Sit, let me finish this before you make a bigger mess."

She wrapped the towel around the handle of the cast-iron pan and slid it to the back of the stove. Using the towel as a fan, she waved the smoke out the open window before heading to the back door to do the same.

Samuel had another towel flipped over his shoulder and egg on his shirt. "I wanted to surprise you, but then I burned my hand, and ...well, you know the rest."

For a split-second, it was like the last six weeks ceased to exist. His boyish grin and dimpled chin charmed her into a smile.

"You're helpless when it comes to women's work. Why would you even try?"

"I was hoping I'd see a smile."

"Well, you saw it, now off with you."

She walked to the bowl on the counter and ran a fork through it. "These eggs are filled with shells. Please, go to your mother's and get some more."

Samuel stood and rolled his hand off the top of his head and bowed. "Your wish is my command, princess."

She slapped him with the towel. "Quit ...just go so I can clean up this mess."

Without a jacket, he stepped in his boots and ran across the yard to his parents' house.

Emma watched his long strides in the deep snow and giggled when he tripped. The sun was glistening off the frozen ground, making its way to meet the bluebird sky that made a beautiful backdrop to the frosted trees.

The coffee started to gurgle against the glass globe, and she turned down the heat and glanced at the clock. Samuel liked his coffee strong, but anything past five minutes would make it bitter. She couldn't remember the last time she'd fixed breakfast, but it felt good to tend to her husband's needs. No sooner had she wiped the table and put fresh bacon in a clean pan, Samuel came bounding in the back door. Cold had added color to his cheeks, and his boots left traces of snow on the floor before he kicked them off in the corner.

He placed the bowl of eggs on the counter and pulled her close. Without saying a word, he held her tight, and she relaxed in his arms as he kissed the top of her head. Tears welled in the corner of her eyes, and she swallowed hard to push all that came between them away. There was so much to explain, but she wasn't ready to give up on their dreams just yet. Stepping back from his embrace, she picked up the eggs and carried them to the stove.

Lifting the porcelain coffee pot, she poured him a cup and set it in front of him. Before she had a chance to walk away, he grabbed her hand. The longing in his eyes was filled with desire. But she moved her head from side to side and pulled her hand from his. Turning her attention back to the bacon, she felt the air in the room turn cold, much like his tone the minute he spoke.

"Bishop Weaver expects us back in church tomorrow. He says six weeks is long enough."

She cracked four eggs in a bowl and whipped them with a fork with her back toward him. She chewed her bottom lip as he continued.

"Church is at the Schrocks'. The paper said the temperature won't be out of the twenties today, so if Eli's hill is still ice-covered, we'll need to go the way of Willow Bridge. Might take us up to an hour, so we'll leave by seven-thirty."

Emma closed her eyes and braced herself for his rebuttal. "I'm not going."

"What?"

Without turning to face him she said, "I'm not going. The last thing I want is a bunch of old women whispering about me behind my back or telling me how I should be feeling."

Samuel stood, pushed his chair in, slammed it against the table, and walked beside her. He cupped her face in his calloused hands. "Emma, James was God's child to give and His to take back. He loved him more than we can ever comprehend."

Emma reached up and tried to pull his hands from her cheeks, but he held tighter and pulled her forehead into his. "We must trust in His plan, and you will go to church tomorrow."

Emma twisted from his grasp and dropped to a chair as he bent to whisper in her ear. "Life goes on, and the sooner you realize that the better. I strongly suggest you get out of this house today. Go to Katie's or visit your *datt*."

She turned her head away from his breath and murmured. "How come you're not angry?"

He slipped his feet back in his boots and pushed his arms through his black wool coat. "Who says I'm not angry? I'm upset at what it's doing to you and to us."

Samuel held his hand on the doorknob and paused. "Anger won't bring him back." A burst of cold air fluttered across her bare feet as he pulled the door shut behind him.

Life was sucked out of the room, and she stood to move the frying pans off the fire. She poured herself a cup of coffee and carried it to the front room.

The purple and white quilt from the back of the rocking chair fell to the floor when she pulled the chair closer to the window with her foot. Setting the cup on the stand, she wrapped the hand-stitched blanket around her shoulders and picked back up the mug. The steam from the dark liquid bounced off her nose when she blew over the rim. Tears spilled over her eyelashes, and she blinked to let them fall. They rolled down her cheeks and landed on the point of the broken star pattern on the quilt. The jagged points of the star matched her brokenness.

Setting the cup back down, she wiped the moisture away from *Mommi* Lillian's tiny stitches on the quilt she'd made for her. She yearned for her grandmother's face. There was a calmness that came over her every time she received a letter. Lillian had a way of seeing past all the bad in the world. Even after *Doddi* Melvin passed, she found things to bring her joy. Oh, how she wished she could find the same peace her grandmother spoke of.

A cardinal outside the window caught her attention as she thought; *losing a husband can't be as bad as losing a child. Can it?* The red bird reminded her of the stained ice she stepped over when Samuel brought her home. He'd spent two hours scraping the spot away as she lay in bed, lost in a fog.

The bird flew away when Ruth walked up to the porch and waved at Emma through the window. Without knocking, she let herself in.

"I was just out to the phone shanty, and there was a message from Marie for you."

Emma grabbed a tissue from the box near her chair. "Did she say what she wanted?"

Ruth looked tenderly toward her daughter-in-law. "I'm sure your birth mother is worried about you like we all are."

Emma stared back out the window and whispered, "I can't give Samuel what he needs."

Ruth slipped out of her coat and headscarf before coming to sit in the chair next to Emma. "You're way too hard on yourself."

Ruth took Emma's hand and squeezed it ever so lightly. "I understand what you are going through. While I didn't lose a baby as far along as you did, I had my fair share of miscarriages between Samuel and Katie."

Emma turned and looked back out the window. "Motherhood won't happen for me ...the way ...I always dreamed it would."

"It will, I promise you that."

Emma choked on a sob and hiccupped between her words. "You can't ...promise me ...that.

"No, I suppose I can't. Emma, you need to reach out to Samuel, he is hurting too, and you need to face this together. You can't let this come between you both."

"But ...he didn't ...bond to James like I ...did."

"True, maybe he didn't. But he loves you, and if you are hurting, so is he."

Emma blew her nose and took in a deep breath. "I don't know how ...to weave past the ...pain."

Emma placed her hand over her chest. "How do I stop ...loving him?"

Ruth's eyes clouded over. "Oh my. You never have to stop loving him. He will always be a part of you, even though he is in his forever home now. Don't expect a day to go by when you don't think about him, especially this early on, nor should you want to. Don't put a time limit on your recovery, but you do have to continue to live."

"But ...you don't ...understand."

"I do. There will be more children. And you and Samuel will get through this, I promise you that."

Emma focused on the birds. "Thank you ...for delivering ...Marie's message."

Ruth laid her hand on Emma's shoulder. "I'm here for you if you need me, but perhaps a phone call to Marie would do you some good. A girl needs her mother in times like this. She's not Stella, but I'm certain she loves you just the same."

The door closed, and Ruth's long black coat swayed behind her as she made her way across the yard. An array of thoughts swirled around Emma's head. *She doesn't understand ...no one can. There will be no more children for me, James was the only son I will ever bear, and I have no one to blame but myself ...and God.*

The words of Dr. Smithson haunted her every day since her two-week checkup. "Emma, you do understand you'll need to wait twenty-four months before getting pregnant again. You need to give your body enough time to heal. If you don't, you could risk the life of another child and have a series of complications that could hinder you from ever conceiving again."

What he was asking her to do was far beyond anything the bishop would approve. The use of birth control was not allowed, no matter the circumstances. In all things, she was taught to look to the Lord to provide and protect. That included bringing children into the world. How would she explain to Samuel she couldn't share their marriage bed for two years? The thought of losing another child far outweighed the disappointment in Samuel's face when he learned of Dr. Smithson's warning.

For days, Samuel had been begging her to come see the progress on their new house. How could she explain the empty rooms would always be void of laughter? His hopes and dreams of little housekeepers and farmhands would never come true. The burden of keeping the doctor's recommendations to herself only added to her state of mind.

Marie wasn't the mother who raised her, but she was, in all rights, her mother. Maybe a visit to her birth mother's home in Sugarcreek was just what she needed.

***

The gray skies of winter hailed a flood of emotions as Emma used straight pins to fasten her black mourning dress closed. Samuel was adamant they attend church service, and no amount of pleading on her part would soften his request. His refusal to listen to her reasoning only added to the distance they now shared.

The long braid she twisted and secured at the nape of her neck matched the knot in her stomach. No amount of covering could calm her nerves as she struggled to pin the starch white *kapp* in place. A quick tug on the curtain revealed Samuel had the family buggy waiting outside. Taking a moment to watch the scene unfold, she yearned for Samuel's touch.

There was a gentleness in the way Samuel ran his hand over Oliver, their buggy horse. The muscular animal leaned into Samuel as he checked his bit and ran a hand over the length of Oliver's mane. Oliver neighed and lifted his head toward Samuel's voice when he whispered something in his ear, which relaxed the horse's posture even more. There was no doubt Samuel and Oliver shared a deep relationship that was built on trust and understanding. A pang of envy coiled around her heart as Samuel readied the horse.

A deep breath filled her lungs, preparing herself to face Samuel. Their late-night argument left her uneasy about the hour-long ride to the Schrocks'. Furthermore, her refusal to answer the door when Maggie and others came calling left her apprehensive about seeing them. Many of her friends were swollen with motherhood which would be like adding salt to an open wound. She was finding it hard to breathe in anticipation of the pain it would cause.

The squeak of the front door preceded Samuel's voice.

"Emma, let's go. We'll be late if we don't leave right now."

He held her coat open, so she could slip her arms in and handed her the heavy brown bonnet to cover her prayer *kapp*.

"*Denki,"* was all she could muster as she followed him down the front steps.

No amount of tension would interfere with Samuel's responsibility to her comfort. Once he helped her inside, he tucked a blanket over her lap and moved the warm bricks he had added to the floorboards closer to her feet to keep her warm.

Before picking up the reins, he reached over and squeezed her gloved hand. With a flick of the leather strap and a click of his tongue, Oliver followed Samuel's lead and moved the carriage forward. How could an animal as large as the dark brown standardbred so easily conform to Samuel's will? The only word that came to mind was *trust.*

Samuel tried his best to lighten the mood as they made their way over the ice-covered driveway. He waved in his father's buggy direction and tipped his hat at Daniel and Katie as they pulled out behind them. "Daniel's been a big help the last couple of weeks. Not sure how I would have gotten so much done on the house without him."

"Jah."

She felt him stiffen a bit before he asked, "Perhaps you might like to see the cabinets your *datt* made for us later today?"

"Nee."

He didn't say a word as he stared motionlessly ahead. His eyebrows curled against each other, and his eyes narrowed with disappointment. "I'll have the house completed in less than a week. You'll need to start packing up our things to move out of the *doddi haus* soon. Most likely before Christmas."

The remainder of their ride was in silence as Emma fought the urge to throw herself from the moving buggy. The last thing she wanted to do was move into their new house without James, let alone face the pitiful eyes of her community that morning.

Samuel pulled up to the young boy in charge of unhitching the horses and parking the buggies. Emma sat still as Samuel walked around the horse to unsnap the brown canvas covering the door and help her down. The line of women forming at Maggie's side door looped around the front porch of the white clapboard farmhouse. Men had gathered at the foot of the stairs waiting for the women to file in first. Without parting words, both she and Samuel headed in different directions.

Katie walked up beside her and wrapped her arm around her shoulders. "I'm glad to see you."

Her elbow brushed Katie's protruding stomach, and she pulled away from her embrace and whispered. "I didn't have much choice in the matter."

"Come now, it won't be that bad. Samuel is only doing what the bishop is instructing him to do. You can't fault him for following the rules of the *Ordnung*."

Emma stopped and grabbed Katie's hand. "How did you know about that?"

"Daniel told me. I suppose Samuel needed a friend to talk to, and he confided in your *bruder*."

Emma clicked her tongue and moved forward. Katie rushed to catch up to her and leaned in so only she could hear. "Isn't that what good friends do? They talk to one another."

Emma didn't respond but continued to make her way through the back door. She stepped around a group of women just inside the door. Making her way to the women's side of the room, Emma took a seat next to the wall. Keeping her hands folded over the *Ausbund* songbook during the first song, she waited until the Lob Lied's first words were sung before joining in. The German hymn was the second song sang at every Amish church service across the country. Typically, she loved its long drawn-out verses, but today she found no comfort when the words echoed off the barren walls; forcing a lump to settle in the back of her throat.

Katie sang the words *...Gib unserm Herzen auch Verstand* and reached over and patted the top of her hand. The words, *give our* *hearts, also, understanding* meant nothing to her, and she pulled her hand away.

A whimper of a small child caught her attention, and she followed the sound to Maggie Schrock, who quietly rocked her two-month-old and patted his small back to calm his cry. Emma gently mimicked her motion, but her arms were empty. She closed her eyes and thought. *My body can't accept it any more than my heart can.*

CHAPTER 4

Samuel pulled the buggy to a stop and secured the reins before jumping down to help Emma. For hours, he studied her from across the room while she endured the message. It wasn't hard to recognize the words were meant solely for her. They matched almost precisely to the conversations he had tried to have with her on several occasions. Letting the words fill the dead space between them on the way home did little to comfort her. He regretted repeating the words, now that she was even more distant than she was earlier. He hoped to remind her that God's ways were not always ours, but we still needed to trust He knows best. It was no help and he found little hope in the words himself.

Unsnapping the heavy yellow canvas, then pulling it aside, he lent a hand while she stepped down from the enclosed buggy. When she slipped and fell into him, she buried her head in his chest and kept it there for a few seconds before pushing herself back. He wrapped his hand around her waist and pulled her close.

"Why pull away? I'm your husband, and there is no shame in leaning on me."

She pushed her hand against his torso. "You invited Daniel and Katie to spend the afternoon with us. I need to make coffee."

"They went home first, so we have a few minutes. He kept one hand firmly pressed on her lower back and took his other hand to place a finger beneath her chin. "Look at me, Emma. I refuse to let our circumstances come between us."

Her beautiful brown eyes were dark, much like the sorrow etched in her expression. He bent down, rested his lips near hers, and breathed, "Please, my love, we need each other."

Without allowing him to kiss her or respond to his plea, she ducked under his arm and headed inside.

Samuel grabbed the harness close to Oliver's neck and guided him to the barn.

"Why can't she be more like you, my friend? You don't cringe at my touch." The horse pulled his head back and let out a soft whinny as if he understood Samuel's question.

After unhitching Oliver from the carriage, he led him to the stall and went to work brushing him down and filling his feed bucket. His smooth coat and gentle response soothed Samuel's lonely soul. He couldn't wrap his head around Emma's reaction to his touch. But more importantly ...how was he going to get them through this?

***

Emma was appalled that Samuel had invited Daniel and Katie to spend the afternoon with them. It was the last thing she wanted to deal with, and she'd rather spend the afternoon in bed. Rummaging through the cupboard for a box of store-bought cookies, she arranged them on a tray and placed four cups on the table.

Katie tapped on the window a few times before she opened the side door and let herself in. "Burr ...I swear the day is getting colder even if the thermometer says different." She shook off her coat, hung it on the peg near the door, and took a seat at the table before slipping out of her boots.

"Thank you so much for inviting us. It's been way too long since we've spent any time together. I miss you."

Emma placed a napkin under each mug around the table. "You can thank Samuel, not me."

Katie raised an eyebrow. "Would you rather I leave?"

"*Nee,* I just wanted to be sure you knew it was Samuel's idea, not mine."

Katie held her cup up while Emma filled it. "I'm not sure how you'll react to anything I say these days. I feel like I have to tread so lightly around you ...it never used to be like that."

Emma put the pot back on the stove and sat down beside her friend. "I'm so sorry. I just can't seem to break free from this dark cloud over me."

Katie reached behind her and rubbed her lower back and rested her hand on her stomach. "We haven't been best friends our whole life for me not to realize how much it bothers you seeing me like this. We've dreamed about this forever ...marriage and motherhood."

Emma propped her elbows up on the table and rested her chin over her clasped fingers. "Yet in our dreams, we never thought we'd have to face something like this."

"True, we didn't, but I can't help to think God is using this experience for a purpose. There just has to be a reason James left this world so soon."

"I can't grasp what that might be. How can taking a child from his mother without even letting her feel his warm body against her skin be for something good?"

"I don't have an answer, but you'll never know what He has planned or how He will use you until you let Him."

Emma dropped her head and rested her forehead on her folded hands and shook her head from side to side. "The pain is too raw to make any sense of it."

Emma sat back in the chair and wrapped her hands around the warm mug. "Everything upsets me. I'm mad when Samuel doesn't hold me, I pull back when he tries, but mostly, I'm heartbroken he seems so callous about it all. He acts like James meant nothing to him, like he didn't even exist."

Katie stirred a spoon of sugar in her coffee. "Now, just wait a minute. You have it all wrong. If you think for one minute he isn't hurting, you're sadly mistaken. I think he's trying to deal with his part in all of it. He blames himself for your fall down the steps in the first place."

"That was an accident and by no means his fault. I was the one who walked outside in my stocking feet. If anyone should be at blame, it should be me."

Emma paused to blow over the rim of her cup. "He's been working so hard on the house. Like he wants to forget James altogether."

"Again, my friend, you have it all wrong. If I haven't learned anything else in the past year being married to your *bruder,* I learned we don't process things the same way."

"What do you mean?"

"Men work through things by doing, not thinking. Women work through things by thinking, not doing. We shut ourselves out, stop doing, so we can work through our pain. Men don't stop to think, but they pick up a saw, or a hammer, or a fence post, and physically work through things with their body."

"I suppose that's why he's been so set on finishing our house, *jah?"*

"Exactly. As women, we hold on to things that could have been. Where a man is driven to "*do*" something to forget the pain."

Emma moved from the table and stared out the window above the sink. "There's more, but I'm not sure I should share it with you before talking to Samuel."

Emma let the room fill with silence while she contemplated whether to tell Katie what Dr. Smithson advised. Before she responded, Katie closed the gap. "If you have something you must share with my *bruder* first, please don't tell me. You need to go to God and then your husband."

Emma turned to face her. "I suppose you're right." She pulled out the drawer beside her and handed Katie the pink envelope that held her mother's letter. "Read this. It was tucked in the box your *mamm* gave me the other day."

Katie unfolded the paper and held it, so the overhead kerosene lamp shed light on the words. After reading through it once, she shook her head from side to side and reread it before asking, "Salvation through Jesus? How is that so?"

Emma took the paper from Katie's outstretched hand and placed it back in its envelope. "I'm not certain, but she wouldn't have left me a letter like that unless she was set on teaching me something."

Katie leaned in and whispered even though no one was in the room but the two of them. "Have you shown Samuel?"

"No, not yet. I wanted to try to make sense of it first."

Katie picked her coffee back up. "Your mother was quite sick that summer while you were away. Maybe she wasn't in her right mind when she wrote it."

"I'm not sure myself, I don't really understand it." Emma quickly changed the subject.

***

Daniel strolled into the barn and waved to Samuel. "Good preaching this morning, *jah*?"

Samuel latched Oliver's stall. "I wouldn't ask your *schwester* that."

Daniel propped his foot upon a rung of the gate. "Yeah, I thought she might find the message a little too close for comfort. It seems when we're struggling, the ministers have a way of saying things to convict us."

Samuel sat the horse brush on a shelf just outside the gate, "I'd say they planned all three sermons around Emma."

Daniel flipped over a five-gallon bucket to use as a stool. "She'll come around, I'm sure of it. You're talking about the girl that found out she was born English, met our birth mother, and then found out our father was Amish. After all we've been through the last few years, she's pretty tough."

Samuel took his hat off and brushed hay off his pant leg. "I thought that too, but she's pulling back pretty hard. There must be more than just losing James. Something ...but I can't seem to put my finger on it yet."

"Have you thought about taking her to Marie's?"

"It crossed my mind, but with trying to finish the house and all, I didn't think I could take the time away. I sure wish her mother, Stella, was still alive. She always knew what to say to help her come to terms with things."

Daniel picked up a piece of straw from the floor and rolled it between his fingers. "Emma hasn't known Marie but for a few years, but she is a mother, maybe she could help. They got pretty close when she stayed in Sugarcreek with her."

Samuel placed his hat back on his head. "It seems like I can't say anything right these days."

"Join the club. Katie's so cranky, it's all I can do to stay out of her way."

Samuel slapped Daniel on the shoulder. "If I had to cart around that basketball all day like she has to, I'd be ornery too."

Daniel chuckled. "It won't be too much longer. That baby should be making his way into the world any day now."

"Hoping for a boy, *jah*?"

"Don't we all?"

Samuel dropped his head and kicked a clump of mud free from his boot. "I know I did."

Daniel stood and stacked the bucket on top of another one by the wall. "The last thing you need is talk of *kinner*."

"There is no need to apologize. Life goes on, and we'll have more *kinner* one day."

Daniel walked to the large double door and pulled it open enough so they could slip through. "Come on, let's go cheer that *schwester* of mine up some."

Samuel led the way back to the house and squared his shoulders as he pushed open the door that led to the kitchen. "I hope coffee's ready. I sure could use something hot."

Emma turned and reached for the white porcelain pot as Samuel and Daniel removed their coats and boots.

Katie tried to push away the heaviness in the room. "Emma and I were just talking about the differences between men and women."

Daniel pulled a chair up next to Katie and put his arm around the back of her chair. "Now that's a topic I'd just as soon ignore. Like the plague."

"You and me both," Samuel added.

Katie reached for a cookie off the platter in the middle of the table. "Maybe we can take a walk to see the new house."

They all turned to Emma, and Samuel asked, "*Jah?*"

Emma's desire to flee outweighed the hopeful look on her husband's face as he pleaded with his eyes for her to agree.

She answered with a sigh. "Sure."

Samuel turned toward his *schwester*. "Can you walk that far?"

Katie pushed away from the table and shot her *bruder* a look. "I'm pregnant, not an invalid."

With the mention of being pregnant, all three looked in Emma's direction and held their breath.

She gestured her hand toward the door. "Go, I'm fine, and you can all stop walking on ice. I'm not going to melt."

A lightness in her tone made them all relax, and Samuel returned a slight smile in her direction.

A crispness in the air filled Emma's lungs as she walked to her new home. Maybe Samuel was right in working so hard to finish it. She couldn't help but be excited at all he'd done, and she chastised herself for not allowing herself the joy of seeing it before this. The sun was trying to make its way through a mirage of darkening clouds to shine a light on the two-story farmhouse that sat down the lane behind Levi and Ruth's farm.

Samuel positioned the front porch at such an angle that they'd be able to watch as the strawberry fields came alive with tiny white flowers in the spring. He was sure she'd be able to enjoy the sweetness through the kitchen window whenever a northwestern wind blew across the field. They planned every window and the wrap-around porch to take in as much of mother nature as possible. Samuel even went as far as to keep in mind the angle of the sun in relationship to the garden, so she wouldn't struggle when it came time to plant.

He took great care in building their new home, and she again scolded herself for not showing any interest in his hard work. They walked down the lane slowly as Katie struggled to keep her balance on the icy lane. Daniel held her elbow and guided each step of their way. Samuel looked over to her and smiled tenderly as Katie reprimanded Daniel for coddling her. Samuel reached down and took Emma's gloved hand and squeezed it ever so lightly. There was a warmth in his touch she couldn't deny, no matter how hard she tried. After everything they'd been through, she treasured the moment before reality came crashing down on her once again.

Samuel dropped her hand and rushed ahead to help Daniel guide his *schwester* up the stairs. "Would you two stop? I'm plenty capable of walking up a few steps."

In unison they said, "They're icy."

Both men took an arm and guided her up the stairs one step at a time. Samuel looked back to Emma and hollered, "Wait! I'll be back for you."

She knew exactly what all the fuss was about and didn't dare proceed without her husband's arm to lean on.

Once Katie was safely inside, Samuel rushed to her side, placed his hand under her elbow, and steadied her up the slippery steps. "Had I known we were coming today, I would have shoveled and salted the walkway."

Emma stopped before they got to the door and pulled him toward her. "It was an accident."

He turned toward her voice. "One that was preventable if I wouldn't have been in such a hurry."

She saw the regret in his eyes that spoke of the pain, much louder than she'd ever noticed before. "I don't blame you."

He pulled her close, and she melted into his chest, letting so much of their hurt blend together as one. He rested his chin on top of her brown bonnet and slowly swayed back and forth and muttered, "His ways are not for us to understand but accept."

Her back stiffened, and she pulled away from his embrace and uttered, "I won't."

She stepped through the door and tried to smile as Katie oohed and ahhed over the polished pine floors. The tender moment they shared before stepping inside was soon a thing of the past as hostility made its way back to the present.

Katie and Daniel, oblivious to her change in demeanor, made their way to the kitchen to admire the cabinets her father made for them. She stayed back and let the empty room remind her there would be no children to run up and down the stairs, no babies to rock to sleep, and no games of checkers in front of the fireplace.

Daniel and Samuel ran their hands over the countertops and explained to Katie the trials they had installing them. Katie's excitement made up for her sudden lack of interest, and she quietly made her way upstairs. At the top of the stairs, she stopped and contemplated which room she wanted to visit first. Two on one side of the hall and three on the other. The first room was the largest of them all, with a small alcove set off to the side that would act as a nursery.

They planned this room especially for their early years when they could keep the littlest of their children close by. When she walked through the door that led to the pale-yellow painted room attached to the master bedroom, she let a ray of sunshine lead her to the window. Staring out over the barren strawberry fields covered in snow, she remembered how they had planned the room, so she could always see Samuel work as she tended to their children.

Moving from their bedroom, she made her way past each room until stopping at the end of the hall. Surprised to find the door locked, she slid her hand over the top of the door frame until her fingers found the key. She furrowed her eyebrows as curiosity forced her to turn the knob against the key.

Light filtered in through the curtainless windows, and her eyes adjusted to the blaring sun. In the center of the room, a braided blue and yellow rug held a rocking chair, James' baby cradle, and a little windup swing to lure him to sleep when she couldn't. Before that moment, she hadn't given the furniture another thought. The rug made a beautiful backdrop to the matching oak chair and cradle, and she crumpled to the floor in front of each. Beside her was a box of baby clothes and brand-new cloth diapers. Everything was waiting in vain. The realization that his little feet or bare bottom would never touch the items in the box was unbearable.

Her husband's voice bounced off the hallway walls.

"Emma?"

The pain in his tone magnified as he knelt beside her. "I locked these things in here so you wouldn't have to face them. I'm sorry, I should have hidden them in the barn."

He wrapped his arms around her. When she leaned into his shoulder, she saw Katie in the doorway. The pity engraved on her face was more than she could stand. She lashed out. "Go! It's not fair." She buried her head in Samuel's shoulder and sobbed. "Please, Daniel, take her home."

CHAPTER 5

Katie rolled to her side and curled up close to Daniel's back, letting the weight of her middle rest in the crook of his spine. Resting her arm across his hip, she snuggled in closer when a deep approving moan escaped his slumber.

For two hours, Katie struggled to find relief from the ache in her lower back. With the restlessness of the child moving inside of her, she let Daniel carry the heaviness of them both when her belly rested against his back.

Without rolling over, he held her hand. "How's my girl this morning?"

"A little achy."

"Anything we need to be concerned with?"

"I'm sure he's just getting anxious to meet his *datt* and is trying to tell me he's had enough of this cocoon."

"How about I go make you breakfast in bed?"

"I don't feel much like eating yet, and besides, that's my job, not yours. What would the bishop think if he found out you were doing woman's work?"

Daniel rolled to his back and moved his arm under Katie's head so she could rest on his shoulder. "I don't care what he or anyone else might think. There is nothing wrong with taking some of my wife's load."

Katie laid her hand on his chest. "I don't think carrying your child is a burden at all. I'm quite fond of a part of you growing inside of me. But I have to say I'd appreciate it if I'd stop getting so big. Not so sure how much more my tiny frame can hold."

He kissed the top of her head. "Not much longer, my love."

"*Nee*, just a couple of weeks and hopefully in time for Christmas."

She closed her eyes and savored the tranquil moment of her husband's heartbeat in her ear. His breath deepened, and a slight snore escaped his lips.

Sleep didn't come for her as she replayed yesterday's explosion with Emma in her head. Her best friend was hurting, and there was nothing she could do or say to help her through this bleak moment. She held no anger toward Emma and silently prayed *God* would reach her friend.

Lord,

I trust you have a purpose in all you do. Please help Emma see that You work all things for the good of those who love you. She's lost and hurting, please my Lord, surround her with a wedge of protection and pull her through this most trying time.

Your will be done, Amen

***

The sky, heavy with clouds and slivers of orange and yellow trying to make their way through the sunrise, greeted Samuel on the porch of the *doddi haus.* One step forward and two steps back was all he could think about. For a short period yesterday, he saw glimpses of Emma returning. Still, after her meltdown, there was no light through the darkness that surrounded her.

At his wit's end, he made the decision to call her birth mother in Sugarcreek. His mother mentioned Marie called the other day, and as far as he could tell, Emma had yet to return her call. Nothing he said or did made any headway, and he prayed his mother-in-law would be willing to give it a try.

The short walk to the phone shanty at the end of the lane helped clear his head and figure out how much he would share with Marie. He couldn't help but think he was betraying Emma by asking Marie for help. His mother-in-law had a young family of her own. Was he asking too much to add one more burden to her already full plate? But again, he had tried everything. Who else could he turn to?

Pulling the door closed, he dialed the number to Marie's husband's business and held his breath as the phone rang on the other end.

"Bouteright Stables, Nathan here."

"Nathan, it's Samuel, Samuel Yoder, Emma's husband."

"Samuel, sorry about your son."

"*Denki*."

"Death is never an easy thing to work through. And Emma, how is she doing?"

"Not good." Samuel cleared his throat. "I'm hoping Marie might be able to help."

"Not sure what she can do two hours away, but she'll do whatever you need. I know she tried to call the other day. Did Emma receive the message?"

"I'm certain of it, but she's not in her right mind lately. I've not been able to get through to her and neither has anyone else around here. We've tried. Even some of the women in the community have reached out to her, but she's shut everyone out."

Nathan paused before asking, "You think Marie can help?"

"I'm not sure, but she's my last hope."

Nathan pushed the silence to an uncomfortable limit. "Sometimes the only thing that helps is time."

"*Jah*."

"Give her time to work through it, but in the meantime, I'm sure Marie would enjoy a visit from Emma."

"*Denki*, I'll hire a driver today."

Samuel didn't wait for Nathan to say goodbye before he disconnected the call. His father-in-law's advice to give her more time fell on deaf ears as he dialed his English driver's number.

***

Emma pulled the quilt over her head when Samuel's heavy boots made their way up the stairs and into their room. The shade slapped against the window just before the mattress shifted under his weight.

"Emma, I know you're awake. I heard you in the bathroom a few minutes ago."

There was no denying his presence, but he'd have to do so behind the darkness of her blanket.

"What do you want?"

"First uncover your head and talk to me." He pulled the quilt away from her face, but she tightened her hold on the fabric and curled into a fetal position.

"Later."

He yanked the bedding from her fingertips, forcing her to face him. She threw her arm over her eyes to shield the morning light spilling into the room.

"What is it? I'm in no mood to deal with you today."

"Regardless, you need to get up and pack a bag. A driver will be here within the hour to take you to Sugarcreek."

"I have no plans to go anywhere today."

"You do now. Your mother is expecting you."

She turned on her side away from him and grabbed the edge of the quilt, pulling it over her bare legs.

"It's time to come back to the real world and find a way to deal with all of this. Maybe your mother will have better luck than me."

He tore the blanket from the bed and tossed it on the floor. "It's one thing to suffer and mourn, but another when you lash out at those who love you. There was no excuse for the way you treated Daniel and Katie yesterday. Some time away is exactly what you need."

"I'll apologize to them if that's what you want, but I'm not going to my mother's."

He walked to the small dresser across the room and pulled items from the drawer. "As I said, you don't have much say in the matter. I've already made plans, and your mother is expecting you."

Emma sat up in bed and pulled her knees to her chest locking them in with her long white nightdress. "So, you're shipping me away just like that? The first real struggle we face, and you pawn me off on someone else? Not the best decision you've made as head of our household."

She waited to gauge his reaction before she continued. "Did the bishop put you up to this?"

He dropped to his knees and pulled a small brown leather suitcase out from under the bed. "The bishop doesn't advise me on all things, and certainly not on my choice to send you to your mother's for a few days."

The stack of clothes he threw on the bed sat in a jumbled mess, and he pushed them aside to open the suitcase. "I don't know what else to do. I've sympathized with you, prayed for you, held you, even begged my mother and Katie to help ...and nothing. You're not getting any better."

In not much more than a whisper, she begged. "Please don't send me away. I just need time."

He sat on the edge of the bed, rested his elbows on his knees, and clasped his hands. "Six weeks is more than enough time to move on. God's will is done ...life goes on. We have a house to finish, the bakery to open, and more children to plan for. What's done is done."

Without looking back at her, he moved to the door. "I'll wait for you downstairs."

The harshness in his voice was alarming. There was no doubt he had lost his patience, and all she could do was comply. With a heavy heart, she dressed then carried the bag to the bottom of the stairs.

Samuel sat in his chair at the head of the table, looking through his wallet. "Funds are tight at the moment, but this should be plenty to pay the driver when you're ready to come home."

"If we can't afford it, then let me stay."

"I've already made my decision. I think you need time away."

It took all she had to reach up and lay her hand across the back of his forearm. "Or do you need time away from me?"

Tires crunching on the frozen driveway alerted them long before the driver blew the horn. He patted the back of her hand. "I'll see you in a few days, *jah*?"

An overwhelming sadness filled her soul as she walked to the door without Samuel following her. She didn't look back and he didn't move from his chair. How could he send her away when he was the one thing, she needed the most? Maybe he was right. A few days away to help her figure out how to tell him there may be no more children for them is just what she needed.

***

The streetlights lining Main Street in Willow Springs were dressed for the holidays and quickly reminded Emma that Christmas was only two weeks away. The first of many events and holidays they would celebrate without James. Every minute of every day was etched in and around the baby boy she longed to hold.

The two-hour car ride to Marie's did little to calm her racing pulse. Even though the driver did his best to pull her into a comfortable conversation, her one-word answers finally deterred him from trying.

She leaned her forehead against the side of the cold window pane and closed her eyes and thought. *Why God? Why my baby?* The warm car and the steady motion made her sleepy, and she gave in to the heaviness behind her eyes.

***

"Emma, we're here."

Caught somewhere between a dream and reality, Emma heard her name being called but fought to stay in a dream like state, singing her baby to sleep.

"Emma, you can wake up now. We made it to Bouteright Stables."

Like water running through her fingers, she felt the small child slip away from her once again. Trying to hold on for a few more moments, she resisted opening her eyes until the driver's voice called to her again.

"Emma, wake up."

She slipped her arms in the sleeves of her coat and looked out the window. Nathan and Marie's home looked the same as it had three years prior. The well-manicured house and stables were a picture of Nathan's success, and she instantly felt at ease.

Marie and Nathan married three years earlier and had already added baby Lydia and Nathaniel Jr. to their growing family. In her mother's letters, she learned Amos and Rachel enjoyed their big brother and big sister roles. Nathan's first wife was killed in a buggy accident, and Marie warmly accepted his *kinner* as her own.

Marie waved her in as she bounced eighteen-month-old Lydia on her hip. A pang of apprehension filled Emma's stomach as she thought about seeing six-month-old Nathaniel. It was too late to turn back now, and if this was what Samuel thought she needed, she would at least entertain his request for a few days.

Marie met her at the base of the stairs and hugged her with her free arm. "I'm so sorry I couldn't come to Willow Springs. Things are so busy at the stables, and Nathan's mother Rosie isn't well these days. To say the least, my days are quite busy."

"Momma, no need to apologize. You have a family to take care of. The last thing you need to worry about is me. Besides, nothing a few days in your busy house won't cure. I'm certain of it."

Marie let a small giggle work in the back of her throat before she replied. "Let's see how you feel after you spend a few sleepless nights listening to my cranky baby."

Her mother wrapped her arm around her shoulders and led her into the kitchen. "Please excuse the mess. I was in the middle of making dinner when Lydia pulled my apron full of eggs off the table. You'd think I'd know better than to leave the string hanging down where she could reach it. It was all I could do to gather eggs; let alone put them away. They are so few and far between this time of year, it made me sick they got wasted."

Emma took her coat off and set her suitcase at her feet. "Here, let me help." She carried the trash can to the table and scooped the runny eggs up off the floor with her hands. Falling right in step with her mother, she helped Marie put dinner on the table, Lydia fed, and Rosie tended to, all before Nathan came in from the stables.

Once they all bowed their heads in silent prayer, Nathan tapped his fork on the side of his plate, and both women lifted their heads. Marie sat back in her chair and let out a slow breath and relaxed her shoulders. "I forgot how smoothly this house runs when Emma's here."

Nathan buttered a slice of bread and dipped it in his stew. "I bet she won't miss the craziness when all the farmhands show up for supper later. We got a reprieve for dinner. I sent them all into town to pick up a big order of fencing supplies."

Marie reached her hand over and patted her daughter's arm. "How are you? Samuel says you've been struggling."

Emma pushed the meat and vegetables around on her plate. "I suppose not any worse than any other mother who loses a child."

Marie held up a finger before she had a chance to elaborate on what she was dealing with. "Hold that thought. I'll be right back."

Nathan tipped his head in the direction of the stairs. "Sounds like Jr. up there has plans to keep his *mamm* away from enjoying a hot meal."

Emma took the napkin off her lap and held her hand out to stop her mother from leaving the table. "Stay, enjoy your dinner."

"Are you sure? You're supposed to be here relaxing, not taking care of my children."

Emma followed the baby's cry up the stairs as her mother hollered after her. "I just fed him, so he probably has a bubble."

Her heart pounded in fear with every step she took closer to the wailing child. Would she be able to comfort the child without turning into a blubbering mess? This certainly would be a test she wasn't so sure she could pass.

Emma slowly opened the door to find the little one had pushed himself up in the corner of the cradle, struggling to find his thumb. Her motherly instinct took over, and she rolled him to his back, swaddled him in a blanket, and settled into the rocking chair near the window. He promptly settled down when she set the chair in motion and rubbed tiny circles between his shoulder blades. Dark wisps of hair tickled her nose, and she took in the fresh baby scent as she buried her cheek in the back of his head. He cooed and squirmed until he found his thumb and went back to sleep.

A fresh set of tears landed on top of his tiny head. She let just a few fall before she tucked them back away, hidden in her own grief.

The sun coming in through the window lured her back to sleep as she held her mother's child close to her heart. It was not until she felt Marie lift the boy from her arms, did she stir.

"I'm sorry. I fell asleep."

"I hated to wake you, but Amos and Rachel are biting at the bit."

Tucking the baby back into the cradle, Marie held her finger to her lips as she motioned for Emma to follow her back downstairs. Only after she quietly closed the door did she explain. "School has parent-teacher meetings this afternoon, so Amos and Rachel only had a half-day of school. They're downstairs having a snack."

She couldn't deny she was excited to visit with Nathan's children. They both ran to her the minute she made it to the bottom of the stairs. "Hold on there, you about knocked me over."

Rachel wrapped her arms around her middle, and Amos pushed his *schwester* aside for a tighter grip. "Let me look at you. You've both grown so much I hardly recognize you."

Amos stood up tall. "I'm seven now, and I come up to *datt's* chest. I'll be as tall as him someday."

Emma patted the top of his head. "I'm sure you will." She pushed Rachel back for a closer look. "Look at you. You're not a little girl anymore. Before long, you'll be going to *singeons* and snagging every boy in the community."

"I'm only ten. Way too young to go to a youth gathering."

"Ten, wow! You look so much older. I'd better have a talk with Marie and tell her to stop making you drink so much milk."

They all giggled and headed back to the table. Emma sat between them, and Lydia held her hands out, begging to be picked up.

Marie picked up a dishcloth and wiped crumbs off Lydia's highchair. "No other word but crazy to describe what goes on around here. I never dreamed four kids would be so much work! Doesn't help I'm in my forties. Most women my age are done with babies by now."

Emma twisted her head until she caught her mother's eye. "Do you regret it?"

"Not for one minute. Days of regretting things I have no control over are long gone. The Lord gave me something I thought I had lost forever. Love, family, and children. What more could a mother ask for?"

No sooner did the words leave her mouth than Marie held her hand to her lips and whispered, "I'm sorry."

CHAPTER 6

Four days had passed since Emma arrived at Marie and Nathan's, and she had yet to get a chance to speak with her mother. The few minutes she did have between spilled milk and making meals was spent helping with the children. There was no doubt Marie had her hands full and the last thing her mother needed was to have her cry on her shoulder. What she did have time for was spending quality time with Rosie. The old woman was wise beyond her years, and Emma took every opportunity to be in her presence.

Crippled with rheumatoid arthritis, Rosie was confined to bed and struggled with a dry cough and shortness of breath. Even the slightest excitement left her in a weakened state.

Emma lightly knocked on Rosie's door before pushing it open to carry her breakfast tray to her bedside.

In not much more than a whisper Emma asked, "Rosie, are you awake? I've brought you some oatmeal and a cup of your favorite tea."

Rosie tilted her head in Emma's direction and pointed to the chair near the bed. "Bless ...you."

Emma set the tray down and carried the steaming cup to her side. "I heard you coughing. How about you take a few sips of tea? I added extra honey to help soothe your throat."

Rosie's distorted fingers grasped the cup, and it splashed over the side as she brought it to her mouth.

Emma moved closer. "Here, let me help."

The lines stamped in the corners of the old woman's eyes were moist, and Emma tried to ease her frustration. "No shame in needing help."

Rosie leaned in and dropped her hands to her lap as Emma held the cup to her lips. Once she had her fill, she rested her head back on the pillows Emma had stacked up around her and asked through a ragged wheeze, "Tell me ...about ...him."

"Who?"

"Your ...baby."

Emma's heart quickened. "You want to know about James?"

"*Jah* ...tell me ...everything."

She sniffled and reached for Rosie's hand. "No one's ever asked to hear about him before."

"His hair ...what ...color?"

Emma gave a slight smile and tilted her head and closed her eyes. "His head was covered in soft wisps of baby fuzz. I remember laying my lips against his head, and the fine hair tickled my nose."

"How ...much...did he weigh?"

"He was born almost two months early, so he was tiny. Just four pounds."

"And ... his eyes?"

Emma pulled her hand from Rosie's and turned to gather the tray. "I didn't see his eyes."

Rosie reached and tried to grab her sleeve. "No ...don't go."

"I should let you rest."

"I can rest ...later ...pleeasse...stay."

Emma's thoughts suddenly became dull, and a rush of emotion filled her head as if a tornado had cleared a path through her heart.

Rosie's disfigured fingers tugged at the fabric of Emma's apron. "You ...know Jesus, *jah*?"

That one question had haunted her for a week or so, and it still held a void in her mind. Did she know Jesus? Is that what Stella was trying to show her? If she did, she surely couldn't feel his presence in her life or understand what it meant.

The desperation in Rosie's voice left her no option but to pacify the woman's plea. "*Jah,* I know of Jesus."

She left the tray and headed to the door.

Without an ounce of rattle in the aging woman's voice, Rosie said, "You're not alone. He's waiting for you to call His name."

She stopped in her tracks and turned in anticipation of seeing Rosie's stare, but instead, she found the old woman's head relaxed on the pillow, drifting off to sleep.

There was a calmness in the room that enticed her to stay. Even the goosebumps forming at the base of her neck wouldn't explain her sudden urge to sink to the floor.

A cry from the other room forced her to turn back to the door but not before she noticed a spectrum of colors bouncing off Rosie's glass, making a beautiful show on the wall. In an instant, she was taken back to sitting on her father's knee as they marveled at a rainbow. The memory was as vivid as the kaleidoscope of colors leaping through the air. She couldn't have been more than six when her *datt* pointed to the sky and whispered in her ear. "Remember, every time you see a rainbow - God is telling you He will always keep His promises."

She wasn't sure she knew what he meant then and wasn't sure she understood its significance now, but the whole scene left her speechless. She had so many questions but didn't know where to turn for the answers.

"Emma! Can you give me a hand?"

Marie's voice beckoned her to the kitchen, and she forced herself to push the memory away until later.

Lydia cried to get out of her highchair while Marie changed the baby on the daybed set up in the corner of the room.

Emma unlocked the tray and picked Lydia up from her seat. Carrying her to the sink to wipe the jelly from her hands, she cooed soothing sounds in the little girl's ear.

"There, there, little one, let's dry up those tears."

As if there was someone over her shoulder, her own words echoed in her ear, *there, there little one, let's dry up those tears.* She quickly turned toward the voice but met nothing but emptiness.

Marie propped Nathaniel over her shoulder and met Emma at the sink. "We haven't had two minutes to ourselves since you walked in the door, but have I told you what a blessing you've been to me the last few days?"

"It's the least I could do since you agreed to let me visit on such short notice. Being busy like this has done more than you can imagine."

"Let's get these two down for a nap, and we can visit some before Nathan and his crew come in for dinner."

Marie balanced both children on her hip and headed up the stairs. "I'll be right back."

Emma moved to the living room and sat in one of the two rockers that faced the front window. She laid her head back and set the chair in motion with her foot. With her eyes closed, she tried to remember exactly what Rosie had said. *He is waiting for you to call His name.* A slight ache deep behind the small incision in her lower abdomen reminded her she probably shouldn't be toting Lydia around. Rubbing small circles around the painful reminder, she thought, *do I know Jesus?* She spoke out loud, "What does that mean?"

Marie laid her hand on her shoulder. "What does what mean?"

Emma reached up and covered her hand with her own. "It's not important."

Marie pulled the chair closer and leaned into Emma. "Talk to me. What's going through that pretty little head of yours?"

"Half my problem is that I can't make much sense of anything these days."

"My heart aches for you, and I wish I knew the words to help you through this. Maybe you need to talk to someone."

"You know as well as I do; it's not our way."

"Maybe not your ways, but you have to remember I've only been Amish for a few years. In the English world, counselors can do a great deal of good. Nathan's district is a little more progressive than yours. Perhaps I can talk to him about finding someone for you."

"Samuel would never allow it."

"I think you're wrong about that. Samuel is at the end of his rope, and I'm sure if he knew how much they could help, he'd agree."

Emma played with a string on the hem of her sleeve. "Maybe so, but I'm not sure that's the answer for what's bothering me most."

"How about you tell me what's troubling you, besides the obvious."

Emma tipped her head back and closed her eyes again. "I think God is punishing us."

Marie furrowed her eyebrows. "God doesn't punish like that. He might use our struggles to teach us something, much like a mother teaches a child, but He doesn't punish us the way you think."

"But He took James, and I may not be able to have more children. That sure seems like a punishment to me."

"What on earth are you talking about? What happened to you was an accident, and no reason you can't conceive again."

Emma grasped the arms of the chair. "You don't understand."

Marie patted her knee. "I don't think I do. What is it?"

"I can't get pregnant for two years, or I'll risk the chance of putting another baby in danger."

"I don't understand the issue in waiting a couple of years to have another child."

Free-flowing tears met Emma's chin. "Momma, I can't deny Samuel and, our marriage bed for ...*two years*."

"Is that what you're so distraught about?"

"I must have done something to God for him to do this to me. How can I put my trust in a God who would take a child from a loving mother's arms?"

Marie moved her chair closer. "We must believe He has a plan in everything He does, and it isn't your fault. This was an accident and God’s will."

Marie picked up the bible from the stand between the two chairs. "I have something for you." She opened the brown leather-lined book to a flowery piece of cardstock tucked between some pages. "Do you remember when I found this in my mother's bible? It was a turning point in my life, and you were right there with me."

Emma took the bookmark from her mother's hand and focused on the words through cloudy eyes. IF YOU SENSE YOUR FAITH IS UNRAVELLING, GO BACK TO WHERE YOU DROPPED THE THREAD OF OBEDIENCE. She handed it back to her mother.

"No, I want you to keep it. If I remember correctly, it was you who asked me how I couldn't see God's hand in my life a few years ago. Now I'm asking you the same. How can you think God doesn't have a hand in this? He orchestrates all things for His good. You told me that, remember? Now, it's time you go back and pick up that thread of obedience. You are doubting God's hand in all of this and all He asks us to do is trust Him and be obedient. We aren't called to understand everything He does, but to have faith to know He sees things we can't. He wants you to be the woman who trusts and says yes to all He asks of you. Which includes accepting this path and moving on."

Marie laid the bible on Emma's lap. "I think you can find a lot of comfort in here."

"I can't take that; we are instructed to read from our German Martin Luther Bible."

"Right now, you're in my house, and around here, we read from the English Bible, and besides, how much of that German version do you understand?

"Not much."

"That's what I thought. Look, I realize your Old Order community is different from our New Order, but maybe it wouldn't hurt for you to read the Lord's words for yourself. You need to learn the truth and understand how He sent His son to die for us so we could live a life without pain and sorrow."

"How can that be? All that's in front of me right now is pain and sorrow."

Marie patted the leather cover of her mother's old bible. "All your answers are in here. Read it, you'll learn this heartache is only temporary. God has so much more planned for you. He has a purpose for your life and I'm certain losing James has something to do with it."

"How can you be so sure?"

"Because I lost you for sixteen years and look what I've gained through all of my troubles. If it wasn't for you forgiving me and showing me how important God was in your life. I wouldn't be where I'm at today."

Marie crossed her legs and leaned closer to Emma. "You're just temporarily lost and confused. You thought you knew God before, but I can guarantee you if you read His word, you'll soon discover a God bigger and better than anything you could imagine. I have a feeling this is His way of leading you into a deeper relationship with Him."

Emma outlined the leather cover with her finger. “Stella left me a letter where she encouraged me to look for the truth in Jesus. What you’re describing is much like what she said.”

“Now if both of your mother’s are saying the same thing, don’t you think that’s something pretty important?”

Emma rubbed her temples and closed her eyes. “I’m still so angry I don’t even know where to start to open my heart back up.”

Marie tapped the Bible on Emma’s lap. “Start here. Then tell Samuel what the doctor advised."

"But he’ll be so disappointed."

Marie leaned back in her chair. "Don't you think you need to discuss it with him before you make any harsh conclusions as to what or how he will think?"

"But I can't risk the life of another child."

"Emma, you're not thinking rationally. You need to talk to Samuel like you should have done the minute you found out. Don't you think he has the right to understand what's really bothering you?"

Emma dropped her head and wiped a lingering tear from her cheek. "I suppose."

Marie laid her hand on Emma’s knee. "I'd say it’s time to go home."

***

Nathan hired a driver to take her back to Willow Springs. The driver, Frank sat patiently in the driveway while she said her goodbyes. It was already late in the day, but Emma wanted to wait until the children came home from school before leaving.

Marie held her close. "Take one day at a time and remember when we walk through trials, He is right there walking them with us if we allow it."

Her mother's hug did little to calm the rolling waves of anxiousness rooted deep inside. "I'll try."

Marie pushed back and tenderly tucked a wisp of Emma's hair under her heavy brown bonnet. "You'll tell Samuel what the doctors advised ...right?"

"*Jah*"

"That's my girl. Now go home to him. I'm sure he's missing you."

Emma picked up her bag and slid into the backseat just as a gust of wind blew through the open door.

Frank turned in his seat. "Looks like a storm's brewing. We best get on the road."

Emma waved at Marie and buckled the belt around her heavy wool coat. "I'd like to make one quick stop before we head out. Do you know where the Shetler farm is?"

"Lillian Shetler?"

"Yes. I'd like to stop and say a quick hello to my grandmother before I leave town."

The driver pulled out into the road. "By the looks of those clouds, I'd say it best be speedy. I'd hate to be stuck on the Turnpike in the storm blowing across Lake Erie."

"I promise I'll make it quick."

Emma sat back and wished she'd found time to visit with *Mommi* Lillian earlier. The long driveway that led to her grandparent's farm was covered in snow with little signs of life. Only a single pair of footprints led from the house to the dairy barn across the yard.

The driver leaned over the steering wheel for a better look at the looming sky. "You've got about ten minutes before we have to get on the road."

"I'll hurry." Emma ran up the stairs and knocked, hoping it wouldn't take her grandmother long to answer. After a few seconds, she rapped a little louder and called out *Mommi* Lillian's name.

A bellowing voice rang out behind her. "She's not home."

Her Uncle Jay walked across the yard, flipping his collar up to block the wind. "Nobody here but me. *Mamm's* visiting her *schwester* in Pinecraft."

Emma wrapped her arms around her middle and walked down the steps. The ache in her heart filled with regret. "How long is she staying?"

"Can't say. *Mamm* said she wasn't coming back until the Robins returned."

Emma snickered. "That won't be for at least three or four months."

"Suppose so."

Jay was a man of few words, plus Emma hadn't said more than a handful of words to him in the three years she'd known him. An uncomfortable silence bounced between them. "Well, if you hear from her, please tell her I stopped by."

Jay nodded his head, and Emma climbed back into the warm car. "I guess we can be on our way now."

Emma settled in for the two-hour ride home. In the back of her mind, she hoped she could talk Lillian into allowing her to stay a few days longer. Her mother meant well, but Emma wasn't ready to go home just yet. Samuel was too quick to send her away, and she wasn't prepared to face the hopelessness that awaited her there.

Frank slowed down at the bend in the road in front of the Sugarcreek Auction house. "I need to make one quick stop at the Bulk Foods Store up here on the right. If you want to grab a drink and a snack, now's the time. I won't be stopping again before we make it to Willow Springs."

"Thanks, I might just do that."

The parking lot was bustling, and a large coach bus sat at the curb. She followed Frank to the front of the store. A poster advertising Sarasota, Florida, took up much of the window as the driver held the door.

"Looks like another load of snowbirds going to Florida," he mentioned.

Emma stopped and looked back outside. Older couples were leaving their suitcases on the curb and rushing onboard and out of the whistling wind. "I forgot my money, is the car unlocked?"

"Sure is. I'll meet you back at the car in about ten minutes."

Two women stood in the line loading the bus when she headed back outside. It was hard not to overhear their conversation.

One woman shook her head from side to side. "Such a shame Ella's not feeling well, it's a shame her ticket will go to waste."

CHAPTER 7

Samuel glanced at the clock when it rang seven chimes. A northeastern gust blew around the house, and he was worried Emma might be caught in the storm. He wouldn't relax until she was safely back home.

It was less than a week until Christmas, and he was excited to tell her they could finally move into their new house. He'd spent the last five days working long hours finishing everything up. Hopefully, the time away gave her a new sense of purpose, and she'd be ready to move on with life.

Stacking a few dishes in the sink, he peered out the window, hoping the lights of a car would pull in the driveway. He pulled a chair close to the window in the front room. After two hours, he put on his coat and boots and headed out to the phone shanty. Maybe the weather-delayed her, and she left a message for him there.

The light on the machine blinked green, and he pressed the play button. He quickly deleted it, realizing he forgot to delete Nathan's earlier message telling him Emma was on her way home. When no other call was recorded, he dialed Bouteright Stables.

After a few rings, Nathan's answering machine picked up and he left a message. "Nathan, Emma's not made it home yet. I wondered if you received any word from the driver." He paused for a moment before continuing. "A storm blew in early this evening. Maybe they got delayed? If you hear any word from the driver, can you call me back?"

After hanging up, he let his headlamp recoil a warm glow on the pine plank walls. He dropped his head and said a silent prayer for Emma's protection.

Samuel checked the phone shanty for messages on the hour, every hour, for the next twenty-four hours. As morning light eased its way over the horizon, an uneasy dread settled between his shoulder blades. It was time he told his parents, along with Emma's father, she was missing. He retrieved Nathan's message explaining his hired driver stopped at a store before they headed out. When he came back to the car, she was gone. He waited for over an hour, but when she didn't return, he assumed she changed her mind about going to Pennsylvania.

He pushed open the door to the small wooden shed at the end of the lane and shielded his eyes from the sun glaring off the white-covered ground. The storm dropped a foot of new snow he had to kick away from the door before opening it. The clip-clop of a horse and buggy stopped short of where he stood. Samuel walked to its side and waited for Daniel to pull the brown canvas covering the door back.

"I'd say that long face has something to do with Emma not being back yet."

Samuel moved closer. "Much worse."

"How much worse can it be than my sister leaving my best friend to fend for himself?"

"I can't find her."

"What do you mean you can't find her? How did you lose your wife?"

"She was supposed to be home yesterday. Nathan left a message saying she was on her way, and I waited up all night and nothing. He even tracked down her driver who said she ditched him at some bulk food store in Sugarcreek."

Daniel raised one eyebrow. "The bulk store near the auction house?"

"I have no idea. The driver said he went in for a drink, and when he came out, she was gone."

"What time was it when they left?"

Samuel's eyes fixed on the frozen ground. "I think Nathan said she left around three or so."

Daniel's lip twitched. "That sister of mine went to Florida."

"Florida? Why on earth would you think that?"

"Because that store is where the bus line picks people up to go south to Florida. If I remember correctly; it departs in the afternoon. I bet she found a way on that bus, and she's already on her way to Sarasota."

"By herself? I can't imagine her going all the way to Florida alone. And besides, I didn't give her enough money for a bus ticket. Let alone lodging."

Daniel snickered. "I know it's not funny, but you have to agree when Emma wants something bad enough, she usually finds a way to get it."

"But Florida? She doesn't even know anyone there."

"She's been pretty depressed the last couple of months. Maybe some warm sunshine is just what she needs."

Samuel kicked an ice mound with the toe of his boot. "I swear that woman is going to get the best of me. How on earth can I help her if I can't even find her?"

"Well, my friend, maybe you need to go after her. A woman wants to feel like she's wanted, and the way you pawned her off on Marie might have left her unwilling to come home."

"I didn't pawn her off!"

"*Nee*? Looks that way to me."

Daniel clicked his tongue to set the horse in motion and hollered over his shoulder. "I think a little sun and sand will do you both some good."

Over the metal wheels crunching snow, Samuel shouted, "But Florida, of all places? I have work to do. I can't take time chasing her all over the country!"

Daniel yelled, "Go get her!"

***

Emma took the ticket from the woman's hand. "Are you sure?"

"*Jah*, maybe the good Lord figured you needed a trip to Florida more than Ella."

Excitement filled Emma as she rushed back to the car to retrieve her suitcase. Everything was happening so fast. Maybe that was good since she didn't have time for second thoughts.

"Let me pay you for it. I don't think I have enough to cover the cost, but I can give you the rest when I get to *Mommi* Lillian's. I'm sure she won't mind giving me a short loan."

"You're Lillian Shetler's granddaughter?"

"I am. How do you know my grandmother?"

"We aren't in the same district, but we quilt together once a month. You wouldn't happen to be Emma from Willow Springs, would you?"

"I am. How do you know about me?" Emma asked.

"Lillian told us all about you and your baby."

The other woman laid her hand on her arm. "It's settled. You'll sit with us, and we won't accept any money for your ticket. It was just going to go to waste anyways with Ella getting sick and all."

Both women grabbed an arm and led her to the bus. "Leave your suitcase on the curb. The driver will put it in the undercarriage."

Emma stopped just before stepping on the bus. "I'm not sure. Maybe I ought to call home first. They're expecting me."

"No time now; the bus is due to leave any minute. You'll have plenty of time to phone home once we reach Pinecraft."

Emma turned back toward the door hoping Frank would come out of the store so she could tell him what she was doing. Hopefully, he would figure it out when she was nowhere to be found.

There was no turning back now. The driver reached for her ticket, then shut the door behind her. Following the two wider women to the middle of the bus, she sat where the first woman pointed. "Here, sit on the aisle seat so you'll be in the middle of us."

Emma sat down and took a deep breath. The bus pulled out of the parking lot just as Frank exited the store. She leaned over the woman by the window, waving to the driver, hoping he saw her on the bus. "I think I should have told my driver at least."

The larger of the two women snickered. "I'm sure he'll figure it out quick enough."

For the next hour, the two women chatted back and forth. At the same time, regret and fear mingled together with anticipation as Emma tried to relax. Finally, she interrupted her seatmates. "I didn't even catch your names."

"Oh my goodness, you're right; we never introduced ourselves. I'm Margaret Troyer."

"And I'm Betty Mullet."

Emma reached out to shake their hands. "So nice to meet you and thank you so much for sharing your ticket with me."

Margaret tucked her purse in the pocket of the seat in front of her. "It's the least we can do for Lillian's granddaughter. She would do the same for us. I'm sure of it."

Betty pulled down the armrest and tilted in Emma's direction. "So, won't Lillian be surprised when we get off the bus in Pinecraft together? She'll be in heaven for sure and certain."

Emma wrung her hands together on her lap. "I sure hope so because my husband's not going to be happy with me."

Betty murmured, "No worries, you'll be able to borrow someone's cell phone as soon as we arrive in Pinecraft. We indulge in such things down there."

Margaret leaned over and gave Betty an alarmed look. "Now Betty, you know what happens in Pinecraft stays in Pinecraft. Those things are best kept quiet." She smiled and then turned to Emma, and whispered, "You're in for quite a treat."

Margaret sat back in her chair. "Might be just what you need to wash those baby blues away."

Emma slipped her arms out of her jacket and pushed the wrinkles out of her black dress. "What makes you think I have the baby blues?"

Margaret patted her knee. "The eyes are the path to your soul, and those dark circles say more than you think. Nothing a few days in the sand and sun won't cure."

"I've never been to the beach."

Betty twisted in her seat. "What? You've never been to the beach? You must go and let all your cares wash out into the ocean."

Margaret added, "You need to go to Siesta Key. The bluish-green water meets the sky and paints a picture that will warm even the saddest soul."

"Oh, it sounds perfect."

Betty tried to cross her leg but gave up when the seat in front of her had already reclined. "We encouraged Lillian to go after Melvin went to his forever home. It helped her, and I'm sure it will help you too."

"I sure hope so because I'm not sure how much longer I can carry around this misery."

Margaret softened her voice. "I lost a baby once too."

"Really? How did you handle it?"

"Not sure I ever did. I still mourn the girl she never grew to be, and that was forty years ago."

"So, the pain never goes away?"

"It never leaves you, but you find ways to live through it. I had a wise old woman tell me once that the Lord weeps with us when we weep because we can't see what He sees. More than once, I heard Him whisper *...this too shall pass*."

Emma felt at ease with the two women. So much so that for a moment, she thought God placed her on the bus for a reason. She couldn't help but think *...was a trip to Pinecraft something He had purposely planned for me?*

An unsettling feeling began welling up inside, and she asked, "How long will it take us to arrive in Pinecraft?"

Betty was quick to answer. "You might as well get comfortable. We won't pull into the church parking lot until noon tomorrow."

Emma shook her head. "*Ohhhh* ...Samuel's not going to be pleased."

Margaret's laugh was full of warmth and life. "I can tell you for a fact it won't be the first time, and I'm sure it won't be the last. Both Betty and I were married for well over fifty years when our husbands passed. And I can tell you we both had a few spats we needed to work through."

"*Jah*, but this one's big. Things are already tense at home between us. This is just going to make it worse."

Betty reached across the aisle and twisted to face Emma. "Might be so, but I have to believe God put you in our path for a reason. Trust in Him. Maybe a visit with your *Mommi* Lillian might be part of His bigger plan."

"Betty's right, He's not forgotten you. He might have withheld a child blessing from you to give you a better one."

Emma looked hard at Margaret and asked, "But you lost a baby. How can you suggest losing a child is a blessing?"

Margaret folded her hands, closed her eyes, and laid her head on the back of the seat. "Count my words, child. There *will* be a bigger blessing, I'm sure of it."

Emma stared straight ahead as both women settled in their seats for a nap. A million thoughts were going through her head, but none made much sense. There was no doubt Margaret's statement left her unsettled, and she closed her eyes to push the irritation away. The steady movement of the bus made her eyes heavy, and she found her thoughts being quieted with the faint sound of her *mamm's* voice ringing in her head.

One of the sweetest memories she had of her Amish *mamm*, Stella, was her voice. More than once, she remembered snuggling up on her lap listening to a song. Struggling to remember the tune; she let herself slip into a dream while Stella sang her to sleep.

In the darkest hour, Emma was startled awake by a nightmare. Samuel was calling her name, but she couldn't see him. The anguish in his cry shook her, and it took a few seconds to realize where she was. The hum of the bus tires was the only sound she heard. Both Margaret and Betty were fast asleep, and only the seat behind her had the overhead light switched on. Needing to wash the dream away, she bounced her way to the back of the bus to the restroom. Once inside, diesel fuel fumes overwhelmed her and the blue chemical in the toilet made her hold her breath as she splashed water on her face. The bus followed the curving road, and she found herself jolted in the small room.

Margaret was right. She did have dark rings under her eyes. She washed the sleep from her eyes and straightened her *kapp* in an upright position. Pressing the creases out of her dress she wished she didn't have to wear a mourning dress. Maybe what she needed was to add some color to her life. Just perhaps being away from the prying eyes of her community would help. In Pinecraft, no one but *Mommi*, Betty, and Margaret would know what she was struggling with. Flushing the portable toilet, she quietly opened the door, hoping not to disturb any sleeping passengers.

While making her way back to her seat, she passed a woman reading in the chair behind her. The young woman reached out and tugged on Emma's sleeve. She held her other hand to her lips and moved her knees and invited Emma to sit down.

The young girl couldn't be much older than herself. She wore a soft lavender dress, much like the Mennonite girls from Sugarcreek. Emma slipped in the seat next to her. Then the girl bent her head close to Emma's ear. "I couldn't help but overhear your plight and was hoping I had a chance to talk to you."

Emma didn't say a word but listened intently.

"I lost my baby girl four months ago, and I understand how hard it is to pick yourself back up and go on as if nothing happened. Often, I laid in bed at night and wondered what I could have done differently, but then I'd remember I wasn't alone. Jesus was grieving right beside me."

Emma focused on keeping her breath steady as the woman shared her darkest moments.

"There were days I'd go to the grocery store just so I could walk down the baby aisle. The pain was so real I couldn't seem to escape it, so I understand what you're going through."

Emma folded her hands. "I can't stop thinking about the little things, like his first wiggly tooth or the first scraped knee I should've been able to kiss away."

The young woman dropped her head and murmured, "It was one of the most horrible days of my life. I never even got to bring her home, but I believe God has a plan in my sorrow."

Emma let out a small gasp and asked, "How can you be so confident our pain comes with a purpose?"

The young woman turned to look at Emma. "Because I believe in a God who spared nothing to send His son to die for us. How can I not believe he would take my child for something much bigger and better as well?"

Emma continued, "But when I remember him being cold, I pulled his little blanket tighter even though I knew it wouldn't warm him, my heart breaks in two. How can that be from God?"

"I can't answer that for you, but you can find your answers in the same place I did."

"Where's that?"

The young girl tapped the bible on her lap. "Right here."

Confusion lingered in the air as Emma tried to make sense of the woman's comment. If she could find the answers in there, why hadn't she been taught that? Yes, the ministers in Willow Springs encouraged her to read the bible, but she couldn't understand most of what was written in German. For the first time in months, she felt hopeful. Just being able to open her heart and talk to someone who understood was encouraging.

The girl pulled a tissue from her bag and handed it to Emma. "Don't keep it all bottled up inside. You need to turn to God and believe me, He will help you heal."

Emma tilted her head in the girl's direction and thought, *there it was again ...how could one lone book hold so many answers. Yes, she believed the Lord could do miraculous things, but help her heal and find peace in such hopelessness? Why did everyone keep pointing her to the bible? What was she missing and why hadn't she been able to fight through her loss with God's help thus far?*

The young woman pulled a pencil and piece of paper from her bag and wrote down an address. "My husband is working in Pinecraft for a few weeks, and this is where I'll be staying. If you would like to talk more, you can find me here."

Emma read the girl's name, Lynette Miller, and then tucked it in her pocket. "I don't know how long I'll be staying, so I'm not sure if I'll have time to reach out to you."

The woman wiped her face. "No worries, I wanted to be sure you knew where I'd be if you needed a friend."

Emma slipped out of her seat and mouthed, "Thank you."

CHAPTER 8

Samuel slammed the phone back in its receiver and rested his chin in his hand. It would be days before he could secure a driver to take him to Sugarcreek and another week before catching the bus to Pinecraft. One week before Christmas, and all southbound routes were booked solid. Seven days without a single word from Emma, and his patience was wearing thin.

The drafty phone shanty left him no choice but to make his way back to the house. The unseasonably cold snap blew around his neck as his chest rose and fell with rapid breaths. He stood in the center of the yard, looking in all directions. He could go sulk in the *doddi haus*, return to their new house and get back to work, check on Katie and Daniel, or retreat to the comforts of his *mamm's* kitchen, he chose the latter.

A welcoming smell of coffee and cinnamon circled his head the minute he opened the door. He removed his hat and raked his fingers through his hair before hollering out.

"*Mamm*, just me."

Ruth called from the top of the stairs. "I made fresh cinnamon rolls this morning. Help yourself. I'll be down in a minute."

Samuel kicked off his boots and hung his coat before taking what his mother had offered. Before he had a chance to sit, a burst of cold air entered the room, followed by his father.

"Samuel?"

"*Jah*?"

"What's up?"

Samuel tilted his head quizzically.

"For as long as I've known you, there are two things I can always count on. One, your jaw twitches when your angry, and two, your strides become mammoth when you've got something on your mind."

Samuel poured himself a cup of coffee. "Guess you got me there."

Levi stomped the snow off his boots before slipping out of them. "How about you tell me what's got you so worked up?"

"Might as well wait for *Mamm* so I can explain it to the both of you."

Ruth dropped an armful of laundry by the basement door. "Explain what?"

Levi poured himself a cup of coffee. "What's got Samuel so worked up today."

Ruth stopped at Samuel's side and rested her hand on his shoulder. "Any word from Emma?"

There was a flicker of irritation in Samuel's response. "Not exactly."

Ruth placed a few of the still-warm rolls on a plate and slid them toward Levi. "Where do you think she is?"

"That's what I'm here about. As far as I can gather, she's in Florida."

Ruth brushed crumbs off the counter and dropped them into the sink. "My heavens! When did she decide to do that?"

"I'm not sure. She was supposed to come home two days ago, but as far as I can figure, she set her eyes on a vacation without me."

Ruth pulled a chair away from the table. "Now, son, she hasn't been herself. Perhaps she wasn't ready to come home and face reality yet."

Samuel swallowed hard. "But she never even called to tell me she wasn't coming home!"

Ruth placed her hand over Samuel's clenched fist. "Time is the only thing that fixes this kind of loss. You have to remember her healing is not on your timetable."

Levi stirred a spoon of sugar in his mug. "But Ruth, not telling him where she'd gone, that's unacceptable."

Ruth's voice tempered. "In whose view?"

Levi brought his cup to his lips, looked over its rim, and then nodded in Samuel's direction. "In his, of course."

Ruth placed a gooey roll on the napkin in front of her. "Have either of you carried a baby under your heart only to have it snatched from you at a moment's notice?"

Silence filled the air as both men swayed their heads from side to side.

"Husband, what you fail to remember is the despair I went through when we lost not one child, but three. How can you forget the months of agony I went through just to get out of bed in the morning?'

Levi lowered his head. "I suppose so. But to run off to Florida without letting your husband know where you've gone. I can't imagine you ever acting so irresponsible."

"No, because I still had Samuel to take care of. What does Emma have to come back to but an empty home?"

Samuel pushed the sticky dessert away. "She has me, our life, and a brand-new house."

"Samuel, I understand how upset you are that she didn't clear it with you first, but as a woman, I sympathize with what's going on inside of her. Here, she has to pretend everything is okay because that's what she's been trained to do, but inside, her heart is torn in two."

Ruth took a bite and waited a few moments before continuing. "Until she finds her way, she's like a wind in a passing storm. This is a season for her, and she has to fight her way back in her own way, in her own time."

"But I wanted us to have a fresh start by moving into the new house before Christmas, and she's gone and upset all my plans."

Ruth's voice took on a new octave. "The major difference between men and women. Men become workaholics, and most times, avoid the issue. Women, on the other hand, mourn the things they can't hold onto ...smells, touches, a baby in their arms."

Ruth took a sip of coffee. "Give her time, but most of all, go after her. Don't let her think she has to do it alone."

Samuel stared into his cup. "I'm to blame."

Levi leaned back in his chair. "There was nothing you could have done any differently to prevent God from calling your son home."

Samuel tapped his fingers on the table. "Perhaps so, but I still feel like I failed my family."

Ruth wiped her mouth with a napkin. "You haven't failed, and you can prove it by finding a way to bring her home. A woman needs her husband to go out of his way for her. Chase her down and show you won't let her battle alone."

***

Emma opened her eyes when Margaret tapped her shoulder. "We're here, sleepyhead, wake up."

The eager voice of her new friend made it impossible to be anything but excited about arriving in Pinecraft. For twenty-two hours, she ran through an array of emotions about her quick decision to veer off course. There was no turning back now. All she could do was embrace her hasty diversion.

The sun burned through her dark stockings and black coverings the minute she stepped off the bus. A bustle of passengers zealous in greeting their friends added to her excitement; clear down to the soles of her black boots.

A display of brightly colored apparel and flip-flops swarmed with smiling faces. There was no doubt the people who came to this small town found joy in their surroundings. Everything around her seemed fresh and inviting, and for a minute, she accepted a new viewpoint on life.

Margaret and Betty stood in front of her, receiving multiple hugs and well wishes from long-time friends. She learned during their late-night conversations that both had been coming to Sarasota every winter for the past ten years. They called it their home ...one step closer to heaven. Emma didn't understand it at the time, but the sunshine and the lingering sweet smell of blooming flowers mingled together with the sea breeze made her grasp the meaning.

She reached out and pulled on Betty's sleeve. "You're right; this place is one step closer to heaven."

Betty warmly smiled and looped her arm through hers. "And the best of what this town has to offer is just a short bus ride away."

Emma tipped her chin toward the older woman. "How can it be any better than this?"

"The ocean, silly girl." Betty pointed to a street sign. "Follow Bahia Vista Street west for two and a half miles, and you'll find yourself in Sarasota Bay. Better yet, catch a city bus, and in less than thirty minutes, you can be to Siesta Key on the Gulf Coast."

Margaret reached down to pick up her bag. "My advice is if you want to see heaven on earth, spend some time digging your toes in the white sand and going for a swim in the Bay."

All thoughts of home fluttered away as Margaret described the pearl white sand and crystal-clear water of the Gulf Coast. For the first time in two months, Emma felt she could restore a little of her life by immersing herself in the beauty of winter in Florida.

From across the parking lot, she heard her name.

"Emma, Emma Yoder."

There was no mistaking the soft voice of *Mommi* Lillian.

Emma broke free of Betty's grip and ran to her grandmother. "How did you know I was coming?"

Lillian held her arms open. "I knew no such thing. I walked up to meet the bus hoping I'd see some friends, and low and behold, you stepped off the bus."

Emma rested her chin on *Mommi* Lillian's shoulder for a long minute and enjoyed the warm embrace. Lillian pushed her away and looked at her with a loving smile. "What a wonderful surprise." She looked over her shoulder. "Where's Samuel? Is he fetching your bags?"

With a twinge of regret she replied, "He didn't come."

Lillian looped her arm through hers and patted her hand, "Maybe a few days away from the cold is just what you need to erase those worry lines from your eyes."

Emma lifted her head and took a deep breath through her nose. "What is that I smell?"

"Winter Jasmine. Isn't it heavenly?"

Emma glanced down at her grandmother. "You have no idea how badly I needed this. I hope you don't mind I came unannounced?"

"Heavens no. My *schwester* Martha and I enjoy the company. Come, pick up your bag and we'll get you settled."

Emma walked back toward the bus and stood beside Lynette, waiting for their bags to be unloaded from the storage compartment.

Lynette leaned in closer. "I'm serious. If you need a friend while you're here, please don't hesitate to call on me. My husband is a minister and is preaching here for the next few weeks. We'd love it if you would join us on Sunday."

Emma looked over the bus toward the stucco building. "A minister? But you're so young."

Lynette smiled and answered, "When the Lot falls upon you; God doesn't take age into account."

"I suppose not."

Lynette nodded her head in the direction of the street behind the bus. "There's Alvin now. Please, reach out to me, but more importantly, join us on Sunday."

Emma watched as Lynette picked up her suitcase and waved at her husband. It was hard for Emma to pull herself away from watching the friendly way Alvin greeted her. How was it her new friend, who had just lost a baby herself, greeted her husband with so much tenderness? With a rush of remorse, she knew she had to find a phone ...and quickly.

Once she found her way back to her grandmother, Lillian was talking with Margaret and Betty. "I hear my quilting friends kept you company and convinced you to come."

"They sure did, and if it wasn't for them, I'd still be in the cold instead of wanting to shed some of these layers before I have a heat-stroke."

"Oh goodness, let's go home so you can change into something lighter."

"That might be a problem since all I have is my heavy winter clothing with me."

Margaret spoke up. "No problem, follow us. My granddaughter is about your size, and she leaves her Florida clothes here. They will be perfect for you to borrow."

"Are you sure?"

"You bet. Besides, she's stuck in Ohio. Baby number three is on the way, and her husband feels they should stay put this winter."

Emma, Lillian, and Betty followed Margaret down the center of Graber Street, chatting about who had arrived at the bus and how long everyone was staying. It was as if the whole community revolved around the bus schedule. The church parking lot cleared out as smiling families made their way to their winter homes throughout the small community.

Lillian turned toward Emma. "What is the long face about all of a sudden?"

Emma whispered, "I need to find a phone to call Samuel."

"As soon as we get to Martha's. She has one of those flip phones in the house for emergencies."

The thought of calling Samuel left her a bit uneasy. They'd left things in such a state before she went to Marie's. This was only going to add to his frustration. Suddenly, a thought came to her. *Maybe she could convince him to come to Florida. "Mommi,* do you think Martha would be okay if Samuel met me here?"

"I think that's a wonderful idea, and I'm sure she would be fine with it. We can ask her as soon as we get home."

Margaret pointed to the house on the corner of Fry and Graber Street. "Here we are. Come in, ladies, while I find a few dresses for Emma."

She unlocked the door, and a cool breeze met them as they followed her inside. The Florida heat forced them to allow the comforts of electric air conditioning even if an oil lamp was positioned in the middle of the kitchen table. Most who visited the area still held tight to their rules and practices, while others enjoyed the temporary reprieve from the strict ordained regulations of their home community. Margaret and Betty were two who opted to follow their New Order ways as much as possible, all while enjoying the sun and warm temperatures of wintering in the south.

Margaret set her suitcase down and disappeared into a small room at the back of the house. When she returned, she carried three light-colored dresses along with a pair of flip-flops dangling from her finger.

"Here you go. These should work for you while you're here."

Emma looked at the pink, yellow, and purple short sleeve dresses. Her features took on a distressed look. "*Denki*, but I'm not sure I should wear things so colorful."

Betty opened a drawer by the back door and took out a yellow plastic grocery bag and held it open so Margaret could slip the stack of dresses inside. "Emma, these colors may not be acceptable at home, but you're in Pinecraft now. And here they are perfectly fine."

"But I'm still in my mourning period."

Lillian wrapped her arm around Emma's shoulders. "The dark circles under your eyes tell the world more than you think. It's completely your choice, but it wouldn't hurt if you traded your heavy winter clothing for something lighter for the short time you'll be here."

Emma took the bag and flip-flops. "I'll think about it."

Lillian squeezed her shoulder into her own. "You do that. In the meantime, let's go home so you can rest some before supper. I'm excited to introduce you to my *schwester*."

***

After introductions, Emma borrowed Martha's cell phone. She escaped to the little porch at the front of *Mommi* Lillian's *schwester's* house. After dialing the number to the phone shanty at the end of the lane at home, she waited, hoping someone would answer. They had the answering machine set to pick up on the fifteenth ring, giving anyone outside plenty of time to respond before she'd have to leave a message.

She held her breath the entire time and only relaxed enough to fill her lungs when she heard it click over so she could record a message. A million thoughts raced through her head before she listened to the beep, and then the line went dead. Confused, she dialed again and waited for fifteen rings for the same thing to happen. She flipped the phone closed and leaned back in the white wicker rocker.

The mid-afternoon sun was high in the sky, and the heat radiating from the rays fluttered across her face as she tilted toward the warmth. She still hadn't decided if she should change into the dress Margaret had loaned her. But after a few minutes, sweat rolled down her back and in the creases of her elbows under the polyester fabric of her long black mourning dress. She scurried off to the bedroom at the back of the house. After laying out all three dresses on the bed, she chose the pale yellow one, took off the heavy dress, and slipped the summery lightweight fabric over her head. She removed her long black stockings and enjoyed the cool tile on her toes before slipping her feet into the simple black sandals. She didn't even pick the pile of clothes off the floor before she tiptoed through the living room trying not to disturb the now napping *schwester's*.

A family on tricycles passed by and waved in her direction as she stepped off the porch. Taking note of Martha's house number, she took off. Free ...if only momentarily from the cold surrounding her soul, she walked down Gilbert Avenue. She wasn't sure what she hoped to find, but for a little while, Emma hoped to shed her anguish much like the crumbled clothes she left behind in exchange for something brighter and more untroublesome.

CHAPTER 9

Heat rose from the pavement, but Emma hardly noticed as she weaved her way through the side streets in and around Martha's house. The small cottages, painted in soft tropical colors, were lined with white picket fences and palm trees. Each yard was as neat as a pin and had a plentiful supply of colorful flowers that added to the landscape. A group of young girls toting a volleyball and picnic basket turned in front of her. Their giggles and chatter made her miss Katie and her twin *schwesters*, Rebecca and Anna. There was a time before her *mamm* died, and long before she found out she was born to an *Englisher,* that the carefree days of her youth were plentiful.

The group of girls kicked their shoes off and dug their feet in the sand at the volleyball court at Pinecraft Park. It only took a few minutes; before each side was packed, a mixture of girls and boys. She leaned on the fence separating the court from the street for only a minute before walking past two older gentlemen playing shuffleboard. Everyone was engrossed in something at the open-air picnic shelter, be it a game of checkers or a mid-afternoon snack.

A playground across the parking lot enticed her to find a seat on a single swing. She kicked off her flip-flops and let white sand spill over her toes. Closing her eyes, she pushed the swing into motion and let the breeze cover her face as she pumped her legs harder and harder. Without realizing it, she felt joy, something she hadn't allowed herself to partake in for a very long time. Jumping off the swing, as she did as a child, she flew through the air and then waited until the seat came to a complete stop before turning away and walking back to a picnic table.

From somewhere behind her, a sweet voice made its way closer. "Now, if I were forty years younger, I might give that a try myself."

Emma turned toward the woman. "*Jah*, I can't believe I did that. It's been a while since I've done anything so childish. I'm surprised I didn't hurt myself." Emma rubbed the spot on her lower stomach, half regretting her impulsive decision.

The petite woman sat down beside her. "Mary, Mary Miller. And you?"

"Emma Yoder."

"I haven't seen you around. Did you just arrive on the bus from Sugarcreek today?"

"I did. How did you know?"

The woman let out a slight snicker before answering. "Not much gets by me around here. You could say I'm the unofficial tour guide of Pinecraft."

The two women sat and watched a group of small children chase a skink under a nearby picnic table. The lizard ran from the squeals and right over Emma's foot. She shrieked, and the small towhead boy stopped in front of her. His big brown eyes looked tenderly at her when he said, "Skinks, don't bite."

Emma patted the little boy on the top of his head, "Thanks for explaining it to me."

His black pants, tiny suspenders, and baby blue shirt ran off; blending into the group of children heading to the playground.

Mary pointed to a family gathered under a big oak tree covered in Spanish moss. "He's the youngest of that family. They have eight *kinner*. Seems like every time they come, they have another one in tow."

Finding it hard to take her eyes away from the young family, she asked, "How long have you been coming?"

"Some twenty years now, but I don't visit; I live here full-time over on Gilbert Avenue. My husband was a minister here before he passed. I love it here so much I couldn't imagine going back to Ohio, so I stayed."

"Miller? Gilbert Avenue? I met a girl on the bus, Lynette Miller."

"Daughter-in-law." Mary shook her head and made a ...tsk-tsk sound with her tongue. "So sad ...she and my son lost their first child a short time ago. My son, Alvin, came down a few weeks ago, but Lynette had to stay behind for a couple of doctor's appointments before they cleared her for travel."

Emma crossed her legs and leaned her arms on the picnic table behind her. "We have a lot in common."

"Who? You and Lynette?"

"*Jah*."

Emma didn't allude to her meaning but instead stood to leave. "It was nice to meet you, Mary."

"And you as well." Mary stood and said, "289."

"Two eighty-nine?"

"Our address, 289 Gilbert Avenue. You're always welcome, and if you want a tour of Pinecraft, stop and see me. I'm sure Lynette would love to visit with you."

Mary Miller had a way about her that told Emma it wouldn't be the last time she'd be seeing Pinecraft's resident tour guide.

***

Samuel stood at the calendar and stared aimlessly at it. How could the love of his life go ten days without finding any way to reach him? He checked the phone almost hourly and practically waited at the end of the lane each day for the mailman. If she did go to Pinecraft, she would have arrived two days ago, plenty of time to call and leave a message for him. With each passing day, the hollow spot to the right of his heart ached a little deeper.

A steady knock broke his stance, and he moved to the front room. As he pulled the door open, Bishop Weaver stood with his hand in the air, ready to announce his arrival again.

"Samuel, may I have a word with you?"

Samuel opened the door wider and let the bishop cross the threshold. After closing the door, he pointed to the two rockers near the front window.

The bishop removed his black felt hat and balanced it on his knee. "I didn't see you or Emma in church yesterday."

"No, sir, you didn't."

Samuel didn't offer an explanation even though Bishop Weaver allowed plenty of time before he posed another statement. "The both of you need the support of your church family as much as you need each other."

Samuel clenched the arms of his chair as he let the bishop continue.

"Been my experience that tragedy like this often triggers some big questions."

Bishop Weaver set the chair in motion as he waited for Samuel to respond. When he didn't, he asked, "Has that happened?"

Samuel followed the bishop's movement and answered, "Could be." He didn't feel it was his place to confess Emma's anger at God or her statement that they must have done something wrong to anger Him. So instead, he let his answer stand.

The bishop looked toward the kitchen. "Is Emma here? I'd like to speak to her."

"She's not. She went to Sugarcreek."

Bishop Weaver crumpled his bushy eyebrows and rested his foot flat on the floor to stop the chair from rocking. "Alone?"

"*Jah*."

Clearing his throat and setting his tone a bit softer he said, "The death of a child can bring a couple closer, or it can isolate them from one another. However, what you need to understand is every marriage will be strained after a loss like this. It's normal, and I don't want either of you to feel ashamed if that happens."

Bishop Weaver had been the head of his church for as long as he could remember, and not once in his twenty-three years had he witnessed this side of him.

Samuel tilted his chin in his direction, unsure how to respond.

The bishop stood and headed to the door. "Samuel, I'm not as coldhearted as you may think, and you aren't the first couple I've seen stumble after the loss of a child."

Samuel stood and turned to look out the window. The older man walked to his side. For a few minutes, they stayed silent, watching the birds outside the window.

Before turning back toward the door, Bishop Weaver changed his tone to something more recognizable. "Marriages only work when two people are together."

Samuel waited until the weathered man stepped outside and shut the door before he mumbled. "One has to have a wife who wants to be home to make things work."

The clock on the kitchen wall chimed ten times just as the hired driver pulled up to the front porch. In three hours, he'd be on a bus to Florida and one day closer to bringing his wife home where she belonged.

***

Lillian and Emma sat at a table on the shaded side of the Coffee Café. Emma stood in line for over twenty minutes, waiting to let her grandmother buy a couple of their signature drinks. According to her *Mommi*, the Iced Honey Lavender Latté was to die for. While waiting, she took notice that everyone she met greeted her with a smile. There definitely was something in the air in Pinecraft, and she hoped she could carry whatever it was back to Willow Springs. After ordering, she headed back to the table to wait for her number to be called. Mary Miller and her daughter-in-law, Lynette, walked up, and Mary pointed to the two empty chairs. "Do you mind if we share your table?"

Emma pulled the chair out closest to her. "Please do."

Lynette brushed a stray hair behind her ear and wiped her hand across her forehead. "It always takes me a few days to get acclimated to the temperature when I first arrive."

Emma snickered before commenting. "*Mommi* had a sweater on this morning, and it was all I could do to keep from sweating."

Mary took a sip of her frosted drink. "Give it a few days, and you'll find the air conditioners are a bit too cold for you as well."

Lynette hung her purse over the chair and moved so she was sitting in the shade. "I hoped Alvin and I could go to the beach this afternoon, but he wanted to work on his sermon for Sunday. He promised we could sneak away tomorrow."

"Order 289."

Emma looked to the pick-up window. "I'll be right back."

Lillian took the opportunity to lean into Lynette to whisper, "Do you think Emma could go to the beach with you?"

Lynette smiled, assuring Lillian it was a great idea.

Emma sipped her drink as she walked back to the table. "*Mommi*, this is wonderful. Thanks for suggesting it."

Lillian took a long drink before she looked warmly at Emma. "Lynette and her husband are going to Siesta Key tomorrow. I think it would be a great way for you to enjoy all that Sarasota has to offer."

Emma pushed her straw around in her drink. "The beach? I've never seen the ocean before, but I'm not sure."

Mary added, "As your official tour guide, I would highly suggest you get out of your comfort zone and take the city bus to the Keys with Alvin and Lynette. You won't be sorry. Something about that white sugar sand chases all worry right out into the ocean."

Emma stayed quiet as Lillian, Mary and Lynette went on talking about the beach. Something didn't feel quite right. Samuel weighed heavy on her mind. She should be sharing this experience with her husband ...not alone. There were too many unsettled things between her and Samuel to relax enough to enjoy her visit. If she could at least talk to Samuel and explain to him why she didn't come home, maybe she could feel better about going off and taking pleasure in a day at the beach. All she could do was keep trying to call him.

Mary placed her phone on the table next to her pocketbook. "Mary, would you mind if I used your phone to try to call my husband?

"No, of course, help yourself."

Emma picked up the phone and excused herself from the table. The ice cream shop across the street wasn't open for business yet, so all the picnic tables out front sat empty. Taking it as an opportunity to escape the busy Coffee Café, she crossed the street to one of the ice cream shop's red umbrellas. Turning her back to the busy street noise, she prayed someone would answer Levi and Ruth's phone. Just like the five or more times she tried over the last few days, the phone rang and rang but didn't allow her to leave a message before disconnecting. She dialed her father's furniture shop in a last-ditch effort to get news to someone in Willow Springs.

On the third ring, a familiar voice answered.

"Byler's Furniture."

"*Datt.*"

Without even so much as a hello, her father began to scold her. "Where are you? You have Samuel and everyone else in this family worried sick about you. We know you've been troubled, but I raised you better than this. This is unacceptable behavior."

"*Datt*, let me explain."

"You owe me no explanation, but you do owe one to Samuel."

"Listen, you have every right to be upset with me, and yes, I need to talk to Samuel, and I've been trying. The phone at Levi's won't let me leave a message. I've tried several times, but before I can leave a message, it hangs up."

"I'll tell Levi to check the answering machine. But again, it shouldn't have even been an issue. You should have come home when you said you would."

"Can you deliver a message to Samuel?"

"*Nee*. He left this morning for Sugarcreek."

"What is he going there for?"

"Why wouldn't he go there? He went to bring you home."

"*Datt*...I'm not in Sugarcreek."

"Daughter, where are you?"

"Florida."

The sigh on the other end of the phone matched the squeak of her father's office chair as he plopped down. Even with being over a thousand miles apart, she could envision the slump of her father's shoulders.

Jacob cleared his throat. "You could have at least let Marie and Nathan know what you had planned."

"I didn't plan any of it. It just happened, and I didn't give it much thought before I stepped on a bus going to Sarasota."

"I half suspect you aren't giving much of anything a thought these days but yourself."

"*Datt,* that's pretty harsh considering all I've been through."

"There comes a time when you need to surrender your life to the Lord's will and quit fighting it."

A stillness laid between them as Emma tried to gauge her words, trying to keep her voice from cracking.

"Even when ...you think ...God is punishing you?"

"Why would you think that?"

"Why else would he take James from us? Samuel or I must have done something to displease Him."

"Emma, God doesn't work like that."

"Then please, *Datt*, explain it to me."

"What's to explain? Our job is to work hard to follow our ways, just like our ancestors have done for hundreds of years. You're not the only woman who has lost a child. How do you think all the women before you handled it?"

"That's just it. I have no idea and that's what I'm struggling with."

"I'll tell you how. They moved on and accepted it as God's will for their life."

Taking a few moments to calm her racing pulse she added, "I can't accept it's all that easy."

"We all have questions on how God works, but it's not our place to question, but to obey. Plus, when our time is up and we face our maker, then we'll truly know whether we've worked hard enough to get our questions answered."

A heaviness pressed on Emma's shoulders. "Oh ...*Datt,* I have so many questions."

"And rightly so, but you need to take those questions to the Lord. Or perhaps you need to get yourself home and meet with Bishop Weaver."

"You're right, but first, I need to track down Samuel. I'll call Nathan's office. Hopefully, Nathan can give Samuel a message from me. I'm sure he'll head to Marie's first."

Her father took in a deep breath and exhaled loudly before replying, "Good."

Emma took in a small breath before asking, "Do you know anything about the letter *Mamm* left with Ruth for me?"

"No, why?"

"Before I left to go to Marie's, Ruth gave me a box with a shawl *Mamm* had crocheted for me, along with a letter instructing me to find the truth in Jesus."

With a deep groan, Jacob answered, "Ohhhh...I prayed she kept that to herself."

"Why would you want her to do that?"

"Have you showed that letter to anyone else?"

"Only Katie. Why are you so upset?"

"Emma, you need to forget that letter ever existed and rely on what you've been taught. Any other notion will only cause turmoil in the community, and I'd hate for you to be the source of that."

"You're scaring me. Why would this upset you so?"

"Please just trust your *Datt*. I know what's best concerning this matter."

Emma's heartbeat quickened. There was something in her father's tone that was alarming. "*Datt*, I need to go; I want to try to reach Samuel."

After saying their goodbyes, Emma closed the phone and played her father's warning over in her head. There had been only one other time in her life when her father's voice took on a hopeless tone, and that was when he told her she wasn't his biological daughter. Now for some reason, his plea took on a whole new level of uneasiness.

Still, deep in thought, she started to cross the street back to the Café when she practically stepped out in front of a passing car. A horn diverted her attention back to the present, and she jumped back on the sidewalk. Her eyes, still fixated on the back of the car, read its license plate. EPH 0289.

CHAPTER 10

Somewhere outside of Columbia, SC, the bus Samuel was on broke down, leaving him stranded. For ten hours, he sat inside a bus terminal, waiting for another to continue his journey to Sarasota.

Three days before Christmas, and he was no closer to getting Emma back home where she belonged than he was twelve days ago. The clock on the wall above the bus departure digital board clicked away. With every passing minute, Samuel's jaw twitched and clenched so hard he gave himself a headache. In the background, Christmas music played, and happy travelers anxiously waited for their connection.

He walked to the electronic board, looking for bus number 289. The ticket agent informed him the board would announce when the new bus arrived. As if on cue, bus 289 blinked on the screen as a woman's voice played over the speaker. "Passengers awaiting Bus 289 to Sarasota can make their way to Loading Zone E."

Swinging the small duffle bag over his shoulder, he mumbled, "About time." Falling in line behind a group of blue and black-clad elderly, he let a woman with small children step in line before him. An array of white prayer *kapps* in all different sizes made their way up the stairs. The stress the delay caused was evident on the mother's face as she tried to calm the littlest one. With one hand on the littlest girl and one around a baby she held tight in her arms, she whispered something in the girl's ear, which in turn made her cry. The woman looked up at Samuel and pleaded. "Sir, would you mind holding my son for a minute? My daughter is dead set against getting on the bus, I need to pick her up."

The woman's eyes pleaded, and he obliged. She placed the sleeping infant in his arms in one swift swoop, and he waited until she led all three of her daughters on the bus. Shuffling the baby to his other arm, he handed the bus driver his ticket and looked to where the driver pointed. "You are in row E, seat 2."

Samuel kicked his bag under his seat, laid the child across his lap, and pulled his arms out of his heavy jacket. South Carolina was already warmer than Ohio, and he wished he would have worn a lighter jacket. The small blue bundle started to squirm, and he instantly brought him to his chest. He followed the sound of a crying child and tried to get the young mother's attention. When she caught his eye, she mouthed, "Thank you."

When the last of the passengers boarded, the driver apologized for the inconvenience and promised they would arrive in Pinecraft by nine that evening. Samuel laid his head against the back of the seat and closed his eyes. Nine o'clock? How would he ever find Emma, let alone lodging for the night? His day was getting worse by the minute.

An hour passed, but Samuel still held the sleeping infant in his lap. When the child started to stir, he glanced over his shoulder to see his mother fast asleep, resting the petite girl over her shoulder. Not sure what he would do if the child was hungry. He gently removed a layer of the blanket and whispered, "Bear with me. It looks like your *mamm* needs a rest. Perhaps you'd like some of these layers off." Not one second after he removed the blanket, the boy shot his hands above his head. The child stretched, arching his back and cooing simultaneously. Samuel smiled before whispering, "I bet that feels good. I wouldn't like to be wound up like a mummy either." Samuel shook the last of the blanket from the boy's feet and propped him over his shoulder. It took only a few minutes for the boy to fall back asleep, and Samuel tried to do the same.

The baby's fine hair rubbed up against Samuel's cheek, and he couldn't help but lean into the softness. He'd never held a baby before, but for some reason, it felt natural. The child, not much more than a few months old, warmed a spot in his heart. He rested his head on the back of the chair and let the hum of the bus tires sway him deep in thought. *We'll have more kinner, I'm sure of it. We're just going through one of those tough spots the bishop spoke of. Things will be better once I get Emma home.*

A light tap to his shoulder brought him out of his head and back to the young woman leaning over him.

"I can't thank you enough; Maryann finally fell asleep, and God willing, the girls will stay settled until we arrive in Pinecraft."

Samuel handed her the blue blanket and shifted the child to his mother's arms.

"It was no trouble, but I was surprised you asked. There are plenty of women on the bus who would have made a better babysitter for sure."

The woman tucked the blanket under her arm. "But none who could rescue me in a moment's notice."

Stretching his legs out in front of him, he asked, "What's his name?"

"James Paul."

The woman turned and headed back to her seat without noticing the deep raspy moan he tried to conceal. It was as if October 15th happened all over again the minute she whispered his name. For the last ten weeks he kept busy, fearing reality would crash down on him if he sat still too long. Holding the woman's child brought all those memories flooding back so fast he had to blow out a couple of long breaths to calm his racing pulse.

***

Promptly at nine o'clock, the bus pulled into Pinecraft, Florida and the overhead lights flashed on. Samuel looked out the window to find a group of people gathered under a nearby streetlight. He assumed most passengers found a way to tell waiting family when their bus would arrive. When he stepped out into the parking lot, he fought to focus past the lights for anything that resembled a hotel. No one knew he was coming, so there wouldn't be anyone to greet him. The parking lot was empty, and the bus pulled away. Leaving him alone in a strange town with no idea how to find Emma. Noise across the street drew his attention, and he wandered toward the sound. Walking through a seating area of the darkened Coffee Café, he found himself in front of the Dairy Bar. Ice cream would have to do in place of a regular meal until he could find his way around.

A group of young men was sitting at the table next to him. "Excuse me, would any of you happen to know Lillian Shetler?"

One of the sandy-haired boys answered, "I don't know that name, but there were quite a few new faces playing volleyball this afternoon. Could she have been one of them?"

Samuel took a bite of his chocolate sundae. "Lillian is my wife's grandmother, so I'm pretty sure she wouldn't have been playing volleyball."

Two boys, in unison, said, "I guess not."

The first boy piped in. "We just arrived last week, so we haven't met too many people yet."

Samuel dropped his head. "Thanks anyway."

Another one of the boys stated, "My parents talked to some lady over on Gilbert Avenue when we first got here. Folks say she is Pinecraft's unofficial tour guide. You might want to pay her a visit. I think her name was Mary or Mildred ...something like that."

Samuel perked up. "You wouldn't happen to know the exact address, would you?"

"Nope. All I know for sure is it was Gilbert Avenue."

"Thanks anyway. Could you point me in the direction of something to eat besides ice cream?"

One of the boys pointed down the street. "Dutch Family Restaurant is right down the road. But they're closed now. Opens back up in the morning at seven."

Samuel took the last bite of his ice cream and threw the dish away and tipped his hat in their direction. "Thanks, boys."

It was too late to go knocking on doors, so he headed back to the church parking lot, used his duffle bag for a pillow, and laid down in the alcove of the church's entrance.

***

The heat from the sand penetrated Emma's thin flip-flops as she struggled to walk through the foreign matter. She carried her heavy beach bag, loaded down with everything her grandmother thought she might need for a day at the beach.

Lynette fell into step with Emma. "We have our favorite spot over by the volleyball court, it's not much further, and hopefully, there will be a free picnic table we can snatch up."

Emma switched her bag to the other arm. "Thank you so much for letting me tag along. It was fun riding the bus over here and having you point out all the landmarks along the way. You're giving me a true feel of Sarasota. I'm starting to realize why everyone loves it here so much."

Alvin piped in, "It has its good points, but I wouldn't trade Sugarcreek for it permanently. I like the snow."

Lynette elbowed Emma and whispered loud enough her husband heard. "Don't let him fool you. He only likes the snow because of hunting."

"My husband Samuel likes to hunt too."

Without missing a beat, Alvin asked, "Why didn't your husband come with you?"

"Alvin, I don't think that's any of our business," Lynette stated.

Emma tried to lighten her response, all while knowing it was more of an issue than she wanted to make it. "Long story, but I came to Pinecraft on the spur of the moment."

Alvin didn't respond and kept moving forward. After they made it to the picnic table under the shade of the oak tree near the volleyball net, Lynette dropped her bag and made a rush to the water. "I've been waiting for this moment all year. I'm wasting no time dipping my toes in the ocean."

Alvin waved his wife on. "Go, enjoy yourself. I'll get things set up here and join you in a minute."

Emma took a blue and white tablecloth from her bag and flipped it over the table before setting a small cooler on the corner to keep it in place.

Alvin arranged their beach supplies in a neat pile and sat facing the ocean, watching his wife splash her feet in the salty water. "Good to see her smile."

Emma sat next to him and took in the picture-perfect view. "It's lovely. How can you not come here and smile?"

For a long while they both sat on the bench, watching Lynette enjoy herself.

Alvin leaned his arms back on the table and stretched his feet out in front of him, crossing them at his ankles. Moments passed before Alvin continued, "Lynette said you lost a baby recently too."

Emma's stomach lurched. "*Jah*."

Something was comforting knowing her new friends understood what she was going through. So much so that she didn't think twice about openly talking about it.

"I still can't believe it. I struggle with thinking there had to be something I could have done differently or some other way to prevent it."

Alvin leaned over and rested his elbows on his knees. "Lynette had the same questions." He waited to gather his thoughts. "I'm always reminded that Jesus pleaded with God for another option just before his death. But in the end, he knew there was no other way."

Emma bounced her foot while contemplating a response. "Everyone keeps telling us there's a reason God put us on this path, but I don't understand what good could come out of taking our child."

Alvin moved his head in her direction. "Most likely, He wants you to draw closer to Him."

"Perhaps, but I'm not feeling very close to God these days."

"Have you tried reaching out to Him? Communication is more than a one-way street."

"Not too much. I just don't feel like God talks to me. I'm not sure how I feel, but right now, there's not much love left in my heart."

Alvin twisted her way. "I'd say the good Lord sent you to Pinecraft, so He could work on that heart of yours."

Emma stood. "Maybe so, but right now, that ocean is looking pretty inviting."

***

As soon as the first ray of sunshine made its way above the horizon, Samuel ate a quick bite at the restaurant the boys had told him about. Afterward, he walked the streets that weaved behind the church. Stopping an older gentleman, Samuel asked how to find Gilbert Avenue. If he had to, he'd knock on every door until he found the tour guide the boys mentioned. Surely this woman would know where he could find Emma's grandmother. Standing at the crossroads of Gilbert Avenue and Fry Street, he looked up and down both ends, hoping something would guide his way.

"Looks like you could use some direction."

Samuel turned toward the petite woman on an adult size tricycle. "I sure could. I'm looking for a woman on Gilbert Avenue with the name of Mary or Mildred."

"My name is Mary, and I live on Gilbert Avenue."

"You wouldn't happen to be the woman they call the tour guide of Pinecraft?"

Mary smiled before responding. "Are you looking for a tour?"

Samuel breathed a sigh of relief. "I'm hoping you might point me to where Lillian Shetler might be staying."

"Family?"

"She's my wife's grandmother."

"Emma?"

"Yes, Emma, have you seen her?"

Mary placed her hand over her chest. "Oh, thank the Lord."

Samuel shifted his duffle bag to the other shoulder. "So, my Emma's here, for certain?"

"*Jah*. She just left to go to Siesta Key to spend the day at the beach."

"The beach? Can you tell me how to get there?"

Mary took a folded map from her bike basket and outlined the path to the closest bus stop. "It will take you about an hour, but I think they're planning on staying all day."

"They? She didn't go alone?"

"Heaven's no. The beach is more fun with friends."

Samuel positioned the map to line up with the direction he needed to go and thanked Mary for her help.

He headed off, but not before Mary stopped him. "Give me your bag and coat and let me drop it off at Lillian's. It's too hot for you to be lugging it to the beach."

After securing his belongings in her basket, he thanked her again and took off in a steady jog toward the bus stop.

***

Palm tree-lined sidewalks and sandy pathways met Samuel as he maneuvered through people making their way to the beach. It was ten o'clock, and the parking lot at the entrance to Siesta Beach was filling up. His eyes darted past the sparsely dressed women. Never had he seen such a display and found himself dropping his chin in hopes of blocking most of it out. When a young group of brightly dressed Amish girls came into view, he hoped Emma might be close by. His heavy work boots dug deep impressions in the sand, and his winter hat felt much out of place. Sweat was running between his shoulder blades, and he stopped for a moment to look up and down the miles of beach that stared back at him.

Choosing to move toward the group of girls, he stopped when Emma's frame came into view. There was no doubt it was her, even though she was dressed in light purple and not her required black mourning dress. Adrenaline mixed with a comforting warmth filled him from head to toe as he walked her way. He had no intention of eavesdropping, but there was something in the way the man's friendliness bothered him. What on earth was she thinking sitting so close to another man in public. His jaw clenched, and he balled his hands tightly.

Emma's words ... *there's not much love left in my heart* ...cut a hole in his stomach, and he swallowed hard. There was nothing he could say, so he turned and walked away.

The path back to the bus stop seemed like an eternity. He played the conversation over in his head. *Why on earth would she share something so personal ...something she needed to share with him first ...something only he should hear? Of course, she didn't feel close to him. She up and left without so much of a word. How could she be seen in public sitting so close to another man?*

The scene blinded his vision so much that his temples throbbed, and he had to blink hard to find his seat back on a bus heading back to Pinecraft.

CHAPTER 11

Samuel tightly wrapped his fingers around the glass of tea Lillian handed him. "I'm sure they'll be back anytime now. Emma will be so happy you're here. She fretted when she couldn't reach you on the phone."

"She tried to call?"

"Of course. At least five or six times. For some reason, it wouldn't let her leave a message. I'm pretty sure she called her father a day or two ago."

Samuel's stomach rolled, but he didn't tell Lillian he saw Emma and her friends at the beach. For all she knew, he couldn't find them and headed back to Pinecraft.

Lillian took a seat on the front porch beside him and used a small paper fan to stir the air. "Do you think you'll be able to stay until after Christmas? It sure would be nice to have family with us this holiday."

He took a long drink and gave Lillian a halfhearted smile. The last thing he wanted to think of was staying any longer than he had to. First and foremost, he needed to have a few words with his wife, and then he would be on his way back to Pennsylvania. With or without her.

Laughter bounced off the small cottages, and he heard Emma's voice long before she came into view. He stiffened his shoulders as she made the way up the sidewalk. Sun kissed her cheekbones, and her shorter than usual dress swayed in the breeze. Her face widened when she caught his eye, and she dropped the beach bag and ran to him. "Samuel, you found me."

He walked to the edge of the step and crossed his arms over his chest. In a harsh tone. "*Jah.*"

Her smile faded, and she turned toward Alvin and Lynette, who waited at the foot of the stairs. "Samuel, these are my new friends,

Alvin and Lynette. They're from Sugarcreek and are visiting Pinecraft for a few weeks."

Alvin extended his hand, but Samuel stood his stance without returning the gesture. After a second, Alvin dropped his hand and focused back on Emma. "We had a nice time today. Hopefully, we can do it again before you head home."

Emma moved back down the steps and picked up her bag, "Thank you again for letting me tag along."

Lynette moved in closer and whispered, "Everything okay?"

Emma squeezed her new friend's hand before saying. "It'll be fine." She waved them on and headed back up the stairs.

Lillian gathered up the empty glasses and headed inside. "I'll let you two catch up while I go start some supper."

Emma tilted her chin toward her husband. "That was pretty rude of you, don't you think? Alvin was only trying to be friendly." Samuel sat back down and grasped the arms of the wicker rocker. The muscles in his jaw quivered, and a bead of sweat rolled down his forehead.

There was no question about it; her comment only added fuel to the fire. She moved the chair closer and laid her hand across his knee. "I know you're upset with me, and you have every right to be."

She followed his glare to Alvin and Lynette walking down the middle of the street. He wiped a bead of sweat from his brow and her heart took on a new rhythm as a shade of red rose from his neck. He jerked his knee away, forcing her hand to fall.

"I thought you were dead in a snowbank somewhere."

"Samuel, please ...I tried to call as soon as I got here."

"You had no right coming all this way without clearing it with me first."

Emma folded her hands in her lap and blew out a long breath. "I know."

Samuel stood and moved toward the steps. "I need to clear my head." He didn't look back as he followed the sidewalk to the street.

Tears pooled on Emma's bottom lashes as the blurred view of Samuel walking away clouded her vision. The disappointment was evident in his slumped shoulders, and she debated whether she should run after him. No matter how much she wanted to erase the last ten weeks, it would take more than one short conversation to ease the hurt they both experienced. For a minute, she questioned his love for her. If he loved her as much as he always claimed, wouldn't it be easier for him to forgive her? But instead, he once again chose to flee when things got tough.

Lillian opened the door. "Supper is just about ready."

"I don't think I have much of an appetite."

"Emma, you have to eat. And Samuel, he must be starving after his long ordeal on his way here." She stepped out on the porch and looked around the yard. "Where did he go? Is he looking at the bushes along the side of the house that I mentioned need trimmed?"

Emma wiped the moisture from her eyes with the back of her hand. "He went for a walk."

Lillian stood at her side and tenderly patted her shoulder. "He'll come around."

"I don't think so, he's pretty mad."

"According to Mary, he couldn't run to the bus stop fast enough to find you at the beach. To me, that's a man in love. Let him figure things out in his own head first, then he'll be ready to talk."

"He went to Siesta Beach?"

"He sure did, but he wasn't gone but a couple of hours after Mary had dropped off his coat and bag. I assumed he couldn't find you and headed back."

"He sat in that chair all day waiting for you to come home. Didn't say but a handful of words. Just sat there all afternoon with the sun beating on his face."

Emma shook her head. "Oh, *Mommi*, I'm not sure how we're ever going to get through this."

Lillian moved to the railing. "I learned many years ago grief knits two hearts together more than any amount of happiness ever can. Men need to sort things out inside. If he went for a walk, he's doing exactly that. When he comes back, he will have calmed down and be ready to face you."

"We're having so much trouble communicating. I have things I need to explain, but every time I try, we end up arguing."

Lillian moved to the rocker next to her. "Perhaps you both need to talk to someone."

"He would never agree to that."

"Have you asked him?"

"No. I thought maybe Alvin and Lynette might be able to help."

Lillian leaned over and rested her hand on Emma's arm. "I think they are exactly what you both need. Spend some time with those two and you'll both go back to Pennsylvania different people."

"How so?"

Lillian smiled before patting her arm again. "Let's just say I've seen it happen before. They're on a mission for the Lord and typically find ways to change people's lives every time they come to Pinecraft."

Her grandmother changed the subject. "So, did you have a good time with them today?"

"I did. Did you know they lost a child too?"

"Mary mentioned that. How is she doing?"

"They both seem to be handling it much better than Samuel and I."

Lillian pushed a strand of gray hair back under her *kapp*. "I'm not surprised."

"Well, let me go finish supper. If you change your mind, I'll keep a plate on the back of the stove for you. Martha's making brownies for dessert. Maybe that will spike Samuel's appetite when he returns."

Emma whispered under her breath. "If he returns."

Pushing herself from the chair, Emma grabbed her beach bag and carried it inside. The smells coming from the kitchen did little to entice her to eat. Instead, she headed to her bedroom for a change of clothes.

Samuel's duffle bag and winter coat sat on the end of the bed. She picked up his jacket and brought it to her nose. The smell of wood and horse filled her senses as she breathed in her husband. She wrapped herself in his coat and curled up in a ball in the center of the bed and thought, *how had they come so far, only to be so far apart?*

***

Samuel rested his foot on the railing at the shuffleboard court and watched four men push yellow pucks back and forth across the painted triangles on the green courts. Mesmerized by the slow slide of the disks, he didn't realize an older gentleman was speaking to him.

"I'm up next but my partner didn't show up. Want to play?"

Samuel looked over his shoulder, expecting to see someone behind him. "Me?"

"*Jah.*"

"Don't know the first thing about the game."

The man gestured for him to crawl over the fence. "You'll catch on quick."

Samuel hesitated but decided it would be better to play a round of shuffleboard rather than head back to face Emma.

The older man extended his hand. "Henry Mast."

Samuel firmly gripped his outstretched hand. "Samuel Yoder."

"Northwest Pennsylvania?"

"How'd you guess?"

"Your shirt and trousers gave it away. My brother owns a lumber mill in Willow Springs. Mast Lumber, do you know it?"

"How about I live a mile from it?"

"Nothing surprises me. We meet folks from all over the country down here. Most times, we find we're related in one way or another."

Samuel took off his heavy black hat and laid it on the bench behind him. He pushed his damp bangs out of his eyes and concentrated on the rules of the game as Henry explained them.

"I think I got it. The object is to move your puck in the scoring zone without going outside the lines."

"I knew you'd catch on quick."

As Samuel took his turn, Henry asked, "So what brings you to Pinecraft? Work or pleasure."

Samuel nodded his chin in Henry's direction as he used the long paddle, or what Henry called the pang, to propel his biscuit to the other end of the court. The yellow puck slid tightly into the eight-position, knocking one of their opponents' biscuits off the board. Henry slapped Samuel on the back. "I think I found myself a new partner!"

Samuel stood off to the side as Henry studied his next move and said, "Lucky shot."

"Lucky shot my foot. It takes most guys weeks to score like that."

Samuel enjoyed the friendly game for the next hour with little conversation other than a few sly remarks about his form and skill level.

After Henry made his last shot, he held up his paddle and said, "That's game, boys. Tomorrow at noon?"

The two men at the far end of the court waved and handed their pangs to the waiting players.

Henry and Samuel did the same and moved to the back of the court under the covered benches. "So how about it? Tomorrow at noon?"

Samuel took a drink from the cold-water bottle Henry pulled from the cooler before responding, "Maybe."

"I'll take that as a yes." Henry swung the canvas bag over his shoulder and walked to where his friends had gathered.

The sun started its descent over Phillippi Creek while Samuel sat viewing a volleyball game in progress. Before long, he'd have to make his way back to Emma's grandmother's house or choose to spend the night on one of the benches in the park. After his night on the steps, he needed a soft bed, regardless of how badly he didn't want to face the truth about Emma. Conflict, especially with his wife, was one thing he hoped he could avoid at all costs.

The short walk back to Graber Avenue did little to calm his apprehension. A slight breeze had cooled the evening temperature to a comfortable setting, and he took refuge back in the rocker on the porch. Off in the distance, someone played a harmonica, and the aroma of grilling meat floated through the air. His stomach growled, and he hoped he could find something to eat without disturbing Lillian or her *schwester*.

As if Emma read his mind, she appeared on the porch, plate in hand. "You missed dinner. Lillian made chicken and biscuits, one of your favorites."

She handed him the plate and set a glass of ice water on the stand between them. "*Denki*," was all he could muster.

"After you eat, can we talk?"

He wasn't in the mood for a lengthy conversation, but he was hungry and bowed his head for a silent prayer without answering her. He pushed a biscuit around on his plate and watched her out of the corner of his eye. In the two weeks, since they'd been apart, she changed. What it was, he couldn't pinpoint. Not yet back to herself, but not so rough around the edges. Maybe the brightly colored dress added color to her cheeks, or it was the day in the sun. Whatever it was, she looked rested. It could be that the time they spent apart transformed her, and if that was the case, he was at his wit's end to know how to fix it.

She calmly sat with her hands folded on her lap, waiting for him to finish without muttering a word. The silence almost drowned out the evening whispers of their surroundings. After taking the last bite, he balanced his plate on the railing in front of him and picked his glass back up. Clearing his throat without looking her way, he asked, "Where are your own clothes?"

She snapped her head in his direction. "We haven't seen each other in almost two weeks, and your only concern is my clothes?"

He took a drink before responding, "It's customary to honor our child for a year. I say your attire would hardly be considered such."

"You sound a lot like Bishop Weaver, and the last time I checked, he's over a thousand miles away."

"Regardless of how far we are from home, I'd prefer you follow our ways."

He knew his wife well enough to know the sudden rise and fall of her chest was an indication she was suppressing her words.

"We have more important things to discuss other than my clothes."

Samuel placed the glass on the table and stood near the railing with his back to her. "We do. Let's start with you going to the beach with Alvin."

"I didn't go alone. Lynette was with us."

"It's not proper."

Emma squeezed her fingers together. "Where's this coming from? You're being unreasonable."

Samuel glared. "Unreasonable? Let's talk about being irresponsible. How about taking off without letting me know where you were going? Or not calling. How about spending the day at the beach like you were on vacation or something?"

Emma looked over her shoulder to the window. "Lower your voice. *Mommi* hasn't gone to bed yet."

He clenched his jaw. "I don't really care who hears me. The fact is you're acting as if you have no responsibility to me or our life in Willow Springs."

"If I remember correctly, it was you who sent me off to my mother's when you didn't know what else to do with me. And you ...who shuts down whenever I want to talk about James. You care more about finishing that house than you do about how I'm feeling."

Samuel sat back down so hard the chair hit the gray stucco wall. "Because life goes on."

Emma sat up straight. "For you, but not me."

"What's that supposed to mean?"

"When life got hard, you pawned me off on someone else and then got mad when I changed course. You wanted me to find a way to deal with everything that happened. Well, this is the way I chose."

Samuel stayed quiet as she spoke to him in a tone unlike herself. Surer of herself and bolder than the Emma he'd known since before she could walk.

She stood and reached for the door. "We're getting nowhere, and I've had just about enough of this day. I'm going to bed."

Samuel stayed on the front porch long after the inside lights were put to sleep. He didn't handle any of it like a true leader of his family and so desperately wanted a do-over. They had been married for a little over a year, and he felt ill-equipped to handle such upheaval. One step forward and five back was the only thing mulling over in his head. There was no denying it; Emma was much better at expressing her feelings than he was. But again, he was a man and typically didn't have an emotion he could put into words. More than once, Emma asked him to express his feelings, but they were foreign to him. When she was broken and begging for his understanding, all he could say was ...*nothing* ...because nothing was typically what was in his head. What had his mother explained to him? *...This is a season for her, and she must fight her way back in her own way, in her own time...* Could this be how she was fighting back? If it was, he didn't like it too much. But again, neither of them liked anything about the last few months.

Like always, he needed something to keep his hands busy. Instead of going inside, he walked off the porch and pulled the overhead roll-top door open to Martha's garage.

He found the chain to the overhead light and walked to the bench along the far wall. A broken bird feeder and half-painted porch sign filled the table. After several attempts to hammer the tiny pieces back together, he sat on a stool next to the workbench. Irritating bugs circled his head and landed on his sweat-filled face. It was past nine o'clock, and even though a slight breeze was evident, it did little to cool him off in the enclosed structure. He switched on a small fan on the table, and it blew the pesky bugs away from his face. If life could only be so easy, he'd flip a switch and blow the ugliness of the day away.

CHAPTER 12

The purr of the air conditioner woke Emma out of her restless sleep. The strange sounds and the illuminated alarm clock forced her to open her eyes. Light made its way through the blinds, just as a shift in the mattress alarmed her. She had no idea when Samuel came to bed, but a layer of uneasiness faded away, knowing he was at least by her side. She turned to face his sleeping features and missed the coziness they shared during the wee hours of the day. Oh, how she wished they could find their way back.

She gently crawled out of bed and moved slowly over the cool tile floor toward the door. Inviting smells lingered in the air as she made her way to the kitchen. Lillian sat at the table peeling apples and smiled at Emma when she poured herself a cup of coffee.

Without saying a word, Lillian pushed a flyer across the table with the point of her knife. "I asked Mary to drop off information about the group Alvin leads at the church. I thought perhaps you and Samuel might want to check it out."

Emma stirred sugar in her cup and picked up the brightly colored brochure. Printed across the top of the flyer was YOUR PERSONAL INVITATION TO MEET JESUS.

Emma flipped the paper over. *Come join us as we gather to glorify God through fellowship to study God's Word. The Bible provides practical answers to life's questions for all willing to listen and obey what it teaches. Enjoy a warm and friendly atmosphere where God's Word is clearly taught and discover the truth of Jesus.*

"*Mommi*, what do you think they mean by discover the truth of Jesus? I've heard that so many times over the last couple weeks."

Lillian peered over her wire-rimmed glasses she wore low on her nose. "Like I said yesterday, I believe you'll go home a different person, and in more ways than one if you spend some time with Alvin and Lynette."

Emma laid the brochure aside and picked back up her mug. "I have the feeling you're trying to tell me something. Can't you just come out and say it?"

Her grandmother continued to peel an apple and paused a few moments before continuing, "Sometimes, what you need to learn needs to grow deep inside your heart."

Emma picked up a slice of apple and nibbled on it before adding, "I'm starting to question bits and pieces of my life that make no sense."

Lillian asked, "Like what?"

"To begin with, why have Lynette and Alvin found it so easy to get over losing their child when Samuel and I are a mess?"

"I doubt they've gotten over it. I think they've ridden the storm through God's Word."

"You think they found comfort in the bible?"

"I do. Security you can only find deep in the chapters of Jesus' story."

Emma fidgeted in her chair. "Have you read the bible?"

"A few times. But it wasn't until I was in my fifties before I picked up an English version."

Emma raised an eyebrow. "Marie gave me hers when I visited."

Lillian popped a slice of apple in her mouth. "Have you started to read it yet?"

"No, I feel like I'm betraying Samuel. We are to read from the German Bible."

Lillian picked up a towel and dried her hands. "Emma, my dear, let me tell you a story about your birth father."

Emma rested her hands around her cup and leaned in. "Does it have anything to do with why he left the Amish in the first place?"

"That it does. What your grandfather told you years ago about him jumping the fence to the English world had little to do with the truth. Yes, he was drinking way too much. But he struggled to understand why our church leaders were so blind to what was clearly outlined in God's Word. He got in trouble for sharing what he read with the young folk around our community. Your birth mother, Marie, was Mennonite and knew the truth."

"I'm confused. What was my father sharing that was so bad it got him excommunicated?"

Lillian folded her hands over Emma's. "He shared the truth of salvation through Jesus Christ."

Emma flipped her hands over and squeezed her grandmother's soft fingers. "Stella left me a note. She spoke of the same thing. She told me I had to search for the truth of Jesus. How is it I've been taught that my only way to heaven was through my works, and I wouldn't learn if I made it to heaven until the day I stand before him?"

"Child, listen to me. Jesus died on the cross to pave your way to heaven, and the only way to get there is to accept Jesus Christ as your Lord and Savior deep in your heart. None of us will find our forever home through our works because none of us will ever be good enough."

"And the bible tells us this, are you sure?"

"I'm surer of it than I am of anything else on this earth."

Emma furrowed her eyebrows. "And my birth father left the Amish because of this?"

"He did. It wasn't until after he died that your grandfather and the other ministers chose to look for the truth on their own. It was your father's shunning that changed the way our leaders shared the Word. Because of your father, our whole community was encouraged to study a bible they understood."

"But *Mommi,* this isn't what Samuel and I were taught, and not what my *datt* believes." Emma brought her fingers to her lips and whispered, "I bet that's why *Datt* got so upset when I told him about *Mamm's* letter. He told me I shouldn't share it with anyone. It would cause too much turmoil in the community."

Lillian lowered her voice and nodded, "It will, for sure and certain."

Emma rested her chin in the palm of her hands. "Between James and this with Samuel, it's just way too much."

Lillian pointed to the flyer on the table. "One thing at a time. Go to the meeting. I'm certain it will help. Then the Lord will find a way to help you accept everything else."

"But what should I do about Samuel? He'll never agree with any of this. Just one more secret I'm keeping from him."

Noise in the hallway hushed them both, and Lillian tapped the brochure and mouthed, "Go."

Emma tucked the flyer in her housecoat pocket.

***

Samuel stood in the hallway, a few feet from the kitchen, and listened in on Emma and her grandmother's conversation. Once again, he heard Emma share things she should be telling him. What happened to the closeness they once had? Shouldn't a wife share things with her husband first? And what was the secret she was keeping from him? One more thing to put a wedge between them. With every passing day, they slipped farther and farther apart. How was he to keep their marriage from sinking?

Clearing his throat, he took the last few steps into the kitchen. He looked past Emma and nodded a warm good morning to Lillian.

Emma stood and rushed to the stove to pour him a cup of coffee. "Are you hungry? I could make you breakfast?"

He pressed his lips together and ran his hand through his hair. "No, just coffee."

All the air seemed to be sucked from the room with his icy response. Emma's tone sounded hopeful when she asked, "It's Christmas Eve, and Alvin invited us to come to their Christmas Eve service. Would you like to go?"

Even the sound of Alvin's name coming from Emma's lips forced his chest muscle to tense. "I have plans today."

"Plans? What might they be?"

His gut response was to lash out, but with Lillian in the room, he brought it down a level and responded, "I just have plans."

Lillian stood to leave. "Help yourself to anything you want; I'll take my coffee out to the front porch."

Samuel waited until Lillian closed the front door before addressing Emma.

"I checked the bus schedule, and the first seat available is next Wednesday. I assume you'll be ready to go home by then?"

Emma leaned against the counter. "There is a meeting next Wednesday night at the church. I was hoping you'd go with me."

"We don't need a meeting; we need to go home."

"Samuel, please. Maybe you don't think you do, but I do."

Samuel leaned over to tie his boot. "What you need to do is move on. God has made it clear James was not ours to keep. We've been over this; how many more times do we need to discuss it?"

Emma laid her hand across his arm. "It's not just James. I have questions, and I think I can only get my answers if we stay in Pinecraft a bit longer. I think Alvin might be able to help us."

The vein at his temple bulged. "What is it about him that you keep bringing his name into our problems?"

"He's a minister, and I think he can help."

"What do you think Bishop Weaver is? I'm sure he would be willing to answer any questions we have. He even told me so before I left."

Samuel folded up his shirt sleeves while she asked, "Told you what?"

"That we might have questions, and we weren't to be ashamed if we did."

Emma played with the hem of her housecoat. "I have things I need to sort out, but I don't think Bishop Weaver can help me with any of them."

In a gruff tone, he replied, "I feel like we're playing cat and mouse. How about you share your questions with me and let me decide if we need to bring them before the bishop."

Emma found a tissue in her pocket and rolled it through her fingers. "We have to sort through a few things, but I need to talk to someone who can help me get past this block I have with God."

He pushed his chair away from the table and towered over her. "Then you'll do it alone. Next Wednesday, I'm leaving for home, with or without you."

The back door slammed shut, and he only glanced back for a moment. Emma's pretty eyes turned dark, and one more layer of distress inched its way between them.

Heading to the garage, a loose sheet of paper blew across the yard in front of him. Stomping his foot on top of the flyer, he picked it up and read the bold letters. *YOUR PERSONAL INVITATION TO MEET JESUS – Come to the picnic shelter at Pinecraft Park on Saturday at 2:00 pm to find out more.* He folded the paper and stuffed it in his pocket before opening the garage door.

***

The sting of Samuel's words weighed heavy on Emma's heart. She placed their cups in the sink and went to get dressed. Everything in her grandmother's house was strange. Even though they still reverted to reading by lantern, everything else in the small cottage screamed English. Both Lillian and Martha told her they indulged in a few more liberties in Pinecraft than in Sugarcreek. She couldn't help but think for once in her life, it would be Pinecraft's liberty that would allow her to explore things her strict Old Order community forbids. For that she felt hopeful.

She opened the dresser drawer and uncovered Marie's bible. The well-worn leather felt smooth in her hands, and she fanned the pages through her fingers. There was no doubt about it. She was about to embrace a new chapter in her life. Deep inside, she struggled to figure out if she was feeling fear or the anticipation of something bigger.

The hair on her arms tingled, and she stopped at the place where Marie's bookmark was tucked in its spine. She read the words from the card over again. *IF YOU SENSE YOUR FAITH IS UNRAVELLING* ...and whispered to herself, "Is that what I'm feeling, my faith unraveling?"

She scanned through the thin pages looking for something, but she didn't know what. Her grandmother wouldn't tell her something that wasn't true, neither would Stella or Marie. She had to find the truth, but where to start.

Samuel's deep voice echoed through the walls, and she scurried to hide Marie's bible under the layer of clothes while his footsteps came closer. She took a yellow dress from the drawer and laid it on the bed just as he opened the door.

He glared at the brightly colored fabric and snarled, "I forgot my hat."

She picked it up from the top of the dresser and handed it to him. He held one side and her the other, neither wanting to break the line between them. "I'll be securing bus tickets today, for next Wednesday."

She dropped her hold on the hat. "I'm not going home yet."

The lines in his jaw protruded, and he turned and walked away.

Emma sat down on the bed and ran her hand across the lightweight dress. If he couldn't come to terms with her wanting to stay, how was he ever going to accept her need to find the truth her mother's spoke of? Or even the issue of them not having children for two years? She laid back on the unmade bed and tucked her legs under the quilt. All she wanted to do was hide under the covers and scream.

***

The small wooden bird feeder fell apart in Samuel's hand when he added more pressure to the flimsy sides than necessary. Emma's defiance frustrated him to no end, and the dull pain behind his eyes magnified every time he pictured the yellow dress.

Samuel felt his presence long before Henry Mast said a word. "Mary Miller said I'd find you here. I wanted to make sure I still had a partner today."

The birdhouse tumbled in pieces in front of him, and Samuel groaned, "Ugh."

Henry stepped off his bike and moved beside him. "Glue would probably work better."

Samuel dug around on the shelf above his head for a bottle of wood glue. "These big hands were meant for farming and framing, not projects like this."

Henry leaned on the workbench. "Young men like you find it hard to sit still down here. Not enough to do, they say."

"I'd have to agree with them. If I could, I'd be on a bus heading home by now."

"Why so fast? You just got here. I'd say by the looks of that feeder, you need to unwind some."

Samuel took a pair of pliers to loosen the cap to the glue. "*Jah*, I made a mess of it."

"Spend some time with us old folks, and the cares of the world won't seem so big."

Samuel put the cap to the bottle aside. "I could only wish."

Henry held the side and bottom of the feeder together as Samuel trailed a glue line along the edge. "Whatever's eating at you is probably not as big as you're making it."

Samuel added a clamp to hold the wood together. "Women."

Henry laughed and said, "Well, that explains it all. When women are involved, I throw all advice out the window."

Samuel picked up a red rag and wiped the glue from his fingers. "Do I need to say more?"

Henry stepped back over his bike, sat on the seat, and used his feet to push it backwards out of the garage. "All I can say is listen."

"Listen?"

"*Jah*, listen. We're hard-headed, and if we listen, instead of trying to find a way to fix things, messes like that bird feeder wouldn't happen."

Henry's words didn't really make sense, but he pushed them aside momentarily as Henry made his way down the driveway. "Noon?"

"Probably."

"Good, and remember you can't fix everything, but you can listen."

Glue was no longer on Samuel's hands, but he continued to run the rag over his fingers while he thought, *It's my job to fix things. I've been listening, but all I've heard is her talking to everyone but me.*

Shaking his head, he moved to the back of the garage in search of hedge trimmers. If he couldn't fix his wife, he could at least take care of some things around the house.

He stuffed the shop rag in his pocket and stopped when the piece of paper touched his fingers. Pulling the flyer from his pocket, he reread the invitation. YOUR PERSONAL INVITATION TO MEET

JESUS. Maybe he'd stick around the park for the afternoon to see what it was all about.

CHAPTER 13

Emma hadn't meant to fall back asleep and only woke when Lillian stood over her.

"Emma, Lynette is here. Should I tell her you're resting?"

Brushing her hair from her face, she asked, "What time is it?"

"It's eleven-thirty."

"Oh my, I slept all morning. Please tell Lynette I'll be right out." Emma reached out to grab her grandmother's sleeve. "I'm sorry you had to listen to Samuel and me this morning."

Lillian touched her hand. "No worries, you're both young, and you'll find a way to work through your differences. I'm sure of it. I think what you need to do is spend some time with Lynette. Both she and Alvin have helped a good many of the young folk around here, and I'm sure they can help you and Samuel as well."

In a hopeful plea she said, "I sure hope so."

"Trust me, child, if you'll both open your hearts to what they have to share, you'll find the peace you need."

"I sure hope so, *Mommi*."

"Now get dressed, and I'll make Lynette some tea while she's waiting."

Lynette and her grandmother had moved to the front porch and were murmuring when she found them. As she opened the door, she heard her grandmother say. "She needs a friend like you."

Emma stepped outside and said, "I do need a friend, that's for sure."

Lynette stood. "Good because I could use a friend to join me at the Coffee Café."

Emma kissed her grandmother on the cheek before saying, "That sounds like a great idea."

Both girls stepped off the porch and waved at Lillian as they headed to the street.

Lynette grabbed Emma's arm to slow down. "Not so fast, we have all day, and there is no reason to rush."

Emma fell into step with her. "I'm sorry I forgot I don't have a list of chores I need to complete. Not that I've been doing many chores lately, I've spent more time sulking around than anything constructive the last couple months."

"I totally agree, but here in Pinecraft, we can indulge in a slower pace."

They walked for a few minutes without saying a word until Emma asked, "My grandmother said you and Alvin help the young folk around here. What do you do?"

"Well, Alvin does a good bit, but all I do is help him wherever I can."

"Like what?"

Lynette pulled a flyer from her purse and handed it to her. "Come see for yourself."

"*Mommi* showed me that flyer this morning. I want to go, but I'm not sure I can convince Samuel to come. He wants to go home on Wednesday."

"Emma, you have to come, and hopefully, we can get Samuel to agree too. It will do you both some good. Alvin is a great teacher. He has gone through training and has a way of helping our people through tough spots by looking to the Bible for answers."

Emma held the flyer up to study it closer. "So what does he teach about?"

"All sorts of things. But mainly, we show you how to turn to Jesus for answers."

Emma handed the brochure back to Lynette and asked, "Do you believe God puts us on a path for a reason?"

"Do I ever. I think you got on that bus in Sugarcreek because he paved your way to Pinecraft. I don't think it was a coincidence that you and I met, and Samuel followed you here. Both of you were meant to hear what Alvin and I have to say. I'm sure of it."

"How can you be so sure?"

"Because you're not the first young couple from an Old Order community that has crossed our path. God lines Alvin and me up with young couples all the time. Most times, they have an issue they need to talk through just like you and Samuel do."

"You sound so confident. How can you be so sure Samuel and I were meant to be here?"

"The good Lord gave Alvin the gift of teaching, and he uses it to open the eyes of many people to the love of Jesus."

Both girls stopped talking long enough to order drinks and find a free table under an umbrella. Once they settled into their seats, Emma continued, "I have to tell you I feel something huge is going to shift in my life. I can't pinpoint what it is, but I'm excited and fearful at the same time."

Lynette smiled. "Emma, you have no idea what's about to happen, but by the grace of God, you will come to understand how trusting in Jesus will change your life; if you'll let Him."

A nervous giggle escaped Emma's lips. "You're scaring me."

Lynette laughed and stirred her drink with the straw. "Trust me, you have nothing to fear. Once you fully understand how Jesus walks with you and you truly trust Him in everything. Your fear will turn into a passion like nothing you've ever experienced."

Emma sat back in her chair and wiped the moisture from the outside of her cup. "But we still have one obstacle."

"What's that?"

"Samuel. He's ready to go home."

Lynette grinned. "I'm not going to worry about that, and neither should you. God will take care of that, I'm sure of it."

"He's pretty set on going home, with or without me, were his exact words."

"Have faith Emma. God works all things for His good, and that includes helping Samuel see how much you both need what we want to share."

Emma tried to embrace Lynette's confidence, but she knew her husband. If he thought they were going against the *Ordnung,* he'd never agree, or that was what she assumed.

Emma changed the subject, hoping to push away her apprehension of Samuel agreeing to stay in Pinecraft longer. "Can I ask you something?"

"Sure, what is it?"

"I know you're still hurting from your own loss, but you don't seem to wear it on your sleeve as obviously as I do. How are you doing that?"

"You can't see it, can you?"

"No, what is it?"

"If I hadn't lost a child just like you, I wouldn't have been led to reach out to you on the bus. You would have slipped right by me without any connection, and we most likely wouldn't be sitting here right now. How can that not be from God?"

Emma opened her hands and waved them through the air. "So, you're saying all of this was to bring us together?"

"I'm certain of it."

Lynette leaned in and whispered, "Look around. All of these people have come from an array of communities. Old Order, New Order, Beachy Amish, and Mennonite. Pinecraft is a melting pot of different beliefs all in one place. Young and old. Believers of salvation through works and believers of salvation through Christ. What better place to spread God's word than right here in Pinecraft? It's no accident you and Samuel are here, and it's no accident we both lost a child to bring us together."

Emma laid a hand on her heart. "I'm still mad at God for taking James and not allowing me to have more children right away."

"He has a bigger plan for you, Emma Yoder. You just can't see it yet. But I promise you before you leave Florida, you'll figure out what that might be."

"Do you have any idea what it is?"

"I have a few thoughts, but that's between you and God, and I'll let Him show you in His own time."

Lynette threw her cup in the trash. "How about we walk to the Park? The old guys should be playing shuffleboard by now, and it's fun to watch."

***

Samuel showed up a few minutes before noon and not one minute before Henry was about to send out a search party. Rounding the corner of the pavilion Henry hollered, "It's about time."

"I had a run-in with a hedge trimmer."

"I entered us into a tournament next Wednesday. Our start time is two, and we are players eight and nine."

Samuel threw his shoulders back. "I was thinking about heading home on Wednesday."

"I don't think so," Henry added as he handed Samuel the paddle.

Samuel picked up the pang and made his first shot. "What makes you so sure?"

"Because you have a tournament to play in, and what's so pressing at home other than shoveling snow?"

Samuel didn't answer but gave the old man a pointed look.

The two played the rest of the game with barely a word between them. When Henry guided the biscuit to the other end of the court, they both hollered when his shot won the game. "See, another reason why you're not going home on Wednesday. That win just moved us up to the next level. We go up against the winning team from last year. No way I'm looking for a new player this late in the season."

Samuel pushed his bangs off his forehead, "Good thing I didn't buy tickets yet, or you'd have no choice but to find another player."

Henry slapped Samuel on the back. "The Lord knows what he's doing, I'm sure of it."

"I'm not so sure a Shuffleboard Tournament is high on his priority list."

"We'll see about that; you can count on it."

"I'm not counting on anything but finding something cold to drink and getting out of this sun."

They handed the pangs off to the following players and walked to a shaded picnic bench. Henry handed him a bottle of water. "There is the team we go up against next week. I think I'll sit right here and see if I can figure out their strategy."

Samuel let out a deep snort. "Strategy? Not so sure there's much skill or advanced planning to push a disk around."

"Maybe so, but let's watch just in case."

Samuel looked up under the picnic shelter, hoping to see some signs of the meeting he wanted to catch, before taking a seat beside Henry.

"Looking for someone?"

Samuel pulled the flyer out of his pocket and showed it to Henry. "Do you know what this is all about?"

"Ah, *jah.* Alvin Miller preaches, and he and his wife Lynette facilitate a bible study. They visit us a few times a year and do an excellent job reaching out to the community while they're here.

"His wife?"

"*Jah*, Lynette. Sweet girl. I hear they lost a baby a few months back, and I was surprised she joined him this time."

Like a freight train, Samuel felt his harsh treatment slap him in his face. "Alvin's a minister?"

"Sure is, and one of the best around, in my books. He might be young, but he's got the voice of God running through his veins."

"How so?"

"Come find out for yourself."

Henry studied Samuel's face before asking, "You're in the same church district as my brother in Willow Springs?"

"*Jah.*"

He made a sound Samuel couldn't quite understand and then Henry asked, "You never did answer what brought you to Pinecraft."

Samuel swirled his hat on his finger and concentrated on the game at the other end of the court. He had no desire to share with Henry the real reason he came to Pinecraft.

Henry stood. "Whatever the reason, I guarantee you'll go home a different man if you stick around a while."

"How so?"

"Take my word for it. You'll see soon enough, I'm sure."

Samuel didn't like puzzles, and Henry's vague warning didn't sit quite right. Following voices from the group, gathering at the far end of the shelter Samuel turned on the bench. He looked at the flyer one more time and crumbled it and threw it in the trash. Something drew him to the crowd, and he waited until his eyes adjusted to the shade before finding a seat near the front.

***

Lynette and Emma stopped at the fence to watch a game in progress before following a group to the covered shelter. "Alvin is going to talk briefly about our meeting on Wednesday night. Let's go listen."

Emma looked ahead and grabbed Lynette's arm. "Samuel's here."

"Where?"

Emma pointed and whispered, "Right there."

"Do you want to go sit with him?"

Emma stopped walking and contemplated what she should do. "No, I don't think so. I want to hear what Alvin has to say, but I'm not sure Samuel would want me to know he's here. He told me he had plans today. Maybe this was what he was referring to."

She pulled Lynette back. "Let's sit back here, so he doesn't see me.

Emma watched as her husband leaned his elbows on his knees and twirled his hat around his fingers; something he did when he was uncomfortable. She closed her eyes and said a silent prayer hoping God would lay something on his heart that would soften his stance about leaving so soon.

A couple dozen people gathered around Alvin and waited for him to begin. Emma wiped her palms on the skirt of her dress and took a seat beside Lynette. A pillar blocked Samuel from her view, and she shielded herself further behind Lynette's shoulder.

Alvin cleared his throat and began. "Who here likes to play baseball?"

Almost everyone under the shelter held their hand up. Samuel, however, kept his head hung low.

"I like to use the game as a metaphor for meeting Jesus. In a game, we all come together to play as a team. Every position is important, and no one can play without relying on each team member to play his part. Agree?"

Everyone nodded in agreement.

"So, who here thinks life has thrown them a curve ball?"

Alvin nodded his head in the direction of those who held their hands up. "Who here would like to think they had someone in their corner to pinch-hit when life threw them out of the game?" Again, just about everyone raised their hand.

Alvin smiled before saying, "Me too!"

"If you showed up here today, then it's your first step in discovering the truth in Jesus and getting in the game."

"First, let me explain. I know how difficult it might be to admit you have something in your life throwing you out. It could be a job, relationship issues, the loss of a loved one, and yes, even addiction. Whatever you're struggling with can be addressed if you put your trust in Jesus for your salvation and have faith you'll make it home through Him."

A sudden hum of whispers filtered around the group. The air under the picnic shelter stopped, and many attendees looked at Alvin, hoping he'd explain further. By the looks of the people who had gathered, many were Old Order and had little knowledge of Jesus's actual plan for their lives. Yes, they believed He existed and would meet Him if they worked hard enough to follow the rules. But trust him in salvation? That was foreign to their ears. Emma cringed when Samuel spoke up. "Many of us were not taught such things. Are you certain you want to expose these young people to these teachings? You do realize what upheaval it will cause to their families."

"Good question and I bet many of you have the same concern. Our Wednesday night Bible study is a tool to help you move forward in your walk with Jesus. Which, in turn, will help you maneuver your way around the bases of ensuring you make it to your forever home. You can only know what God offers us if you study the bible in greater detail."

Emma's sensed Samuel's jaw tense even if she couldn't see his face. She thought for sure he was about to leave, but he settled back down as Alvin continued.

"What I'm trying to share is that there are many scriptures that have been kept from you. A truth that can only be found when you look deep in the pages of the bible. A truth that will set you free. What I'm about to share will cause an awakening in your heart that may change your life forever." Alvin held a bible above his head and asked, "How many of you have read this book?' A few young girls raised their hands but quickly put them down when everyone turned their way. Alvin smiled and continued, "There's no shame in admitting you've found yourself drawn to the pages of this book. It's the one place where you can find many answers to the questions you have and the one place where you'll find comfort like no other. The place where you'll find Jesus."

Emma bumped Lynette with her shoulder. "Samuel's going to flee. I can see how uneasy he is."

Lynette touched her arm. "Relax, let him finish. You'll be surprised at how he can draw people in."

"I'm not here to tell you I have all the answers, but I am here to say you don't have to go it alone. Life is hard, and things can be challenging, but I know of something bigger that can work in my life and yours. If you have something weighing you down, I invite you to join us on Wednesday evening. I promise to answer all of your questions then."

Emma sunk down when Samuel stood and spoke up. "You're asking many of these people to go against their church."

Alvin didn't back down and directed his following comment to Samuel. "I certainly understand your apprehension, and you have every right to question what I'm saying. But don't you owe it to yourself and your family to know the truth?"

In a huff, Samuel added, "You're setting these young people up for conflict within their own community."

“You're correct, it may. But studying the Word will help restore their faith in God, and they have major choices to make in their walk with Jesus. As followers of Christ, we aren't called to stand on the sidelines but to suit up and get in the game. "

Emma crawled under the picnic table. Her heart was about to burst out of her chest when Samuel's voice got louder as he stomped by. "You're just asking for trouble."

Emma watched as her husband's heavy boots passed by the table while she stayed hidden.

CHAPTER 14

Lillian and Martha moved in harmony around the kitchen, putting supper on the table. Their lighthearted chatter filled the air despite Emma trying to pull Samuel out of his solemn mood. He had no idea she witnessed his outburst earlier, and she prayed she could find a way to ease the surrounding tension.

Lillian filled his glass with ice water and asked, "Martha and I are going to the Christmas Eve service at the Mennonite Church. Would you and Emma like to go with us?"

Emma held her breath, waiting for him to respond. "I don't think it would be wise for us to attend but thank you for the invitation."

She knew it would cause a great deal of strife between them even before she said, "I want to go."

Lines etched around Samuel's eyes. "Bishop Weaver wouldn't approve"

A million thoughts rang through her head, but the one thing that gnawed at her soul was that her husband cared more about keeping face with the bishop than he did about learning the truth. On the other hand, she needed to find the peace and joy Lynette and Alvin carried with them, regardless of the cost.

Lillian put a casserole dish in the center of the table. "If you change your mind, it starts at seven."

Emma pushed potatoes and ham around on her plate as she tried to come up with the words needed to convince her husband to change his mind. There were times like this when she wished she could be more like her best friend, Katie. She would never go against Daniel in matters like this. Completely and without a doubt, Katie followed Daniel's lead in every aspect of their life. Katie was a much better Amish wife than she was.

No doubt about it, she had a mind of her own and often challenged Samuel in matters where he was to make the decisions. He often teased her that she favored her birth mother far more than she did her Amish *mamm*. This was one of those times when she knew she had to go against his wishes and follow her heart.

After Lillian and Martha excused themselves to the front room, Emma poured Samuel a cup of coffee and finished cleaning up the kitchen. Samuel sat at the head of the table reading through the Budget Newspaper. Words toyed around in Emma's head until she said, "I don't mean to go against your wishes, and I certainly don't want to upset you more than you are already, but I feel I have to go tonight."

He snapped the paper and lowered it below his chin, "What do you want from me? How can I lead us if you argue with me about everything?"

In a tone that resembled hopelessness, he continued, "I'm really at my wit's end. I suppose I can't stop you if you want to go, but I'll not be joining you, and I will be bringing this up with the bishop when we return home."

For a moment, Emma sympathized with him, until he brought the bishop back up. "If I have to hear one more time about what Bishop Weaver thinks one more time, I'll go crazy. Since when do you hold on to his every word for guidance? Maybe Alvin is right. Don't you owe it to yourself and our family to know the truth?"

Samuel laid the paper aside. "Where were you this afternoon?"

"In the park, just like you."

"I don't need some young Mennonite preacher to tell me how I should lead my family and what I should be reading in scripture."

Lowering her voice Emma said, "Exactly why I felt drawn to him and what he has to say."

"Something is telling me I need to find out what Alvin is talking about. Samuel, I want to study the bible, but I can't do that at home. Please come with me. There has to be a reason God brought us here."

For a moment, she thought he might concede. His eyes darted around the room then settled on hers. "It goes against everything we've been taught. How can you expect me to throw twenty-three years of instruction out the window? Once you pick up that Bible, all things will change."

Emma rubbed her fingers across his forearm. "How can that be a bad thing?"

"Because we made a promise to God and our community to follow the ways of our forefathers."

"But Samuel, we're encouraged to look for instruction in the Bible. How can that go against anything we've been taught? I want to know everything. I can't explain it, but I have a feeling God is trying to show us something."

Samuel leaned back in his chair and squared his shoulders, "I'm certain the ministers will tell us anything we want to know."

She gave him a few minutes to ponder his thoughts before adding, "I'm not so sure they'll tell us everything." She stood and said, "Wait here, I want to show you something."

Emma went to her room to find the letter Stella had left for her. Within seconds, she returned and removed the letter from the pink envelope and handed it to him.

Her pulse quickened when his expression didn't change, and he handed it back to her. "This truth your *mamm* speaks of will change us."

"So, you know what she's talking about? Why haven't you shared it with me? For weeks I've been trying to figure out what it means. Marie told me about it, Nathan's mother Rosie spoke of it. Lynette has been hinting about it, and even *Mommi* talks about salvation through Christ. Why haven't we been taught that?"

He stood and moved to the backdoor. "You need to drop it. I don't think either one of us is ready to face the turmoil this will cause."

"Samuel, please, I feel like we were sent here for a reason. This has to be God's answer for taking James from us. He wants us to learn the truth. Why else would he pave the way for us to come all the way to Pinecraft?"

There was a heaviness in the way Samuel opened the door. "You're asking for trouble for sure and certain."

When the door closed, Emma folded her arms on the table, rested her head in their creases, and prayed. "*Please, Lord, show me what you want me to do. I know going against my husband is not what you have in store for me. But I need to know what everyone is trying to teach me. They all can't be wrong, can they?"*

***

Samuel followed the street until he made his way back to Pinecraft Park. The path along the banks of Phillippi Creek called to him, and he maneuvered his way around a group of young men deep in a heated conversation about Alvin's earlier meeting.

"If my *datt* finds out, he'll put a stop to it right quick."

"Mine too. But what if that preacher is right?"

"My folks are pressuring me to take my kneeling vow, but before I do, I want to know the whole truth."

One of the boys hollered toward Samuel. "Hey, you were there this afternoon. What do you think? Is he right?"

Without answering right away, Samuel played his response over in his head. Had someone told him the truth before he promised God and his community to live by the rules of the *Ordnung,* he might have chosen otherwise. But now, he had no other choice but to abide by the rules he promised to uphold. Could he help this group of young men not make the same mistake?

He turned to face the group. "If you haven't already been baptized, I'd say you owe it to yourself to find the truth and then make your own decision."

His comment left the boys speechless, and he walked away.

There was no hesitation in speaking what he knew was real to the young boys. He knew what the truth would do to their lives, and it wasn't too late for them. But for him, it meant division and separation from his family. Hard as he might try, he knew he couldn't keep Emma from the truth much longer. He felt it the minute he heard Alvin speak. Emma wasn't the only one that was keeping secrets. He'd kept his bible reading from her for the past year and found himself sneaking away to read the words printed in English as often as he could. He knew she thought he accepted God's will to take James, but all along, Samuel knew God had bigger plans. It wasn't until the eager faces of the young people gathered under the picnic shelter that God revealed His plan.

He knew what he had to do, and that was to come clean with Emma. In his attempt to keep them from facing ex-communication, he made Emma feel like their current strife was her fault. But in retrospect, it was his way of keeping them safe. But is that what God wanted him to do? He knew for a fact Emma was correct. God did bring them to Pinecraft for a reason, and that was to push him into revealing his true beliefs to Emma; to find the strength to step out in faith and go against everything he'd been taught. Even if it meant they would become outcasts from everyone and everything they held so dear.

As he sat on the banks of the creek, he opened his heart to God in a way he never had. It was time to be the true leader of his family and show Emma what Daniel had shown him so many months ago. To teach her the meaning of being a Christian was more than following a set a rules and outward appearances. It was laying her whole life at His feet and trusting He would guide her every step. All at once a wind blew across the waters of Phillippi Creek and he knew his old life was to be never more. A new life had been given to him regardless of what trouble it would cause when they returned to Willow Springs.

***

Emma sat on the edge of the bed and combed out her waist-length hair before coiling it up at the base of her neck. Taking a clean *kapp* from the top of the dresser, she pinned it in place and prayed Samuel wouldn't be too mad she disobeyed him.

Lillian knocked lightly on the door before pushing it open, "Are you sure you want to go with us? It might cause more trouble between the two of you."

“I have to go. Do you think I'm wrong?"

"I can't say one way or another, but we are to follow the lead of our husbands; the Bible tells us that."

Emma sat back down on the bed and asked, "Did you ever go against *Doddi* Melvin?"

Lillian sat down beside her. "Did I ever. And for this exact reason. When he and the other ministers refused to seek the truth about salvation, I questioned him. Your father showed me in his English Bible where God told us that we will be saved not by our works but through faith. Melvin was angry with me for a long time. He was certain if we read from the English bible, we would surely be misled."

"But you continued to search for the truth, didn't you?"

"What I did was continued to ask Melvin to prove to me that what we'd been taught was right. After months of him looking for answers, he finally admitted he couldn't prove your father was wrong."

Emma moved to the edge of the mattress and picked up her grandmother's hands. "You gave me an idea. You and Martha go without me. I need to find Samuel."

Lillian squeezed her fingers. "Good girl, go to your husband and work through it together. I'm certain God will show you what you need to do if you only listen."

Emma went to the dresser and pulled Marie's bible from beneath a stack of clothes. "Can you show me in the bible where God tells us about salvation through Christ?"

"I don't need to find it; I know exactly where it is. Read Ephesians Chapter 2: verses 8 and 9."

Emma snapped her head back in surprise. Chapter 2, 8, and 9?"

Lillian looked at her quizzically, "*Jah*, why?"

"Ever since I got here, those numbers keep showing up. Everywhere I turn, I see two, eight, and nine."

Lillian smiled before saying, "I'm not surprised. God never ceases to reveal things to us He wants us to see."

Emma kissed her grandmother on the cheek, picked up her mother's bible, and ran out the door. It had to be a sign from God; it just had to be.

***

After making his way back to Pinecraft Park, Samuel sat beneath a large oak tree covered in moss. A group of young people sat under the shade of the picnic shelter singing. The slow and drawn-out songs from home soothed his soul. Tomorrow was Christmas, and all hopes of spending it in their new home were as far away as the miles that separated them. After hearing Alvin speak, he understood that what he overheard that day at the beach and then later at Emma’s grandmother’s house was a misunderstanding. He was just as guilty at keeping secrets as she was. He refused to admit it, but he had questions too; and that forced Emma to think he held Bishop Weaver's position higher than the Lord's. But all in all, he used the bishop as a cover for his own sin of not being honest with her.

"Samuel, can I sit with you?"

Startled by Emma's arrival, he followed her voice. The light green dress she wore made her features sparkle in the sun illuminated behind her head. Her big brown eyes were filled with love as she pointed to the spot in the grass next to him. "I think we need to talk."

He cleared a twig in the grass and held out his hand to help her sit. Energy sparked between them when their fingers touched. "I'm sorry," he whispered.

"No, I'm sorry I caused so much tension between us. I should have never come here without you, and I should have gone home."

He closed his eyes and took in a deep breath through his teeth before exhaling. "God called us here. I know that now."

She laid the bible down in the grass and turned to face him. "You feel it too?"

"I do, but there's something I need to explain first."

Emma folded her hands on her lap and lowered her chin. "No, me first. I kept something from you that I need to tell you before we go any further."

He didn't say a word and gave her the time she needed to compile her words. "First, I have to explain to you how mad I was at God for the last couple of months. I thought I must have done something wrong, or we must have not followed the rules well enough, and we were being punished."

He picked her fingers up and rubbed small circles over the back of her hand. "That's not true; God doesn't punish us like that. And believe me when you mentioned that before, I had to look for the truth myself."

"You did? Did you talk to Bishop Weaver?"

He picked up the bible and moved it to his lap. "No, I looked here."

"Did you find the answer in the bible? What does it say?"

"That bad things often happen so the works of God might be displayed."

"So, Lynette was right. She said things often happen so God can set us up for something bigger. Like me and her meeting, and Alvin sharing with us the true meaning of salvation with us."

"*Jah*."

Emma sat up straight. "Wait, you read the bible? An English version?"

"*Jah*."

"But why didn't you share it with me?"

"I couldn't. How could I encourage you to go against the promises you made? If word got out, we would be excommunicated or be made to go before the church to repent. I couldn't subject you to that. You were going through so much already."

"Is this what you wanted to tell me? Why have you been against me going to a bible study if you have questions yourself?"

He picked both of her hands up and turned to face her. "Emma, do you realize what will happen when we return home? If the bishop gets word of this, we'll not be able to see our families. We will be exiled in our own community. Is that what you want?"

Tears teetered on her bottom lashes. "I want to follow God's word. How can that be wrong?"

He reached up and pulled her face to his and rested his forehead on hers. "There will be no going back, you understand that, right?"

"What other choice do we have?"

"Believe me, I have tried to find a way around it for the last couple of weeks. I keep asking myself what I want to teach our *kinner*."

Emma pulled her head away and put distance between them, but he pulled her close again. "Emma, we'll have more children, I'm sure of it."

"There may not be more. I've kept something from you. Something I should have told you a long time ago."

"What is it?"

"Dr. Smithson warned me not to get pregnant again for at least two years. If I did, there would be a chance I wouldn't carry it to term. We could lose another child."

Samuel let out a sigh. "Is this what's been bothering you for so long? Two years will go by quick, and I see no problem in waiting."

She dropped her head and whispered, "But Samuel, you don't understand. We can't share our marriage bed."

He lifted her chin up with his finger. "If the doctor said it would not be wise to conceive a child, so be it. I'm not worried about that, and neither should you be."

She twisted her eyes away from him. "But we can't use birth control."

Pulling her chin back in front of him he said, "We'll figure it out ...*together*."

Emma pulled the bible to her lap and ran her fingers through the pages until she found Ephesians. "I have to show you what *Mommi* shared with me."

When he saw her flip to Chapter 2, he placed his hands on the page and recited the verse. *"For by grace are ye saved through faith; and that not of yourselves: it is the gift of God: Not of works, lest any man should boast."*

Emma clasped his hand. "Ever since I got on the bus in Sugarcreek, the numbers two, eight, and nine have been showing up everywhere I turn."

He smiled and pulled her close. "Me too, but I tried to ignore their meaning. Instead, I looked for every opportunity to question your loyalty to me and let the devil play tricks in my head. He led me to believe you were sharing secrets with Alvin and your grandmother and put jealousy in my heart. It took Henry Mast to remind me to listen before I figured out what God was trying to tell me. I thought Henry was telling me to listen to you, but really, God used the old guy to remind me to listen to Him."

Samuel stood and helped Emma up. "It's time we both started listening to what He's trying to teach us. I'm certain He sent us to Pinecraft to prepare us for a battle much bigger than we can fight on our own."

"A battle?"

"*Jah.* He is preparing us to be His disciples, and that comes with a price. Once we learn what He has sent us here for, we won't be able to keep it to ourselves. Much like Alvin and Lynette, we'll have to share it. And that, my love, will cause friction at home, I'm sure of it."

Emma twisted the ribbon to her *kapp* between her fingers, "It already has?"

"How so?"

"Stella's letter. I mentioned it to my *datt,* and he was adamant I forget about it and keep it to myself."

"I'm sure he did. Have you told anyone else?"

"*Jah*, Katie."

"I'm not concerned with Katie."

"*Nee*, why?"

"Because Daniel believes the truth."

"He does?"

"Where do you think I got the bible? Why do you think he has so much trouble making it to church? He's already been questioned by the bishop more than once, and I'm confident they're second-guessing letting him join the church in the first place. Why do you think they try so hard to keep the English away? They don't want our young people to learn the truth. Daniel's been a threat from day one. If they weren't afraid of losing Katie to the English world, they might never have allowed them to marry."

Emma tucked her arm in the crook of his elbow. "What are we going to do?"

"To start with, we're going to church, and we may even stay to go to one of Alvin's bible studies. After that, I'm not sure, but we'll take it one day at a time and trust in the Lord and have faith he will pave our way."

Emma leaned her head on his shoulder. "I've missed you."

He smiled down at her. "I can't dispute that, but we had to go through all of this to get here."

CHAPTER 15

Daniel wore a path from the house to the barn. The brim of his hat was so snow-covered that he stopped to shake it off before entering the house. Katie, deep in the throes of labor, moaned a piercing cry that made him shudder.

"Are you sure there is nothing we can do to ease her pain?"

Ruth, Katie's mother, stood at the counter cutting slices of bread from a fresh loaf she'd brought over earlier. "Shouldn't be too much longer now. Maybe you should stay outside and tend to that mare about to foal. Strange as it is to have that mare birth in the winter; I think you're needed more outside. Besides, the midwife and I have everything under control in here."

Stomping the snow from his boots Daniel said. "I think I should stay, and besides, Levi is watching over the barn. I do wish Samuel was here. I could use his help right about now. Have you heard from him?"

Ruth brushed crumbs from the counter into her hand. "I checked the phone shanty early this afternoon, but still no word. I'm sure if Samuel hadn't found her, he would have called by now."

Daniel hung his coat on the back of the chair. "Katie was asking for Emma this morning. She knew her time was near and wanted her close by."

Ruth added jam to a slice of bread and handed it to Daniel. "They've always been so close. I'm sure she misses her."

Daniel licked a dollop of jam off the side of the bread but dropped it on the table when Katie's groan cut through the air. All color drained from his face as he looked at his mother-in-law when she exclaimed, "Trust me, you best go to the barn. I'll ring the bell when you should come back inside."

"Maybe you're right. I can't handle Katie in so much pain without being able to do anything about it."

Ruth giggled and wiped up the overturned bread from the table. "Not so sure watching your horse in labor will be any better, but it will keep your mind occupied."

Dusk added layers of gray to the snow-filled sky as Daniel made his way across the yard and back to the barn. Still void of life, Samuel and Emma's house sat as a cold reminder of the pain his best friend and sister endured. For days, he hid in the loft of the barn, praying and pleading with God to spare Katie and him the same sorrow. Snow collected on his short beard as he petitioned God one more time for a safe delivery for their new child.

Levi, Katie's father, had a headlamp secured to the brim of his hat and positioned it so the light illuminated the white and gray mare in the stall. Her labored breath danced in the filtered light.

"How's it going in there?" Levi asked.

"About the same as out here. I had to leave. Not sure how anyone can handle listening to that."

Levi lifted his foot and rested it on the rung of the gated fence. "When Samuel and Katie were born, I stayed far away from those birthing sounds. Too much for even a tough guy like me to handle."

Daniel let out a deep groan and shook his head. "And Katie thinks she wants a house full of *kinner*. I'm not too sure of that."

The mare rolled her head back, and they watched a contraction push the new foal's foot into view. "Much like in the house, all we can do is stand by and let nature take its course."

"*Jah*, but it's much easier watching a horse give birth than listening to my wife cry out in agony."

Levi lifted his chin. "God knew what he was doing when he put women in charge of childbearing. I don't think any of us could withstand labor, no matter how tough we were."

Heat rose from the freshly wet straw-covered floor as the mare continued to work through rolls of contractions, tightening her stomach. In a final push, the white sac covering the new foal came into view, and they both held their breath as its tiny head broke free.

"Amazing, isn't it? Just like that, new life makes its way into the world." Daniel nodded in agreement at the same time the dinner bell bounced off its cast-iron frame.

Levi lifted his chin in the direction of the house. "That's your call, go meet your new family. I'll stay here and make sure old Betsy takes to her new foal."

The walk back across the road took less than a few minutes, giving Daniel enough time to calm his racing pulse. Shedding his jacket and hat before he even opened the door, he threw them on the table while shuffling out of his boots.

A warm glow from the upstairs oil lamp seeped down the stairs, and Ruth waved him up with a smile. "All is well."

Relief outlined Daniel's jaw as he took the stairs two at a time. When he stepped into their room, Katie's face was flushed, and wisps of dark hair were painted on her forehead with moisture. Her voice cracked. "Come meet your daughter."

"A girl? We have a daughter?"

Daniel sat on the side of the bed and kissed Katie on the forehead. "Are you okay?"

"Better than okay, look at her. Isn't she beautiful?"

"Are you sure she's okay?"

"Yes, we're both perfect."

He let out a long sigh and ran his fingers through his hair. "I was so worried."

Katie tilted her chin in his direction. "Didn't you have faith God would protect us?'

"No, it wasn't that at all ...it was ...well you know ...everything Emma went through and all."

"You can breathe now. I'm good, and so is Elizabeth."

"Elizabeth?"

Katie looked up at Daniel. "What do you think?"

"You want to name her after Emma's birth name?"

"I want to clear it with Emma and Samuel first, but I can't think of any other name that suits her better."

Daniel touched his daughter's dark downy hair. "It might mean we can't officially name her until they return home. I'm not sure when that might be. Can you wait?"

"I can and will. Emma is like a *schwester* to me, and I can't think of any other name that would suit us either."

"But what if she comes back, but she still doesn't want to have anything to do with us?"

"Oh Daniel, that won't happen. She just went through a rough spot. When she lays eyes on Elizabeth and holds her in her arms, all will be well, I'm certain of it."

Daniel squeezed his wife's hand. "This is the best Christmas present ever."

***

After over twenty hours on the bus, Samuel and Emma stepped off. They leaned into one another to block the wind whipping around the bus terminal in Pittsburgh. Samuel arranged for a driver to pick them up and even agreed to the increased fair since it was the first of January.

"Samuel, maybe we should have stayed in Florida until winter broke. I say we turn around and hop back on a bus going south."

Samuel wrapped his arm around her shoulder. "We'll go back, but right now, we need to start this new year with a fresh start."

"My stomach is churning."

Samuel gulped a lungful of frosty air, "Are you ill?"

"No, nothing like that," Emma placed her hand over her stomach, "I'm nervous."

They headed toward their driver's familiar sedan, and Samuel added, "We need to separate what we feel from the One we serve."

They both placed their bags in the open trunk. "You're right, but I'm still scared."

Samuel opened her door and waited until she slid across the backseat. "And rightly so. God never told us being one of his disciples would be easy."

Emma rubbed her hands together. "*Jah*, I suppose not."

Samuel and Emma stayed quiet in the hour it took to get from the bus depot to their home in Willow Springs. Both lost in their own thoughts about what the future might bring. Since Christmas, Alvin and Lynette had spent almost every day sharing different passages and stories from the bible to help them understand what God wanted them to see. So much truth had been kept from them, and they now felt it was their mission to spread the Word. How or when that might happen was still a mystery, but they agreed they would take one day at a time and wait for God to pave their way.

Snow gathered on the front porch of the *doddi haus,* and Samuel held Emma's arm tightly while she made it up the stairs. "Perhaps tomorrow we can start moving into the new house, *jah*?"

Emma pushed open the door and stomped her feet before stepping inside. "I'd like that, for sure and certain."

Emma snickered when she saw the sink filled with dirty dishes. "My punishment for leaving you alone for two weeks."

"Sorry about that; I meant to take care of those."

She slipped out of her jacket and kissed her husband's cheek. "Give me a few minutes, and I'll fix us some dinner. Maybe after that, we can go visit with Daniel and Katie. I have some apologies to make."

It was good to have his Emma back. He didn't want to do anything but keep her to himself all evening. But he knew their family missed them, and they would be anxious to see them both. Emma stood in front of the calendar to flip it to the New Year, brought her hand to her mouth, and gasped, "Katie will have had her baby by now."

Samuel's voice, filled with concern, asked, "Would you rather not go over?"

Emma stammered, "It will be hard, I'm sure, and I pray she'll forgive me for my unacceptable behavior."

Samuel smiled tenderly at his wife. "I know my *schwester,* and that's the last thing you need to worry about."

"Can dinner wait? I'd really like to go see them now."

Samuel held out her coat, and she slipped her arms back in the still warm lining. "As long as you keep that smile on your face, my stomach can wait as long as you need."

***

Katie sat in a rocker near the front window and watched a dark car pull into her parent's driveway. Curious as to why her parents would call for a driver on New Year's Day, she tucked Elizabeth in the crook of her arm and moved to the kitchen window. From her view across Mystic Mill Road, she watched as her best friend stepped out of the car. The tenderness of the way her *bruder* helped her up the stairs revealed so much more than words could say.

"Daniel, come quick."

Daniel ran up the stairs from the basement and breathlessly asked, "What is it? What do you need?"

'Look, Emma's back."

"Well, I'll be."

"Hurry, put your boots on and go ask them to come to visit."

"Now Katie, are you sure? How about we let them settle first. They'll come to see us when they're ready. And besides, I don't think you or the *baby* need any excitement yet."

"No, please, I want Emma to meet her."

Daniel took Katie's elbow and guided her back to the living room. "Let's see how Emma's state of mind is first. Perhaps it's too soon for her to see our child."

Katie's bluebird eyes fluttered in hopes she could change his mind. "I'm certain she's better. I can feel it."

"Now, don't go batting those eyelashes at me; you know I can't say no to you when you do that."

Katie blushed. "Please, Daniel, go ask them to come over." He mumbled as he headed to the boot rack. "If she says one word to upset you, I'll send her home."

"Quit, she won't, I'm sure of it."

No sooner did Daniel get his boots on than Samuel knocked on the back door.

Surprised at their guests, Daniel stepped back and waved them in. "I was just heading your way. Katie was adamant you come to visit."

Emma removed her coat. "The baby?"

"Yep, she was born on Christmas Eve."

Emma put both hands over her heart. "A girl?"

"*Jah*, go see for yourself. Katie's dying for you to meet her."

Emma moved closer to her brother. "Please forgive me for the way I treated you both. It was uncalled for, and I'm so sorry."

Daniel pulled her into a big bear hug. "You have nothing to worry about here; all is good."

Emma pushed through the lump forming in the back of her throat and whispered, "*Denki*."

"Now go meet your niece," Daniel pointed to the front room.

Samuel followed close on Emma's heels and stopped a few feet from where his *schwester* sat in the rocker. "You can come closer, Samuel." Katie shifted and turned the baby's face in their direction.

Emma held her hands out. "May I?"

The room seemed warm, and Emma was cautious not to lose her footing in her dream-like state. Everything around her faded away as she picked up the tightly wrapped bundle from Katie's arms. She backed up toward the twin rocker to Katie's left and kissed the child's forehead. "Well, hello there, Miss..." she looked toward Katie, "What did you name her?"

"That's just it. We wanted to wait until you got back to officially reveal her name."

"Why? It doesn't matter to me what you call her."

Katie patted Emma's knee. "But it does because we couldn't think of a better fitting name than Elizabeth."

Emma's chest tightened. "You want to give her my biological birth name?"

Unsure of Emma's response, Katie asked, "Would you mind?"

"Heaven's no, unless Samuel has any objection."

Both women looked Samuel's way. "None from me."

"Wonderful, then Elizabeth it is." Emma ran her fingers along the side of the baby girl's face. "Hello there, Elizabeth, I'm your Aunt Emma." The baby cooed and stretched out her hand until it touched Emma's chin. Emma took her tiny fingers and kissed them as they gripped her thumb. For the first time in months, Emma felt true joy. Holding her niece set a longing in her heart. But at that moment, sharing in the beauty of new life with her best friend didn't compare to anything else she'd ever experienced.

Daniel elbowed Samuel. "Want to see what I'm working on downstairs?"

Samuel looked in Emma's direction. "You good?"

"Better than good, I'm perfect. Go, do whatever you two do in the basement. Katie and I have some catching up to do."

After the men's heavy footsteps faded, Katie leaned into Emma and asked, "How are you?"

Emma replied, "Better, not great but better." Without looking up from Elizabeth's face.

"Daniel said you went to Florida. Is that true?"

"*Jah*, I went to Pinecraft. I stayed with my *Mommi* Shetler and her *schwester*.

Katie's eyebrows raised. "Your biological father's mother? How was that?"

"It was good. *Mommi* Lillian helped me work through some things."

A comforting hush filled the room while both women found their footing in their life-long friendship. "Katie, can you forgive me for being so ugly with you?"

"You have already been forgiven, and we don't need to speak of it again."

Emma pulled Elizabeth's tiny fingers to her lips. She whispered, "It was easier for me to allow myself to be consumed by my grief. But I finally had to face the fact that God had bigger plans."

Katie asked in a wistful tone. "So you're not mad at God anymore?"

"I'm not saying I understand all of what he has in store, but I'm better equipped to accept it now. If nothing else, losing James made me aware of my own mortality."

Confused, Katie asked, "How so?"

"Let's just say I figured out I could spend my life mourning over what I lost, or I could find ways to rejoice at what I've gained. In this case, I choose the latter. And sometimes I have to find that joy multiple times throughout the day."

"I'm proud of you Emma. I can't imagine what I'd feel like if we lost Elizabeth, but I'll thank the Lord for every day we have with her."

The baby started to fuss, and Emma handed her back to Katie. "Part of me didn't understand the array of emotions I was dealing with, and I blamed both God and Samuel. It was easier to distance myself from you and my family rather than face the exhausting reality."

Katie waited until Elizabeth latched onto her swollen bosom before answering, "I'm sorry I didn't insist you let me help you through all of that."

"There is no need to have any regret. I don't think I was in any state of mind to graciously accept even if you offered."

Katie pulled a blanket over the baby's head. "I'm sure the Lord has a reason for everything He put you through."

Emma crossed her legs and lifted her heel from the floor to set her chair in motion. "You'll never comprehend how God will use you until you let Him."

Katie took a sip from a drink on her stand before asking, "Do you have any idea what He has planned?"

"A lot of things were revealed to Samuel and me when we were in Florida. We met a young couple who lost a child as well, and they were wonderful in helping us see through losing James."

"Oh, how wonderful. I can sympathize with you, but to truly understand your pain, I just couldn't, no matter how hard I tried."

"I understand, really I do. Lynette showed me that God hears when we cry out to him and if He has to tell us no, it's for our protection." Emma paused long enough to decide whether she wanted to share her next thought with the one person, other than Samuel she trusted with her life.

"Protection? What would He be protecting you from?"

"Maybe protecting isn't the right word, but He wants us to grow...*grow in Christ*."

Katie shook her head. "Must be mommy brain kicking in, but I really don't understand what you're trying to say."

Emma moved toward the kitchen. "It doesn't matter right now. How about I fix dinner? I bet you have more in your refrigerator than I do. Things are pretty slim at my house."

"That would be wonderful. There's a slew of casseroles in there and way too much food for just Daniel and me."

Making herself at home in Katie's kitchen, Emma worked on getting a meal on the table. Her heart swelled at wanting to share everything she and Samuel learned in Pinecraft, but Alvin's warning about taking it slow weighed on her mind. Katie took her baptism vows seriously, and it would take more than a few words to show her the true meaning of salvation through Christ. The excitement that kept building in her chest about sharing the truth with those she loved mingled deep in her stomach, making it hard to concentrate on anything else.

***

Daniel pulled an extra stool up to the workbench in the basement and nodded his head for Samuel to take a seat.

"So good to see Emma smile."

"*Jah*, Florida was good for her."

"And you?"

"I'm good."

"Are you sure about that?"

Samuel pushed the towel away from the bible Daniel kept hidden in the basement. "Emma's been reading."

"An English bible?"

"*Jah*."

"Have you told her about us studying together?"

"*Jah*."

Daniel picked up a chisel and started to smooth out a piece of wood. "Do you think she'll tell Katie?"

"It's not her place."

Daniel brushed wood chips into the bin under the bench, "True."

"You'll need to tell her sooner than later."

"Katie won't be as open as we are about going against the *Ordnung*."

"Daniel, Bishop Weaver is already questioning you about your motives for joining the Amish church. As soon as he gets word of us attending a bible study, he'll certainly blame you."

"But I didn't tell you to do that."

"No, you didn't, but I can bet the Amish grapevine will make its way up here from Pinecraft before too long. We didn't hide spending almost every day with Alvin and Lynette Miller for the last week. It's sure to make its way back to Willow Springs. I even met old man Mast's *bruder*."

"That's not good. Who are the Millers?"

"A Mennonite couple who ministers to young people. They say their mission in life is to convert Old Order teens into discovering the truth of Jesus. Lynette got a hold of Emma, and ... well, you know the rest of the story."

"So that explains Emma's change."

"I can't take any credit for that. In fact, I made things pretty difficult the first few days I was there."

Daniel shook his head. "This isn't going to go well for any of us, is it?"

"You're not telling me anything I don't already know. I just hope we can keep it to ourselves for a while until I figure out what to do."

"Don't think you have to carry that weight yourself. I was the one who brought it to your attention in the first place."

"I didn't have to read it. That was my choice."

Daniel picked up a piece of sandpaper and ran it the length of the wood in his hands. "Let me figure out how I'm going to tell Katie first, then we can go from there."

"We can't turn back now. Emma and I have already made up our minds about it. If it comes between serving God or adhering to the *Ordnung*, we will choose God."

"As you should."

"I had some intense conversations with Alvin while in Pinecraft. He helped me see my first responsibility is to God and then my family. Knowing what I know now, how can I raise my family in believing the only way to get to heaven is by following a set of rules and guidelines someone other than God dictates to us?"

Daniel stopped sanding long enough to say. "Exactly what I've been struggling with for the past two years."

Samuel opened the bible and started to fan through the pages. "It will get worse. I feel it. Now that Emma and I know the truth, how can we follow anything else?"

"You can't."

Samuel closed the book, "I'm not sure how you've gone on all this time sidestepping the truth when it's right here in black and white."

"At the time, I didn't think it would be so much of an issue. I've never told Katie what I truly believe. If I did, she might not have married me."

"Man, you can't keep something like this from her. You have to tell her before Bishop Weaver pays us all a visit."

"*Jah*, I know you're right, but man, I hope we can hold off for a few weeks. She just had Elizabeth last week."

CHAPTER 16

Somewhere in the wee hours of the morning, Emma rolled over and wrapped her arm around Samuel's middle. Not realizing he was awake, she snuggled into the curve of his spine just as he brought her hand to his lips. Without saying a word, he rolled to his back and tucked his arm under her head and kissed her forehead. The rooster was already making morning known even before the first rays of light filtered through the blue pleated curtains. For so long, she denied the warmth of his love. She took advantage of every ounce of the day to be in his embrace. His strong arms squeezed her tight one last time before he rolled out of bed.

She rubbed a circle in the warm spot. "So soon?"

His raspy voice said more than just a few words. "I best put distance between us."

There was no denying what he meant, and she felt him pull away from their closeness more than once over the last couple of weeks. She folded her arm under her head and wiped away a tear from her cheek. There had to be another way; she couldn't imagine turning him away for two years.

After his bare feet made it down their newly sanded stairs, she pushed aside the covers and dressed. They'd spent the last few days moving out of the *doddi haus* and into their new one, and it would be the first day she could put some routine back in her life. Samuel, Levi, and Daniel were getting back to building a bigger counter at the bakery, and she ...well ...she wasn't quite sure what she'd do. Perhaps she'd visit with her *datt* and *schwesters*, or better yet, she'd see if she could see Dr. Smithson. The smell of coffee floated up the stairs, and she followed it to the kitchen.

She pulled the curtain above the sink to the side and asked, "I need to go to town, and I thought I'd visit my *datt*."

"Not a problem, I'll hitch Oliver up for you. What do you need in town?"

She continued to stare out the window, hoping to find the right words so as not to alarm him. "I ...I want to see Dr. Smithson."

Samuel stopped his cup in midair. "Why? Is something wrong?"

"No, not exactly."

"Then what is it?"

"I didn't ask him enough questions last time, and I want to see what our options might be."

"Options for what?"

She walked over and pulled out a chair at the table beside him. "You know ...our ...*options*."

His upper lip turned to a thin line. "We know what our options are; there's no reason why we have to look for others."

She laid her hand across his forearm. "Marie said we had other choices. I have to learn what they might be."

"If it's anything we have to go to the bishop about, I'd just as soon stay under his radar."

"Why? Has he already come to call on you?"

"No, not yet, but let's keep it that way."

"Let me go talk to Dr. Smithson. I can't believe I'm the first Amish woman who needed other alternatives to prevent pregnancy."

"But you know as well as I do; we are to put these things in God's hand."

"Samuel, we can't put another child in harm's way. We must listen to Dr. Smithson's advice. Besides, if we're going to upturn the apple cart around here, we'll be in no position to bring a child into that. When word gets out about us being re-baptized in Florida, it won't only be the bishop who calls on us. We can count on that."

"I suppose no one will think twice about you going to see the doctor again. But just remember I won't be going to clear anything with the bishop."

She stood and pushed her chair in. "Let me see what he has to say first. There may not be anything we can do, but I have to find out for sure first."

Their chocolate lab, Someday, started to bark at the front door a few seconds before a knock announced an arrival. Emma patted the dog on its head before opening it to see who stood on the porch. "*Datt,* what a nice surprise. I was planning to stop by today."

He kicked the toe of each boot on the door frame before he stepped inside. "Levi stopped by yesterday and said you made it back."

"*Jah*, we did. We've spent the last couple of days moving in." She kissed his cheek before saying, "Come see how nice the cupboards you made us look. I just love them."

"I can't stay long. I have a couple of orders I need to finish, but I have a matter I want to discuss with you."

"Okay, come sit down. Can I get you anything? A cup of coffee or cocoa?"

"*Nee*, really, I can't stay."

"What is it, *datt*?"

Her father looked at her and then to Samuel, "I want to see the letter your *mamm* left you."

Emma moved to the drawer near the sink, "The one she left with the shawl?"

"*Jah*, that's the one."

She handed her father the pink envelope, and he looked to Samuel and asked, "Have you read this?"

"*Jah*."

His stern voice spoke in not much more than a whisper, "You both need to forget it ever existed." Before Emma could protest, her father walked to the sink, took a lighter from his pocket, and set it on fire.

Emma ran to his side and tried to grab it from his hands. He twisted away and watched it wither away in flames. "*Datt*, what are you doing!"

"No good will come from this, and it will only cause separation."

"But *Datt*, that was my letter, not yours! *Mamm* left it for me, not you."

"And she did so against my wishes."

Samuel moved to his wife's side. "I mean no disrespect Jacob, but that was uncalled for. If Stella's last dying wish was for Emma to find out the truth about Jesus, what right do you have to take that away from her?"

Emma squeezed Samuel's hand. "It doesn't matter now. I have her words etched right here." She laid her hand over her heart. "I don't need a piece of paper to remind me what she wanted to teach me."

Her father picked his hat up from the table and said, "While my job with you has long been completed, I have to leave your fate in your husband's hands. However, I warn you if I hear you've shared this with your *schwesters,* you won't have to worry about being excommunicated. I'll do that myself."

Emma lowered her head and tried to appeal to her father's softer side. "You can't be serious?"

"When it comes to matters like this, I am. You both have made promises before God and the church. To go back on them now will force my hand in more ways than one. You realize what it would mean if you pursued this, don't you?"

Samuel stiffened his shoulders and stood face to face with Jacob. "Emma is my concern now, and I'll deal with this in my own way."

Jacob didn't move his eyes from Samuel's face. "Just as my household is my concern. Even though Rebecca and Anna are older than Emma by three years, they still live under my roof, which means they fall under my care."

He turned to face Emma. "You will not be permitted to see your *schwesters* or me if you share this with them."

Jacob let himself out and they didn't breathe until his footsteps left the porch. Emma turned and let Samuel pull her into a hug. "We can't promise him we won't speak the truth, can we?"

"*Nee*, my love, we can't. If Rebecca and Anna want to learn the truth, God will make it possible with or without us."

She looked up and found his eyes. "It will happen, I'm sure of it."

"How can you be so sure?"

"Because *Mamm* left the same letter for both of them as well. In due time they will go through something in their lives that Ruth will be called on to hand them a gift, much like she handed me mine."

Samuel ran his finger along her jawline. "Then you see, my love, it is already out of our hands."

Emma buried her head in his chest. "It's starting already, isn't it?"

"*Jah*, we're being called into battle in the name of Jesus Christ."

***

Levi started a fire in the woodstove that sat in the bakery corner long before Samuel and Daniel showed up to help. In three short months, the girls would need to open back up Yoder's Bakery. For the past two years, they'd only opened from March until October. But starting soon, they would be opened year-round. A much bigger counter and the addition of seating meant the community could enjoy fresh pies and cookies whenever they wanted.

The front door sprung opened, and he waved the bishop in. "Bishop Weaver, what do I owe this visit to?"

"Good morning, Levi. I see you are making headway with opening the bakery soon." The old man patted his stomach. "I know for sure I'll be making it one of my favorite stops again."

"*Jah*, you and me both."

Bishop Weaver pulled over a paint bucket and took a seat. He pointed to another. "Join me."

Levi straddled the other bucket and took a red shop rag out of his back pocket to wipe paint from his hands. "Something on your mind?"

The bishop rested his folded arms across his belly. "You know we are down two ministers. Abe Stutzman moved to Byler's District, and Harvey Hershberger is on his way to his forever home."

Levi's shoulders slumped. "Don't tell me you feel my name may be added to the list of nominees to fill one of those spots."

"It very well may be. Both you and Jacob Byler are well-respected members of our church, and I have all faith the congregation will nominate you both once again."

"Jacob? Have you told him yet?"

"I stopped by and talked with Jacob and his new wife early this morning. I reminded him as I am reminding you the responsibility that comes with such a calling. We won't know for sure until Sunday who the community chooses, but in the end, God will have the final say."

Levi was at a loss for words. There was no other time in an Amish man's life that was so disturbing than to hear he was to be called into a life of service. The responsibility didn't come lightly, and most times, it came with a heavy burden. He'd seen it more than once. When a man's Lot was chosen, you often heard his wife cry in agony. Life as they'd known it ...was gone *...forever.*

Bishop Weaver stood and extended his hand. "May God's calling be upon you, and may you accept it in service to the Lord."

Levi stood and shook the man's hand even though his insides were burdensome. Not for himself, but for Ruth and his family. If his name was called, his family would be under strict scrutiny. Everything they did would be watched, and they would be expected to uphold every ounce of the *Ordnung*, with no exceptions.

There would be no doubt about it. Levi would have to pull his family together that evening and explain what being called into ministry would mean to them all. His concern wasn't with Samuel, Katie, or even Emma, but he worried about Daniel. The boy had been raised English, and it would fall much harder on his ears than anyone else. He already had his doubts about him following their strict conservative order. But he knew Daniel loved his daughter Katie, so he was sure he would comply.

***

Emma tied a blue scarf over her *kapp* and picked up two plates of pie. "I'm going to take dessert out to Samuel and Daniel. I'll be back in a few minutes."

Katie was busy changing Elizabeth's diaper in the front room. She hollered toward the kitchen. "I'm sure they'll be back in a few minutes. They said they wanted to just check on the new foal."

"I don't mind; I'll be right back." Emma hurried out the door before Katie could protest again. After Levi's announcement after supper, she knew exactly why her husband and *bruder* retreated to the barn before dessert. Thank goodness Ruth had a headache and left as soon as supper was over. She needed to talk to Daniel and Samuel. She balanced the two plates in one hand and pushed the heavy barn door aside. Light filtered in the tack room, and she followed the glow. Standing in the doorway, she waited until both men turned her way. "This is horrible news, isn't it?"

Samuel was the first to speak. "Regardless, there are two spots. One or both of our fathers may soon be ministers."

She handed them each a dish and took forks from her pocket. "This has to be why my *datt* was so adamant this morning."

Daniel picked up a bite of pie but stopped to ask, "What happened?"

Samuel spoke up. "He made sure we both knew we were to bury Stella's letter and never bring it up to anyone. He so much as already told us he would excommunicate us, regardless of if we were family or not."

Emma leaned on the workbench. "He's worried I might say something to Rebecca or Anna."

Daniel propped his foot on the wall and leaned back as he finished his pie. Scooping the last bite in his mouth, he set the plate on the bench. "I haven't found the right time to tell Katie yet."

"Tell me what?"

Emma stood up straight, and Samuel moved aside, so she could come into the tack room with them.

"Daniel, what do you need to tell me, and why does everyone know but me?"

Daniel reached out and took her hand. "We can talk about it later."

Snapping away from his grasp. "No, we can talk about it now. If there is something the three of you are keeping from me, I want to know it now."

Emma walked to her. "Come on, Katie, let's go check on Elizabeth. Daniel can explain it to you after we leave."

Her voice squeaked, "No, now."

Emma pulled her shoulders up and looked at Daniel. "She needs to know; it affects us all."

Samuel pulled out a stool and patted its seat. Daniel cleared his throat and buried his hands deep in his pockets. "Samuel and Emma have been studying the bible."

"Why would that be a big secret?"

Daniel pushed a clump of straw around on the floor with the toe of his boot. "I gave Samuel an English bible."

Katie covered her ears with both hands. "No, I can't hear this."

Daniel pulled her hands away and looked her in the eye. "Katie, I've been reading it as well."

Katie moaned, "Whhyyy?"

"Because I've been questioning the *Ordnung* and what it stands for. I don't believe my only way to heaven is how well I follow a set of rules. God tells us the only way we can make it to heaven is through Jesus."

She grabbed his hands and held on tight as he cupped her face and she asked, "How on earth can we get to heaven through Jesus? This isn't right. We made a promise, we can't go back on our word."

Samuel stated, "We can, and we must."

She pulled his hand away and looked to Emma. "Please, talk some sense into them. We can't read any bible, but our High German one. We promised."

Emma came and knelt in front of her best friend. "But Katie, we don't understand that one. I learned we can be rest assured of our salvation through Christ. There is no other way to the Lord but through Jesus. Samuel and I both have been re-baptized as Amish Christians."

"What do you mean re-baptized?"

"Our friends Alvin and Lynette opened a whole new world to us. One where we don't even have to guess if we'll make it to heaven. Don't you want the same thing?"

Katie wiped her nose on her coat sleeve. "Daniel, how could you?"

"I tried to keep it from you for as long as I could. But it's the truth, and you have to know it as well. I want us to rely on God's Word, not on a set of rules."

"That's just it. You shouldn't have kept it from me at all. How long have you doubted your vows?"

Daniel tried to reach out, but she pulled away. "Did you feel this way on our wedding day?"

"*Jah.*"

"Then why did you marry me and agree to raise our family in the ways of our Old Order community?"

"Because I love you."

"You lied to me, ...to God ...and to our family!"

"I didn't lie to God. He knew my heart."

"A lie is a sin, Daniel, don't try to play it off that one is any less offensive than another."

"Katie, please listen to me. I didn't plan any of this. I had no idea Emma was going to figure out the truth. I didn't tell her or convince her to believe anything."

Emma took Katie's hand. "He didn't. This was all my doing. Samuel didn't even tell me he and Daniel had been studying the bible together until a couple of weeks ago."

"You poisoned my *bruder* against the church too?"

Samuel declared, "He did no such thing, and he didn't twist my arm. I did it all on my own. All we did together was talk about what we read."

Katie turned, threw her arms up in the air. "We'll be put in the *bann* for sure."

CHAPTER 17

Sunday morning brought an onslaught of unseasonably warm weather. A bright January sun glistened through the trees as Samuel guided Oliver to fall into step behind Levi and Daniel's buggies. The slow and steady procession gave them all plenty of time to contemplate how the Lot would fall. The process of opening one of the three books that soon would be set in front of Jacob, Levi, and Henry Schrock added a heaviness to the day. Each man would put their fate in the hands of the Lord and respectively would accept the outcome without complaint.

Earlier, Emma noticed Ruth held tightly to a handkerchief as she crawled inside Levi's buggy. If they only knew the secret they shared with Daniel and Katie, her tears would be much harder to control.

The landscape was dotted with brown-topped buggies as they made their way to Bishop Weaver's farm on the outskirts of Willow Springs. Samuel reached over and squeezed Emma's gloved hand. "What are you so deep in thought about?"

Emma took her other hand and laid it over her husband's. "I'm a little anxious about what this will do to my *datt*. He already suspects we have questions. If he is one of the chosen, it may add a deeper wedge between us. How can he accept his calling knowing his daughter and son-in-law may challenge his position?"

"Emma, I'm not going to worry about today or what might happen. The best thing we can do is keep what we are learning to ourselves for now. God will show us when the time is right to share what we know. Just like Alvin and Lynette were put in our path, He will line other people up with us when the time is right."

"What about Katie? She's so upset with Daniel. I already sense strife between them." Emma said.

"Again, we can't fret about that. Daniel will lead her and Elizabeth in his own manner. I know my *schwester*, she'll come around, just give her time. All we can do is pray for them and get out of God's way. He'll do the rest."

Emma nodded, "You're right." She leaned in and nudged his shoulder. "How did you get so smart about things like this?"

He grinned and elbowed her. "You see ...I've been reading this book that's teaching me such things."

She wrapped her arm around his and hugged it tightly. "I love our evening studies. But more than that, I enjoy hearing how you interpret God's word."

He snuggled close without taking his eyes off the road or letting up on the reins. "God is preparing us. I can feel it."

"How can you be sure?"

Samuel paused a few seconds before responding. "It's like a burning feeling way down deep in my belly. An ache that won't go away until I tell someone. But the thing is, I don't want it to go away. I want it to grow bigger and better. Does that make sense?"

Emma gave it some thought. "It does because I feel the same way. It really started the day we went to the ocean, so Alvin could re-baptize us. When I came up out of the water, something happened inside of me. It was like the bright sun could finally reach the spot in my heart covered in the shade. I felt like one of my sunflowers that turn their face to the sun all summer long. I want that warm feeling every day of my life."

Emma got quiet for a few minutes and then added, "I hope Katie will experience that someday too."

Samuel snapped his tongue at Oliver. "She will, I'm sure of it. We just need to give God time to work on her heart, much like he did ours."

***

Katie held on tightly to Elizabeth when the buggy shifted, forcing her to slide closer to Daniel. "Sorry."

"There is no need to say sorry. I like my girls sitting close."

Katie took a hand and pushed herself closer to the canvas door. The air was thick inside the enclosed buggy, and Katie wished they could find a way to fix what was between them. No matter how many times they tried to discuss the issue, she couldn't get past how betrayed she felt. He had turned into something Katie was afraid to embrace. What he was asking her to believe was so far from what she'd been taught that she saw no outcome but complete isolation from her family and friends.

When Daniel left late last night, she watched as he walked across the road and onto Samuel and Emma's porch. There was no doubt in her mind they had a plan to study the bible together. He didn't ask her if she wanted to join them. Instead, he slipped out of bed after he assumed she was asleep. The treachery of their secret meeting etched a deep void in her heart.

She stole a glance his way as he concentrated on the slushy road. There was no doubt she was in love with him, but what he was doing would cause heartache at some point. How could he go against her and what they stood for? A sudden glimpse of life without him flashed before her eyes. Would he walk away from her and Elizabeth to follow the ways of his English background? In the Amish world, divorce was not an option. But Daniel was not Amish. He was just an English man in Amish clothing. Would she or Elizabeth be enough to hold on to him, or would she have to give up everything she held so dear to be with him? If only she knew what to do. A small gasp escaped her lips, and she swallowed hard to stop tears from taking hold.

"What is it, Katie? Something is bothering you this morning."

She turned her head away from his stare. "Nothing I can't figure out on my own."

"But you don't need to figure things out on your own; I'm here to help."

Katie focused her eyes on the road. "Really? How can you say we figure things out together? You didn't come to me when you decided to slip out of bed last night and turn to Samuel and Emma instead of me."

Daniel stiffened his shoulders. "In all fairness, you've not been very receptive to what we want to share with you."

"I'm not and never will be. You chose to explore these things behind my back. That was your decision, not mine. So don't tell me we figure things out together."

Her hands shook when she tucked the blanket around Elizabeth. She never raised her voice to Daniel before, and Elizabeth squirmed with her tone. He didn't utter a word in response to her outburst but kept his eyes fixated on her father's buggy in front of them.

***

Ruth twisted the thin white layer of linen in her hands. "My heart is full this morning."

Levi patted his wife's knee. "Mine too, my love, but we'll thank the Lord for whatever he puts in front of us today, agreed?"

"Agreed, and I have faith you'll be ready for whatever He asks of you, even if it means life as we know it, will be no more."

Levi tried to lighten the mood by adding, "Now, now, Ruth, it won't be that bad. I might have to give up our Saturday night Scrabble game, but besides that, I can't see things changing much."

Ruth gave him a nervous smile before asking, "Who are you trying to convince, you or me?"

"A little of both. We have to remember God makes no mistakes, and He is already aware of the outcome of today's Lot assignment."

Ruth turned to glance over her shoulder. "I'm worried about Katie. Something's off, but I can't pinpoint it. I think maybe she has some post-baby blues."

"I haven't noticed, but again I've been preoccupied the last few days. Maybe Katie just needs a long visit from her *mamm*."

"Maybe so, I'll walk over this afternoon and see if I can take care of Elizabeth, so she can take a nap or something."

Levi pulled back on the reins to slow his horse to turn into Bishop Weaver's long driveway. "Here goes. Are you ready?"

Ruth sucked in a long breath. "Is it wrong I've been praying someone else's name will be on the list today other than yours?"

"If it is, then I'm just as guilty."

"The Lord is with us all," Ruth added as they came to a stop in front of the procession, making their way to Bishop Weaver's white farmhouse.

***

Emma and Katie fell into step behind the line of women making their way into the kitchen. Bishop Weaver's wife stood at the back door, welcoming each inside with a holy kiss and a warm smile. As Emma made her way to the women's side, she noted three empty chairs placed at the front of the room. A small table sat off to the side with three *Ausbund* songbooks neatly tied closed with a string. Two of the black leather hymnals contained a small slip of paper with a scripture written on it. Whichever man chose the book with the bible verse inside would commit his life into service to the Lord.

She let Katie step in front of her when she stopped to ponder over what it might mean if her father was one of the chosen. Rebecca, her older *schwester,* gave her a slight shove to take her seat beside Katie and Elizabeth. There was a coldness in Katie's greeting that she half expected. Once again, Emma found herself at odds with her best friend, but the coolness came from Katie this time. She had to find a way to clear the air between them. Perhaps she'd go visit with her that afternoon. All they needed to do was talk it out, and all would be well again. She was sure of it.

Rebecca leaned in and muttered in Emma's ear. "*Datt* seemed nervous this morning. I'm not sure why. If his name gets added to the Lot today, it's what God had in store for his life, and he needs to just accept it." The tone of her older *schwester's* voice always grated on Emma's nerves. No matter what it was, Rebecca had a way of using the nip in her voice to emphasize the negative of a situation.

Emma hushed her and replied, "Did you ever stop to think he may feel the pressure of what being a minister would mean to all of us?"

Rebecca wouldn't be quieted and added, "We don't have anything to hide. I think him being chosen would be an honor to our family. Don't you?"

Again, Emma tried to quiet Rebecca and replied through gritted teeth, "Do you need to speak so loudly?"

Rebecca sat up straight and opened the *Ausbund* to the first song, "But don't you think he would be respected by the community if he was a minister? And besides, he should have been chosen the last time."

"Rebecca, you know as well as I do it would be prideful to think that way. *Datt* isn't like that. He's a humble man and will want to uphold the guidelines of our community just like his ancestors did before him. He will take the job seriously and won't act like nobility, I'm certain of it."

Rebecca turned away from Emma in defiance at her rebuttal. "Oh, that's right, all-mighty Emma has all the answers like always."

Emma said a silent prayer that God would change Rebecca's prideful heart, and he'd make her and Samuel's path clear. Her heart ached with the thought it might come down to her father's charge to excommunicate them if their secret was ever revealed.

Nearly three hours later, after the last minister spoke, Bishop Weaver stood and directed his comments to the whole congregation. "God instructs all men to be in good standing with the church to accept the Lot. Before I read the names of those nominated, let me remind you that each of these men is known to be filled with faith, exhibit blameless self-control, and are good managers of their household. At the time of the adult baptism, each man here agreed to uphold the position of minister, if he should be called."

The entire congregation followed Bishop Weaver's lead and dropped to their knees. Each member silently prayed for the men whose names would soon be revealed. When the bishop cleared his throat, each person quietly slipped back on their bench and waited.

The communion service fell way into the afternoon as each man held his breath, praying his name would not fall from their bishop's lips. "As I call each name, please walk to the front of the room. Retrieve a book from the table and take a seat in one of the chairs in front of me."

Not a single sound was heard, not even a whimper from a hungry toddler or restless infant. It was as if they knew God's hand would fall among them.

Without so much as an introduction, the bishop read the names before him; "Henry Schrock, ...Levi Yoder, and ...Jacob Byler."

Emma looked across the room to Samuel and Daniel. Samuel's face fell an ashen gray, and Daniel's followed suit. Rebecca reached over and tapped Emma's knee as if she was waiting for her own name to be called. While everyone else in the room felt the burden for the three men, it was as if Rebecca found pleasure in her father's nomination. Emma twisted her leg away from her *schwester's* touch and turned toward Katie just in time to see her wipe moisture from her cheek. Katie felt it too. Soon one of their fathers would be called into service, and its heaviness hit them both.

Like in slow motion, Emma watched her father walk to the table and pick up one of the books. As he turned to look out over the congregation, he locked his eyes on her. Somewhere deep behind his dark lashes, her father pleaded with her without saying a word. When he turned to take a chair, her heart picked up its rhythm, and tears began to build behind her eyes.

After the three men had selected a book, Bishop Weaver moved in front of Henry Schrock. Holding his hand out, he took the book, pulled the string, and searched for a single slip of paper. When his fingers stopped where the page was marked, he pulled the paper and handed it back to Henry. In the seat right in front of Emma, Maggie Schrock inhaled and dropped her head. It was evident to everyone around her that she felt the responsibility her husband was just handed. Next, the bishop moved to Levi. When no scripture-filled paper was found in his book, he handed it back and moved to her father. It was already known that the second slip of paper would be found in her father's songbook, and Rebecca once again reached over and squeezed Emma's knee. Bishop Weaver instructed both men to stand and accept their charge. He greeted both her father and Henry with a holy kiss and let the congregation extend their expression of sympathy and support one by one.

Katie slipped out of the room, making the excuse she needed to nurse Elizabeth, but Emma read the anguish on her face. It was evident she was on the verge of a meltdown.

Emma headed to the kitchen to help with serving, but not before Samuel held her elbow and whispered in her ear. "Daniel wants us to come over this afternoon."

Emma whispered, "I'm not sure Katie is ready for that. She's pretty upset this morning."

"Exactly why Daniel wants us to come over. He's hoping you can ease Katie's concerns."

Jacob came up behind them and stopped their conversation. "I'm calling a family meeting this afternoon and expect you both to be there."

Emma looked at Samuel and waited for him to answer. "We'll be there. What time?"

Jacob looked across the room toward Rebecca and Anna. "Three and tell your *schwesters* not to make any plans.

They waited for him to depart the room before commenting. Emma muttered, "This is not ...going to be good."

Samuel clutched her elbow tighter. "I bet not, but what else can we do but abide by his wishes ...for now at least."

"You might want to tell Daniel we can't come until later."

"I will."

Emma retreated to the kitchen just in time to hear Rebecca gloat about their father's appointment. A hush fell over the room as the women in the kitchen stopped what they were doing and stared back in disbelief. Emma pulled her *schwester* off to the side and squeezed her arm while whispering, "What are you thinking? Do you want our father's first charge to be to make you repent for your prideful manner in front of the whole congregation?"

Rebecca twisted from her grasp. "Oh, quit being so dramatic. I just said what everyone else is thinking. What harm is that?"

Emma felt heat rise to her cheeks. "You can think things all you want, but when you voice them out in the open like this, you are only causing yourself trouble."

Rebecca waved her off by making a tisk-tisk sound with her tongue.

Emma carried a stack of bowls to the front room and started to set them out across the benches turned into tables. If she and Samuel didn't push the limits with her father's new appointment, Rebecca was sure to test the waters. Out of the corner of her eye, she saw Katie and Ruth huddled in the corner of the room. Katie handed Elizabeth's diaper bag to Ruth and followed Daniel's voice across the room. The seriousness on both of their faces alarmed her, and she wondered if maybe she and Samuel should forgo visiting.

After Katie and Daniel left, Ruth carried the baby her way and stopped at her side. "Katie wasn't feeling well. Daniel's taking her home. I volunteered to watch this little one for the afternoon."

Elizabeth stretched, and Emma reached out to rub the child's belly. "I bet she'll love spending the afternoon with her *Mommi*."

Ruth flipped Elizabeth up over her shoulder and asked, "Has Katie said anything to you? Something is bothering her, but she won't open up for the life of me. I asked her again just now, and she got this far away look in her eyes and changed the subject."

Emma patted Ruth's arm, "Maybe she just needs some sleep. I bet this little one has been keeping her up at night. Nothing a long afternoon nap won't cure."

"I suppose, but I don't think so. Please promise me you'll talk to her. If anyone can figure her out, you can."

Emma smiled in Ruth's direction and went back to setting the table up for the noon-shared meal.

CHAPTER 18

At three o'clock sharp, Samuel pulled into Jacob's driveway and stopped at the front steps to let Emma out. Jacob stood on the porch. "No need to unhook your buggy. This shouldn't take long."

Emma looked over at Samuel and shrugged. "Short, and to the point, I guess."

"Okay. We don't want to give him time to start asking us too many questions. We'd never lie to him, best we keep the conversation short and sweet as well for the time being."

"I suppose so, but I hate seeing him like this. Ever since *Mamm* passed, he's been so aloof. So much different from when we were *kinner*."

"Come on, my love, give the man some grace. It's not like the last three years have been easy on him."

"*Nee*, they've not been. Having to tell me I wasn't his biological daughter and then *Mamm* dying at the same time took its toll on him."

"At least he has your older *bruder* Matthew living close by and the twins still at home. If it wasn't for them, I'm sure he'd be even more lonely and detached."

Emma snickered as he unrolled the canvas-covered door and added, "Rebecca probably still pushes his buttons, and that in itself would make anyone irritable."

"Now, now, be nice. Rebecca is your *schwester*."

She laid her finger on her chin and replied playfully, "If you want to get technical, she's not really."

"Emma Yoder, be kind."

Both were still laughing when they walked in the front door. Her father had moved to his chair at the head of the table, and Anna,

Rebecca, Matthew, and his wife Sarah, looked their way as they continued to giggle.

Samuel took his hat off and nodded in Matthew's direction. Anna stood and carried a kettle to the table and poured the hot water in two waiting cups.

Emma hung her coat on the back of a chair and pulled it closer to Samuel. She was the first to speak. "So *Datt*, what do you think about your new appointment?"

He leaned back in the chair, rested his elbows on the arms, and folded his fingers together. "Challenged."

She measured a few hearty spoons of hot chocolate mix in her cup and asked, "Challenged? How so?"

Without responding to her personally, he addressed them all. "I have a few words I want to share with each of you. But before I do, let me say this. I take this charge seriously, and I expect each of you to do the same. The community will watch our every move. As a minister, I'm expected to have my house in good order."

Taking a few moments to gather his thoughts, Jacob focused first on Samuel, then Matthew. "In the eyes of the church, my house extends to the both of you as well. I anticipate you will take heed to your own households. All should follow the *Ordnung* as you promised the day you accepted membership into the church."

Matthew nodded, "I will see to it that Sarah, and I give you no reason to be concerned."

Jacob dipped his chin in his son's direction, turned toward Samuel, and asked, "And you? Can I count on you to stay true to the teachings of our forefathers?"

Samuel took in a deep breath through his nose and straightened his back before answering. "I will do my best to follow the ways of the Lord."

Emma breathed a sigh of relief. Samuel found a way to answer his question without lying, but her father was not satisfied. "That's not what I requested. I asked if your household would stay true to the *Ordnung*?"

Emma watched color make its way up under Samuel's starched white shirt, not stopping until it reached his forehead. Standing firm to his answer, he replied, "I will guide my family in the way of God's

Word. If it lines up to what our forefathers held so dear, then you can rest assured we will cause you no trouble."

Her father's demeanor changed at Samuel's response. He was not pleased, but he let it pass. Without moving his glare from Samuel, he continued, "As I said, we will be watched, and I don't want any undue attention. I expect each of you to adhere to your baptismal vows."

Everyone at the table, besides Rebecca, had a solemn look. The weight of the responsibility their father would need to endure fell heavily on each of them. Rebecca however, gleamed at her father's appointment and proudly stated, "I, for one, will follow the *Ordnung* to a tee. You'll never need to worry about me."

In a harsh tone, Jacob replied, "Starting with you, Rebecca. I have one word that is meant as a warning. I've witnessed each of your weaknesses. At some point, they may cause contention in your walk with the Lord."

The snarl in her father's forehead caused Emma's stomach to flip as he uncovered six pieces of paper before him. Each of their names was printed clearly across the folded sheets. He handed Rebecca hers first. "It's totally up to you if you want to share it or keep it to yourself. Regardless, it is the one thing I see in each of you that may cause me to bring you in front of the congregation for repentance."

Rebecca boldly stood. "I have nothing to be ashamed of." She unfolded the paper and turned it around so everyone could see.

Emma read it aloud. "*Pride.*" Rebecca glared toward her father. "Pride, my word is pride? Well, I never!" she sat down in a huff.

Each of them took the sheet of paper that held their perceived fate. One by one, they read their word and sat quietly. Rebecca was the only one to share their father's warning openly.

Rebecca snarled, "Come on! I shared mine with all of you."

Emma covered her warning with her hand and said, "Unlike you Rebecca, I think each of us is taking *Datt's* warning with a bit more seriousness."

Anna, Rebecca's twin, laid her hand on Rebecca's arm and said, "I think we should pray in private about our weakness. Only then can we hope to overcome our shortcomings." Anna was the only one who could ever get a word in edgewise with Rebecca's sharp tongue.

Jacob pushed himself away from the table. "That's all I have to say for now."

No one moved from their seat, and all let out a sigh when the back door closed. Rebecca tried to take the slip of paper out of Emma's hand. "I can only imagine what you got ... I bet it was ...*perfect.*"

Emma closed her hand around the paper. Samuel reached over and patted her knee under the table before she responded, "I bet this is harder on him than we realize. If *Datt* sees something in us, it's his job to bring it to our attention."

Rebecca crossed her arms over her chest and grumbled, "Leave it to you ...know it all!"

"Leave what to me?"

"Thinking you're better than any of us."

Emma's voice cracked. "When have I ever made anyone feel like I was any better than any other member of this family?"

Matthew slapped his hand on the table. "Rebecca enough. Don't think for one minute *Datt* didn't think long and hard about what he had to share." He reached for Sarah's hand, and they stood. "For me and my family, we will be praying that God works on our flaws."

Rebecca raised and snatched the paper from Emma's grip and picked Samuel's up from the table and sneered. "Oh no, you don't. No one is leaving until I know everyone's shortcomings."

Samuel stood and grabbed Rebecca's arm, and she screeched, "Get your hands off me!"

Throwing his hands up, he stepped back just as Rebecca's mouth curved in a satisfying grin before announcing Emma's word, "*Submission.*"

She handed the sheet of paper back to Emma and said, "Well, isn't that fitting for the girl who's only half Amish. I'd say you should've run off when you had the chance. If you did, you wouldn't have to worry about submitting to anyone but yourself."

Anna covered her mouth and gasped, "Rebecca, please stop." She turned to Emma and continued, "Don't listen to a word she says. She doesn't mean it."

Rebecca spewed out her words as if the devil himself possessed her. "She should have stayed in Sugarcreek with her other family."

Without giving anyone a chance to recover from her outburst, Rebecca unfolded Samuel's paper and smirked before saying, "*Loyalty*."

Emma picked the paper off the floor and faced Rebecca, eye to eye. "I will take my word to the only one who can help me overcome it, and I propose you do the same."

Matthew shook his head and pulled Sarah toward the door, "You keep this up, and you'll be the first one bowing a knee in front of the church."

Samuel seized the note from Rebecca's fingers and then held out Emma's coat while she slipped her arms in the sleeves, as he warned, "Rebecca, I'd hold your tongue if I were you."

She waved him off and growled, "You made your choice, now deal with it!"

Emma stepped in front of Samuel when he opened the door and asked, "What did she mean by that?"

He glanced back over his shoulder before shutting the door. "I've long given up trying to figure that one out."

Emma pulled the wool blanket up over her lap as soon as she crawled inside their buggy. She waited for Samuel to check on Oliver's harness before joining her inside. Once he did, she asked, "Rebecca acted like you should know what she's talking about."

"Oh ...I have an idea."

"You do? What's that?"

Samuel tightened Oliver's reins for him to move away from the hitching post. "When you were in Sugarcreek a few years ago, she tried to stir up trouble between us, which I put a stop to quickly."

Emma sighed, "Every time I think she's gotten over whatever it is that eats away at her about me, it pops back up when I least expect it."

He molded his hand around hers. "Rebecca is the least of our worries. I think we need to tell Daniel about your *datt's* warning. Not sure why he pointed out loyalty to me. Unless he already knows more than he's letting on."

Emma cupped her free hand over his and said, "Oh Samuel, I bet Henry Mast from Pinecraft said something to Sarah's father."

"I'm not sure about that. Henry acted like he and his brother didn't speak often. And besides, Henry's New Order believes as we do now. Why would he purposely stir up trouble for us?"

Emma twisted toward him. "But you know the Amish grapevine, it spreads like wildfire, no matter where it starts."

"We need to keep our bible studying to ourselves for now. I'm half inclined to put a stop to Daniel coming over as well. The way your father questioned me makes me think he already knows something. Let's let the dust settle for the time being."

Emma moved closer and laid her head on his shoulder. "I'm sorry I haven't always been totally submissive to you."

Samuel kissed the top of her *kapp*. "Listen to me, I knew way back when we were catching tadpoles in the creek, you had a mind of your own. If I wanted something else in a wife, I had plenty of time to look elsewhere. Now, I'm not giving you a pass on the whole thing about tramping off to Pinecraft without me, but looking back, it was all for a good reason. If you hadn't gone, we wouldn't have met Alvin and Lynette, and we surely wouldn't have found Jesus."

She wrapped her hand around his arm. "But I think we would have, because you and Daniel were already questioning things. I can't imagine you not finding a way to eventually share that with me."

"I suppose you're right. It wouldn't have been something I could have kept from you forever."

Samuel pulled up to the front porch and secured the reins as Emma asked, "How can the ministers expect us to do as they say if it's not what the bible instructs?"

Samuel shifted toward her. "There are many discrepancies between the bible and what we were taught. But we can only go by what we read is true. Look at Henry Mast, he found the truth, and it forced him to leave his Old Order community to seek fellowship elsewhere."

Emma added, "And look at Alvin's parents; they did the same thing. They left and joined a Mennonite Church. Will we have to do that?"

"I wish I had an answer, but for right now, we'll keep seeking the truth and let God reveal to us what door he'll open and which he'll close.

When we walk in faith, he will guide our way. I'm confident of that, for sure."

"I'm scared."

He pulled her close. "No reason to be fearful. We can only control the choices we make at this very moment. God had it all planned out, even before we took our first breath."

She looked into his eyes and asked, "He even knew James wasn't meant to be with us, didn't He?"

"He did, just like He knows when he'll send us another. And He will provide us more when the time is right, even if it means we have to use some of Dr. Smithson's natural prevention recommendations."

Emma's cheeks took on a rosy hue and asked, "Do you think God is preventing us from having more *kinner* right now because He wants us to be free to work for Him?"

Samuel lifted her chin and warmed her chilled lips before saying, "I believe that's exactly what He's doing. But his calling is not only to salvation; it's also to a life of serving him and our fellow believers."

Samuel reached under his seat and brought out a small black bible. "Let me show you what I found last night." He flipped the pages until he stopped on the scripture he had highlighted in yellow, and read it aloud, "*Go into all the world and preach the gospel to all creation*."

Emma laid her hand on the page. "He's calling us to share what we're learning with our community, isn't he?"

Samuel shut the book and tucked it back under his seat. "He is, and how can we deny that. I feel so strongly about our calling; I can't think of anything else."

"Is this the battle you spoke about?"

"It is. Like Alvin told us, challenging our Old Order ways will cause great division in this community, and we must be prepared for what is to come. All we need to do is plant the seed and then get out of God's way. He'll do the rest."

Emma smiled before saying, "I take my comment about being scared back. I'm not scared; I'm excited to see what God will do in this community and with us. The more we talk about it, the more I believe James was just a stepping-stone for God to use us for His greater mission. Marie told me once that I needed to be a woman who says *yes* to God. I want to be that woman."

Samuel pulled her back into his embrace. "And I want to be a man of God who leads his family to the Lord according to all of His Word, not just selected bits and pieces."

***

Daniel sat on the edge of the bed and rested his elbows on his knees. "Katie, I don't know what else to say. I've apologized a dozen times for keeping this from you. But I had to make a choice, and I chose to marry you, even when I knew the church was not teaching you everything."

Katie rested her arm over her eyes, trying to ease the pounding in her head. "But you lied to God and to me."

"I didn't lie to God. He knew my heart."

"But a lie is a lie, and a sin is a sin, regardless of how you rationalize it in your head."

Daniel sat up straight and moved her arm away from her face. "Then tell me. If I had told you what the ministers were teaching was not the whole truth, would you have left your family and friends for me?"

Katie turned her face to him. "You know the answer to that. I was already baptized. I would have had no other choice but to let you go."

"Exactly, you would have chosen the Amish church over me."

She rolled off the bed and walked to the window. "This is all too much. I don't even know how I feel about any of it. Why would they steer us wrong? They are men of God, put in charge of nurturing our spiritual lives. I can't believe Bishop Weaver would do anything that didn't line up with God."

Daniel walked to her. "I'm not trying to turn you against the leaders of the church, I'm not, I promise. But as the head of this family, I want you and Elizabeth to know the whole truth, not just selected verses."

Katie wiped her chin with the back of her hand. "Bishop Weaver and the ministers are good teachers. They share God's Word with us all the time."

"They do, but they don't teach us everything. I don't want to be a bits and pieces Christian; I want to be an all-in follower of Jesus."

"See what I mean? You call yourself a Christian, not Amish."

Daniel picked up her hands. "Because I am a Christian — an Amish Christian."

She pulled her hands from his, "We're going to be shunned, I know it."

He placed his hands on her shoulders and turned her back to face him. "Jesus never said following Him would be easy, and even if it comes down to that, I know without a doubt it will be worth it."

She twisted from his grasp. "How can you say that? My parents will be forbidden to talk to us or sit at our table. I can't do it. I won't take that kind of chance. Please, Daniel, you must get rid of your English bible before someone finds out. It will be the death of our family, for sure and certain."

Daniel turned toward the window and stood silent.

Katie pleaded, "Please don't do this to us. I can't ask you to stop believing, but you must keep those thoughts to yourself. You must stop studying with Samuel and Emma. If Jacob gets word of it, he'll have to bring his own daughter in front of the church, and that would be heart-wrenching."

Without looking in her direction, he muttered, "I'll stop meeting with Samuel and Emma if that's what you want."

"And the bible? You'll dispose of it?"

He didn't say a word but continued to stare out the window.

She walked over to him and touched his arm. "What about your bible?"

His stance hardened, and the muscles in his jaw twitched at her question. When he refused to answer, she turned and ran downstairs.

Her bare feet against the stairs reaffirmed her frustration, but he couldn't make a promise he couldn't keep. Refraining from spending time at Samuel's was one thing, but getting rid of his bible; that was asking too much.

***

Katie curled up in a rocking chair and wrapped a blanket around her shoulders. A few lingering rays of sunshine spilled through the window as they made their way closer to the horizon. Smoke swirled from her parent's roof as she watched her father walk to the barn. She couldn't help but wonder if he knew of what Daniel spoke of. Salvation through Christ, how was that even possible?

She saw both her father and mother as faithful followers of the *Ordnung*. They had a happy life, full of friends and family, along with sharing the burden of their fellow church members without complaint. Not once in her life had she heard either of them complain or wonder what life would be outside of their faith? If it worked for them, why would Daniel think it couldn't work for them as well?

When the blanket slipped from her shoulder; she bound it tighter and pulled her knees up to her chest. There was a stillness in the room that made the pulsation over her eyes feel like boulders. Laying her head in her folded arms over her knees, she saw no way out of the inevitable doom lingering over them. She had to stop it, but how?

With her eyes still closed and her head buried, she heard Daniel's footsteps stopping near her. "I'll do anything for you, you know that, but I won't stop reading."

Without lifting her head, she willed herself to keep quiet. She wanted to lash out, but her spirit held back in submission. A surge of cold air swirled around her chair when he opened the door. After the squeak of the hinges quelled, she opened her eyes and followed him across the yard and into the barn. Her heart cried out to him, even in her pain.

***

Daniel filled each grain bucket and broke the ice free from the troughs before retreating to the tack room at the back of the barn. His Sunday church clothes prevented him from doing anything but contemplate what Katie was asking of him. Perhaps once she calmed down, he could reason with her. They had only been married a little over a year, but it was long enough to know he wasn't wrong in putting God first. That was the one thing his Amish community did right. They put God first, then family, and then community. How could she be asking him to put her first?

"Daniel, are you in here?" Samuel hollered.

Daniel followed Samuel's voice. "*Jah.*"

"I saw your footprints headed this way. Emma went up to the house."

"Not sure Katie's up for company, but if anyone can get through to her, it's Emma."

"How did it go at Jacob's?"

"Let's just say he gave us all a warning."

"A warning?"

"*Jah*, a warning to let us know he will be watching us, and he won't think twice about bringing us in front of the church to repent if he sees us stepping outside the *Ordnung*."

"You have Jacob; I have Katie. I promised her I wouldn't be studying with you and Emma anymore. She's terrified of being shunned."

Samuel gripped his best friend's shoulder and tapped his chest with his other hand. "For now, we can honor their wishes, but it won't stop what we already know in here."

"I agree, and in time I pray the Lord will help me find a way to get Katie to feel it too."

Samuel added, "Remember you can't be her Holy Spirit. Only God can put that desire in her heart. The way I see it, she's fighting it because her spirit is already trying to convict her."

Daniel leaned back on the workbench. "Man I hope you're right."

***

Emma stepped inside the kitchen and pushed the basement door shut as she entered, calling out, "Katie?"

When Katie didn't answer, she removed her coat and boots and called her name through the house. Back in the kitchen, she tilted her head, turning an ear to a muffled cry. She opened the basement door and listened. In the distance, she heard Katie moan, "I won't let him do it," and then the sound of ripping paper, "I won't let him shame us," and more tearing of paper.

Emma followed her voice to the back of the basement near the coal furnace. There, on her knees, in front of the open furnace door, Katie ripped page after page of Daniel's bible and tossed it in the fire.

Emma dropped to the floor and grabbed the half-torn book from her hands. "What are you doing?"

Katie tugged it back. "I won't let him take me away from my family. Elizabeth needs to know her grandparents."

Emma lowered her voice. "You're not thinking clearly. Daniel would never do that."

"But he would, and he has. He is going against the rules he agreed to when he became a member of the church. If the leaders find out, they'll shun us. I'll be forced to choose between him and the church."

Emma shut the glass door of the furnace and took the leather-bound book from her hands. "Daniel only wants you to know the truth."

In a frenzied manner, Katie scooped a few loose pages off the floor and held them tight to her chest and turned back to the fire. Emma grabbed her arm and pulled her away. "Stop, you're not thinking this through. Burning his bible isn't going to do anything. He already knows what is written. You can't burn it from his heart."

Katie recoiled from her grip. "I'm so sick of hearing about all this truth you're all talking about. The only truth I need to hear is Daniel giving up this silly notion and staying true to the promises he made to both me and God."

Emma flipped to the back of the bible to Ephesians and followed her finger until it stopped on Chapter 2, where verses eight and nine were underlined in red ink. "Read this." She handed Katie the tattered book.

Katie pushed Emma's hand away. "I don't need to, I already have. He had that page marked."

"Then you know the truth. Why would you still want to burn it?"

"Our marriage is built on nothing but lies."

Emma sat on the floor in front of her and took both of her hands. "Your marriage was built on love, not lies, and you can't really believe that."

"But Emma, you don't understand. He never intended to follow the *Ordnung.* And he married me knowing he couldn't agree with what was being taught. Daniel lied, and I can't forgive that."

"Katie, listen to yourself. You're condemning Daniel for lying, but you're committing a sin just as great as his by not forgiving him. How can one sin be any less than the other?"

"Oh, Emma, what are we going to do?"

Emma stood and reached out her hand to help her up off the floor, "To begin with, we're both going to trust in the Lord and then trust in our husbands. God gave them the authority over us, and we have to leave any decision like this up to them."

"But if we do, we may be excommunicated."

"I can't say that might not happen. But if I didn't learn anything else from my time spent in Florida, I learned we can only concern ourselves with this very moment. Once I realized I have no control over anything that might or might not happen, it was like a huge weight was lifted from my shoulders."

Katie took a tissue from her pocket and wiped her eyes. "I'm so confused," she pointed to the book Emma held. "Are there other things in there that were kept from us?"

"I'm sure of it, but we're only going to discover more if we study it for ourselves."

"But Emma."

"But nothing, this is much bigger than either of us can fathom. You don't think the Lord orchestrated this to happen? He wants our community to understand the truth of Jesus and not just a bunch of rules and regulations created by man. I agree we need to stand in unity and keep ourselves separated from the outside world. That's what keeps us focused on God, and I wouldn't want it any other way. But I also realize we can continue to live a simple life, serving the Lord and loving our neighbors all while sharing the truth in why Jesus died for us."

Katie sniffled. "But we aren't supposed to evangelize; it goes against everything we believe in."

Emma picked up the bible and held it out to her. "Show me in here where it says that, and I'll show you where Jesus instructs us to go out and spread his name to the world."

"What? We're told to talk to people about Jesus."

"We are, and He may have appointed Samuel, Daniel, and even you and me to be His messengers. And how can we say no to God?"

Emma wrapped her arms around her middle, and Katie rested her head on her shoulder and whispered, "I don't want to."

"And neither do I. I know how hard this must be for you and it is for me too. But we must let our husbands lead their families the way they see fit, even if it means it goes against our Old Order ways."

"But Emma, do you understand what this means for us? We will be forced to live as strangers to our family."

"It might very well mean that, but we'll always have each other. And who knows? It may be the special gift God gave us to serve Him."

"A special gift?"

"Yes, God gives each of us spiritual gifts that we are to use to better the Kingdom of God."

"How do you know that?"

Emma took the tattered book from her hand and said, "Here, let me show you where He teaches us about our spiritual gifts."

EPILOGUE

Wrapping herself tightly with her cream-colored shawl, Emma walked the fifteen minutes to the cemetery.

"My sweet boy, it's been six months since I visited you here at your graveside. I still cringe when I think about your tiny body lying in this cold earth. But I've learned so much since I held your lifeless body in my arms. I've learned that healing can come in many forms from many other people. Healing doesn't mean I've stopped feeling sad or miss what could have been if you had lived. No, it means by losing you, I gained so much more. It turns out in the depths of despair, and in the wake of loss, it isn't the end, but just the beginning.

So many times, I have thanked God for allowing me the time I felt you grow inside of me. But more than that, I thank Him for finally showing me that your precious soul is in heaven for eternity, and I will see you again. Don't get me wrong, we lost a lot when we lost you, and I hope and pray your *datt* and I will never have to endure such loss again. But the bittersweet reality is, we have grown so much through this journey.

I don't know if the hole in our hearts will ever close, but I do know that we have more of Jesus in there than we ever had before. All because God chose to carry you into eternity. Had you not been taken from us; we would have never found the truth in Jesus. I will always find comfort in that. I've finally found peace, and I'm ready to move on. I'm a vastly different person from the one who carried your tiny body under my heart for seven months.

God never promised us an easy passage, but he does promise to always walk beside us. You'd be so proud of your *datt*. He's been called into service for the Lord, and he has taken his charge with honor. I'm not sure what will happen once we step out in faith to our community, but we both trust the Lord to pave our path. Your *datt* and I have made a promise to God to share the word of salvation through Jesus. We won't stop until we have shared His promises with as many people as we can.

I read somewhere that it's not how we get to heaven but how many people we take with us that matters most. My relationship with heaven has always been a strange, hopeful plea, that Lord willing, I will be good enough to walk through those pearly gates. But because of you, I can rest assured my name is written in His book, right beside yours. Heaven is a place I think about every day and a place I want to be.

Right here beside you lies my *Mamm*, and I'm so comforted she is there with you.

Mamm, you have no idea what your note has done for me. It took me months to truly understand what your words meant, but they saved my life. One of the biggest things I've learned over the past six months was that God wants to share both in our joys and our sorrows. He wants us to be content in trusting His plans, and He wants others to see Christ in us. Even though I never saw that in you while you were alive, I am so honored your last words to me were those that helped me search for the truth. Without knowing I had a God who wanted a personal relationship with me centered around love and not works, it was a miracle. Because of your note, a burden was lifted that literally saved me from drowning in the depths of despair.

So, until we meet again, I will be faithful in the wait and know there is more to life on the other side waiting for me. See you both soon."

Rebecca's

Amish Heart Restored

THE AMISH WOMEN OF
LAWRENCE COUNTY SERIES - BOOK 2

PROLOGUE

May – Willow Springs, Pennsylvania

The rhythmic movement of Rebecca Byler's spinning wheel picked up speed as she thought about her run-in with her younger *schwester*, Emma. In all her twenty-three years, she'd never been more aggravated than she was at that moment. When the roving of alpaca fiber she let slide through her thumb and index finger hit a clump of dark matter, she pulled back and let the draft of yarn fall to the floor. "Ugh! I don't have time for this."

Rebecca's twin, Anna, stopped the drum roller and turned her way. "Now what?"

"I'm still finding bits of hay in the roving. You're not getting it clean enough."

Anna stooped down and picked up the tan cloud of fiber and held it toward the light of the window. "I don't see anything."

"I felt it. Look closer."

Anna held it out. "I don't see a thing; show me."

Rebecca waved her off. "Just be more careful when you're picking and carding. We can't afford to have our customers complain our yarn isn't clean enough."

Anna threw the clump back in the carding box and asked, "What's got you all worked up today?"

Irritation crept up Rebecca's neck as she replayed the argument that she had at the bakery earlier that morning. "Can you believe Emma had the nerve to tell me I was hateful?"

"Why did she say that?"

"Things would be so much better around here if she would've stayed in Sugarcreek."

Anna tilted her head. "I bet you provoked her. It doesn't sound like something Emma would say."

Rebecca snarled, "Why do you always insist on taking her side?"

"I'm not taking anyone's side, but I know how you get."

"What's that supposed to mean?"

"You tell me. You've been harping on Emma for months and nit-picking about every little thing. If you don't watch it, word is going to get back to *datt,* and then you'll really have something to fuss about."

"Me? It's Emma who should be worried. I don't know what she and Samuel are up to, but they've got something they're hiding, and I'll figure it out one way or another."

"Rebecca, why are you so set on causing them trouble?"

"She's the one who thinks she's better than everyone else."

"How do you figure?"

"Think about it. First, she runs off to Sugarcreek to spend time with her birth family and leaves *Mamm* when she needed her most. In my books, *Mamm* would still be alive if she hadn't spent the last few months of her life worrying about Emma. Next, she strings Samuel along for months only to come back assuming he'd drop everything and take her back."

Anna laid a cloud of fiber in front of the teeth of the drum. She turned the handle to feed the batt through, combing it in long, smooth batches. "Why are you harping on this? That was three years ago."

"Because it was the start of her prancing around like we all owe her something."

"You're exaggerating. Emma doesn't act like that at all. You don't give her enough credit. How do you think you would have felt if you found out *Mamm* and *Datt* weren't really your parents after sixteen years?"

Rebecca snarled, "Elated that she wasn't really my *schwester*!"

Anna gasped. "You take that back. You don't really mean it."

"I won't, and I do."

"You are hateful, and I can see why Emma said that to you. You best take your attitude to the Lord before it gets you in trouble."

The bell above the door to their father's shop jingled, and Rebecca snapped, "I'll get it."

Their father built a room off the side of his furniture shop for them to sell the yarn they produced from the alpacas raised on their farm. A divider kept the washing, sorting, and spinning area separate from the display floor and the customers. In the two years since they'd opened their store, *Stitch 'n Time,* their alpaca and specialty wool yarns had become a popular stop for both the Amish and English. They even started offering hand-made products, on consignment, from the women in their community.

Rebecca made her way around two spinning wheels and pulled the curtain aside to step out into the store. Their father had built display racks along the outside wall to hold the hand-dyed fiber. An array of baskets sat on the worktable in the middle of the room that contained mittens, hats, socks, and scarves available for sale. Canisters of different sized crochet hooks and knitting needles adorned the counter by the cash register.

It didn't take her but a second to recognize Samuel's broad shoulders and wisps of hair that flipped up from behind his straw hat. "Samuel?"

He turned toward her and in an irritated tone, stated, "I'd like a word with you."

"What about?"

"Let's step outside."

Her lip turned upward before saying, "The porch? Not so sure that would be the honorable thing to do with your wife's *schwester*."

"I'm in no mood for your shenanigans," he moved her way and whispered, "I can air your dirty laundry right here so Anna and your *datt* can hear, or we can take this outside."

She moved to the door and to the far end of the porch. "So, what is so important that we had to come out here?"

"We can start with your visit to the bakery this morning. Don't you think Emma's had enough to deal with the last six months? She doesn't need your verbal abuse to add to it."

Rebecca crossed her arms over her chest. "I only spoke the truth."

"I don't believe a word that comes from your mouth. It wouldn't be the first time you've stirred up trouble for your own benefit."

She snapped her head in his direction. "Like I've said before, if you bring any of that back up, I'll tell your sweet little Emma exactly how her wonder boy behaved while she was away."

He moved closer and snarled, "Don't threaten me."

She backed up. "*Ohhh* ...did I hit a nerve?"

"Don't think for a minute that I'll stand by and watch you harass my wife. Whatever you think she's done is no concern of yours, and I'll warn you one last time. Keep your snide remarks and accusations to yourself."

"Or what? You'll tell whom, the bishop?"

"I mean it, Rebecca, don't go there."

Rebecca walked back to the door, held her hand on the knob, and said, "The way I see it, you have a lot more to lose than I do."

He walked toward her, stopped at her shoulder, and muttered in her ear. "That's where you're wrong. I've already made my peace with God ...have you?"

She snapped back. "But have you made your peace with my *schwester*?"

He didn't respond to her question but walked off the porch and into his waiting buggy.

Her nails dug into the palm of her hand, and she clenched her teeth at his comment. She'd kept his secret for years, holding onto it until just the right time when it could cause the most pain. If he thought for one minute that, she wouldn't use it to get her revenge, then he was sadly mistaken. If she planned it right, her little *schwester* would be sorry she ever stepped foot back in Willow Springs.

CHAPTER 1

Through the shop window Rebecca could see Wilma hanging clothes. Just the sight of her stepmother unleashed a series of not so flattering thoughts.

For the life of me, I don't see what Datt sees in that woman. She's as dreary as an early spring sky. For certain, he only married her for fear Anna and I would leave him to fend for himself. I'm not sure why men think they have to have a woman around to take care of them. I, for one, don't ever plan on getting married, and God forbid a man thinks he has the right to tell me what to do, and how or what I should be thinking. I won't have it, that's for sure, Amish or not.

I learned soon after Mamm died that I couldn't count on anyone but myself. I've even put myself out there a time or two and let a few boys give me a ride home from a singeon. But they are all the same. They want their wives to be some milly-mouse, yes-sir, shell of a human being. Even Emma has become that to Samuel. I can see how she follows him around and tends to his every need.

I must admit there are days I see Mamm in Emma more so than in either Anna or me. As much as I hate to admit it, even though Emma is not my biological schwester, Emma favors Mamm's mannerisms more than I do. I sure do miss mamm's sweet disposition, even though I tested it more than once growing up.

Datt's new wife, of just six months is nothing like my mamm. She's brassy and a tad bit bossy, and I fail to understand why he married the old spinster in the first place.

With no children of her own, she's taken to telling Datt how to deal with Anna and me. She has no right, that's for sure and certain. If I'd known his Sunday afternoon visits to Willow Brook, ten miles north of Willow Springs, would produce a stepmother, I would have kept his mind occupied on things that really mattered. Perhaps I should have done more to convince him my yarn business needed to include a kiosk at the Grove City Mall.

As it stands, Wilma has made it clear that no young woman should have thoughts of growing a business when her mind should be concentrating on securing a husband and raising babies. She thinks business should be left to the head of the household, and no talk of such things should be left to a woman. What does Wilma know anyway? It's not like she ever did either of those things in her fifty-five years on this earth.

Just the thought of her adding her two cents makes my skin crawl. I guess it's best I spend all my time here in the store and let her have the run of the house like she wants. If anything, it helps Anna's anxiety if I keep my mouth shut and my opinions to myself.

To be quite honest, I couldn't care less about what Wilma thinks. The only thing that matters is that I protect my twin. I might only be minutes older than Anna, but she's not as strong-willed as me and gets frazzled quickly. It's been almost five years since Mamm passed, and Anna continues to battle with anxiety over the smallest things. Anything out of the normal will send her into a bout of heart palpitations and stomach pains.

Datt and Wilma are trying to force her into facing her fears, but I know my schwester best. Anna needs to let me continue to shelter her like I always have. We've worked things out; why can't they just leave things alone?

"Isn't that right, *schwester*?"

Anna pulled the curtain aside that kept her shielded from the customers in the front of the yarn shop. "Were you talking to me?"

"Not so much you, but myself. I was just thinking that *Datt* and Wilma don't need to butt their noses into our arrangements. We have everything worked out between the two of us, and it's none of their business how we manage the shop."

Anna stood and carried an armful of yarn to the display rack beside the front counter. "Well, to be quite honest, as long as our shop is inside of *Datt's* furniture store, and we still live under his roof, I'd say he still has some say in the matter."

Anna's bold statement made heat fill Rebecca's face and retreat in the wake of cold frustration. "But we've worked hard making this shop what it is today. *Datt* didn't help us with that. We did it on our own. It was us shearing the alpacas, and it was us working day and night creating the right natural dyes that have made the shop so successful."

Anna replied, pointing to an array of pink and purple skeins in a basket on the counter. "I do love how we figured out beetroot and the right amount of vinegar would result in this beautiful dark pink."

"See, that was us, not *Datt*. He didn't spend hours boiling goldenrod, pokeberry, and black walnuts until his hands and fingernails were stained beyond recognition."

Rebecca bounced a pencil on the counter and Anna quickly laid her hand over it before saying, "No, he didn't. But he did build us this shop and provide the financial support to get it off the ground. In my books, he has every right to tell us how and what we should be doing."

Rebecca snatched her hand from Anna's grasp. "Not you too! Here I am trying to protect you, and you're turning on me."

"Oh, *schwester,* I'm not turning on you; I'm only trying to get you to see *Datt* has our best interest in mind. I don't even know what's got you so worked up this morning."

"Wilma, that's what. She prances into our life and thinks she knows what's best for us. We were doing just fine on our own all these years. Why did *Datt* have to go and upset the apple cart?"

"Rebecca, come on, can't you see he's changed since Wilma came to live with us? He's much happier. He's not nearly as short with us, and not once since he sat us all down to warn us about his new position as minister, has he taken on such a harsh tone. I contribute that to Wilma.

I can see he's finally found his way back to the man we knew long before *Mamm* passed and long before we found out Emma had another family other than our own. How can you fault him for finding happiness in someone other than his children?"

Rebecca walked back to the window and thought. *I don't have to like it, and I'm not about to back down without a fight.* She'd poured her heart and soul into *Stitch 'n Time* and wasn't about to let her stepmother have any say in how she ran it.

Turning from the window, Rebecca straightened a basket of patterns and said, "I should have known you'd side with her. Your quest to be peacemaker grates on my nerves to a point I don't even want to discuss things with you. Did you know she told *Datt* it wasn't a woman's place to make business decisions?"

"What decision is that?"

"I want to expand our business to the mall, but Wilma butted in and convinced *Datt* I should be looking for a husband instead. She even went as far as telling me that I need to let you help the customers more. They think I coddle you too much."

Anna tucked a loose strand of chestnut brown hair under her *kapp*. "I certainly appreciate you taking on that role, but you aren't doing either one of us any good stewing about everything that comes out of Wilma's mouth." Anna picked up a bucket of clean fiber and headed back to the spinning wheel concealed by the heavy curtain that kept her hidden from the public.

Rebecca sat on the stool near the counter and rested her head in her hands. She rubbed both of her temples and thought. *I can't think about Wilma right now. I have to find a way to support myself.*

If living under her parent's roof meant she didn't have a say in the outcome of her life, she would need to find a way to branch out on her own. Her idea of selling their all-natural dyed and handspun yarn at the mall was the perfect solution. Even if it meant she would have to go against her Amish upbringing and decline the prospect of marriage in place of her independence. Wasn't it God who said singleness was a gift? If it was good enough for Jesus, why couldn't it be good enough for her? Besides, being single would allow her time to devote more of herself to God. *That's perfect ... I'll tell that to Datt and Wilma. How can they chastise me for wanting to serve God and the community?*

Rebecca pulled out a stack of receipts and entered them in the ledger with a new plan in place.

***

Anna set the table as Wilma and her father spoke in hushed whispers in the front room. She passed Eli Bricker, their neighbor, on her way into the house. He tipped his hat her way but didn't speak a word. Wondering if something had happened to his grandmother, Mary, she strained to hear what her parents talked about. It was announced at church a month ago the elderly woman suffered a stroke. The last she heard; Mary was in a rehabilitation hospital in Mercer.

Wilma removed the lid from the pot simmering on the stove and asked, "Is Rebecca on her way in?"

Anna started to slice a loaf of fresh bread that was cooling on the counter. "I believe so. She was just about done washing a batch of fiber and said she'd be in as soon as she hung it to dry."

"Your father and I have some things we want to discuss with you before you head back out to the shop."

Anna took a deep breath, taking in the savory aroma of chicken stew. "Oh, that smells good!" She broke off a piece of bread and dipped it in the thick gravy.

Wilma batted her hand away, but not before she plopped the bread in her mouth. "I swear, for such a little thing, you sure do have an appetite."

Anna wiped her mouth with the back of her hand and went back to slicing bread. "I saw Eli leave. Did he mention how Mary was doing?"

"That's what we want to talk to you girls about. Let's wait for your father and Rebecca."

Anna lost herself in her own thoughts as she finished with the bread. There was a time when she thought Rebecca and Eli might be courting, but that was short-lived and long before their *mamm* passed away and Emma married Samuel. With all of them being around the same age, she wasn't sure if Eli attended *singeons* any longer. While twenty-four was anything but old, neither Rebecca, Eli, nor herself went out of their way to find a mate. One thing was for sure, she was happy Eli was there to take care of Mary.

Mary Bricker was one of the sweetest women she knew. Her husband died five years ago, and when he did, Eli left his father's home in Lancaster and moved to Willow Springs to care for his grandmother. That spoke mountains of truth into Eli's character. She wondered why Rebecca or any other young girl in Lawrence County hadn't noticed.

***

Jacob took his place at the head of the table and waited until Wilma and his daughters sat before bowing his head. Clearing his throat to signal prayer was over, he handed his bowl to his wife and said, "Eli stopped by earlier to tell us he brought Mary home the other day. He needs a nursemaid to assist her with some womanly things he's not comfortable doing."

Anna spoke up. "I would be more than happy to help. I'm sure Eli couldn't help her bathe and such."

Jacob took his filled bowl back from Wilma and turned to respond to Anna. "While I'm pleased, you're so willing to help our neighbor in need, I think I'd like Rebecca to go instead."

Rebecca stopped her spoon in mid-air as a wince of disappointment flashed across Anna's face. Without thinking of the consequences, words flew from Rebecca's lips. "What would make you consider anything so utterly ridiculous?" A hush filled the room as Anna and Wilma held their breath. The vein at Jacob's temple pulsed, and he wiped his mouth with a napkin before responding.

"Exactly why you'll be the one tending to Mary Bricker. Your lack of compassion to see past your own needs is something I've warned you about. It's high time you put your own selfish desires to rest and think about someone else for a change."

Her tone was grated. "But what about the yarn shop?"

Rebecca was positively trembling. Just when she thought she had everything planned out, *Datt* upset the apple cart again.

Without letting her father even answer, she continued, "Anna isn't comfortable helping the customers like I am. I think I would be better suited to care for the shop than Mary."

Jacob dipped his bread in his bowl. "My decision is final. You will help Eli with Mary starting tomorrow."

Rebecca's heart pounded in anger as she thought. *Doesn't anyone in this family have a bit of common sense? Sending me to help an old woman will end in disaster, I'm sure of it.*

***

Tears welled up in Anna's eyes, but she refused to let them drop at the table, let alone in front of her family. Rebecca was correct in saying she wasn't comfortable dealing with the customers. The mere thought of talking to strangers sent her into a panic attack. Why couldn't *Datt* see her *schwester* was better suited to run the shop.

Rebecca left the table and slammed the front door, leaving Anna to face her father alone. In not much more than a whisper, she stated, "*Datt*, I really wouldn't mind helping Mary. I'd much prefer that than running the shop."

In a soothing tone, he replied, "I know, but you need to trust me on this one. I know what's right for both of my daughters. Someday you'll thank me."

Anna rose slowly and cleared the table, her head down. Her eyes burned at the cruel irony. The dream she never told anyone was within reach, all to be snatched away. Tending to her own mother's illness awoke a deep-rooted desire to be a nurse. Even the agonizing thoughts of dealing with people was overshadowed by her desire to give comfort to the sick. All she could hope for in her Amish community, who didn't believe in higher education, was serving her community as a nursemaid. Yet again, she was thrown into situations that tested her anxiety levels, much like running the yarn shop. That was Rebecca's vision, not hers.

Trembling again, she leaned back against the kitchen counter, reeling herself through the disappointment.

***

Rebecca clenched her teeth as she made her way back to the yarn shop. There was no reasoning with her father, and she was sure Wilma put him up to this. Since when did either of them believe she had the patience to care for an old lady? Let alone spend time with Eli Bricker. That time had long passed. He was the one that said her tongue was a bit too sharp for his liking. Whatever that meant. Now she was being forced to take care of his grandmother. This is not what she had planned, and she'd have to find a way to put a stop to it and fast. It was time she started making her own decisions, one way or another. Inhaling through her nose, she released her breath slowly to calm herself. Like a wave of fog on a chilly spring morning, old resentments started to simmer as the past flooded her mind.

Sitting behind the spinning wheel, she coiled fiber between her fingers and started to pump the treadle that spun the soft fleece around the bobbin. Speaking as if there was someone in the shop to answer, she asked, "Why God? I've prayed and prayed, but still, you don't answer my prayers. I attend church regularly; I've committed myself to the *Ordnung,* I drop things in the sunshine box whenever I can, and I even go as far as attending work frolics even though I hate them. What more do I have to do to get what I want?"

Rebecca frowned in annoyance, thinking about all she'd done to gain God's favor despite the sin surrounding her past.

With a sense of conviction, she heard the following words echo between her ears …*you can start with honoring your father.*

There wasn't an ounce of breath she was going to breathe into the fleeting words that left her head as quickly as they entered.

Lord, I see no way out of this. What should I do?

***

After a day of listening to Rebecca voice her complaints and a supper of utter silence, Anna sat cross-legged in the middle of her bed, clutching a pillow against her chest. Why did Rebecca always make things so complicated?

Oh, God, you know how much I want to follow you and never want to second guess your plans. But just once, I'd like Rebecca to see what she does to this family. I've tried to understand her, really, I have. Please help her see it doesn't always have to be about her.

Anna whispered to herself. "Does loving your neighbor as yourself always mean you have to give up on your dreams for the sake of living out someone else's?"

The last thing Anna wanted to do was let bitterness toward her *schwester* fester too deep, but she was so frustrated. For once, couldn't

Rebecca just do what she was asked without making life miserable for everyone around her?

Anna wanted to love her *schwester* as God instructed her to do, but it was getting harder and harder. After the day they had, she could barely endure the thought of spending another evening listening to Rebecca. Like always, her thoughts were tucked deep inside in hopes of extinguishing any fire her words might ignite. Hopefully, she'd be fast asleep before Rebecca came to bed.

***

If Rebecca Byler was good at one thing, it was holding grudges. She kept a list of grievances against every hurt she'd ever suffered, regardless of who caused it. She never forgot, and God forbid if she forgave quickly. The past was like the ledger in her shop, offenses were deposited often, and withdraws came few and far between.

Much like Samuel's sharp words engraved so deep in her soul, she still remembered them word for word, as if it were yesterday.

"Rebecca Byler, there's going to come a time when your self-centeredness is going to cause you great harm. Always thinking about yourself with no regard for how your actions may affect someone else is going to keep you away from God."

She didn't remember the molten words she poured back at him, but she recalled what happened next. The night that would forever be etched in her memory and one she was sure kept God from hearing her prayers.

CHAPTER 2

Mary Bricker took a few labored steps from the table to the kitchen sink. Her entire right side was limp from a stroke she suffered four weeks earlier. She leaned into the quad stick and dragged her right foot until she could steady her poor balance at the counter.

The house sat quiet, and only the wall clock bonged softly from the living room. Eli headed to the barn hours ago and she yearned to open the window above the sink. The sun was just making its way above the horizon, and the sky was filled with pinks and yellows, welcoming the spring day into view. Though her home was closed up tight, she could faintly hear the cooing of a pair of mourning doves outside the window.

Loving the sounds of springtime and the smell of the hyacinths planted below the window, she longed to let God's beauty fill the air. Pushing her hip into the counter and reclaiming her posture with her good hand, she looked at her gnarled hand and gave up hope. Instead, she stared out over the kitchen garden. Normally, Eli would have already plowed and tended to the soil. Leaving her to plant the tender spring lettuce and early radishes that would adorn their dinner table for weeks.

Other than some arthritis settling in her knees, she felt spry and full of life before the stroke. Even after her husband died five years earlier, she didn't stop enjoying life. Her grandson, Eli, coming to live with her only added more joy to her home. Her outwardly bubbly personality suffered only after the unexpected decline in her health. Now all she could think of was how she had become a burden to Eli. Sadness filled her, and loneliness deepened with each passing day.

Eli was young and ill-prepared to take care of his aging grandmother. His unease at helping her with womanly things became apparent when she soiled herself and needed his help. While he was patient and kind, his posture spoke a million words of discomfort. He was just twenty-four and without any *schwesters* of his own, he was ill-equipped to tend to her more personal needs.

Making her way back to her chair, she rubbed her hand over the well-used oak table that had been a wedding present from her husband, Noah. Their marriage, one of convenience, grew into a sweet reminder of God's undying provisions. The life they lived in Willow Springs glorified God in every way imaginable, even after an unspeakable sin sealed their fate.

The quietness was almost deafening as her mind drifted to those troubled times when their one and only child, Andy, left Willow Springs to live with his grandfather in Lancaster. The pain and brokenness stayed planted on her husband's face for years. They vowed they wouldn't share their secret with Andy; the pain of his betrayal was still too raw to verbalize. However, Mary felt an overwhelming desire to share their story with Andy. He had to know the truth before it was buried deep in the grave beside her.

Eli, unlike his father, didn't idolize their family's heritage and would be quick to defend one ill-spoken word against herself or Noah. Her husband's final words spoken on his death bed still rang in her ears, as clear as his undying love for her.

"You've been good to my family, Mary."

Though not always easy, Mary learned early on that she mustn't harbor any unresolved bitterness or unconfessed sin if she wanted to hear from the Lord. She had long forgiven her husband's family and spent her life upholding the name of God to all those around her.

Resentment stayed rooted in Andy's heart, so much that he refused to attend his own father's funeral. Mary blinked, hurt lodged deep in the back of her throat.

Oh Lord, will Andy even care when I'm gone? Will he shed a single tear? What more could I have done? I love my son as you do; how can I make him see what sacrifice his father made for him?

For years, she tried to keep her family together and failed in all attempts to reunite her son with his father.

Tears bristled Mary's eyes, blurring her vision. Her heart ached. Andy was always too busy to write, too busy to visit, just too busy to fulfill a dying man's wish.

Rubbing the knuckles on her useless hand, she winced in pain as she stretched her arthritis-filled knee straight.

From where she sat, she could view her long-abandoned flower garden through the picture window at the back of the kitchen.

The ache in her heart matched the tangled rose vines and unkempt bushes. Once a place of renewal, the shaggy garden was overrun with patches of dandelions and dead seed pods. Empty pots sat, still filled with soil, and were waiting for a new life springtime had always promised.

For years, Noah and she shared a love of gardening. They spent countless hours combing through an array of seed catalogs that would arrive every January like clockwork. Oh, how much fun they had sketching out new garden beds and planning new color themes. Now the stack of beautiful glossy pages sat untouched in a basket near her late husband's chair. Much like their life, awaiting the first signs of life after a long Northwestern Pennsylvania winter.

Stretching her fingers slowly, Mary reached for the Budget newspaper. The scribes shared snippets of life much like that in Willow Springs, a constant reminder of how life went on. She often found herself looking forward to the weekly subscription. Still, since her weakened stance prohibited her from holding the pages upright, the strain of reading the words was tiresome.

An unfamiliar grumpiness took over, and she pushed the paper aside and mumbled, "It's the same old stuff week after week. Why would I want to read it anyway?"

Lord, look at me. I've become a cranky old woman, reminiscing about things I have no control over. Why don't you just take me home now?

The nurses at the rehab center told her she should exercise her mind as much as her body, and she reached for the crossword puzzle book. The last thing she needed to put on Eli's already full shoulders was a bad case of Alzheimer's. Heaven help her if she wandered outside without any clothes on, and Eli had to cover her.

She pulled the book closer with her strong hand and struggled to hold the pen. She lifted her weak arm and used it as a paperweight on the flimsy pages. Even if she knew the answer to the puzzle, her left hand would prove useless in writing legible letters. In a fit of frustration, she pushed the book aside, making it land on the floor as the pen rolled under the stove.

Tears burned Mary's eyes as she stared down at the book. Unable to retrieve it, she laid her head on the table, letting defeat and grief envelop her. Unable to think of anything else, she lost herself in thoughts of Andy's betrayal. Would he have acted the same if they'd told him the truth? Look what the secret had cost them and what burden it put upon Eli.

I kept our secret, my darling, just as you asked. But it's time Andy knows the truth about his grandfather. Please forgive me, but it's the only way I see to let Eli live the life he so deserves. Andy must step up and assume responsibility to me in my weakened state.

She clung to hope as Eli's heavy boots stomped off layers of mud before opening the door.

"*Mommi*, what are you doing at the table? Let me help you back to your chair in the front room."

Mary lifted her head and wiped the moisture from the corners of her eyes. "I wanted to hear the birds and smell the flowers."

"You can do that from the living room. I'll open the front window for you."

Mary leaned into Eli's firm grip as he guided her back to the rocker near the window. "You are a good boy, Eli, and I'm not sure what I would have done had you not been here to look after me."

"Now, *Mommi,* don't go getting all sentimental on me. I'm only doing what any good grandson would do for his favorite grandmother."

"I'm your only grandmother, if I'm not mistaken."

"And that makes you my favorite."

Eli tucked a lap blanket around her legs and unleashed the window sash to let in the early spring breeze.

"I stopped by Jacob Byler's this morning, and he's agreed to send one of the twins by to help you get ready for the day."

"Did you let him know I prefer Rebecca over Anna?"

"I did, even though I'm not sure why you would choose Rebecca. I would think Anna would be more compatible with you than Rebecca."

"If you remember, I quite enjoyed Rebecca's company until, for some unknown reason, she stopped coming by."

Eli's face took on a flash of color that changed the temperature in the room as quickly as a wildfire.

Mary looked up at her grandson's lofty stature and asked. "Whatever happened between the two of you?"

"I can't remember what day it is, let alone what happened five years ago."

Mary smiled at his outright lie. There was no doubt by the way he refused to look her in the eye that he was putting her off for his own protection.

"Now, how about I make you a cup of tea before I head back outside? I have two ewes about ready to lamb."

Mary smoothed out the quilt on her lap. "Maybe Rebecca can help you when she comes tomorrow. I won't need her by my side all day. Besides, if she's going to buy the wool from shearing this year, she might want to see what it takes to raise sheep."

Eli patted his grandmother's shoulder. "Oh no, you don't. You're not sticking her on me. You're the one who wanted her over Anna. She can stay right here in the house out of my way. The last thing I want is a know-it-all woman telling me how to tend my flock."

Mary snickered. "Looks like I touched a sore spot."

Eli picked his hat up from the chair and headed back to the kitchen, contemplating his grandmother's words.

The sounds of Eli making tea instantly faded as Mary lovingly stared at her husband's chair. For weeks after his death, the only comfort she found was when she sank down in it. His smell lingered on the blanket thrown over the back, and the well-worn wooden arms soothed her. When she closed her eyes, she could feel his warmth surrounding her. Over time, the smell faded, and eventually, she made new chair covers and replaced the tattered lap blanket with a new one.

Now, in the light of a new day, she had become him. Sitting, staring, and waiting for her time to pass. They talked little in those final months of his life, but no words could fill their already full life. They were blessed beyond belief, and they had no regrets. Well, she thought so anyway. That was until Eli gave up his life to take care of hers. One that he could get back. If only she could shed light on the darkness of a secret, she swore to never tell.

Lord, what's the point? Maybe it would be better if I got Alzheimer's. Then I wouldn't realize my only son refuses to acknowledge me. What if I did forget everything? Wouldn't that be better than the sting of his rejection?

Mary pressed her lips together and let the sweet smell of spring flutter across her nose.

***

The heat continued to warm Eli's cheeks long after escaping his grandmother's questions. His short-lived courtship with Rebecca Byler left a sour taste in his mouth that forced him to give up all hopes of finding a woman to share his life with. He always thought he was a good judge of character, but Rebecca proved him wrong. From catching her in a compromising situation to trying to curb her overpowering personality, he'd given up on all women. Especially when he'd lost his heart to the chestnut brown-haired, green-eyed beauty.

Even the thought of Rebecca spending time on his farm made anger bloom deep in his belly. It was one thing to see her at church or tip his hat at her passing buggy, but here in his kitchen, sharing a meal was going a bit too far for his liking.

Maybe he needed to try calling his father one more time. Mary's care was too much for him to handle on his own, but the thought of listening to his father give one more excuse as to why he or his mother couldn't be bothered left him restless. Didn't they realize she was fading fast, and soon the brightness in her eyes would fade for good? Not for one minute did he want to believe the explanations they hurled at him.

For years, his parent's tone changed to muted mumbles anytime his grandparents' names were mentioned. He never understood the distance between them, but after his grandfather died, he took it upon himself to come look after the farm. Totally against the wishes of his own parents, and in time, the distance he recognized as he was growing up extended to include him. His younger *bruders* took up the slack on his father's dairy farm, and his absence was barely noticed within months.

His grandmother, on the other hand, was gracious and loving and provided him with the most God-centered home he'd ever experienced. It was under her loving guidance that he came to discover the truth of Jesus, even though their Old-Order community failed to teach them the complete truth. In the wee hours of the morning, long before he headed to the barn to care for the sheep, they studied God's word in secret.

He'd long given up hope Rebecca could be the wife he longed for. The seasons came and passed, one merging into another until time stood still in that exact moment.

Steam escaped through the small holes in the teakettle, whistling a tune as his thoughts drifted back to the present. Bouncing a tea bag up and down in the hot liquid, the bold black tea scent filled his nose as he carried the cup to the front room.

"Here you go *Mommi*, this should hold you over until I come in for dinner. Do you need anything?"

Mary's eyelids brimmed with tears, and she looked toward the bathroom. The chair toilet Eli carried in from the barn sat to her left. He lifted the chair and placed it inside the small room without saying anything. Easing her anxiousness, he put her quad stick in her left hand and guided her toward the door.

Mary felt the warmth before Eli noticed the puddle on the floor. She gasped and whispered through broken gurgles. "I'm sorry you have to deal with this again."

"It's my job to take care of you, and that's exactly what I plan on doing."

"But cleaning up an old woman is not in your job title."

"And taking in your grandson wasn't in your job title either, but you did it anyway."

Once in the bathroom, Eli wrapped a strong arm around her waist, pulled her skirt up, and turned his head as she struggled to pull her soiled undergarments out from underneath the long, dark fabric. Once they fell past her knees, he helped her sit. It took every ounce of control Mary had to keep the situation dignified. In a manner, much like his personality, he lovingly prepared a warm washcloth, laid it on the counter close to her, and picked up the soiled underwear off the floor. Tears teetered and toppled over her lashes as she lost so much of her life.

***

Filling the bucket at the sink, Eli reminisced about the times his grandmother cared for him over the years. Why she felt she had become a burden to him was beyond him. The look etched on her face spoke of broken dreams and shattered independence. Maybe she was right in forcing him to hire Rebecca. Perhaps she wouldn't feel so embarrassed with a woman looking after her personal needs. He needed to get out of his own head and put aside his reservations about Rebecca being underfoot and doing what was best for his grandmother. But could Rebecca be trusted with the one person that meant more to him than life itself?

After throwing the water out, he hung the mop on the hook and waited for his grandmother to call his name.

In not much more than a whisper, he heard, "Eli, are you still in the house?"

He walked to the door. "I am. Are you finished?"

"I need clean undergarments. Can you fetch them for me?"

Without answering, he moved to her room and retrieved what she required before opening the bathroom door.

"Do you need my help?"

Biting her bottom lip, Mary nodded and took a deep breath to calm herself.

Eli placed her feet in each leg opening and pulled them up to her knees. In one swift movement, he pulled her to her feet, held her skirt up, and turned his head while she maneuvered her undergarment in place. Her frail body quivered in his arms, and without asking permission, he slid his arms under her knees and carried her to the bedroom.

No words were shared as he tucked her beneath a quilt and kissed her forehead before he left.

Eli softly shut the door, slipped back in his boots, and headed to the barn. The herd of sheep waiting to be fed could go on about their day with little knowledge of his presence. Still, his grandmother would be a constant reminder of what God's steadfast love meant to another human being. Mary was his life, and he wasn't sure he could trust her well-being to just anyone, especially Rebecca Byler.

CHAPTER 3

Rebecca walked to the Bricker house, irritated and tense. The ten minutes it took her to walk up Mystic Mill Road, Eli's Hill, as many called it, did little to calm her racing pulse. There was no changing her father's mind even after she pleaded with him during breakfast.

Taking in the early morning chill, she filled her lungs and hoped she wouldn't have to run into Eli. If only her father knew Eli couldn't stand the sight of her, he might have allowed Anna to come instead. But that would require her to explain their sordid past, which was nobody's business but her own.

Mouth tight, Rebecca knocked on the front door. While she waited, she took note of the overgrown rose bushes near the porch and the weeds that covered the kitchen garden. There was a time when the Bricker house was well-cared for, but by the looks of it, Eli had bitten off more than he could chew with Mary's stroke. A pair of rockers sat on the far end of the porch, and she recalled Mary and her late husband spending many evenings there. Two hanging pots hung above the railing, connected by a giant garden spider. The flowerpots contained last summer's ferns, now brown and scraggly.

Rebecca knocked on the door again and moved to the front window. The panes of glass needed a good washing, and she used her finger to wipe a spot away to peek inside. The living room sat empty.
"I believe I hired a nursemaid, not a peeping tom."

Suddenly agitated, Rebecca turned toward Eli's voice. "I knocked on the door a couple of times, and when no one answered, I wanted to make sure Mary was okay."

Eli opened the door and motioned her to follow him inside. "I'm pretty sure she's sleeping. She had a rough morning, and I helped her back to bed before I went to the barn."

Rebecca hung her sweater on the peg by the door and wiped her black sneakers on the rug. She tried not to look around and judge Eli's cleaning abilities, but by the grime on the floor and the clutter in the corner, she could tell he kept his work to the outside of the house only. In an instant, heat rose inside of Rebecca like steam from a teapot. *If he thought she'd be doing more than tending to Mary's personal needs for one minute, he had another thing coming. She was a lot of things, but a maid wasn't one of them.*

Eli looked aghast as she clicked her tongue at the pile of dirty dishes on the counter.

"For one thing, you can get that look off your face. I do the best I can, but it's spring, and I have lambs popping out left and right around here. The last thing I have time for is a stack of dirty dishes. I'll get to them later. For now, all I care to talk about is my grandmother's care."

Rebecca threw her hands up. "I didn't say a word, now did I?"

"You didn't have to. It was written all over your face."

Rebecca saw a hint of annoyance in his blue-green eyes. For a swift moment, his cheeks took on the color of the red onion skinned dye she made for her latest batch of fiber. Forcing herself to turn her face from his, she moved a stack of newspapers off a chair and sat down.

"How about you tell me what your expectations are, and I'll tell you if they match mine."

Eli crossed his arms over his chest and leaned back on the counter. "Excuse me. I do believe I'm paying you. So, it's you who must live up to my expectations, not the other way around."

Rebecca crossed her legs and bounced her foot up and down. She didn't like being reprimanded, especially by Eli Bricker. Too much water had passed under their bridge for her to tolerate his arrogance.

"Whatever! Just tell me what you want me to do."

Eli paused long enough to let the sting of her words settle. "Look, for some reason, my grandmother insisted you be the one to take care of her. So, no matter what we think of each other, we need to make this work for her. All I care about is that she is fed, happy, and well cared for – understood?"

The lines on Rebecca's forehead magnified. "Why would she want me and not Anna?"

"I have no idea. But as you know, she has a mind of her own, and there's no changing it."

Rebecca lifted her chin and stared him straight in the eye. He might tower over her, but she needed to set a few things straight right from the start. "I'm here only because my father gave me no other option, but I'm here against my will. I will take care of Mary and Mary alone. I won't be washing your clothes or cleaning up after you. As for your meals, if I make enough, you are more than welcome to clean up Mary's leftovers, but other than that, I'm here only to take care of her. Understood?"

He opened his mouth, but she didn't give him the chance to respond.

"Either that works for you, or I go back and tell my father you fired me."

Pressing his lips together, he headed to the door, reached for the doorknob, and stopped and turned her way. "I do believe you told me once that I was the rudest boy you'd ever met. Well, guess what? You're the meanest spirited woman I've ever known, and I can see five years did nothing to curb your ugly disposition."

Rebecca's stomach flipped as she remembered the exact moment she told him that. It was the first time he'd shown any interest in her. And it was at the same time he told her that a girl as pretty as her should wear more smiles. She'd never admit it to anyone, but a part of her missed the carefree days of her youth and the way Eli Bricker used to look at her. But that was long before secrets and accusations clouded her heart, much like the film covering the yellowed linoleum under her feet.

"Maybe you're just as much to blame. If I remember correctly, you once told me that you liked a girl with a little spit and fire."

***

The door bounced against its frame as Eli marched from the back porch to the barn. He had done his best to control his anger and mumbled under his breath as he fought the urge to look back at the house. No matter how much time had passed or how many nights he lay awake trying to push her face from his mind, the woman still held a spell over his heart. There was something he saw in her that she refused to see herself. From the first day he saw her, he knew there was more to Rebecca Byler than the harsh exterior she showed to everyone else.

***

Smiling slightly, Rebecca waited until his feet exited the porch before moving to the window. There was no doubt about it. She still got under his skin and, for some reason, that pleased her. Was it that she could always count on having the last word, or was it the purple hue his face took on whenever she pushed a little too hard?

She turned from the window and walked to Mary's bedroom through the front room. Gently opening the door, she peered in and was greeted by Mary's soft snores. Pulling the door closed, she turned and rested her hands on her hips and thought. *What now? I don't like chaos, and this house is full of it.*

Stifling her irritation, she picked up an empty cup, straightened a stack of magazines, and headed to the kitchen. How could she tackle the dishes when she clearly told Eli she wasn't his housemaid? *I'm not doing it for him; I'm doing them to help Mary. Maybe she was being unreasonable. There were more important things she could argue about than refusing to wash up a few dishes or sweep the floor. Why did she let him get to her so?*

Opening the refrigerator, she took inventory of what was available to make dinner once Mary woke up. She failed to ask Eli if she had eaten breakfast, but by the look of the plates on the table and the smell of bacon in the air, she assumed she had.

Frustrated and restless, she moved around the kitchen, stacking the dirty dishes next to the basin. She retrieved a tub of hot water from the water reservoir at the back of the wood stove and poured it over a stack of plates in the sink. Once she sunk her hands in the sudsy water, her mind drifted back to a time when she and Eli had high hopes for their future. His certainty and commanding attitude attracted him to her in the first place. Her heart melted into his from the first time he insisted on walking her home. The scene played in her head, and she ached to have a do-over with her life.

Spring five years earlier…

Eli squared his shoulders. "I'm going to walk you home."

"Not may I walk you home,' but 'I'm going to walk you home?' That's a little presumptuous of you, isn't it? What if I don't want you to walk me home?"

Rebecca tucked a piece of hair behind her ear that escaped her kapp and looked down, trying to hide a smirk.

"Look, smarty-pants, I've waited for you to say anything to me that was halfway civil for months now," Eli retorted. "I'm getting tired of waiting. If I'm going to get past your nasty comments, I'm just going to have to take the bull by the horns and get to know you better. My mommi told me that I couldn't sit around and wait forever for what I wanted. If I want something bad enough, I should go after it."

Removing his hat and wiping the sweat from his brow with the back of his forearm, he said, "Look, I know there are a lot of other girls in our community, but that's not what I want. I like a little spit and fire, and I figure you're just about the only one I know that can keep up with me. So, are you interested or not?"

"That's a pretty unflattering way to tell a girl you're interested in her, don't ya think?"

"Maybe, but as I said, I'm tired of beating around the bush and playing it safe. I decided to go all in. Are you in or not?"

"Can I at least think about it for a minute?"

"I'll give you one minute. Sixty, fifty-nine, fifty-eight, fifty-seven, fifty-six ..."

"Stop! I'll let you walk me home, but that's all I'm promising right now."

"All right, I guess that's a start. But I'm tired of waiting and I'm not going to give you long to make up your mind."

Catching up to his long strides, Rebecca fell in step beside him. Anna and Emma were snickering as she passed, and she put a quick finger to her lips, pleading with them to keep quiet.

"Why did you have to pick the most public place around to go after what you want? We'll be the topic of conversation tomorrow at church."

"I figured I'd put my claim on you since I wasn't getting anywhere talking to you all gentleman-like. Every time I tried to strike up a conversation, you looked like you'd rather bite my head off. A guy wants a girl to give him a friendly smile once in a while, and the way I see it, smiles aren't in your repertoire, and I'm about to change that."

"What makes you think I want you to change it?"

"And you don't?"

She stopped dead in her tracks, waiting for him to notice she wasn't walking beside him. She gave up when he didn't slow down and ran to catch up to him.

"You didn't answer me."

With a huff, she asked, "I'm not sure what I'm supposed to be answering; you've thrown so many things at me."

"To start with, why don't you smile? What makes you look so sour all the time?"

Rebecca felt her nose start to tingle and a lump form in her throat. Taking in a deep breath, she willed herself not to cry in front of him. She wouldn't give him the satisfaction of letting him know he had upset her.

"You are the rudest boy I know."

"I suppose so, but I've tried to be nice and look where it got me. Months of trying to get your attention and nothing. Today was the first day that you've given me even a hint of a smile, and I took it as my only chance."

Stopping in the middle of the road, Eli grabbed her arm and made her stop and turn toward him. As she jerked his hand off her arm, he noticed she had big tears spilling down her cheeks. His stomach flipped, and he wasn't sure if it was from the spark that ignited when he touched her or the fact that he had made her cry.

"I'm only going to say one more thing, and then I'll let you be," he said as he tugged on the same piece of hair that she had tucked behind her ear earlier. "A girl as pretty as you should wear more smiles."

He turned and walked away, leaving her at the end of her parent's driveway. There were so many things she wanted to say, but the lump in her throat had prevented her from saying a word. She was mad that he held nothing back and told her just what he thought of her. She was sad that he saw her as a sourpuss because that wasn't how she wanted the world to see her, especially him. It was his grandmother that made her realize that a smile could make a difference. But most of all, she wanted him to know that she was interested, and that she'd love to learn to keep up with both his snide remarks and his long strides.

Rebecca wiped her eyes with her sleeve, remembering the warmth she felt when Eli grabbed her arm. He thinks I'm pretty. She felt a smile replace her tears. He's right! I should wear more smiles.

She stood and watched him walk away until she could only see the top of his straw hat over the crest of the hill. Feeling hopeful and determined, she turned and walked down her parents' driveway, thinking of everything she'd say to him if she got a chance. And maybe if she gave him one of her prettiest smiles, he'd offer to take her home from the singeon tomorrow night.

But now, standing in his grandmother's kitchen, she knew a do-over wasn't in the cards. She had said too much, betrayed his loyalty, and let him believe she was in love with another. All to protect him from the inevitable doom that was sure to follow her throughout the rest of her life.

History was repeating itself. She was sure of it. The undisclosed secret sin she harbored was pushing its way through her soul just like the dandelions that invaded Mary's garden.

Thinking back on how much peace her father found when he finally told Emma of her biological family, she wondered if she could see the same peace. Perhaps if she confessed the sin that put a wedge between Eli and herself, she could find relief.

But she was sure her secret would be too much for even Eli's forgiving heart to accept. It was too much for her to bear; how could she expect anyone else to understand what her selfishness had caused? No, she couldn't do it. It was better to keep pushing everyone she loved away in hopes of protecting them from the dreadfulness that followed her.

Drying her hands on a towel, she heard Mary's small voice carry through the house. "Eli, are you there?"

Rebecca pushed open the bedroom door and moved to Mary's side.

"Oh, Rebecca, you came."

She replied, placing her hand under Mary's elbow, and helping her stand. "I did, even though I'm not sure why you requested me and not Anna. She is much more suited to care for you."

Mary's eyes narrowed as she winced in pain. "But it's not Anna I want taking care of me; it's you."

Moving Mary's cane closer to her grip, Rebecca asked, "For heaven's sake. Why?"

"All in good time, my child. For now, get this old woman to the bathroom. I'm in dire need of a bath, and that's your task for the day."

Rebecca guided Mary to the bathroom, still trying to make sense of the woman's chatter about choosing her over Anna. Hoping she could gain more insight into her comment, she inquired, "I still don't understand why you would want me and not Anna."

Mary stopped moving and looked up at her. "Not now." There was an edge to her voice. "I need a bath."

Rebecca had never seen this side of Mary. Sharp, to the point, and impatient. Mary was full of life and a true joy to be around in the past. It was she who gave her reason to smile all those years ago.

As she readied Mary for a long soak in the tub, she drifted off to a time so many years ago when Mary explained her outlook on life.

Five years earlier…

Rebecca pulled a chair closer to Mary and asked, "How do you stay so happy? You always have a smile on your face."

The older woman just smiled. Pausing for a few minutes, she finally answered, "I guess I believe if you can't have the best of everything, you make the best of everything you have. As I see it, God wants us to see the good around us, and there is no sense in being unhappy; it's not going to change anything other than make us blue. And I don't like to feel that way."

Mary stopped talking long enough to pop a juicy strawberry in her mouth and turned toward Rebecca.

"I feel blessed, and to me, that's enough to keep a smile on my face," Mary continued, "I may not have a lot of money, but I figure a smile is free, and I give them away whenever I can. You never know when someone you meet might be having a rough day. A friendly smile could be just what they need."

The frail woman in front of her was but a mere image of the woman she first met five years ago. Gone was the welcoming smile and bubbly personality she had come to love. After filling the bathtub, she helped Mary undress, and all but lifted her into the warm water. Her petite frame was easy to maneuver, and she dutifully washed her hair and transparent skin. It was all Rebecca could do to pray that she would once again witness the part of Mary that her stroke shamelessly took away.

CHAPTER 4

Eli's mother voice cracked, "I knew this would happen. If you had only listened to us, you wouldn't find yourself in this predicament now."

Eli sighed. "But *Mamm*, if I had listened to you, *Mommi* wouldn't have anyone here taking care of her."

"Eli, your father and I only wanted the best for you. It was your choice to leave Lancaster to tend to your grandfather's failing sheep farm. You made your bed; now you must lie in it."

His mother's voice took on a familiar edge. "When are you going to come to your senses and come home? It's high time you start living your own life and stop living for her. I'd say it's about time you find yourself a wife."

Eli rubbed his forehead and switched the receiver to his other hand. He knew there was an underlying bitterness between his grandmother and his parents that he never entirely understood. It was exhausting trying to keep peace on the never-ending teeter-totter of grudges and secrets he wasn't privy to. Would it ever end? Why couldn't they both understand God instructs them to forgive and forget and move on? *Mommi* Mary didn't have much time left on this earth, and they all needed to get past this.

"Look, *Mamm,* all I'm asking is for you to get *Datt* to come visit her. She keeps asking for him, and I could use some help around here for a few weeks."

"I doubt your *datt* will be up for that. He has his hands full on this farm, and besides, it's planting season. He'll want to be here supervising your *bruders*. How about we send you some money?"

"I don't need money. What I need is for the both of you to act like you care."

Maybe calling his parents wasn't such a good idea. What made him think his *datt* would care about anyone but himself? He proved that more than once over the last few years.

"I'll give your *datt* your message, but I wouldn't count on him breaking free from the farm to come to Willow Springs anytime soon."

"*Mamm,* God called me here."

When she didn't say anything, he knew he had surprised her. Did her silence denote her displeasure in his comment?

"Son, I know you felt called to take care of your grandmother, but what you don't understand goes so far back in history; I don't even understand it myself."

"What is it that tore *Datt* away from Willow Springs? Why is there so much animosity toward *Mommi*? She has such a kind heart. What on earth could have ever happened that he can't even stomach coming to visit her?"

"I'm not really sure. But perhaps your grandmother holds the key. I learned long ago not to press your *datt* on the subject."

He was quiet for a moment. "It makes no sense."

"I agree, son. But often, when things like this fester for so long, it's best to leave them buried in the past and move on."

"That's just it. If whatever it is that's keeping *Datt* from spending time with his mother stays buried, the woman will have no peace. Please, *Mamm*, try to convince him to come see her."

"I'll do what I can, but I won't make any promises."

"That's all I can ask for. One more thing."

"What's that?"

"What do you know about *Mommi's* family from Lancaster?"

"Not much. Only bits and pieces. She didn't have any siblings since her mother died in childbirth. Her father left to serve in a field hospital in France during World War II. Before he left, he sent Mary to live with his neighbor, your Great-Grandfather Bricker. Shortly after her father returned, Mary and your grandfather married and moved to Willow Springs. As far as I know, she doesn't have any family left here in Lancaster."

"Why did they move so far from home? The Bricker Farm was huge even back then. There would have been plenty of work for him."

She gave a dry laugh. "Eli, you know as well as I do it's not best to dig things up from the past. No good will come from it."

Eli sighed heavily. "Okay, I'll leave it alone. But there is something that just doesn't sit just right. I think if I could get to the bottom of it…"

"You've spent too much time with your grandmother. Her white-picket-fence syndrome she has just isn't going to happen, so leave it in the past."

After they said their goodbyes, Eli sat in the phone shanty and thought. *What could have happened to cause so much animosity on his father's part? His mother made it sound like she knew more than she let on. Could the estrangement between his grandmother and his father be more than a minor family squabble? Or was there something far deeper that could be resolved if it was only addressed?*

***

After a warm bath and a hot cup of tea, Mary sat near the window. From across the yard, she watched as Eli shut the door of the phone shanty and headed back toward the barn. His slumped shoulders reminded her of the heavy burden he carried. If it was the last thing she'd do, she would find a way to bring Rebecca and him back together. He needed a wife to share his heavy load. There had to be more to their short romance since either of them failed to find someone else to share their life with.

Rebecca's footsteps stopped short of her chair. "I was going to start some dinner. Anything you have a liking for?"

It didn't take but a second for her response. "Chicken and dumplings."

"But that will take hours."

"If you didn't want me to give you my desire, why ask?"

"True. I'll think twice next time."

Mary smiled as Rebecca walked away and tapped her quad stick on the floor to get her attention. "Remember, I'm paying you, so I'd put a smile on your face and get to it."

It didn't take but a few minutes for the clang of pots and pans to make an awful racket from the other room. With each sound, Mary smiled broader, she had tricked Rebecca into making Eli's favorite meal. One thing for sure was the best way to a man's heart was through his stomach, and she was sure it was the same for her grandson as well.

***

Rebecca mumbled under her breath as she unwrapped the chicken and added onion, celery, carrots, and a bay leaf to a pot. Rummaging through cupboards, looking for the correct array of spices, she added the mix to the pan and filled it with water.

Adding a few pieces of kindling to the wood stove, she moved the pan to the burner and finished putting away the dishes she'd washed earlier. Without realizing it, she caught herself peering out the kitchen window, hoping to catch a glimpse of Eli. Disgusted with herself for even caring where he was, she moved away from the window and picked up Mary's recipe box, fingering through the well-worn cards. Stopping on the second chocolate-stained card, it read *Eli's Favorite Brownies.*

A good dose of chocolate was precisely what the day called for, regardless of if it was Eli's favorite or not.

Just before noon, the house was filled with the rich aroma of a family dinner, and she looked forward to Mary and Eli joining her in the kitchen. Eli could be heard on the back porch stomping the mud off his boots.

With her back toward the door, she held her breath and waited for him to say something before she turned around.

***

Eli watched the clock in the barn and wondered if Rebecca had made enough dinner for both him and Mary. The mere thought of the girl he prayed so fervently for taking up residence in his kitchen left him bewildered. He really didn't want to go down that path again with Rebecca, but at this point, he would do anything his grandmother wanted to ensure she was well cared for.

Eli kicked the mud off his boots before opening the kitchen door. Shocked at the kitchen's transformation in such a short time, he stated, "I do believe you clearly said you wouldn't be cleaning up after me or making me any meals."

She swung around and dried her hands on a towel. "I didn't. I made Mary dinner, and if I wanted to do so, I had to wash the dishes first."

He moved to the stove and picked up the lid from the simmering pot. "Chicken and dumplings?"

"That's pretty obvious, isn't it?"

Eli snapped his head in her direction in hopes of a smile to soften her sharp words. Instead, he was met with a sneer that would chase any logical man for the hills.

He replaced the lid and moved to the sink. The cool water flowing over his hands did little to settle the hairs on the back of his neck. For his grandmother's sake, he needed to find a way to make this new arrangement work. With Rebecca's feral cat-like tendencies, it was going to be a challenge, to say the least.

Before he could comment on her snide remarks, Mary's long slow shuffle made its way to the table. He scurried to pull her chair out and placed his hand under her good elbow to help her ease down. Her limp arm hung at her waist, and she pulled it to her lap.

Eli pushed her chair in closer to the table and moved her quad stick to the side of the counter before taking a seat.

He patted the back of her hand. "So, how is my favorite *Mommi* today?"

In a slightly slurred mumble, Mary replied, "First, I'm anything but good with being so incapable of tending to myself. However, Rebecca helped me with a bath, and I feel like a new woman. Or as much as I can with this broken body."

"Well, she definitely earned her keep if she's made you feel like a new woman again."

He raised his eyebrow in Rebecca's direction, and she made a loud TSK sound as she placed a steaming bowl in front of him.

After they bowed their heads and Eli tapped his spoon on the side of his bowl, indicating he was through, Rebecca tucked a napkin on

Mary's lap. The small gesture touched Eli, but he refused to acknowledge it for fear she'd lash out in front of his grandmother.

Turning his attention to Mary, he said, "I called my *mamm* this morning and invited them to come for a visit as you requested. She wasn't too hopeful that they could pull themselves away from the farm during planting season."

Mary stirred her spoon around the bowl and struggled to take a bite without spilling it down her dress. Both Eli and Rebecca watched and were ready to offer assistance if need be. When she let her spoon sink to the side of the dish, she whispered, "I really didn't think they could, but I appreciate you asking. I know how busy they are these days."

Eli took a drink. "I'm sorry, but *Datt* shouldn't be too busy to visit with his mother. I'll never understand him."

Mary picked up her napkin. "Andy bowed out of my life long before any of this happened."

"But it's just not right."

"Maybe so, but it's just how it is," Mary said the words, but down deep inside, she was crying at the loss of her son. If he only knew the sacrifices his father made on his behalf, things might have been different. But was it her place to go back on the promises she made to her husband and take their secret to the grave? It seemed like the right thing to do when she made that vow. *But don't Andy and Eli deserve to know the truth?* She couldn't help but think. *Oh, Andy, how could you do this to me after everything your father gave up for you? We loved you and were there for you every step of the way, and this is the thanks I get. Total abandonment. You pushed my care onto your own son when it should be you taking care of me. Eli has a life of his own to live. He should be settling down with a family, not caring for an ailing grandmother.*

"*Mommi*?" Her grandson's voice pulled her back to the present. Nothing he could say would cure the deeply etched pain she anguished over. Only God could take her pain away, and she wished for that more and more with each passing day.

"*Mommi*, what is it?"

"Nothing a nice long nap won't cure. You finish eating. Rebecca, if you'll help me to my room, I think I should lay down for a spell."

Eli laid his spoon down and started to get up, but Rebecca stopped him. "I got this. Do as your grandmother said and finish eating." He gave in to both strong-willed women. He waited until Rebecca led her away from the table before finishing his meal.

The underlying pain followed the creases on his grandmother's face so deep that he instantly became annoyed with his father all over again. Why couldn't he see that it was his mother's last wish to see him, perhaps for the last time? He carried his bowl to the sink, cut a brownie from the pan near the stove, and headed back to the barn.

Once outside, he gathered his bucket of fencing supplies and headed out to walk the fence line. He thought over everything he knew about his Great-Grandfather Bricker and what he'd heard about his own father going to live with him right before he died. Why did he leave the farm to his father and not one of his own sons?

Nothing made much sense, and what did wasn't good. There was an underlying hostility between his father and his grandparents throughout his whole life. He had the feeling he should go see his father, no matter the cost. And that cost would be high. He could count on that. His father was pretty set in his ways, and he didn't like anyone to challenge him, especially his own son.

Still, seeds of unrest were taking root and growing inside of him that wouldn't be put to rest until he figured out what happened to make his father turn on his own mother like he had. But he couldn't do that during lambing season. It would have to wait until summer at the earliest. He prayed his *mommi* would stay strong until then.

***

Rebecca helped Mary sit on the edge of the bed and removed her black sneakers before she lifted her legs to the mattress. "Is there anything I can bring you?"

"No, dear, I think a nap is all I need. Thank you for making dinner. I'm sure Eli enjoyed it."

"I don't really care if Eli did. I made it for you, and you didn't even eat anything."

Mary laid her head back on her pillow. "You do care, and you're not fooling this old woman for one minute."

Rebecca pulled a blanket up over her and shook her head. "I have no idea what you're talking about. Whatever notions you have about Eli and me, they can fly right out the window. I'm here for you only, and if I could have figured out a way to get out of that, I would have."

"Whatever you say, my dear. But remember, God's plans are not always our own."

"Mary, you're talking nonsense, and you're living in the past. Whatever you thought would happen five years ago is all dead and gone. Too much time has passed, and too much water has flowed under that bridge."

When she stood to leave, Mary's eyes were already fluttering closed, and she waved her off with her good hand. After all these years, why do Mary's comments affect her so, and why does the pain of giving everything up to protect Eli matter now? It was nobody's fault but her own, and no amount of wishful thinking from a dying woman should make a hill of beans now.

She pulled Mary's bedroom door closed softly and stood at the front window watching a cluster of robins peck at the thawing ground. She couldn't help but think her life was much like those birds poking and prodding for just one juicy worm. Hopping from one hole to the next, hoping it would be the one to fill her up.

Over the last five years, she'd pushed everyone away, put on a rugged exterior that no one could break through, and was determined to keep the sins of her past hidden so deep they wouldn't show their ugly head to anyone she held dear.

But that was just it. Everyone she loved didn't love her. And whose fault was that? Hers, of course. It was better that way. Or so she thought.

She moved the chicken pot to the warming spot on the stove and walked to the counter. Eli had tipped the sugar dish on its side and wrote *THANK YOU!* in the fine white crystals.

A gentle nudging softened her heart for a split second before it became a push, and she focused on the exclamation point. Was that his way of being sarcastic? She brushed the sugar back in the bowl and tried to figure out what was bothering her so.

Not that God ever answered her prayers in the past, but she felt drawn to lift her questions to Him.

Why now? That part of my heart has been closed tight for years. Is this your way of punishing me? Haven't I sacrificed enough? What more do you want from me?

CHAPTER 5

Emma poured Samuel a cup of coffee and stirred in the right amount of sugar and cream to add a smile to his face before handing it to him.

She sat down beside him at the table and brushed a few loose toast crumbs off the table in her hand. "I'm not so sure Rebecca will be open to the idea of spending any more time with me than she absolutely has to.

"I'm not high on her list of casual acquaintances these days."

"Now Emma, she's your *schwester,* and if we can't offer our own kin grace, how can we expect God to offer it to us?"

"But she can't stand the sight of me. Everything that comes out of my mouth infuriates her, and I'm not sure why."

"Like I said before, her secrets built a wall around her heart, keeping her from finding peace. I'm sure of it."

"You keep saying that, but what are those secrets? Maybe if I knew, I could help her work her way through them."

"They're not mine to tell. The only one I can reveal is the one that affected me personally."

Emma emptied the crumbs onto a napkin and anxiously waited for Samuel's explanation.

Samuel reached out and took her hands in his. "Now, before I tell you about my part in all this, please know I'm as much to blame as Rebecca. I don't want you to hold any ill feelings toward your *schwester*. It was my fault for letting it go on for as long as it did. I have made my peace with God, but I know I need to make my peace with Eli as well."

"Eli, why Eli?"

"Hold on, give me a minute to explain."

"You're worrying me. What could have happened that was so bad you had to make it right with God?"

Samuel squeezed her fingertips. "Believe me, I've carried around enough guilt about that summer for a lifetime. But God showed me there is no room in my life for Him and guilt."

Emma moved in closer. "Please, Samuel, tell me. What is it?"

"Okay, here goes. Remember the summer you went to Sugarcreek to get to know your birth mother?"

"*Jah*."

"Well, that was also the summer Rebecca and Eli were seen leaving the *singeons* together. It was no news to anyone that Eli had his eyes set on her. But then something happened, and suddenly, Rebecca begged me to help her end it."

"But why would she need your help? Since when does a girl need help to end a courtship?"

Samuel averted his eyes from Emma's and whispered, "I had witnessed something and kept it to myself. I became just as guilty by not acknowledging my part in it, and she held it over me. I felt I had no choice but to do her bidding."

Emma pulled her hands from his grip. "You let my *schwester* blackmail you?"

"There's so much more to all this, but again, it's not my story to tell. It's hers, and until Rebecca does, she will always be stuck in this vicious cycle of hurt and anger."

"But what did you do, and why do you need to make peace with Eli?"

"That's just it. What I took part in affected Eli in a big way."

"Please, Samuel, just spit it out. What did you do?"

Samuel leaned back and grabbed the arms of the polished oak chair. "I made Eli believe I was in love with her."

"You what? Why on earth would you do that?"

"Rebecca didn't want him to think there was any chance for them. I helped her make him believe we were courting."

Emma rubbed her fingers over both temples. "So let me get this straight. My *schwester*, who knew how I felt about you, went behind my back and forced you into deceiving someone who cared for her. What kind of *schwester* does that?"

Samuel reached out and picked up her hand again. "The kind of girl who is lost in her own pain."

"But she's been mad at me for what reason? She has been acting like I'm the one who's done something wrong all these years. With all due respect, she's the one who's been harboring an unresolved secret. It put a wedge between us. She's blamed it on me when it's been her own doing all along."

"Emma, calm down. I've given it a lot of thought and prayer over the years. I believe secrets can cause a great deal of harm to a person, which is what I think has happened with Rebecca."

Emma took in a labored breath and blew it out before responding. "We think secrets can lay dormant in our mind, forever buried deep in the past, but at some point, they come alive and have a will of their own. They destroy our lives, and until we turn them over to God and fully find redemption, they will eat away at us until we have no choice but to surrender them to Jesus."

She leaned her elbows on the table. "I don't understand. If it's just one secret, why wouldn't she want to confess and be done with it?"

"That's just it. My involvement in helping her convince Eli there was no hope for them was just one little aspect of a much larger problem. Until she finds it in her heart to confess the whole truth to the Lord and all those involved, she won't get much relief from her past."

"But what can I do? Rebecca has her own agenda. Spending time with me is at the bottom of her list. She never has time for anyone but herself."

"Exactly why we are on the mission we're on. If we haven't learned anything else in the past six months, it's that God will continue to lead our way if we are open to following Him. I believe we're meant to be the light in Rebecca's darkness. And I know for a fact I already failed miserably at that."

"How so?"

"To begin with, I laid into her the other day about how she treated you at the bakery. All that did was ruffle her feathers even more. But more importantly, it made me hear God even clearer. It's not our job to change her heart; it's God's. All we can do is help her grow in Christ."

"But Samuel, do you know what that means?"

"I do. It means there may come a time when we can show her that her past doesn't define her future, and if she turns her life over to Jesus, she can find the peace she is longing for."

Emma stood and carried their cups to the sink. "But it also means we open up our private bible studies to her, and that may open up a whole new can of worms."

Samuel walked to the sink, wrapped his arms around her waist, rested his chin on top of her starched white *kapp,* and whispered, "I am the vine; you are the branches..."

Emma laid her hands on his chest and pushed him back enough so she could look into his eyes. "I understand we are to be God's branches, but how can we do anything to help her if she's not willing to confess whatever is haunting her?"

"That's just it. Secrets want out. They have a way of trying to escape."

Emma pulled away from his hold and picked up more of the breakfast dishes from the table. "By keeping it hidden, she's pushed everyone away in the process. All she has ever wanted is to be accepted, but that can't happen as long as there are parts of her that she's keeping under lock and key. That's why there's never been any hope for her and Eli. As long as she keeps things from him, there will never be any hope for a future."

Samuel leaned back on the counter and crossed his arms over his chest. "Exactly. The very act of secrecy makes us inaccessible to love."

"Oh, Samuel, it's like history is repeating itself. Remember when my *datt* kept my true identity a secret for so long? When the time came and he needed to tell me, he became impossible to live with. He pushed me away and became angry. It's the same thing Rebecca is doing. Why can't she see it?"

"Because she's too deep in it to realize what's happening."

Emma ran hot water over the stack of dishes and tossed Samuel a towel. "But what can we do?"

"Pray and remember what Alvin and Lynette taught us. Without faith, a person can't understand spiritual problems."

Emma handed him a wet plate. "And we can't counsel an unbeliever. All we can do is evangelize to them. And that's exactly what we can do for Rebecca. She might not enjoy it, but I'll pray God gives us the wisdom to make a difference in her life."

***

In the distance, Rebecca heard a rooster announcing the first rays of light above the horizon. Caught somewhere between a dream and reality, she heard laughter. Fighting to remain in the peace of slumber, she let her mind follow the sound.

Walking through a field of clover, she stopped short of the row of maple trees that lined Willow Creek and watched three young girls playing by the bank. As if she was watching the scene for the first time, she stood back and remembered the day as if it were yesterday.

"Come on, Rebecca, Mamm won't mind if we're a few minutes late for dinner. As long as we stay near the bank and don't go in too deep, we'll be fine."

"But we were supposed to go to Shetler's Grocery and come right home. If we're late, she'll be worried, and I'll be the one who gets in trouble."

Rebecca watched the younger version of herself walk to the creek's edge. "Emma, Anna, come on, we have to go."

"But Rebecca, it's hot. Please...just for a few minutes? We'll wrap our skirts up high, so they don't get wet. Mamm will never know."

The young girl looked over her shoulder toward the field where their datt was plowing. "All right, but just for a few minutes. Mamm will come looking for us if we don't get back soon. If she finds out I let you go in the creek after yesterday's heavy rain, she'll have my tail."

In a flash, the day turned dark, and the murky waters of Willow Creek swam through her lungs as she thrashed her arms, trying to find her footing on the muddy banks. Under the water, her schwester's screams bounced off the ripples. In an instant, a log appeared, and she wrapped her arm around the floating limb and pulled herself to the surface. Floating in the fast current, she let the log pull her downstream, all while watching Emma and Anna run along the bank, hollering in her direction.

Anna took off toward the field, and Emma's little feet tried hard to keep up with her in the water. "Hold tight, Rebecca. Please ... Rebecca, hold on. Anna went to get Datt!

The sound of Emma's voice faded even though Rebecca fought to remain in the past. When the rooster's call became louder than the cries of her youngest *schwester,* the reality of what she lost became all too real. Rebecca pulled her quilt up over her head and sunk down deep under the covers. Once she threw back the covers and faced the day, she knew that the memory of what she used to have would be lost again forever.

She ignored the knock on her bedroom door for as long as she could. Anna pushed open the door and walked to the edge of her bed, shaking her from her dream-like state.

"Rebecca, you better get up. *Datt* and Wilma are waiting for breakfast, and you need to get to Mary's. Best not be late on your second day."

Anna pulled the blanket from her head, and she retaliated. "Stop! I'll get up when I'm good and ready, and I'm not there yet."

Anna threw her arms up. "Suit yourself. Just figured you'd rather get a visit from me than Wilma. She's already in a mood because the eggs are getting cold."

Rebecca tossed the blanket to the bottom of the bed and sat up. "All right already. I'm up. Now get out of here, so I can get dressed. I'll be down in a minute."

The first rays of the sun were starting to shine their way into her room; a heaviness surrounded her thoughts. *Love like that doesn't last forever, I'm sure of it. Emma wouldn't care at all about me drowning these days.*

She walked into the kitchen without saying a word, lured by the aroma of fresh coffee and salted ham. Taking her seat and bowing her head, she ignored the irritated glare from her stepmother. She waited until her father cleared his throat before opening her eyes.

Anna reached for a slice of toast and asked, "How was Mary yesterday?"

Rebecca added a scoop of eggs to her plate. "There aren't a lot of things she can do by herself, let alone take care of that house. I'm not sure why she is so set on staying put in Willow Springs when her son lives in Lancaster. Surely, he's better equipped to take care of her than Eli is."

Wilma passed the plate of ham and added, "Hence why they need a nursemaid. I surely hope you're treating them both kindly."

Rebecca's heart pounded; anger poured through her before she responded, "Who do you think I am?"

The table fell quiet, and a wave of remorse brushed by her like an annoying fly. Had she overreacted to Wilma's comment, or was it the shame she felt by her harsh treatment of Eli yesterday? If her father found out how she spoke to him, he'd have more than a few choice words to say.

Jacob pounded his fork on the table. "You apologize to Wilma. There was no need to speak to her in that tone."

"She automatically thinks the worst of me."

Her father picked up his knife and cut his ham. "And have you given her reason to believe otherwise?"

"That doesn't matter. What matters is she's always free to offer her opinion even when it's not asked for!"

Wilma laid her hand on Jacob's forearm. "It's fine. Rebecca's old enough to know that if she lets one bad weed grow in her garden, it will choke all the good from growing and taking root."

Rebecca rolled her eyes and pushed her plate away. "What's that supposed to mean?"

Anna took a sip of her tea before saying, "She's trying to say it's your responsibility to plant your garden with seeds of kindness."

Without saying a word, Rebecca carried her plate to the sink and headed out the back door. The early morning breeze made her wish she would have grabbed a sweater, but instead of going back inside, she picked up her pace. The short walk to Eli and Mary's did little to calm her frustration at Anna taking Wilma's side. The one person she could always count on having her back just turned on her as well.

As she walked past Emma and Samuel's, their chocolate lab, Someday, ran out to greet her. She stopped, knelt, hugged his furry coat, and let him nuzzle her neck.

"How's my big guy today?"

Someday used his nose to force her hand into a back scratch, and she giggled as he leaned into her fingertips. "That feels good, doesn't it, big guy?"

Emma walked up beside her. "He sure does love his back scratched. I've never seen a dog who can force a stranger into a good back rub."

Rebecca stood back up and sneered. "I'm anything but a stranger."

Emma patted the top of the dog's head. "I didn't mean you were a stranger. I just meant that he could encourage anyone to love on him a bit."

Emma sucked in a calming breath, trying to remember everything Samuel and she had just spoken about. "I'm glad I caught you this morning. I was hoping you might like to come to supper sometime this week. It's been a long time since we've spent any time together, and I'd hoped we might find a way to clear the air between us."

"Why would you think I'd want to do that?"

"I don't know. Maybe because I miss you, and I'd love to figure out what's eating at you."

Both women stood in the middle of the road waiting for the other to speak first. When the silence became uncomfortable, Emma turned and walked away saying, "The invitation stands. You are welcome at my table anytime."

Rebecca watched as Emma returned to the basket waiting for her at the clothesline. After she was sure she wasn't going to turn back around, she headed back down the road toward Eli's.

After the horrible way she had treated her earlier in the week, she was astonished that her little *schwester* still wanted anything to do with her. If the roles were reversed, she was confident that inviting her to share a meal would be the last thing on her mind.

Not one prone to cry, Rebecca blinked back tears and looked down at the road. She wished things could be different. She wished she could tell Emma how she had betrayed her trust and forced Samuel to lie for her.

Some things were better off left buried deep in the past. Much like the one lie that would haunt her the rest of her life. Even if she wanted to confess, too much time had passed. God had already punished

Emma and Samuel by taking their child before he even had a chance to live. It was all her fault.

It was too late. Her fate was sealed. She would continue to push everyone away, so when it came time for God to punish her, no one would miss her, and life could go on without her.

CHAPTER 6

The aftermath of Emma's invitation still burned on Rebecca's cheeks as she walked up Eli's driveway. Along both sides of the loose gravel path were fenced-in pastures with abundant herds of sheep. Eli had turned every ounce of his grandfather's farm into pasture except the acre-sized yard. A weed-filled kitchen and flower garden and an array of flowerpots dotted the landscape surrounding the white clapboard one-story farmhouse.

Walking down the path that led to the kitchen door, she stopped to pinch a stem of mint pushing its way through a patch of weeds and gathered a cluster of Johnny Jump-ups. She pulled the mint to her nose, and it reminded her of the Sweet Meadow Tea her *mamm* used to make.

Still lost in a time long gone, she didn't hear Eli step up beside her and leaped at his voice.

Eli grinned. "Didn't mean to startle you."

Rebecca rolled her eyes. "Oh, no, you didn't."

Both stood looking out over the weed patch that was once a reflection of Mary's love for plants.

Eli sighed. "Not much time left in the day after I tend to two hundred sheep to take care of such things."

Rebecca didn't look up at Eli. "I suppose if I have time, I could at least get some of the weeds pulled." Before she even got the words out of her mouth, she regretted doing so. What did she know about gardening? To be honest, half the time, she couldn't tell a weed from a plant. That was always Emma's job growing up. She preferred to be in the barn tending to her alpacas than working in the gardens.

Rebecca looked up, stricken, hoping he wouldn't take her up on the offer.

Eli pointed to the bench alongside the garden. "I bet *Mommi* Mary would love to sit outside with you when it warms up."

He walked past her and around to the back of the house. Leaving her standing in the same spot where she wished she could turn back the minutes. *What have I done now? Always opening my mouth before I think. I have no desire to play in the dirt, that's for sure and certain.*

***

Eli grinned from ear to ear as he left Rebecca standing, trying to take her words back. He remembered a lot about Rebecca Byler, including her dislike of gardening. But if anyone could teach someone about tending a garden, it would be his grandmother. And besides, a little sunshine would do them both some good.

When he pushed the wheelbarrow filled with a rake, shovel, and pruning shears around the house, her mouth fell open, but no words escaped. "I think you should have everything you might need. Let me know if you don't, and I'll get on it."

"Now hold on just a minute. When you hired me, you didn't say anything about cleaning up an overgrown garden. I doubt that's in my job duties. I take back my offer. I wasn't thinking."

He gave her a halfhearted grin as he brushed by her but refused to answer. Her tone spoke a thousand words, and he knew better than to engage in a sparring match with her. In the back of his mind, he kept hearing his grandmother tell him … *just cultivate a friendship with her…*

He wasn't sure what that meant other than he knew the heart of Rebecca Byler held more than the brassy exterior she showed to everyone else. He'd been given a second chance to be around the green-eyed beauty that captured his heart so many years ago. And in the dark of the night, he proclaimed before God that he wasn't about to let the few daggers she kept throwing at him wear him down. If He gave him another chance to fix what was broken with his Becca, he'd do as God bid.

He didn't dare turn around as he walked back to the barn. He could feel her eyes burning a hole through his shirt as clearly as if she held a knife in her hand. Thinking to himself, *She offered; I only took her up on the idea before she had a chance to change her mind.*

No sooner did he make his way through the opened double doors than he heard his neighbor, Samuel Yoder, call his name.

"Hello, Eli. Are you in here?"

"*Jah*, back here."

Eli lifted his head above the gate where he was stooped down, checking on a pregnant ewe. He opened and closed the gate and latched it tight before extending his hand in Samuel's direction. "What do I owe this visit to?"

Samuel drew in a long breath and replied, "This visit is way overdue. I'm hoping you have a few minutes so we could discuss a matter I should've cleared up years ago."

Eli had no idea what Samuel was referring to. By the way Samuel's forehead was crunched together; he assumed it was serious.

***

Heart still thumping, Rebecca pushed open the back door, laid the handful of miniature pansies on the counter, and slipped out of her mud-caked black shoes. Mary sat in a chair pulled up close to the window that overlooked the backyard. In not much more than a whisper, she said, "It really was quite glorious in the spring."

Rebecca walked beside her. "What's that?"

"When in bloom, the pink rhododendrons cover the fence so much that you can't see the fence through the flowers. They don't bloom until June, though."

Rebecca stooped down so she could see what Mary was pointing to. All they both could see were barren branches with just a hint of green buds starting to change the landscape. Mary knew she didn't know the difference, but she acted as she did for her sake.

Mary couldn't speak past the lump in her throat as she watched Rebecca add the small bouquet of pansies to a tiny juice glass and set it on the windowsill. Mary's throat closed tight, and she gasped for air.

Rebecca snapped around at the sound and ran to her side. "What is it?" The room fell silent, and tears streamed down Mary's cheeks.

Rebecca looked deep into Mary's eyes but couldn't read her expression. Was she in pain? For the first time in a long time, Rebecca felt something that resembled compassion, and her heart sank.

The old woman's eyes misted over and focused on the small vase on the windowsill. "Where did you find those?"

"They were at the edge of the garden right beside a patch of mint."

Through a labored hiccup, she asked, "Bring them to me."

Rebecca carried the tiny glass container to her side and handed it off to her. When she thought Mary had a good grip on the glass, she let go, and it slipped from her frail fingers and shattered on the floor. Mary dropped her head, and her shoulders sank, pulling her petite frame into a childlike form.

Rebecca's eyes flickered, and she tried to keep her irritation at the unexpected mess under control. When she bent down to pick up the shattered glass, she felt Mary's eyes looking down at her. Rebecca felt her pain long before she saw the darkness in her eyes. Did she dare pry?

Before she had a chance to say a word, Mary pointed to the bathroom, and they went on about their day. Rebecca took care of Mary's needs for the rest of the morning, tidied up the house, and made dinner. For the first time, someone other than herself occupied her mind. Something in Mary's eyes spoke of a deep-etched sadness that bothered Rebecca. It was as if they shared the same cell in a darkened room for a split second. What was it, and how could she explain it?

When Eli didn't come in for the noon-time meal, she wandered from window to window throughout the house, hoping to catch sight of him. An edge of bitterness and resentment welled up inside her because she went out of her way to make enough for him, and he didn't come in to eat. A spark of anger lit inside her just as the screen door slammed.

She had her back to the kitchen, sitting on the living room floor sorting through years' worth of seed catalogs as Eli rummaged through the kitchen. He didn't say a word and moved throughout the room without acknowledging her. Something was wrong; she could feel it. There was a tension in the air that was much different from their early morning interaction.

Stacking the most recent issues on the stand next to Mary's chair, she picked up a large stack of old magazines and carried them to the trash in the kitchen.

In a gruff voice, Eli said, "Just leave them by the door. I'll take care of them."

Dropping the stack on the floor by the back door, Rebecca placed both hands on her hips and replied, "Is it something I said?"

Eli buttered two slices of bread, forked a slice of meatloaf up off the plate, and made a sandwich before pushing the plate aside.

Rebecca clicked her tongue when he laid the butter-filled knife on the clean table and wiped up the mess before saying, "If you had come in at noon, you wouldn't have to eat cold meatloaf."

After taking a bite, Eli rubbed his temple with his free hand.

"Do you have a headache? I could find you an aspirin if you like."

"No, I'm fine. How's *Mommi* Mary today?

Rebecca felt a little uncomfortable telling him his grandmother soiled herself again that morning and that she caused the old woman to cry. So, instead, she told him she was napping comfortably.

Whatever had happened between the time she had arrived that morning and the present was troubling him. The way he glared at her when she spoke made her want to run and hide, but she didn't know from what. She pressed her lips together, hoping to prevent herself from spitting out some snide remark that would only add to his mood.

After wiping his mouth on a napkin, Eli walked to the back door, picked up the magazines, and said, "I have to run an errand. Can you stay until I get back?"

He didn't wait for her answer before he headed out the door. Rebecca closed her eyes just as the door slammed shut. Eli was struggling with something; she could see it in the lines around his eyes.

Rebecca couldn't speak. It wasn't that she didn't have any words. It was that she had too many, all of which would just add fuel to whatever fire was already burning in Eli's soul.

Eli's long strides marched with determination toward the barn. Rebecca wanted to run after him and find out what was bothering him. Still, the undercurrents of the past kept her planted securely to the yellow linoleum under her feet. What were all these feelings being stirred up inside of her? And what would they matter now? She made her choice a long time ago, and there was no turning back now.

***

"Rebecca?"

Mary's frail voice tumbled through the house until it reached Rebecca's ears. Pulling herself away from Eli's form, she followed Mary's call.

"Was that Eli I heard a few minutes ago? Why didn't he join us for dinner?"

Rebecca reached for Mary's hand and helped her sit up, moving her legs over the edge of the bed. "I'm not sure. He didn't say."

"That's not like him. I'd like to speak to him. Can you go get him?"

"He's running an errand. I'm sure he has already headed on his way."

Both women turned toward the window when Eli's buggy passed Mary's bedroom window on its way down the driveway.

"I'm sure he won't be long. Would you like to sit in your chair or out in the front room so you can watch the birds?"

"I wanted him to retrieve a box from the attic."

Rebecca handed Mary the quad stick and helped guide her to the front room. "I can get what you need. Tell me what I'm looking for."

"No, Eli can fetch it later."

"Suit yourself."

Rebecca sat in the rocking chair next to Mary, and both women let the steady sounds from the clock on the wall fill the silence.

"Would you like to go outside? The sun's warmed the day, and the fresh air might do you some good. I could carry a blanket out to the bench, and you could sit near the garden."

Rebecca watched Mary's face change, but she didn't answer right away. Mary's bottom lip quivered as she struggled to form a yes. When no words escaped her lips, she nodded her head instead.

Once she had Mary settled on the bench and covered her legs with a quilt, Rebecca stood and faced the years of weeds that had been left to capture the garden.

Rebecca let out her breath slowly and dropped to her knees. Hopefully, if she started to pull something that wasn't a weed, Mary would stop her. She would tug and pull on everything and anything that looked out of place until then.

Rebecca filled the wheelbarrow with so many early spring weeds and the remnants of previous gardens that they spilled over the sides within an hour. When the afternoon sun started to ascend over the rooftop, leaving Mary sitting in the shade, Rebecca helped her to her feet and led her back inside.

Mary hadn't said a word the whole time they were outside, and the long silence left Rebecca wondering if she had indeed said something to offend Mary as well. After settling Mary back in her chair, she looked out the window, hoping Eli had made it back, so she could head home. The silent treatment left her yearning to go home and away from both Bricker's for the day.

Walking through the front room on her way back to the kitchen to start supper, Rebecca heard Mary whisper, "My husband sprinkled those Johnny Jump-Up seeds in the garden the first year we moved here. They haven't bloomed in years. You pulled them all out and tossed them in the wheelbarrow with the weeds."

Rebecca's mouth flattened. "Why didn't you stop me? I don't know a flower from a weed! I didn't see any purple and yellow petals."

Mary's eyes darkened. "They hadn't bloomed yet."

When she didn't say more, Rebecca walked from the room and went to wash her hands in the kitchen sink. The strangest feeling was stirring inside of her. One of regret and sadness. It was different from the self-inflicted pain she caused herself by pushing everyone away. No, this was different. It was like nothing she'd ever felt. The agonizing betrayal of an old woman's memory was on her hands, and no amount of soap and water would wash it away.

The sun was starting to set over the horizon when Eli made it back home. Rebecca was sitting at the table working on a word search when he came in the back door.

He flipped his straw hat off and hung it on the peg as he entered. Rebecca laid her pencil aside and closed the book. "Your grandmother is already sleeping. She should be good until I return in the morning. Is there anything else you need before I leave?"

Eli moved to the sink to wash up. "I didn't unhook the buggy, so I could take you home."

"There's no need to do that. I can walk just the same."

"I didn't say you couldn't, but there's a storm rolling in, and you'll get soaking wet before you make it home."

The fire in his eyes died, and Rebecca almost felt sorry for him. Whatever was on his mind weighed heavily, and she was confident that taking her home wasn't high on his list.

She followed him out the side door and to his waiting buggy.

***

Eli studied her as she climbed inside and folded her hands neatly on her lap. He had learned way too much about what made her tick that afternoon, and it was all he could do to stop himself from lashing out at her. Eli knew better. Her sharp tongue would win against him every time if he pushed too hard. How much did he really know? Not enough for sure.

Samuel spent the better part of the morning confessing to his role in convincing him Rebecca didn't have feelings for him so many years ago. So much that it left him reliving the pain all over again. The muscle in his jaw twitched, and he snapped the reins moving his horse forward. The sudden jerk made him glance in her direction, but she kept her eyes focused ahead.

Call it compassion or plain stupidity on his part, but a small voice in the back of his mind told him to keep his thoughts to himself. It wasn't the right time. He needed to gain Rebecca's trust again before he could press her into admitting the truth. *It's up to you, Lord, isn't it? It's your will, not mine.*

***

Rebecca desperately wanted to believe the tension in the buggy had nothing to do with her. But for the life of her, she couldn't think of one thing she might have said or done to cause such an icy response. Eli clicked his tongue and called his mare by name to encourage the horse to pick up the pace. The brown-topped buggy rocked back and forth in a steady response to Eli's command. The clip-clop of the horses' hooves echoed off the blacktop as dark clouds rolled overhead. When a car behind them passed too close, it made the horse pull to the side; the buggy swayed, and she voiced her concern. "Eli, what's the big hurry?"

Eli pulled in beside the Byler's Furniture Sign and stopped short of *Stitch 'n Time's* front door without barely slowing down. For years, he had hung on her every word and took every opportunity to steal a glance her way. But at that exact moment, the mere sight of her left him wondering if he really wanted to go out of his way to find the truth. But again, that small voice told him to be still.

When the buggy rolled to a stop, Rebecca waited before stepping down. She looked toward Eli and asked. "Do you want to tell me what that was all about?

He didn't move his head toward her voice but kept his eyes focused ahead. "Not now, Becca."

The deep growl of his voice told her he was in no mood to explain himself, so she stepped from the buggy and watched him pull away. No one ever called her Becca but him. But why now?

CHAPTER 7

Mary worried all day on Sunday that Rebecca wouldn't return come Monday morning. Despite how Eli tried to convince her otherwise, she didn't think she'd be back. Mary tried to read her bible to take her mind off the ill manner in which she treated Rebecca, but she couldn't concentrate on a word she read. Thank goodness it was a no church Sunday, so she had time to gather her thoughts and figure out how she would make it up to the girl.

Even Eli was in a mood that Mary couldn't explain. It was all she could do to get him to give her more than a grunt for the few questions she'd asked him that morning. Mary closed the book and rested her hand on the top of the well-worn leather binding. Not wanting to leave her alone for any longer than need be, Eli headed to the barn to check on his pregnant ewes and promised he would be back in shortly. Taking advantage of the quietness of the morning, Mary closed her eyes.

Lord, you know I've been giving myself a pity party for the last few weeks, and it's not something I've enjoyed. I know you have a plan for all of this, even though I can't see or understand what that might be. For some reason, you put Rebecca on my mind and have tasked me with helping the girl. I don't know how this old woman can help, but I'm up for the job, whatever it might be. Please give me another chance with her. It wasn't her fault she destroyed what was left of those flowers. She didn't know any better, and I should have spoken up. What is it you want me to see? And whatever is bothering Eli this morning, can you help him find peace in his troubles? Amen

When she opened her eyes, Eli was standing near her chair.

"I didn't hear you come in."

He stood staring out the window next to her chair.

Mary moved the bible to the stand, pulled up her lap blanket over her knees with her good hand, and asked, "Is something bothering you?"

"Samuel stopped by to see me yesterday morning."

"That's nice, dear. How's Emma doing?"

"Fine, I guess. He stopped to make a confession of sorts."

"A confession, that's an odd basis for a visit."

Eli sat in the rocker next to her, rested his elbows on his knees, and clasped his hands together.

"What is it, Eli?"

"I'm not really sure what to make of it, but it has to do with Rebecca. It seems she hasn't always been honest with me, and I'm not sure what I want to do about it."

"Does this have anything to do with why she stopped coming around?"

"*Jah*. And it's been so long that I'm not too sure I even want to figure it all out."

Mary waited and watched her grandson's face. Whatever Samuel had shared weighed heavy on his mind.

Eli sighed. "I don't know what to do."

Mary put a trembling hand on his arm. "Often, the best thing you can do is nothing."

"Nothing? But shouldn't I let her know what I know?"

Mary squeezed his forearm. "Would it change things now?"

"At one point, it might have. But no, not now when too much time has passed."

"Then perhaps the best thing to do is nothing."

"*Mommi*, I'm angry she lied to me."

"And she's the one who had to live with that lie all these years. I guarantee she harbors more grief from the lie than you do just finding out about it. Secrets tend to eat away at a person until they become more miserable until the pain of hiding the truth becomes worse than the pain of revealing them."

"So, I do nothing?"

"*Jah*, nothing."

"But you don't even know what she did."

"And I don't care to know. The good Lord put that girl back in our lives for a reason. How about we stop trying to figure out why and let God work His plan like He sees fit."

"I suppose you're right."

"This time, I think I might be. Let's just pray she shows back up tomorrow."

Eli stood and picked up his grandmother's empty cup. "I'm sure Jacob won't give her any other option but to do so."

***

Anna flipped the blue shawl around her shoulders and asked again. "You sure you don't want to walk over to Emma's with me?"

Rebecca took a sip of tea. "I'm not in any mood to watch her and Samuel swoon over each other."

"Oh, Rebecca, you're exaggerating. They do no such thing."

"What do you call it then?"

Anna moved to the edge of the step. "Two people in love."

Rebecca pushed the rocker into motion with her foot. "It's sickening in my books."

"Come on, Rebecca. It would do you some good to stop in for a visit. What else are you going to do today? *Datt* and Wilma went to visit her family in Willow Brook, so you'll be here all alone."

"Suits me just fine. Maybe I'll take a walk or something. But the thought of spending the afternoon with Emma doesn't sound fun at all."

Rebecca noticed the eagerness in her *schwester's* eyes pleading with her to change her mind. For a moment, she felt she might weaken, but Anna bounced down the step and waved her off before she had a chance.

The early April morning gave way to pleasant temperatures. Rebecca placed her cup on the railing and followed Anna down the driveway. Anna didn't notice she was following her, even after turning into Samuel and Emma's.

Rebecca stopped at the Yoder Strawberry Acres sign. She paused only for a moment before she continued down Mystic Mill Road. She wasn't sure where she was going, but a long walk was just what she needed on such a lovely spring morning.

Thick green moss covered the north side of the trees, and the lush fields gave way to cows and sheep alike enjoying the sweet, abundant pastures of clover. The back roads of Lawrence County were quiet, and she could lose herself in her own thoughts.

Ever since Eli dropped her off the night before, her mind was fixated on his odd behavior. Between his lightning speed and the look on Mary's face after she had pulled out the row of flowers, there was an uncomfortable nagging in the pit of her stomach. Why she should care what either one of them thought was beyond her.

One step fell into another, and before she realized it, she had stopped at the white picket fence that separated Eli's sheep pasture from the barn. The barn's double doors were swung open, and she could hear the rustling of sheep and Eli's calming voice inside.

Seconds turned into minutes, and Rebecca found herself following Eli's voice in the barn. She stopped short of the gated padlock and watched as Eli had his hand inside a lambing ewe trying to turn the half-born lamb. Rebecca stepped on a paper feed sack, and the rustle alerted Eli to her presence.

He snapped his head in her direction. "I could use a hand."

Rebecca moved swiftly in his direction and dropped to her knees at the ewe's head. "Keep her calm while I try to push this lamb back inside. Its legs are in the wrong direction."

Rebecca spoke calming words in the sheep's ear and pushed its head in her lap. The ewes stomach contracted with a new wave of labor, and Eli worked to free the lamb. With a flick of his wrist, he pushed the lamb back into the birth canal and released its twisted legs. It took a few seconds for the lamb to wiggle free and fall to the floor.

Eli squeezed the lamb's nose and swung it around for the mother to lick it clean. Rebecca moved from the sheep's head and started to stand.

"Not so fast." Eli spat out. "She's not done yet."

Rebecca let the ewe tend to her lamb but stayed right by her side. With another wave, Eli checked the position of the next lamb. "Looks like this momma is having twins."

When Rebecca got too close to the new lamb, the ewe swung her head and knocked Rebecca to the floor. Eli rubbed the ewe's stomach and waited until she pushed the next lamb out on her own. "Looks like she didn't need my help this time."

Eli squeezed the new lamb's nose to open its airway, positioned the lamb next to its twin, and moved aside.

Eli stood and reached out a hand to help Rebecca to her feet. When the slime on his hand gave way, she fell back to the floor again. This time she rolled over and helped herself up.

They both moved from the stall and stood watching the ewe clean both identical white lambs. Rays of the morning sun were bouncing light off the pair, and the serenity of the scene left them speechless.

Eli moved to a bucket at the side of the stall and washed his hands. "One down, ten more to go."

"You have ten ready to lamb?"

Eli walked back to the gate and rested his foot on the bottom rung. "As far as I can tell."

"I'm glad I came along when I did. How do you do that all by yourself each time?"

"Most times, they don't need my help. They're self-sufficient. But that's a new momma, and she had me worried."

"What would have happened if you weren't there to help her out?"

"We might have lost the lambs or the ewe and the lambs. The next couple of weeks will be busy around here with lambing season. I'll be staying pretty close to the barn as much as I can."

"Well, I guess it's good I'm here to help you with Mary then, isn't it?"

Eli nodded his head once and moved to the next stall to check on another ewe. Without looking her way, Eli asked, "Did you need something?"

Rebecca brushed the straw off her blue dress and replied, "No, I was out for a walk and heard you in here. It was more me being nosy than anything else."

"Rebecca Byler, nosy? I would have never guessed."

"Is that a hint of sarcasm I detect?"

"Call it what you may, but if I know one thing about you, it's that you like to be in everyone else's business. But you don't like anyone else in yours. Isn't that right, Becca?"

Heat rose from her shoulders to the top of her head. Not because he called her on the table about her nosiness, but because he called her Becca again.

She hadn't moved from her stance at the gate when he moved back past her. When he stopped at her shoulder, he whispered in her ear. "I'm bound and determined to figure you out. I won't be lied to so easily this time."

The rueful look on Eli's face was warning enough. What happened next left her gasping for breath. He reached up and pulled a loose hair that had escaped her *kapp* and in a raspy voice, said, "Fool me once, shame on you, fool me twice, shame on me."

He moved from her side and walked to the house. After he was far enough away, she exhaled as she watched him move across the yard. Her heart pounded, and she couldn't fathom what he was referring to. She had told herself and him so many lies over the years that she couldn't be sure which one he might be referring to. But it really didn't matter because every one of them was to protect him. One secret led to another, which led to a lie. The vicious cycle continued for years until he finally gave up on her and any hope they had for a future. After a few minutes, Rebecca left the barn and headed toward home.

Everything felt like it was spinning out of control. For years, she'd been able to keep everyone at arm's length for fear her true shame would be revealed. But the run-in she just had with Eli left her shaken. Why suddenly, and what did Eli know?

The warm sun on Rebecca's shoulders did little to calm her nerves. When she made it to Emma and Samuel's driveway, she stood at the end and tried to figure out how to speak to Samuel alone. He was the only other person in Willow Springs that had any idea what tormented her. But speaking to him alone without Emma present would be highly unlikely.

When Anna and Emma saw her standing near the mailbox, they hollered in unison. "Rebecca, come join us."

It was too late to go unseen, so she followed their voices to Emma's front porch. Anna was the first to notice her shaken state. "Are you okay? You look like you have the weight of the world on your shoulders."

Rebecca looked over her shoulder toward the barn. "Is Samuel around?"

Emma pointed across the road to her *bruder,* Daniel's. "Why would you need to speak to Samuel?"

Rebecca shuddered. "I … I have a question about … well, never mind, it can wait for another day."

Emma furrowed her eyebrows together. "I'm sure he won't mind you stopping over at Daniel's if it's something important."

"Perhaps I'll do that. Thank you."

Anna stood and moved an empty chair closer to hers. "Are you in a hurry? Would you like to have a glass of Meadow Tea with us? Mint in the garden is coming in fast and Emma made a fresh batch yesterday. It's about as good as *Mamm's* was."

"No, I don't think so. I best go ask Samuel my question and get home. I feel a headache coming on, and I'd like to take a nap."

Rebecca prayed all the way to Daniel's that she would be able to catch Samuel alone long enough to ask him about Eli.

***

Daniel pulled a stool up to the workbench and took his English Bible from its hiding spot behind his toolbox. "So, how did it go with Eli yesterday?"

Samuel took his Sunday wool hat off and brushed his bangs off his forehead. "About as well as I expected. He was shocked that I played along with her for as long as I did. I wished I could tell him the whole story, but I have to trust Rebecca will come to her senses one of these days and go to the Lord with her confession."

Looking down at the bible, Daniel turned to the place they had left off the week before and waited until Samuel finished. "I'm almost sure Eli will be joining us soon for our study. Just as I suspected, his liberal upbringing in Lancaster allowed a more in-depth study of God's word. I think he will be a great addition to our time together."

Daniel shifted on the stool. "I suspected he had a better understanding of scripture than he let on."

"*Jah*, I didn't ask too many questions. He was more concerned with understanding why Rebecca was so set on making him believe we were courting than anything else."

Daniel rubbed the short beard on his chin with one hand. "That makes two of us, I guess. I don't understand it myself."

"It's a long story and one only Rebecca can tell. But I took care of my part in it, and now we have to wait and see how long Rebecca will carry the rest of the burden herself."

Samuel patted the open bible. "Before we get started, tell me how you made out with the Kauffman boys."

Daniel propped his elbow on the table and began. "Just as we suspected, they've been visiting the Mennonite Church in town on our visiting Sunday. Word is spreading through the younger members of the district, just like we prayed."

Samuel looked toward the door when he thought he heard a sound. When nothing else alerted his attention, he continued, "I spoke to Emma last week about what this might mean for us. If the bishop and the ministers, especially her father, get word of us studying the English Bible, we'll all be shunned."

Daniel tilted his ear toward the door and put his finger to his lip to quiet Samuel. He walked to the entrance of the tack shop and opened the door. "Must be one of the barn cats making a ruckus."

Once Daniel retook his seat, Samuel added, "Eli is a crucial player. He's been reading God's word a lot longer than I have, and he will be a good influence on some of the younger men in the community."

"I'd like to say I had an influence, but with being raised English, I think you or Eli have a better chance in convincing the men to be open to what we want to teach them."

"*Jah*, I think you're right. More and more of the younger people want to know more beyond the three-hour service on Sunday morning. They are thirsty for Jesus, and I want to show them that being a

Christian means more than following a set of rules handed down from generation to generation. God wants so much more from us."

Daniel stood and walked to the door again when a noise drew his attention back to the central part of the shop. "So, how is Emma making out with reaching out to some of the younger women?"

"The bakery is the perfect cover. She is cautious with whom she speaks and keeps things to a particular age group. The bishop doesn't realize it, but hopefully, by the time they find out what we're up to, we will have enough families ready to break off from our Old Order and start a New Order."

Daniel pulled the door closed. "You do realize that the bishop is going to blame this all on the English kid turned Amish."

Samuel slapped Daniel on the shoulder. "I'm sure of it. But don't worry, we're in this together. If one falls, we all fall. But in my books, if we are falling in the name of Jesus, we are doing precisely what God instructs us to do."

***

Rebecca held her hand over her mouth as she crouched down behind a stack of strawberry baskets, listening to their conversation. What on earth were they up to, and what were they doing talking to people about Jesus? Didn't they know they'd be put in the *bann* if the bishop ever found out?

She knew her *schwester* and Samuel were up to something, but she never dreamed it would involve going against their ways this far. Forget talking to Samuel about Eli. As much as she could tell, Eli had a stake in the matter as well.

How dare Eli talk to her about secrets. By the sounds of it, he had a few hidden away as well.

CHAPTER 8

Rebecca tossed and turned all night with the thought of facing Eli. Would he press her more, and would she be able to hold her tongue on what she overheard in the barn? Before taking off to Mary's, she stopped into *Stitch 'n Time* to check on Anna.

Anna was out the door and in the shop long before Rebecca had come downstairs. Wilma and their father had left early for town, so she grabbed a biscuit and headed to find her *schwester.*

The shop door was propped open, and the tangy smell of vinegar and cooked spinach filled the air. A propane burner on the porch had a big pot of freshly chopped spinach simmering. A tub near the steps held a vat of fiber soaking in a vinegar and water solution. Rebecca popped a bit of biscuit in her mouth and pushed the fiber underneath the water.

"How long has this been soaking?"

Anna waved her away. "I've got it under control. I know how long it takes."

Rebecca nodded her head in the direction of the simmering pot of fresh greens. "You'll want to make sure you keep the time on both the dye and vinegar solution. If you make a few batches, you want to ensure the color lot stays the same. Measure things precisely, so you get the same dye lot for each batch."

Anna pushed her away from the pan. "Aren't you going to be late?"

"A few minutes here or there isn't going to make a bit of difference."

Rebecca stepped in the shop and pulled the ledger book out from under the counter. "Are you keeping good records?"

"For heaven's sake, Rebecca, you've only been gone a couple of days. I believe I'm more than capable of taking care of the shop in your absence. I've recorded everything down to the last penny." Anna pulled the black leather book from Rebecca's hand and put it back under the counter. "Now get out of here. You're in my way."

Rebecca moved about the storeroom and pointed to an almost empty hook. "You'll need to pick up some purple cabbage and work on dyeing more of this color. You know how the *Englishers* love pink."

Anna moved toward her *schwester,* took her by the arm, and directed her to the door. "I don't need you second-guessing my ability; now go. *Datt* put me in charge of the shop, and I'll run things as I see fit."

Rebecca grabbed the door frame. "But let me help you strain that pot of spinach, then I'll be on my way."

"*Nee*, I've got it. What you can do …is talk to Eli about buying more raw wool. I bet he'll start shearing soon and we'll need to get our order in. We certainly aren't going to have enough with our four alpacas." She pointed to a basket near the wall. "That's the last vat of fiber we have from last year's shearing."

Both women walked to the porch, and Anna lifted the lid from the simmering pot and used the wooden spoon to check the depth of color. "This should make a nice spring color to add to our line."

Rebecca peered in the pot. "I think you need to boil it down some more. And don't forget to record the time. Boil all batches the exact amount of time."

"Would you please just go and quit telling what I already know."

"All right already. I'm going."

Rebecca skipped down the steps and hollered over her shoulder. "Don't forget to order a crate of red cabbage from The Mercantile."

Anna raised her hand and waved her off before getting back to work dyeing the last of the white alpaca fiber. It was easy to convince Rebecca she was doing fine, especially with no customers in the shop. But her hands were sweating. Let alone the uneasiness creeping up her chest. The mere thought of turning the open sign around left her gasping for air.

***

Eli sat at the kitchen table, enjoying the last few sips of coffee when Rebecca tapped on the side door and let herself in. He couldn't keep his annoyance from his tone when she showed up over an hour late. He had work to do and tending to his grandmother's personal needs kept him from checking on a few missing sheep.

"Good morning." His disgruntled response didn't faze her. Moving to the stove, she poured herself a cup of coffee before leaning back on the counter and bringing the steaming mug to her mouth.

"Take a seat, Becca."

Something about the way he said Becca made her cringe. But she took a seat and waited for him to gather his thoughts.

He cleared his throat and set his coffee cup aside. "I do believe when I hired you, we agreed you would get here in plenty of time to get Mary up and ready for the day. I have a herd of missing sheep, and your tardiness kept me from my work."

"It's just an hour! Don't you think you're being a bit dramatic?"

Eli sucked in a breath through his nose, and his chest puffed up like a strutting rooster. "The point is, I expect you to be here when you say you will. No, ifs, ands, or buts about it."

Rebecca picked up his cup and carried it to the sink. "Okay, okay, I get it. It won't happen again."

Eli stood and pushed his chair in harder than necessary. "*Mommi* Mary wants you to wake her at precisely nine o'clock. You are to bring that notebook and pencil to her room and be ready to take notes."

She sipped her coffee and raised her eyebrows at his strange request. "Take notes for what?"

"I'm not sure, but she has something she wants to get down on paper, and you're going to help her do it."

Rebecca stayed quiet for a long moment as he watched her wheels turn. No doubt she was trying to find an excuse, any excuse to deny his request. She was treading on thin ice, and he hoped she wouldn't test him more.

He steadied his eyes on her for a few moments longer than usual. She had disappointed him in so many ways. Still, a twinge of longing edged in between the layers of past mistakes. Why did her eyes have to awaken something he thought he'd gotten over?

Seeing her mouth tighten, he added, "I may need your help this afternoon."

She rinsed her cup and set it upside down on the drainboard. "Is that in my job duties?"

He had the feeling that she was baiting him into another battle of wills, but instead of responding, he opened the door and headed to the barn.

***

At nine o'clock, Rebecca carried a tray of tea to Mary's room and lightly knocked on the door before opening it.

With the notebook tucked under her arm, she set the tray down on the dresser before going to Mary's bedside.

Rebecca laid her hand on Mary's shoulder and gently shook her. "Eli said you wanted me to wake you at nine."

Mary opened her eyes but didn't move. "I was having the sweetest dream."

"Do you want me to come back later?"

"*Nee*, I want you to help me sit up."

Rebecca helped her to a sitting position and reached for the brush. She pulled it through Mary's thin, waist-length gray hair. After brushing the knots out, she parted it down the middle and coiled it up tight to the back of her head, covering it with a *kapp*.

"Would you like to get out of your nightdress?"

A frown flickered across her face. "I suppose not. That would require too much energy, and I best keep all my strength for what I have planned for us today."

"Eli told me you have some things you want to get down on paper. I brought in the notebook and pen like you asked."

"Good. We will get started in a few minutes. How about you pour us a cup of tea first."

"I brewed a pot of Earl Grey. Will that do?"

"It will."

Rebecca watched the old woman out of the corner of her eye and half suspected she was trying to work up to something.

Mary blew over the rim of her cup. "Tell me what happened between you and Eli."

Rebecca stiffened her shoulders. "I do believe that's between Eli and me."

Mary raised her eyebrows. "Well, let's get something straight, starting right here and now. The good Lord laid you on my heart, and we are to share this season together for some reason. Starting right here, right now."

Rebecca's heart drummed in her ears, and she sat still for a few seconds. Why on earth was Mary suddenly interested? "I'm not sure what you are referring to, but I still don't see any reason to bring up the past."

Why should she feel guilty of something that happened so long ago? But the way Mary asked her to explain left her scrambling for a logical answer. *So what if she pushed Eli away with a lie. What did it matter now?*

Mary handed Rebecca her cup and pointed to the notebook laying on the bed. Rebecca tried to change the subject. "So, what is it you want me to write down for you?"

Mary's eyes narrowed slightly, but she said nothing.

"Eli said you wanted me to record something for you?"

Mary sighed softly, looking weary. "I want to tell someone my story before it's lost. Forever buried in my grave so deep my son Andy will never know the truth."

Mary's eyes took on a look of regret. One moment she was bold and direct about demanding Rebecca tell her about Eli, and the next, her face took on a deep pain, just dying to be released. Rebecca was confused at the array of emotions the old woman displayed.

Rebecca picked up the notebook. "I will do my best."

Mary stiffened at Rebecca's statement. "I'm sure you will. But this will be a journey for both of us. What you will soon learn will be hard for you to comprehend, but I am trusting you to write my words in such a way that there will be no doubt Andy will understand the magnitude of his past."

Rebecca tilted her head in Mary's direction, almost unsure she wanted to walk through this journey with her. While she was intrigued by the secret Mary alluded to, she could feel herself being drawn into revealing more of herself than she was comfortable doing.

Rebecca crossed her legs and balanced the notebook on her knee. "Where would you like to start?"

"With you answering my first question. What happened between you and Eli?"

"Mary, again, I don't think that is any of your concern."

Mary tilted her head and whispered, "But you see, my dear, it has everything to do with where we need to start."

Heat surged into Rebecca's cheeks. "I'm not going there. And besides, it's your story you want to tell, not mine."

In a more serious tone than Rebecca had ever heard come out of Mary's mouth, she said, "Confession is risky. I'm not blinded by the mask you've been wearing around Eli for years."

Mary rubbed her useless hand and took in a calming breath. "The only way to completely and utterly trust another person is to share some of your darkest moments. I'm about to share things with you that I've only told one other person, and I have to know that you can be trusted."

"Trusted with what?" Rebecca asked.

"With a series of events that will change my son's life forever. It's the one thing I can leave him; an explanation."

"How is me telling you what happened with Eli going to change a thing?"

"Because I'm here to show you that even the darkest secrets can turn bright. That some people's worst mistakes can turn into a beacon of hope for others."

Rebecca rubbed her temple and shook her head. "Mary, you're talking in circles. I have no idea what you're trying to tell me."

Mary sat taller. "Think about this. When you're trapped by secrecy, you don't want the advice of people who have never walked in your shoes. You want someone who has been where you've walked and made it back alive. That person is me. That's why I'm pushing you to confide in me. You need to know that I walked in the murky waters of denial and self-loathing, much like I've seen in you over the last few years."

Mary looked out the window and took a few minutes before continuing. "I wasted many years pushing my husband away, fearing he wouldn't understand the depth of my despair. He often said all it would take was time to heal all things. But when I was in the midst of it, I wouldn't allow myself to believe it."

Mary's expression grew serious. "Perhaps you can start recording my words later. I've become quite tired all of the sudden." She laid her head back on her pillow and closed her eyes.

Rebecca sat still for a few minutes, waiting to be dismissed, only to hear her labored breathing take on a soft snore.

She laid the notebook on the dresser, still void of any words, and retreated to the kitchen.

The clock on the living room wall chimed ten, and she sat at the table trying to make sense of the rambling words of the old woman. *What was all that about? Half of what she said seemed more like a riddle than anything that made a bit of sense.*

Everything was so confusing. Eli's mumbled warning about once a fool, to Samuel and Daniel's secret bible study, and now Mary's cryptic message left her senses on edge.

She picked up the basket of laundry she had gathered earlier and headed to the basement. Sorting the darks from the whites, Rebecca picked up one of Eli's Sunday white shirts and brought it to her nose. *What a strange thing to do*, she thought. His musky smell tickled her nose, and she quickly dropped it back in the basket.

"Becca, are you down there?"

"*Jah*, what is it?"

"I could really use a hand in the barn."

Before she had a chance to answer, the screen door slammed. She turned off the washing machine, ran up the steps, and rushed to follow Eli across the yard and into one of the gated pens.

"I'm afraid we are going to lose this young ewe. My hand is way too big to turn this lamb. I'm going to need you to reach inside and do it.

"Me? You want me to turn the lamb?"

"*Jah*, we don't have much time. Your hand is much smaller than mine. I will keep her calm, and I'll walk you through it."

Eli quickly tied an apron around Rebecca's blue dress and pointed to the floor. "You'll need to get your footing in case she kicks. Steady yourself on one knee and lean into her belly."

"I don't know if I can do this; what if I hurt her?"

"It's either we turn the lamb and help her deliver it, or we lose both the ewe and the lamb."

Rebecca took each one of Eli's instructions and performed it with care. The young ewe was clearly tired and gave Rebecca little resistance. When Eli told Rebecca to wait until a natural contraction began again, she took in a deep breath. She exhaled loudly like she was in labor herself. Rebecca pulled the lamb from the mother's womb with one swift push and squeezed its nose to remove the mucus, just like she had seen Eli do the other day. She moved the lamb to its mother's nose and moved away so the ewe could lick it clean.

Rebecca fell back on her heels. "Oh, my goodness. That was intense."

Eli stood and reached his hand out to help Rebecca stand. "It typically is. This is the first year I've had to help many young ewes deliver. Normally, I'm a pesky standby to nature's natural rhythm."

"Why are so many having issues?"

"Mere numbers, I'm sure. I've grown the herd this year, so it's just the fact that there are more lambing."

They backed out of the pen and leaned on the gate, watching the mother take to her baby. "How many more will lamb?"

"It's hard to tell. But at least a dozen or so. Hopefully, by May, we should see the pastures filled with lambs, and I can start shearing in June and July."

"Speaking of shearing, have you given any more thought to Anna and I buying raw fiber from you? I know you've contracted with a fiber wholesaler for the bulk of it. Still, we would really like to promote our yarn being supplied locally."

"It depends."

Rebecca looked his way and asked, "Depends on what?"

"How much help I can get with shearing."

"You want me to help?"

"I suppose if you want the best of the lot, you best be right in the midst of it."

"I don't know the first thing about shearing sheep."

"Who shears your alpacas?"

"We've always hired someone to come do it for us."

"Well then, I guess you have a choice to make. You can continue to hire someone to shear your alpacas and buy your raw fiber from a sheep farmer you don't know. Or you can learn how to shear them yourself. I'd say you'd want to cut the middle-man out of the picture as best as you can."

His expression altered. "So, what do you think? Are you up to learning how to be a sheep farmer?"

Rebecca tilted her head in his direction and added, "So let me get this straight. You want me to care for your grandmother, cook your meals, wash your clothes, and now you want me to add sheep shearing to my list of duties. Oh, and let me add being your grandmother's memoir writer to the list."

He looked at her again and shook his head. "If that's not enough, I can hand you off some of my chores as well."

"I think I have plenty if you don't mind. This certainly isn't what I signed up for." She made a loud TSK sound, sighed, and left him standing in the barn.

CHAPTER 9

Rebecca carried the clothes basket to the side yard and watched Eli out of the corner of her eye while she hung rows of blue and black. He had rolled up his shirt sleeves and fixed the fence close to the road. The post driver he was using to hammer in a new fence post bounced off the metal, making a series of precisely timed clangs ring through the air. The sight left her having a hard time turning her face from the scene.

Walking around the side of the house, she stepped over a cluster of tulips before heading inside. The warm sunshine was drying out the soggy ground, and she couldn't help but try to envision what Mary's gardens once looked like.

Something was changing with her, but she couldn't quite put her finger on it. In the four days she had spent at Eli and Mary's, she found herself caring more about Mary than herself. On the other hand, Eli still drove her crazy, but there was a softness she felt anytime he came to mind.

What was it she was feeling? A calmness, a belonging, a hope for the future? Could she really think time could heal all things like Mary said?

Pushing the screen door open, she stepped inside the kitchen to find Mary sitting at the table.

"You should have waited for me to help you."

"I might not get around as well as I used to, but so far, I can still find my way to the table, even if it does take me twice as long."

"Still, you should have waited until I came back inside."

"No sense in worrying about it now. I'm here, and I can stay right in this seat until after dinner. I'd like to get some writing done if you have time later."

"Rebecca, sometimes I wonder…"

"What's that?"

"If maybe we could bring my garden back."

"I don't know the first thing about gardening." Rebecca lifted her hands in the air. "Hence pulling out all your flowers last week."

Rebecca let out a raspy chuckle. "Emma got all the green thumbs in the family."

Mary snorted. "Perhaps we could at least clean up the porch and wash the windows."

Groaning inwardly, Rebecca asked, "What do you want me to do first? Fix dinner, clean the porch, or help you get your thoughts on paper?"

"I suppose we have been asking you to do a good bit around here. It's just that this old house has needed a young woman's touch for a good long time."

Rebecca mumbled under her breath, "Lucky me."

"What was that dear?"

"Nothing."

Rebecca moved to the stove, pulled the casserole out of the oven, and placed it in the center of the table. It was a good thing *Mamm* taught her to cook; she could at least keep them fed if she couldn't bring Mary's gardens back to life.

She moved to the back porch and rang the dinner bell. Eli was nowhere in sight, but she was confident the sound would lure him to the house.

Within minutes, he was at the sink telling his grandmother about the three new lambs and what a great help Rebecca had been.

Rebecca stifled her irritation. She shook her head and thought. *What's the matter with me? He was trying to give me a compliment, and all I could think about was the list of chores he kept giving me.*

Dinner was all but a blur to Rebecca as she tried to stop the conversation in her head. Eli and Mary were in their own little world, trying to pull her in every chance they got. It was like a raging war taking place inside with nowhere to retreat but further inside herself.

She didn't understand how Eli could act like he didn't mind her around when she had done nothing but discourage him in the five years she'd known him. And then Mary, how could she still be smiling after a stroke took every ounce of dignity the woman had left? For goodness' sake, the poor woman couldn't even go to the bathroom herself. Something was different between the two of them, but what was it? Maybe she could figure it out once she started writing Mary's story. Perhaps then she could figure out what made the two of them tick.

Eli leaned back in his chair and patted his stomach. "Thanks for the meal, but I best get back to work."

Mary lifted her limp arm on the table and rubbed her gnarled fingertips with her good hand. "Rebecca's going to clean the porch and wash the front windows this afternoon."

Eli grabbed his straw hat off the peg by the back door. "*Jah*, I'd been meaning to do that. But there's never been enough time in the day for such things." The screen door bounced behind him.

Rebecca didn't respond to his comment and gathered the plates and silverware from the table and carried them to the sink. "Do you want me to help you to the living room while I clean up the kitchen?"

"No, I think I'd like to sit right here until you're finished."

"Suit yourself."

Rebecca made a mental note of everything she needed to get done before heading home. Thank goodness Wilma took care of running the Byler house now, or she'd have a full day's work to do once she returned home. She ran her hands under the warm water and thought. *I guess Datt marrying her didn't turn out so bad after all. Oh, my gosh! There I go again. Where are these thoughts coming from?*

Rebecca pulled a bucket from beneath the sink and two rags to tackle the front window and rocking chairs on the porch. A layer of winter grime covered the white rockers, and a film covered the front windowpanes.

Mary settled herself comfortably in the chair near the window. "Thank you. Now I'll be able to make sure you get all the streaks."

"You're welcome," she said through gritted teeth and went to work sweeping dead leaves off the covered porch. The half-smile on Mary's face warmed her heart as she tackled cleaning the windows. After getting most of the dirt cleaned from the two identical rockers, Rebecca returned inside. "Would you like to sit outside for a spell?"

Mary's lopsided smile said all she needed to hear, and she helped the woman move outside. "Bring me the notebook, would you?"

Rebecca tucked a lap blanket around Mary's knees and returned after the pen and paper.

After she settled in the chair beside her, she asked, "So, what is it you want me to take notes on?"

Mary stared off in the distance and then pointed to the maple tree at the edge of the property. "See that tree over there? My husband planted it the week we arrived in Willow Springs. That was sixty-five years ago."

Rebecca looked at the tree and gave a curious nod. "Do you want me to write that down?"

"*Nee*, I'm just remembering that's all."

Rebecca tapped the pen on the notebook. "I'm not trying to be difficult, but I'm not sure what you want from me."

"Patience, child. Give this old woman a chance to gather her thoughts. The story I need you to record spans back some sixty-plus years, and it will take me a little bit to get my facts straight. I mustn't leave anything out."

Rebecca let the seconds turn into minutes as she waited for Mary to begin. Inpatient as she was, she couldn't wait a minute longer before she asked, "What was your husband like?"

"Noah was a good man," Mary said firmly. He had a big heart and cared about many things. He was just . . .quiet."

Rebecca wrote down Mary's exact words. "Did you court long before you married?"

Mary took in a long breath and closed her eyes as if a painful memory surfaced too close for comfort. "*Nee*."

"So, was it love, at first sight?"

Again, Mary sighed. "Perhaps it was for him and his first love. But not for me."

Rebecca clicked the pen. "I'm confused. Did Noah love another before you?"

"Not before me, but despite me."

"If he didn't love you, why did he ask you to marry him?"

"All in good time. I need to start from the beginning not in the middle for it to make sense."

Rebecca made a small note on the side of the paper to go back and ask Mary the question again when she felt it might fit into her story. "Where do you want to start?"

Mary opened her eyes and boldly replied, "1944"

"What happened in 1944?"

"My father went to France to serve in a hospital during World War II."

Rebecca let out a small gasp. "Your father served in the military? How is that so?"

"He felt the Lord was leading him to serve our troops in France right after D-day. My father had a servant's heart, and he knew he couldn't fight in the war, so he volunteered to work in the field hospital."

"But where did that leave you? You couldn't have been more than thirteen or fourteen in 1944."

"I was thirteen to be exact, and he left me with his best friend and neighbor, Amos Bricker. Eli's Great-Grandfather."

"What happened then?"

Mary pulled the quilt tight on her lap. "The Japanese bombed Pearl Harbor, and my father was gone for over a year."

Rebecca wrote down Mary's response and leaned in closer. "Were you scared for him?"

"I loved my *datt*. It was just him and me for so long I was beside myself with worry. I wasn't sure if I'd ever see him again. My mother died having me, so my father was all the family I ever had."

"I don't understand why you want to write this all down. Doesn't Eli and his family already know all of this?"

"They only know bits and pieces, and I need to set things straight."

"Were you mad your father left you behind to go support the troops? How did that go over with your district in Lancaster? Wasn't serving in the military frowned upon, much like it is here?"

"At the time, I understood he felt God calling him to help, and I loved him for his dedication. After almost eight months of worrying that he wouldn't return, I realized there were things much worse than my father not coming home from war."

"But he did come home, right?"

"He did, but life was never the same once he returned."

Rebecca scurried to catch up with Mary's words while the old woman wiped the moisture from her eyes.

Rebecca positioned her pen and asked, "Why were things not the same? Did he get hurt?"

"Physically hurt? No. Emotionally devastated? Yes."

"How so?"

Mary rubbed her limp arm. "I think I've had enough for one day. Perhaps I should go lie down for a spell."

Rebecca was disappointed by Mary's lack of energy to continue with the story. It was just starting to get good, and she was dying to see what was so emotionally devastating for Mary's father.

Rebecca laid the notebook and pen aside and helped Mary stand to move inside.

***

After setting a pot of vegetable beef soup on the stove's warming burner, she proceeded outside to tell Eli she was leaving.

The afternoon sun had already receded behind the barn, and the cool spring breeze whipped around the open door and under her skirt. She pushed the hem of her blue dress back down and stepped in out of the wind.

"Eli?"

"Back here." She followed his voice to the back of the barn and into the tack shop. He stood at his workbench, sharpening a pair of shearers.

He tipped his head in her direction. "Done for the day?"

"*Jah*, I left a pot of soup on the stove for you both."

"*Denki*."

Rebecca leaned up against the door frame and asked, "Have you ever talked to your grandmother about her father?"

"Not too much. She keeps a lot of her past under lock and key. Why do you ask?"

"I think something traumatic happened to her when she was younger. She started to tell me about your grandfather going to France to help in World War II, but she got tired, and we quit for the day."

Eli sat down on a stool and ran the blade over a sharpening stone he moved with a pedal on the floor. "I've asked my mother if she knew anything, but what she does know, she wasn't too keen on sharing with me."

"What do you know about your grandfather Noah?"

"I only met him once."

Rebecca pulled her chin to her chest. "You only met your grandfather once?"

"We didn't visit much. When he was fifteen, my father left Willow Springs to work on my Great-Grandfather Bricker's dairy farm. By the time I came along, he had already taken over the daily operation, and it left us little time to visit."

"Didn't your grandmother ever go back to Lancaster?"

"Nope, not that I knew of. For that matter, I don't think they were ever invited to come visit us."

"That's a shame."

"It's just how it was, I guess."

Rebecca studied him from her spot near the door. When Eli stopped to test the blade's sharpness, he looked her way. Rebecca saw something in his expression that made her want to stay. Perhaps her probing questions gave him reason to share what he knew with someone who might be interested in what he had to say.

Rebecca's mouth tightened. "Why do you think your father wouldn't want his parents to visit? You would think they would like their sons to know their grandparents."

Eli blew sharpening dust off the blade and said, "My *datt* was more concerned with getting the best milk price than making sure his *kinner* knew anything about their family heritage."

She crossed her arms over her chest, pondering his reply.

Eli laid the knife on the bench. "I suppose he did the best he could, considering the circumstances."

"What circumstances?"

"My *datt's* uncles were furious that my great-grandfather would leave the farm to his grandson and not them. It always put a real wedge between any family dynamics the Bricker family had."

"TSK. TSK."

Eli glared in her direction after her judgmental response.

"I'm sorry. I didn't mean any slight against your father. I guess I just don't understand, I might not always agree with my own father, but he made sure we knew our extended family as best as we could."

"No offense taken. The way I see it, maybe you'll discover the big secret that has plagued this family for years. I'm too close to the situation, and I only get frustrated by the lame excuses I'm thrown. Besides, my *datt* and I aren't on the best of terms. He was furious when I moved to Willow Springs to take care of *Mommi* Mary. He felt I had a responsibility to him and the legacy of Bricker Farms."

"And you didn't?"

"You know how it works. The farm goes to the youngest son. I was the oldest, and my hopes of a future in the Bricker Dairy Farm fell way down the line for me."

"Then why did he get so upset when you moved to Willow Springs?"

Eli picked up his straw hat and brushed it across his thigh before putting it back on his head. "Perhaps you'll help me figure that all out by recording whatever *Mommi* has on her mind."

Rebecca let him pass her in the door frame and followed him through the barn, stopping at the pen where the young ewe was nursing her lamb. "Looks like she took to her baby fine." Eli rested his elbows on the gate. "I'd say it was a good day all around."

"I better be heading home."

Eli followed her outside. "Do you want a ride?"

She waved over her shoulder and headed to the road. "*Nee*, I can make it home before it gets dark."

***

The mystery Mary started to unravel was playing havoc in Rebecca's head. What on earth would force Eli's grandfather to marry his grandmother unless he was in love with her? She'd heard of arranged marriages before. Could that be what happened? Did her father already arrange for her to marry Noah long before he left for the war? Or was it something else? She could hardly wait to return to Mary's story the next day.

Picking up the pace of her twenty-minute walk, she played every scenario over in her mind. What was so important that Mary needed to tell her story now? And why was Eli's father so upset that he chose to come to northwestern Pennsylvania when there was no hope for him to take over the farm. It only made sense that Eli came here to help Mary. She had no one else. Something just didn't add up, and her inquisitive mind was working overtime trying to make sense of it all.

Rebecca couldn't wait to get home and tell Anna all she'd learned that day. But even before she could figure out where to start, her conscience caught up to her, and she decided it wasn't her story to tell. Again, her day at Mary and Eli's was something she didn't want to share with anyone. It was like they were letting her into their world, and she liked being part of something outside of the Byler household for some unknown reason.

CHAPTER 10

It was all Rebecca could do to get out of the house and to Eli's on time the following day. She practically ran all the way to his farm and stepped into the kitchen, out of breath.

Eli glanced at the clock on the wall and covered his bible with a newspaper. "So, I see you do know how to tell time after all."

Rebecca removed the blue scarf from her head and hung it on the hook near the door. After rearranging her *kapp* and smoothing a wrinkle from her skirt, she moved to the stove.

Picking up a bowl of eggs, she cracked a few in another bowl and asked, "Is Mary awake?"

"She hasn't hollered for me yet. Perhaps she's waiting for you. She's getting pretty particular about hanging on until you're here to help."

"Let me go check on her real quick."

Eli waited until she had made her way into the other room before he moved the English bible to the top of the hutch at the side of the room. The last thing he needed was for Rebecca to catch him reading such a version. He needed to get to the bottom of many things with her but sharing his private bible studies wasn't high on his priority list quite yet.

Rebecca stopped at Mary's door and looked over her shoulder into the kitchen. She watched as Eli placed a book on the top of the cabinet. Curious, she thought. *Why would he hide his bible from her? Unless it had something to do with what she overheard Samuel and Daniel talking about. Just one more thing she needed to get to the bottom of.*

***

Mary sat on the edge of the bed, hair askew and feeling forlorn. A ray of sun shone in through her window, bouncing a rainbow of colors off a glass of water sitting on her nightstand. How many years had she sat on the edge of the same bed, looking forward to another day? Lately, each passing day seemed longer than the next, and she fought harder each day to keep a lighthearted outlook.

Without taking her eyes from the window, she mumbled, "What day is it?"

Rebecca moved to her side. "It's Tuesday, April twelfth." Letting out a small giggle, Rebecca added. "Do you have somewhere you need to be today?"

Mary didn't answer but thought. *How had old age caught up to me so quickly? Seems just like yesterday I had enough energy for ten women. Now I can't even go pee by myself.* She felt a wave of grumpiness overcome her but pushed it aside.

Giving up every ounce of her independence was heart-wrenching. Even after Noah died, she found peace and solitude by spending time with God in her garden. Now she couldn't even do that. She dropped her head and closed her eyes.

Rebecca stooped down to her level. "Are you feeling ill?"

Mary looked around the room as if she were looking for someone. "Noah, did he go to the barn already? I haven't made his breakfast yet."

Rebecca's blank stare, along with her voice taking on a high octave, alarmed Mary when she asked, "Noah?"

She looked up into the girl's green and brown flecked eyes. For a moment, she couldn't place her name. The rising sun added a halo around her head, and she had trouble remembering her name. Tears unexpectedly pooled on her bottom lashes.

"I'll be right back. Let me go get Eli."

As soon as Rebecca left the room, Mary wiped the moisture from her face, and things became clear.

Within a few minutes, Eli sat on the edge of her bed. "*Mommi*, are you feeling all right? Rebecca said you were asking about grandfather."

Mary patted Eli's arm. "Don't mind the ramblings of this old woman. I just got confused for a minute."

Eli looked over at Rebecca and shrugged his shoulders.

"Now go and get out of here. You have sheep to tend to, and Rebecca and I have things to do."

Eli walked out of the room and motioned for Rebecca to follow him. "What was that all about?"

Rebecca whispered, "I have no idea, but she clearly thought your grandfather was still living. And I swear she didn't know who I was for a minute."

"How about you get her ready for the day, and I'll go start breakfast."

Rebecca looked over her shoulder into Mary's room. "Let's not confuse her any more than we have to. If she sees you in the kitchen, she'll really be out of sorts. Go to the barn, and I'll ring the bell when I have breakfast on the table."

Rebecca didn't know what to think of Mary's odd behavior. But she went about taking care of her personal needs and sat her at the table right next to Eli's chair while she finished breakfast.

***

After breakfast, Rebecca brought out the notebook and sat down beside Mary. "Do you feel up to telling more of your story?"

Mary tipped her head and gave Rebecca a strange look. "It will take God to change your heart."

Confused at Mary's odd statement, she pointed to the notebook. "Do you want me to write that down?"

Mary continued without answering. "A heart change will mean a transformed life."

Rebecca picked up her pen and scrambled to write down Mary's comments.

Mary's bottom lip started to quiver. "My father was furious with me."

Rebecca crossed her legs and pulled the lined paper closer. "How so?"

"I embarrassed him."

"By doing what? Because you married Noah?"

"I was a little girl when he left for the war. I was a woman when he returned."

"But why would that embarrass him? Time doesn't standstill. It was bound to happen."

"But not the way he had envisioned it."

"I don't understand. I'm getting confused. If you want me to record things, I have to understand what it is you're trying to explain."

Rebecca flipped back through the notes she had taken the day before. "Let's start where we ended off yesterday. You had just told me that your father was emotionally hurt when he returned. How was that so?"

"I cried enough tears for a lifetime during that time. All I wanted to do was find a reason to laugh again. Noah saved me from my own fate."

"Did he save you from your father? And why was your *datt* so upset when he came home?"

Mary closed her eyes and rested her forehead on her hand. "I couldn't tell him the truth. It would kill him for sure. So, I kept my secret from everyone except Noah. He was my only chance for any hope."

"What kind of secret would be so bad that it would have killed your father? You're talking in bits and pieces and I'm having trouble putting it all together."

Mary's low voice was barely audible. "Secrets ruin a family."

Mary looked at Rebecca and asked, "Did you hear what I said?"

"*Jah*, you said secrets ruin a family."

Silence filled the air and Rebecca waited for her to respond.

Mary turned her attention to the window and thought. *Lord, is it your will I take this secret to my grave? Will it really do any good if Andy and Eli know the truth?* She watched as a pair of mourning doves landed underneath the bird feeder, and the words she was dying to hear landed on her ears. *I am the truth, and the truth will set you free. Tell her Mary ...tell Rebecca the truth, it will set her free.*

Mary cleared her throat. "The truth will set you free."

"Excuse me?"

Mary smiled as Rebecca repeated. "The truth will set *me* free. Don't you mean the truth will set *you* free? Should I write that down?"

Mary reached for her quad stick and pointed to the bathroom. Rebecca laid the pen aside and helped Mary to the small room off the kitchen.

Rebecca held her elbow and asked, "Did whatever secret you kept from your father ruin your family?"

With an edge to her voice, Mary replied, "You don't see my son caring for me, do you? What do you think?"

Rebecca didn't know how to respond but wanted to be sure she remembered Mary's exact words when they returned to the table.

Instead of returning to the kitchen, Mary made Rebecca take her to the living room. Their time in Mary's story ended for yet another day, leaving her to ponder why she was so intent on telling her that the truth would set her free. Did Mary know more about her past than she gave the old woman credit for? Or had Eli confided things in his grandmother that should have been kept private?

Mary's soft snores matched the clock's pendulum, and Rebecca left her to nap and went outside. Carrying a glass of iced tea to the front porch, she lost herself in things of the past.

Laying her head on the back of the chair, she transported herself to the Farmers Market five years earlier. It was the start of her demise, and her jaw tightened as she remembered that hot June day.

Samuel had just delivered a load of strawberries to her father's furniture booth at the market, and she got bossy with him in an unladylike manner. When Anna pointed out her behavior, she became angry and left the booth in a fit of rage. How dare Anna embarrass her in front of the customers and in front of Samuel as well?

As the sights and sounds of the busy vegetable market played in her head, she tried to remember what Anna said to make her so mad. She remembered pushing a young mother aside as she blasted through a group of people and didn't look back when she heard the young woman scream.

Eli's heavy boots alerted her, and she opened her eyes when she felt him nearby.

Eli leaned on the porch railing. "Any more strange episodes with *Mommi* this morning?"

Rebecca stopped rocking the chair with her foot and looked up and thought. *Should I tell him what she said about secrets ruining a family.*

"*Nee*, but she did start to tell me about a secret that she was sure would upset her father had he found out."

"What secret is that?"

"I don't know. She had to pee, and then I lost her to a nap. She keeps saying bits and pieces but nothing that makes much sense."

Eli sighed. "May I make a suggestion?"

"Sure."

"Stop trying to make sense of it right now. Just let her talk."

"That's what I'm trying to do."

"Are you?"

"Okay, maybe I'm rushing her along too much. There is something she is trying to say, but she keeps beating around the bush about it."

"Maybe you're reading too much into it. Perhaps the message is more about something you are supposed to learn than letting some long-ago dark secret out."

His words hit a chord, and she nibbled on her bottom lip. Something in his eyes told her he was trying to tell her something. But just like his grandmother, he brushed by the true meaning with a riddle.

She picked up her glass and moved to the door. "I need to make dinner."

Eli continued to lean on the railing as he watched her move past him. Her gaze shifted back to him when he said, "Did I hit a nerve?"

"You tell me. Seems like you're trying to tell me something yourself."

Eli raised one eyebrow. "You're the one who has a few secrets in her past that might be prohibiting you from moving on. Ain't so?"

Rebecca snapped her head in his direction. "What's that supposed to mean?"

"Come on, Becca. We both know things didn't turn out between us like either of us hoped. When are you going to come clean with your part in it?"

He waited for her to respond, but she just looked at him with a perplexed frown. She closed the door behind her and leaned back on the door, thinking. *It's not that easy, Eli. I only did what I had to do to protect you from a fate worse than death. Nobody should have to suffer from my sins. Especially you.*

***

After Mary woke from her forenoon nap, Rebecca helped her to the kitchen. Then she proceeded to put dinner on the table.

Eli said few words during dinner and what he did say was directed at his grandmother. A heaviness hung in the air from their earlier conversation. A look of distress filled Mary's face when Eli asked her if he should make another appointment with the doctor.

"Heavens no. I'm in my eighties, and a little confusion comes with the territory."

Rebecca grinned at her statement, and Eli rolled his eyes and sighed. "I guess you got me there. But if Rebecca sees anything out of the normal, I'll be calling Dr. Smithson right away."

Mary tucked a tissue up under her sleeve. "You have better things to worry about than a senile old woman."

"And none are as important as you."

Rebecca changed the subject. "It's a lovely afternoon. How about we go sit in the garden, and we can get back to recording your story."

After Eli bowed his head for the second prayer, Rebecca took the chance to notice how his sandy blond hair was pushed tight against his temples. His jaw twitched as his lips moved silently. When he lifted his head, their eyes met, and she hoped he didn't notice she had failed to close her eyes at all.

Rebecca blushed. Something she didn't think she had ever done before. What was it about Eli that left her speechless? Rebecca felt Mary watching them. She dropped her head, gathered up his plate, and carried it to the sink. Oh, how she wished she could erase the past.

***

Rebecca followed Eli and Mary to the garden. She tucked the notebook and a lap quilt under her arm. After Eli had her situated on the bench, he glanced her way. "I'll be heading to the back pasture to fix a row of fence if you should need anything."

A flock of robins landed in the loose soil in the garden, digging for a worm or two. Both women stayed quiet as they watched the scene unfold.

Rebecca crossed her ankles and folded her hands on top of the notebook waiting for Mary to begin. In the silence, Rebecca started to remember how angry Eli had been when he caught Samuel and her together all those years ago. At the time, it was completely innocent. Still, she was sure it was precisely what Eli referred to in their earlier conversation. She didn't want to think about the past, but more importantly, she didn't want to talk about it, especially with Eli.

Mary's words rang in her head. *The truth will set you free.*

How could they? No one would understand and no one would care what haunted her so. She turned her attention back to Mary. As if the old woman knew exactly what was playing through her head, she said, "We all deserve to be happy."

Rebecca clenched her hands and studied Mary's face. She couldn't look into her eyes but for a moment before she had to turn away. Didn't she realize ...she *didn't* deserve to be happy?

Ignoring her comment, she opened the notebook. "Do you want to pick up where you left off? You just told me that secrets ruin a family. How so?"

"When *Datt* came back from the war, things were different. I was no longer his little girl. I had shamed him."

"How so? You were barely a young woman. How did you shame him?"

Lowering her head, Mary whispered, "I was with child."

A small gasp escaped Rebecca's lips, and she covered her mouth.

Mary continued, "There was no hiding my condition. Noah and I were sent to Willow Springs, where no one knew us."

"So is Eli's father, Andy, that child?"

"*Jah.*"

Rebecca wrote Mary's responses on the lined paper and waited patiently. She had so many questions, but she took Eli's advice and didn't rush her.

Mary brushed a drop from her nose with her sleeve. "Do you believe?"

"Do I believe what? In Jesus?" Rebecca creased her forehead. "*Jah*. Of course, I do. Do you?"

Mary waited for a few seconds then rubbed her temple.

"But do you really believe in Jesus?"

Mary's questions turned back to a riddle tale, and Rebecca tried to keep her frustration under control as she answered.

"I believe there is a Jesus." She paused and tapped the pen on the paper. "Do you want me to write these questions down?"

"If you need to." Mary pulled the lap quilt up with her good hand and tucked her limp arm under the quilted fabric.

"God doesn't want just a part of you now. He wants all of you, all the time."

Rebecca recorded Mary's words down and waited until Mary began again. "Things were different here in Willow Springs. No one knew Noah and me, and we could pretend we were a happily married couple. No one was the wiser."

"But I thought you said you were happy."

"As happy as you can be being married to a man who really didn't love you and only agreed to marry you to save face for his family."

"Mary? I'm so confused."

"It was just the beginning of a life full of lies and secrets. One lie turned into another, and before we knew it, we were living it like there was no way out."

"Did you ever go back to Lancaster?"

"*Nee*, and I never saw my father again. He died the same month Andy was born."

Rebecca noticed Mary started to tremble. "Are you cold? Do you need to go inside?"

"*Nee*. It's just sometimes the past is harder to face than the future." Mary pointed to the paper. "Keep writing."

Mary turned her face to the sun and closed her eyes and repeated. "Secrets ruin a family."

Rebecca's tone took on an edge. "*Jah*, you said that a couple of times now."

Mary opened her eyes and glared at Rebecca. "But do you believe it? That one small secret cost me dearly, but I had kept my promise up until now."

"What promise was that?"

"That I would never share with Andy who his father was."

CHAPTER 11

Mary's house took on an eerie silence as Rebecca sprayed potato starch on Eli's Sunday shirt and ironed it. Lost in an array of confusing thoughts, she couldn't get past wondering why it was so important Mary kept Andy's father a secret. Eli's father had to be in his sixties, and she was dying to ask Eli if he knew what his grandmother was referring to.

What was it that Mary asked her? *Do you believe in Jesus?* That was a funny thing to ask her in mid-sentence. Of course, she believed in Jesus; she was baptized and all. It was all a mystery to her. The way Mary went back and forth from talking about Noah to asking her what and who she believed in. Not only was she confused, but she also felt Mary was getting more and more disoriented as the days went on. If she wanted to get to the bottom of Mary's story, she would need to keep her talking.

The screen door squeaked, and Rebecca let out a little yelp. "For heaven's sake, Eli, you startled me."

"How's *Mommi* this afternoon?"

"She's resting again. I'm afraid she hasn't been making much sense today. She goes from one subject to the next. In and out of thoughts with no order to any of them."

"Well, then I guess it's a good thing she has you to decipher things for her."

Eli didn't bother asking her any specific questions, and it was all she could do to keep what she'd been told to herself for the time being.

Eli popped a cookie in his mouth from the container on the counter before asking, "I need to run into town to get some more fencing supplies. Is there anything you need from Shetler's Grocery while I'm out?"

She moved to the refrigerator and rattled off a few items before turning to face him.

His eyebrows arched. "Would you like to go with me?"

Rebecca felt a surge in her cheeks. "I think I should stay around in case Mary wakes up."

He shrugged without saying a word, turned, and walked back out the door.

Was that a look of disappointment etched on his face? There she goes again. Not allowing herself to enjoy even the simplest of things. *What harm would it have done for her to ride along?*

***

Eli opted to take the open wagon and looked back toward the house one last time in hopes she changed her mind. Was he crazy to think she might let her guard down for even a few minutes to enjoy the spring day with him? *Mommi* would have been fine for the hour it would take them to get to town and back. Two steps ahead and one step back. Maybe he was chasing a dream, thinking she'd ever fess up and clear the air with him.

How would he ever get her to confide in him? There had to be more to the story than Samuel's confession. Perhaps another visit with Samuel would help him understand.

***

No matter the forlorn look on Eli's face, Rebecca knew she was doing exactly what she was meant to do. She couldn't help it; her father and Mary threw the two of them back together again. Nothing either of them could say or do would help correct the past. There was a rightness to keeping him at arm's length. She couldn't allow anything to get in her way of going forward with the life she planned out. Especially allowing herself to have a family of her own. She couldn't chance it. Not for one minute.

Turning her head toward Mary's room, she placed the iron back on the heat plate and followed the quiet whispers.

Mary was moving her head from side to side, mumbling. "Don't punish Noah."

Hoping to gain more insight into Mary's story, Rebecca waited and listened carefully.

Mary's voice rattled in a sleep-like state. "It's not fair. It's your fault . . .you're the one who . . ."

Not sure if she should wake Mary, she sat on the floor near the foot of the bed and listened.

As straightforward as the dust particles dancing in the ray of sunshine, Mary's following words flipped in her stomach to a point she covered her mouth. She pushed herself up from her knees and backed out of Mary's room, leaving the old woman to relive the pain in a dream. Rebecca's heart pounded in her ears. How long had Mary carried that horrible secret? And how could anyone as sweet as Mary Bricker be forced to live with such memories? And why did she feel the need to share such things now? For the life of her, she couldn't see how sharing any of it would make a difference now. *Oh*, she needed to talk to Eli. She had to tell him. Or did she?

Rebecca pulled her sweater around her tighter and sat in a rocker on the front porch, loathing a man she'd never met. Shock ran cold and deep inside Rebecca, and her heart ached for what Mary endured. She drew in a nose full of air and blew it out slowly. The peonies at the edge of the porch blew a sweet aroma by her, and it awoke her senses. She closed her eyes and tried to remember what Mary had shared with her about Noah.

Eli's grandfather didn't love Mary, but he sacrificed his life to give Mary and Andy the life they deserved. What kind of man did that? She knew Eli's character was cut from the same cloth without answering herself. He had done everything all those years ago to convince her to give them another shot. More than once, he told her he didn't care what she had done. He loved her and could forgive and forget anything as long as she would be honest with him. All he wanted was for her to be his wife.

At the time, she couldn't fathom any man forgiving a woman for such things. Her sins were unforgivable. But here again, a man much like Eli was willing to put genuine love aside to do the right thing. Noah had forgiven Mary, even though it wasn't Mary who needed forgiveness.

Moisture pooled in the corner of Rebecca's eyes, and she wiped it away while taking herself back to the screech of the truck tires and the cries of the young Amish woman at the market. It was the same dream she relived every day of her life. One of selfishness and ignorance at the cost of a woman and her child. If the woman at the market couldn't hold her child because of her carelessness, she would never allow herself any happiness either.

The scene played over in her head. *An argument with her schwester made her push her way through the crowd and separated the woman from her small child. When the woman's voice echoed off the open-air market, Rebecca ignored her cries and let the small toddler run in front of her and out into the parking lot.*

Rebecca's memory was engraved with the horrible sound. *The screeching tires and the thud of the toddler hitting the pavement a few feet away. Watching the commotion from the shadow of a delivery truck, she remembered Samuel looking up at her as he held the small child in his arms. His pleas to call 911 fell on deaf ears as she ran through the market.*

For days, Samuel pleaded with her to go to the bishop and confess what she had or hadn't done to save the young boy's life. After a month had gone by, Samuel felt responsible for his part. He succumbed to her blackmailing tactics to deceive Eli.

After so long, Rebecca reasoned away any role she played and used her life to sacrifice any meaningful happiness. Much like Noah did for Mary. But he held no fault for her secret.

The cooing of two doves forced Rebecca to open her eyes and follow the sound. She struggled against the resentment rising to overwhelming guilt that left a bad taste in her mouth. Why was God so intent on making her relive the woman's screams so often? Wasn't it enough that Emma and Samuel lost James, most likely as a pretense to her sin? When was enough, enough?

Lord help me. I don't want to be as old as Mary and still reliving the same old dream over and over again.

Following the doves, she marveled at how they gave no care in the world to her presence. They were perfectly content in picking up the leftover seeds the cardinals had pushed out of the bird feeder above.

She let out another breath and thought. *Is it too late for me? Much like it's probably too late for Eli and Andy. How will they ever understand? But it's not my secret to tell; it's Mary's.*

The air stood still as if someone stood in front of her to block the breeze, and she heard. *Rise up and step out of the darkness. The truth will set you free.*

Suddenly calm inside, Rebecca knew what she must do.

***

For a few moments, Mary opened her eyes and let the warmth of the sun land on her face. A strange buzzing in her ears pounded against her temples. A stab of pain warmed her ear and then settled over her forehead. The sensation forced her to bury her head deeper in her pillow, she called out.

"Noah."

Thoughts of her late husband filled her head, and an outstretched hand beckoned her forward. *Oh Lord, I've waited so long. Is it real?* Her weakened body lay beneath her as she floated toward the light. A voice was all around her, soothing her arrival. *Come, my daughter, look what I've prepared for you.*

Still, a part of her resisted. "But I need to explain things to Andy, and I haven't gotten through to Rebecca yet. She has so much to live for if she'll only let go."

He held His arms wide. *"You've set the seed; now trust me, my child. It's time."*

With a sigh of submission, Mary Bricker went home.

***

A sudden breeze blew through the wind chime at the end of the porch. Rebecca stood and watched the clapper bang against the tubes. Perhaps a short walk around the farm would clear her mind and help her find a way to set things right.

The quick thought of checking on Mary first floated away with the hollow sound at the end of the porch. Picking up her pace, she took the stairs two at a time and walked behind the barn to follow the fence line. New lambs abounded through the green fields without regard to anything but play.

Thinking of her carefree days as a child, she whispered, "Life had been so much easier then. To romp and play with no regard to what the future might bring. Oh, how I miss those days."

The afternoon sun cast shadows on the trees, and she stepped out in the sun to warm her shoulders. After turning the corner and stepping across a ditch, she moved to the side of the road just as she heard the dinner bell on the back of the porch clang repeatedly.

"What on earth?" she mumbled and took off, running toward the house.

Her heart sunk when she finally reached the back door. Eli stopped the bell and didn't say a word. The reason for the commotion was written all over his face.

"I was only gone for thirty minutes."

Eli sank to the steps and laid his face in his hands. Rebecca moved past him and ran to Mary's bed. There was a heaviness in the room, and Mary's distorted face took on a shade of gray.

Rebecca laid her fingertips on the side of Mary's wrist, even though she knew she'd feel no movement. When she stood, Eli was at her side. "I shouldn't have left her. I was only gone for a short time. I'm so sorry."

"You had no way of knowing."

Hadn't she? Once again, she put her selfish desires above her responsibilities.

"It's all my fault. God is punishing me, and you and Mary had to pay the price."

Rebecca turned to walk from the room, and Eli caught her arm. She stopped for a moment and looked into his eyes as she laid her hand on top of his. "I'll go get my father. He'll know what to do."

"Please don't go." Rebecca bit her lip. "I have to get someone."

"I'll go with you."

Rebecca moved his hand off her arm. "*Nee*, you stay."

The pleading in his sunken eyes did little to convince her otherwise. All she wanted to do was get as far away from Eli and his grandmother as she could. The dark cloud following her struck again. And no amount of assuring herself things weren't her fault did nothing to ease the pain behind Eli's blond lashes. The screen door slammed behind her.

***

Rebecca, Anna, and Emma helped clean Mary's house from top to bottom for the next two days while Eli, Samuel, and Daniel cleaned out the barn, making room for the furniture.

As Eli carried the last living room chair to the barn, making room for the rows of benches, a black sedan pulled into the driveway. An older version of Eli stepped out first, followed by who she assumed was Eli's mother. The older couple stood in the middle of the driveway and waited until the car pulled away before moving toward the porch. Rebecca watched Eli from across the yard and prayed he'd follow them to the house. When Eli called his father's name, the man stopped and changed his footing.

"*Datt*?"

"*Jah*, why are you so surprised?"

"I didn't think you'd make it in time."

"I'm not saying it was the ideal time to leave your *bruders* with all the planting, but out of respect for my mother, I came."

It didn't take much to notice Eli's jaw tighten at his father's response, even as far away as she was on the porch. His mother wrapped her arms around his middle and tenderly kissed Eli's cheek.

"It's good to see you, son."

"Thank you for coming. I do believe we have just about everything ready, and *Mommi's* body has been prepared, and her grave dug."

His father's voice, void of any emotion, replied, "Good I will need to head out tomorrow afternoon. Hopefully, you'll come to your senses and return to Lancaster with me."

Rebecca's hand began to cramp, and she loosened the hold she had on the bottle of window cleaner. For what seemed like an eternity, she held her breath, waiting for Eli to answer his father.

Eli hollered to her. “Becca, will you show my mother to my room?”

She set down the cleaner and rag, waved Eli’s mother her way, and greeted her once she made it to her side.

“Becca Byler?”

“Rebecca.”

The stout woman raised her chin and suppressed a slight smile in her direction. “Eli has spoken of you.”

Without acknowledging the woman’s probing, she led Mrs. Bricker to the back bedroom.

***

Eli turned on his heels. “I’m in no mood to discuss this with you now. As I have said a million times, I’m not moving back to Lancaster.” Pushing his hands out before himself, he stated, “Besides, who will take care of all these sheep?”

His father stepped up his pace beside him. “I’m sure we could find some young farmer to take it over. It would be the perfect starter farm for any young family.”

Eli stopped dead in his tracks. “Starter farm? I’ve poured more sweat and tears into this farm than any person I know. How could you think I would be ready to walk away from it all?”

The older man rolled his eyes. “It’s a sheep farm! No son of mine should be tending sheep like a shepherd when he has a profitable dairy farm at his fingertips.”

Pulling his father to the side of the barn and away from the group of men who gathered near the double barn doors, Eli stammered, “I can’t believe we are having this conversation now. You haven’t even paid your respect to your mother, and you’re badgering me about leaving Willow Springs. For the final time, I’m not leaving this farm.”

In a moment, he understood where his father stood, and his heart burst with what his father really thought of his *Mommi* Mary. “Couldn’t you have thought of anyone but yourself for a minute?”

“I’m here, aren’t I?”

"For face only. Had I known you'd be like this, I may not have called you until way after the funeral."

His father tipped his hat at the group of men heading their way and said, "You fail to forget this farm is mine, and I've only let you play farmer until the time came when I could take back what was rightfully mine."

Eli let out a slight groan and sucked in a deep breath as his father whispered, "Playtime is over."

Eli fought to move his feet but couldn't take his eyes off the man who walked across the yard. Had he been so blind all these years to see his father cared about no one but himself? How could a woman as sweet as his grandmother raise a child who was so outright evil? He swore right there and then that there wasn't an ounce of Andy Bricker he wanted to claim as his own.

CHAPTER 12

Rain pounded against the windowpane as Rebecca tried to concentrate on her father's words. As one of the newest ministers, he delivered Mary's funeral service. Eli's tiny home was bursting with one hundred or more neighbors and friends who came to pay their final respects.

Anna sat to her left and tapped her knee when she leaned on the cool glass. Even having her *schwester* close wouldn't stop the urge to run home and far away from prying eyes. While they didn't say it, she was sure each one was blaming her for Mary's death. She had been hired as her nursemaid, and she wasn't there when the old woman took her last breath.

Even Eli's typically soft and endearing eyes were cold and lifeless when he looked her way. For a fleeting moment, two days ago, Rebecca was sure she knew what she needed to do to move her life forward. God proved she wasn't worth His forgiveness. Once again, she was responsible for another person's death. It was time she left Willow Springs for good. The further she was away from those she cared about, the less likely God would take vengeance on those she loved. Rebecca twisted the tissue in her hands and closed her eyes.

First, it was the toddler at the market. I didn't stop him from running through the crowd when I could have. Next, it was Mamm. She died on my watch. If I hadn't gone outside to brush the straw out of the alpacas, I would have been there to ease her last breaths. Then Emma's James. And now, Mary. How could I be so selfish as to not be by her side when she needed me the most?

The doctor said nothing could have stopped another stroke from taking her life. But I don't believe it. I should have been there. If not for her, then for Eli.

Anna reached down and squeezed Rebecca's hand when she failed to stand. It was their turn to file past Mary's body. As the row in front of them emptied, Rebecca noticed Eli's mother wiping a tear from her cheek.

Frowning slightly, Rebecca chastised the woman in her head. What did Eli's mother know about Mary? Did she really have the right to mourn? Something dark was working beneath the surface. The change that had been taking place in Rebecca's heart since coming to care for Mary hardened with one look at Eli's parents.

Rage raced up the back of her neck, and it was all she could do to keep the words from spilling off her tongue. If it hadn't been for Anna's warm hand in hers, she might have marched right up to the woman. Regardless of the backlash she would have gotten from her father and the bishop.

Anna leaned in close. "What is it? You're trembling."

Rebecca pulled her hand away and nudged her *schwester* to move forward. "It's nothing. I just need some air."

Rebecca fell into step in line, filing past Mary's body, and looked around the room until she laid eyes on Eli. His head was dropped, and his hands were folded in his lap. The starched white shirt she had just ironed the other day looked stiff and unnatural on his slumped shoulders. His father sat to his left with his head held high.

Taking in a deep breath and letting it out again, she felt Eli's anguish. There was no doubt he loved his grandmother and would miss her terribly. It was evident to anyone who knew them that Mary was more a mother to Eli than his own. Well, it was at least obvious to her. The room started to close in around her, and it was all she could do to make it to the porch. The rain had slowed, and only a few sprinkles were left in the air. The harmonious dark cloud had moved to the east, and tiny slivers of blue could be seen edging their way among the budding trees.

It would still be an hour before Mary's body moved to a pine box and taken to the Willow Springs cemetery only a mile away. Too many times over the last five years had she walked past the field lined with small white grave markers a short distance away.

Stepping off the porch, Rebecca moved to the side of the house and past the kitchen garden. Peeking up through a mound of dirt was a cluster of the same Johnny Jump-ups she had destroyed just a week ago. The small yellow and purple petals lifted their faces toward the sky and greeted her with a smile as she knelt to run her fingers over the velvety petals.

A warmth penetrated her fingers, and Mary's voice echoed in her ears. *Secrets are simply part of our life stories that have been forced into hiding. Secrets ruined my family, don't let it ruin yours.*

A sob settled into the back of Rebecca's throat, and she got her foot caught in the hem of her black dress when she tried to stand.

A strong hand cupped her elbow. "I'd hate for your good clothes to be caked with mud from a fall into *Mommi's* garden."

She saw the muscles in his face tense slightly after he spoke. She stayed quiet as he swallowed hard and moved to the side, so she could get her footing.

"*Mommi* loved this place. I should have done more to keep it up for her."

Eli Bricker had the tenderest heart of anyone she knew. Much too sweet for the likes of her. "She understood, I'm sure of it. You had your hands full with running the farm."

She was sorry she said anything when his jaw clenched again, and he looked off in the direction of the barn. "It's not my farm; it's my father's."

A new wave of tightness filled her chest. "What do you mean, your father's? You made this land what it is today. Your father didn't."

He didn't answer but looked toward the row of buggies starting to form a line down Mystic Mill Road. "I suppose it's time."

She stood still and watched him walk to the barn. The blond curls at the nape of his neck wrapped up to the rim of his black felt hat, and it was there she said her goodbyes. Both to Mary and to Eli.

***

Spring turned into early summer as Rebecca resumed her duties at *Stitch 'n Time*. On the other hand, Anna fell back into step with staying behind the curtain while Rebecca handled the customers. Even walking past Eli's house left Rebecca in a state of disarray, so it was better she pushed any thoughts of him far away.

The bell above the door chimed, and Rebecca looked up from her seat at the counter. Her eyes widened when Eli's broad shoulders encased the doorway.

He moved his attention to Anna, who sat at the spinning wheel and back to her. "May I have a word with you?"

She bit her bottom lip and waited for him to continue. She hadn't laid eyes on him in almost four weeks and went out of her way to stay clear of any chance of running into him. Her mind was still swarming with a way to leave Willow Springs, but a plan hadn't presented itself yet.

He pushed the door back open. "Can we step out on the porch?"

She glanced over her shoulder toward Anna and shrugged before heading to the door.

Eli held the door open until she passed through. Once the door closed, he took off his hat and twirled it in his fingers. He moved to the edge of the stairs and stared off toward her father's house.

"It's out of my hands."

The tone of his voice was unlike anything she had ever heard. The pain in his words spoke so much, even without her knowing what he was referring to. She never realized a person could communicate a feeling in so few words.

She walked to his side and looked at him bleakly. "What's out of your hands?"

"*Mommi* Mary left the farm and all of its acreage to me with a stipulation."

Rebecca folded her hands, brought them to her chin, and sighed. "That's good news, *jah*?"

"Depends."

"Depends on what?"

"It depends on the person she left it to. And she'll need to agree to something that she has no desire for. It's the only way to keep the farm away from my father."

There was no doubt he was referring to her the way he said *she*. Rebecca felt a heaviness in the pit of her stomach, and she was afraid to ask. "*Me?*"

Eli sat on the top step and motioned his head for her to sit beside him. "You'd better sit, or you may fall once I explain."

Rebecca scooped her dress behind her knees and sat on the wooden step. "You're starting to worry me. What is it, and how can I help you keep the farm?"

Eli secured his hat on his knee and rested his forearms on his thighs. "Seems *Mommi* Mary had this planned for a long time. Even before she had her first stroke. About this time last year by the looks of it."

With an edge of impatience, Rebecca asked, "Had what planned?"

"To sign the farm over to me."

"But that's good news. It won't go to your father like he threatened. How can that be a bad thing? You won't be forced to go back to Lancaster."

Eli looked straight ahead. "Lancaster was never an option."

He drew a shaky breath and let it out slowly. "The farm comes with a clause. And that clause is you."

She pressed her hand to her temple. "Eli, you're making no sense."

"The only way I can keep the farm is if I marry you. The farm, house, and land will become mine the day I marry. And then it will become ours."

Breath escaped Rebecca's lips, and she shook her head from side to side. "What?"

Eli reached into his back pocket and pulled two letters from his trousers. "She explains it in these. She left a letter for both of us. I found them in her room last week when I was searching for any paperwork for the house."

She took the white envelope from his hands with her name clearly printed across the front.

"I didn't open yours, but I'm sure it's similar to mine."

"And if I don't agree?"

"The farm and the land go back to my father."

"Why? I don't understand. Why would your grandmother do such a thing?"

Eli stood. "I'm sure she explains everything in your letter. I didn't come here to beg you to marry me. Especially since I know it's the last thing you want to do. But I had to tell you what I'm up against."

Rebecca looked at him, eyes troubled. "I don't even know what to say."

"Don't say anything right now. Read the letter. You know where to find me when you want to talk."

The white envelope had a cluster of pansies faded into the background and smelled like Mary's almond cherry hand lotion. When she brought it to her nose, she was transported back into Mary's room, and her soothing voice played in her head.

A songbird cooed overhead as Eli backed his buggy away from the shop and clicked his tongue to get the horse to pick up its pace. The clip-clop of its hooves kept time to the wagon wheels as it pulled out onto Mystic Mill Road. The hardened blacktop set the steady beat of the horse's metal shoes in motion. As it faded, all that could be heard was the bird perched on the maple tree beside the porch.

Rebecca was afraid to slide her fingers along the seal and reveal her future. The loneliness she had felt over the last five years of keeping everyone at bay tried to escape. She desperately wanted to keep her true identity hidden far away from anyone it might hurt. How could Mary do such a thing? She could hardly breathe as she slipped her fingers under the flap. The riddles Mary kept twisting around their conversations played in her head like the television she'd seen at The Sandwich Shoppe in downtown Willow Springs. Repeating itself repeatedly until the same message was embedded in your brain.

The white-lined paper had deep creases like they were ironed in to make a point. When she unfolded it, Mary's perfect penmanship pulled her in.

Rebecca,

As this may come as a shock to you, please know my decision concerning my grandson didn't come lightly. I may be an old woman and one who should keep her nose out of the affairs of my grandson, but when it comes to knowing what is best for him, I do.

You may think you've kept yourself hidden beneath layers of lies and secrets, but you're only fooling yourself.

I've watched you throw away your life, and I refuse to let this one last chance I have to save it pass me by.

If you're reading this letter, I assume I could not help you and Eli see you were meant for each other while I was alive. If that is the case, I have set a plan to force you two to realize there is more to life than what you're both running from.

There is no hiding from me, as there is no way to hide from God. I was there, and I saw it all. I watched from afar as you faded into the shadows filled with shame and guilt. Quit hiding Rebecca; it's time to face the truth. It's time to call on Jesus and ask for forgiveness. His truth will set you free.

I've spent my life running from the truth, and it cost me my son. Don't make the same mistakes. My God is your God, and he has a forgiving heart. He sent his son to die for our sins, which means yours too.

I may not be the best with words, and I can only speak of my own experiences, but I've learned in my long life that if God has placed me near a dry well, it's for a reason. At every turn, He's preparing me for something bigger. A new spiritual place beside Him. In those dark and dreadful times when I felt the furthest from Him, isolated and alone, I heard Him the loudest.

Find yourself, Rebecca, step out of the shadows. Let God direct you, even push you if need be, to a place where you feel His presence in your life. It's only there that you will find the peace you are chasing.

Now onto the purpose of this letter…

Andy will do everything in his power to take this farm away from Eli, and I'm bound to stop that from happening. I refuse to make excuses for my son's actions, and he will face his maker one day, the same as me.

Eli's great-grandfather bought us this farm, and it came with a similar stipulation. The only way Noah could get a farm of his own was to agree to marry me in the process. At the time, it was a great burden for him to leave the woman he loved to save me from a tarnished reputation. But Noah had the heart of a saint, and he sacrificed himself to protect me. I've always felt this house was blessed by the Lord because Noah put his wants and desires aside to do His work.

I see Noah in Eli. I know this is so much to ask. But step out in faith and give Eli a chance to show you a life you so deserve.

Remember, Rebecca, you are only fooling yourself. God sees your heart, and it's His job to restore it if you let Him.

Often God will not allow us to continue in a place that seems safe and secure. But shows us a path that takes us places that leaves us uncomfortable and vulnerable. This is the place God has put on my heart to show you. He wants your faith primed, ready to be His ambassador when you are called into service. He'll often call us to a place in waiting to prepare us for bigger things.

This is my blessing to you, Rebecca. Take this house beside Eli and make it a home. Love will follow, I promise.

Mary

A nagging fear coursed through her. She could hear her inner bell chime a warning to run away. Rebecca shivered inside. *I can't do it. Eli will suffer just like Mary did. It worked out for Mary, but it won't for me. A dark cloud will follow us, I'm sure of it.*

This was too much to ask. Regardless of whether Eli would lose the farm or not, how could he agree to marry her? He didn't even love her. She was shocked he would even consider it. Rebecca flipped the letter over and found Mary's words. *Eli's great-grandfather bought us this little farm, and it came with a similar stipulation.*

Defensive anger welled up inside of her, and she mumbled, "He bought you a farm to keep your mouth shut, and you let him! How could you, after what he did to you?"

A torrent of angry words spilled from her mouth as she tried to wrap her head around what Mary was asking her to do. And Eli, how could he even consider it? She rubbed the back of her neck with her free hand and shoved the letter in her apron pocket with the other. Letting a long breath escape her lips, she whispered. *"If you see my heart, Lord, then you can see this is plain crazy. I'd just as soon stay alone than agree to a loveless marriage. It might have worked for Noah and Mary, but there is no way it would work for Eli and me."*

She stood, placed her hands on her hips, and stretched her back out just as Mary's voice rang in her ears. *The truth will set you free.*

In a disgusted tone, she yelped, Ugh!

CHAPTER 13

Wilma's voice etched a piercing tone as Rebecca's name rang across the yard.

"What?"

"Your father wants a word with you."

Tucking Mary's letter down deep in her pocket, she stepped off the porch and tried to swallow down her frustration. The last thing she needed was a lecture, and she murmured her complaint on the way to the house. "What have I done now?"

The squeak of the screen door announced her arrival, and her father called to her from the kitchen. "In here."

"Wilma said you wanted to talk to me."

Wilma sat to his left and had her hands wrapped around a mug. Her father pushed away his glass of tea and sat back in his chair. The way he took in a breath and puffed out his chest told Rebecca that she wouldn't like what he had to say.

"I see Anna isn't helping the customers anymore since you returned to the shop."

Rebecca took a seat at the table. "She's more comfortable behind the curtain."

"In whose opinion? Yours or hers?"

"I suppose hers, but I didn't ask. We just took back our original places once I was done working at Mary's."

Her father leaned his elbows on the arm of the chair and laced his fingers together. "That's a problem."

"Why so?"

"We were noticing Anna was starting to come out of her shell while you were away. Now that you're back, she's reverting to her old ways."

Rebecca crossed her legs and folded her arms across her chest. "Anna's always been a bit timid around people. Why is that an issue?"

Wilma was quick to add. "Because she hides behind you, and that's not healthy."

Raising her head in the woman's direction, she answered, "So you think that I purposely hinder my own *schwester*? And stop looking at me that way!"

Jacob cleared his throat. "We're only trying to say that Anna was doing so well in your absence."

Rebecca's shoulders hunched slightly. "And you feel I'm holding her back?"

Her father picked up his glass and took a long drink before answering. "*Jah*."

Wilma pushed a letter across the table in her direction. "My family in Willow Brook needs help at their farm stand this summer, and we think it best you leave Willow Springs for a short time."

"*Datt*?"

"Now get that look off your face. It's only for a short time, and it will give Anna the time she needs to step out on her own. She can't hide behind you her whole life."

Rebecca stopped and stared. She couldn't believe what they were suggesting. *Stitch 'n Time* was her idea, and now they wanted her to walk away from her business to work a farm stand twenty miles away.

Wilma pushed the letter closer. "My *schwester* says you can stay with her for the summer. They have a lovely farm at the edge of town, and it's only a short thirty-minute walk to the market."

"No way!" Her eyes were hot.

The frown on her father's face and the way he straightened his shoulders told her more than words could express.

A coldness seeped into the room and sent a chill up her arms. "You can't be serious."

"Look, we didn't come to this decision easily. We could have just as quickly sent Anna away, but you are the stronger of the two. We are afraid your *schwester* wouldn't fare well away from home."

"I can't believe it. You're really suggesting I move away from Willow Springs?" Rebecca sprang up and paced the kitchen. "This is my life, not yours."

Shame gripped her. Not that she hadn't tried to figure out how to leave Willow Springs herself, but being forced to leave? That was like she was being backed into a corner with no way out.

Wilma pulled the letter back into her possession and folded it neatly on the table. "For heaven's sake, Rebecca, you're being over dramatic. It's only for the summer. It's not like we're sending you off forever."

"The summer? That's when we are the busiest with preparing fiber for the rest of the year. The shop slows down in the summer, and it gives us time to clean and spin enough yarn to get us through the winter. Besides, I've already agreed to buy more wool from Eli. Anna could never take care of that all on her own."

Her father pushed his chair out and stood. "Then Anna can hire someone to help her."

Rebecca stopped in her tracks and faced her father. "I can't go to Willow Brook."

He turned and looked her straight in the eye. "Give me one good reason why."

Without thinking about what she was about to say, she blurted out. "Eli asked me to marry him."

Wilma let out a gasp. "Thank the Lord."

Her father's lip turned upward. "And when was he going to speak to me about this?"

Rebecca dropped her head. "I suppose after I gave him my answer."

Jacob grabbed his straw hat off the table and headed to the door. "I guess this changes a good many things."

Wilma seemed to be enjoying herself, and the smirk on her face moved to a solemn look. "Oh my, we have so much to do."

Rebecca hadn't given one thought to the plans she just put in motion. In the span of just two weeks and after the bishop published them at church the next day, she would be Mrs. Eli Bricker. Sitting back down in her chair, she rested her hands on the table and covered her eyes with the palm of her hands. *What had she done?*

Wilma moved to the drawer at the end of the counter and pulled out a pad of paper and ink pen.

"A dress, we need to go buy fabric. And you'll need a new white apron. You'll want royal blue for your wedding dress, right? And the meal. I'll need to meet with the neighbors and see who can help make pies. Oh, and the cleaning. This farm hasn't been cleaned from top to bottom in a good long time. The invitations. You and Anna will need to get started on them right away. You and Eli will need to begin hand-delivering them on Monday. Do you think his parents will come from Lancaster?"

Rebecca flipped her head back and blew out a long breath from her lips in an unladylike manner. "Stop! I can't talk about this right now."

Wilma squared her shoulders. "But we must. We only have two weeks before the wedding. There is so much to do. But first, I'll need to write my *schwester* and tell her you won't be coming to help at the market."

Rebecca stood and moved to the sink. She ran a cool glass of water and downed it all before walking back outside. Something inside her ruptured, leaving a wave of sorrow in its path. She had just agreed to marry Eli, knowing full and well he didn't love her. Mary's plan was put in motion, and there was nothing she could do now but accept her fate.

***

Eli walked home, knowing Rebecca had most likely read *Mommi's* letter. Once he reached the barn, he sat on a bale of straw and pulled his grandmother's letter from his pocket. He still couldn't believe Rebecca held his future in her hands. Would she realize what it would cost her for him to stay in Willow Springs? Or better yet, would she even care?

My Dearest Eli,

My heart aches to know you most likely are dealing with an array of emotions right now. You are so much like my Noah. He wore his heart on his sleeve, much like you do. I can't thank you enough for coming to care for me all these years. I most likely would have perished long ago from loneliness had you not come along. You were an answer to my prayers.

There are so many things I had hoped to explain to you before I left, but if you are reading this letter, I didn't get that chance. First, I want to say how sorry I am that you had to be in the middle of your father's and my problems. Please don't hold any ill feelings for your father. Andy is a good man; he just had the influence of your Great-Grandfather Bricker longer than he did Noah.

Eli stopped and read the line over again. Why wouldn't *Mommi* refer to Noah as my grandfather? So many things I don't understand. He shook his head and continued reading.

I know for sure your heart is on the right path. We have studied the bible together, and I'm confident you are a follower of Jesus. So many of the young people here in Willow Springs are not taught the truth in Jesus. They're still following our past ways of works over faith. Our leaders don't know any better, and I pray someday that will change. I believe it will come about with your help. I'm not sure how I know that, but I think it will happen in your lifetime. Please continue to study your English bible and break the cycle starting with your family. Teach them the truth from the beginning, and that begins with Rebecca.

By now, you have found the deed to this house and farm. You will see that I have left it both to you and Rebecca. If you are reading this letter, I failed at getting you past the things that kept you apart. You can't hide your feelings from me. I saw it on your face every time you looked her way. Just as Rebecca hasn't been able to hide them either. I know what has caused her great pain, and it's your place to get to the bottom of it. The woman loves you and always has. She just can't see it through years of lies and secrets. If anyone is going to pull her from the depths of her despair, it's Jesus and you.

Please forgive me for putting you in a position of having to force Rebecca's hand in marriage. I'm not sure if she will accept your proposal, but I know she has the heart to do the right thing. And if she can't see that, God will continue to work on restoring the spirit He gave her. Please see past her hard exterior and know all she has done was to save you from what she thinks she is protecting you from.

I had hoped that I could have helped her see the path God wanted her to walk on by the time I passed. But again, if you are reading this letter, I failed, and now it's up to you.

She will balk at an arranged marriage, but it's the only way I could convince your father to allow you to stay in Willow Springs and on this farm. He agreed to my wishes, only if you were married. As you can see in the agreement, the farm reverts to Andy if you are not married within three months of my passing.

Eli, please know that not all marriages start out with love. Often our plans are not what God intended. But it's our job to lay our lives at his feet and accept whatever season he puts us in.

God has put you in a position of great sacrifice. You may think you have no other option than to concede to your father's wishes. But please, Eli, don't think of it as a great burden but as a great gift. Rebecca needs a man of God to lead her, and God chose you. Why else do you think no other woman has crossed your path in the last five years? God knows how to work through the most challenging circumstances to better his kingdom.

I promised to take the most disturbing secret to my grave, and it cost me my family. Please don't let Rebecca succumb to the same fate. Show her that she deserves to be loved, first by her heavenly father and then by you.

All my love,
Mommi Mary

The clip-clop of an approaching buggy pulled his attention away from the letter, and he slipped it in his back pocket as he walked to the opened barn door.

Jacob Byler pulled his buggy to a stop at Eli's feet, and Eli led the horse to the hitching post. Jacob stepped down from the buggy and wrapped the reins around the iron stake.

Silence reigned for several seconds as both men found their footing. Jacob removed his hat and motioned toward the house. "May I have a few moments with you?"

"Of course." Eli raised his hand and let the older gentleman step before him.

Once inside, Eli pointed toward the table. "Can I offer you something to drink?"

"No, I won't be long. What I have to say will only take a few minutes."

Eli felt his legs buckle under his weight and chose to sit to hear Jacob out. By the look on the man's face, he wasn't sure he'd like what he had to say.

"Rebecca tells me you asked her to marry you?"

Eli jerked his head in Rebecca's father's direction. "In a roundabout way, I did. But she has not given me her answer yet."

Jacob took a seat at the table. "I'm certain she will. If not, she will be leaving for Willow Brook in the morning."

"Willow Brook? For what?"

"*Jah*. To work."

Fear gripped Eli for a split-second. "I'm confident she'll choose to stay."

Jacob laid his hat on the table. "The girl is troubled. You know that, *jah*?"

Eli could hardly believe his ears. Had Rebecca's father come to tell him to stay clear of his daughter by pointing out her flaws?

"Excuse me?"

"The girl has some issues, and I want to be sure you are aware of her shortcomings long before you are stuck with her for life."

Eli leaned back in his chair and tried to understand why Jacob would speak so ill of his own daughter. "I'm fully aware of Rebecca's shortcomings. But to be quite honest, I'm bothered you felt the need to come and point them out to me. Could it be that you're part of the problem?"

"Son, I didn't come here to talk you out of marrying her or get in a disagreement with you. I just want to be sure you are fully aware of what you are taking on when it comes to Rebecca."

Eli smiled wryly. "How about you tell me then?"

Jacob crossed his hands over his chest. "To begin, her tongue gets her in trouble most days."

"Nothing I can't handle."

"Next, she has a prideful nature and steps out of line more often than not."

Eli smirked. "I quite like to be challenged on occasion."

"Lastly, she'd much rather be in the barn than in the kitchen. Won't get many good meals out of that one."

Eli tapped his thumbs on the arm of his chair. "I didn't starve when she was here taking care of my grandmother. I didn't find her meals displeasing."

Jacob stood and put his hat back on. "I guess you know what you're getting into then. I assume you'll give the bishop a date before tomorrow so you can be published properly?"

"As soon as I know, you'll know too."

For the first time in his life, he felt like a man. Standing up to Rebecca's father had felt good. Maybe *Mommi* Mary was on to something. Perhaps it was his job to save the girl, and it didn't hurt that he genuinely cared for her. Just listening to her father talk wrongly about her left a sour taste in his mouth. He didn't see Jacob out but stayed planted in his chair until a soft knock pulled his attention to the front door.

***

Rebecca ducked around her father's buggy and quietly walked around the backside of the house, hoping to eavesdrop on her father and Eli's conversation. Had she known her father was heading to Eli's, she would have stayed clear until he returned. But now that she was here, her curiosity got the better of her.

The warm spring day meant Eli had the windows opened to let a fresh breeze air out the house. It would be easy for her to stoop under the kitchen window to hear what her father had come to say.

Hearing how her father talked about her behind her back made her sink to the ground. Yes, he said nothing she didn't already know, but to hear her own father speak so unkindly of her tore at her soul. She went numb from the top of her head to the soles of her shoes.

Out of pure embarrassment, she let tears fall to her chin and thought. *Oh Datt, how could you? Eli already knows all those things, but did you have to point them out so harshly?*

After hearing Eli defend her, she knew what she needed to do. If she couldn't trust her own father's love to come to her defense, how could she expect God or even Eli to forgive her for her past mistakes?

She waited for her father's buggy to pull away before she left her hiding spot and headed to the front door. She pushed a few loose strands of her chestnut hair back under her *kapp*, softly tapped on the door, and waited.

The scrape of Eli's chair across the linoleum sent shivers up her arms. In a swift moment, she closed her eyes and prayed. *Lord, please help me do right by Eli.*

CHAPTER 14

Eli looked over Rebecca's shoulder as he opened the door. How long had she been standing there, and had she heard the conversation he had with her father? Every window in the house was open, and it wouldn't have been hard to overhear. He noticed she held his grandmother's letter in her hand.

Glancing down at the paper she gripped between her fingers, he asked, "Are you okay?"

"*Nee*."

He tipped his chin, his eyes tender. "Would you like to come in?"

Rebecca ducked past him and waited until he guided her to the pair of rockers in the front room. "Your father was just here."

"*Jah*, I saw."

"You told him I asked you to marry me?"

"*Jah*."

He raked his fingers through his hair, and his tone was flat. "It would have been nice if you had told me first."

Her eyes grew moist as she lowered herself to the chair. "I've made a terrible mistake by blurting that out before I gave it much thought. I had just read Mary's letter, and then *Datt* and Wilma told me they were sending me off to Willow Brook for the summer."

Eli took a seat in the adjoining chair and rested his elbows on his knees. "So your answer?"

The tears fell harder. "Eli, I just don't know. I thought I could live with what Mary was asking me to do, but listening to my *datt* just now, why would you want me?"

Leaning forward, he clasped his hands between his knees. "I was afraid you might have heard us."

Rebecca wiped a tear from her chin and stared out the window. "Why did you leave Lancaster?"

He propped his elbows back on his knees and rested his chin in his hands. "I knew if I stayed one day longer, I would give into my father's dream and not wait on what God had planned for me."

He unfolded himself from the chair and moved to the window. "I suppose to my family, I made the biggest mistake of my life."

Rebecca set the chair in motion. "And if you went back now?"

Without an ounce of hesitation, he replied, "I'd be miserable. God called me to Willow Springs for a purpose."

"A purpose?"

His brows rose. "*Jah*, I'm just not sure what it is yet."

She looked at him in defeat. "I'm certain your purpose wasn't to get tangled up with the likes of me."

He grinned wickedly. "I'd do it all over again if it meant we would cross paths again."

"How can you say such things after my father just pointed out all of my shortcomings?"

"I don't need your father telling me anything. I know all there is to know about Becca Byler."

She darted out of her chair and headed to the door. "You're wrong. You only know a few surface things. You don't know anything about the real Rebecca Byler." She found the doorknob and struggled to get it opened.

He rushed to her side and grabbed her arm to turn her around. When she stumbled, she fell against the wall, and he towered over her with his arm holding himself up above her head. "How about you tell me then?"

She tried to duck under his arm, but he put his leg out to stop her and pulled her back into his hold. She leaned back on the wall and moved her head to the side, so he couldn't see her eyes.

With a gentle nudge, he pulled her chin forward. She ducked out of his grip. He pulled her chin back to the center and said, "Tell me all the things you've kept hidden in that pretty little head of yours. I want to hear it all. Nothing you say will shock me or change how I feel."

She cringed at his last statement and sucked in a deep breath chastising herself again.

"Isn't it enough my own father can see all my faults? Why would I need to point them out again to you?"

He cupped her face tenderly. "Because I don't care what your father thinks." He took his finger and tapped her chest. "I know what's in here."

She tried to twist from his hold. "You know no such thing."

Eli dropped his hands and wrapped his fingers around her wrists. A flash of red moved from her neck to her cheeks and settled on her lips. Her heart took a leap as he leaned in closer.

"What are you afraid of?"

Her green-flecked eyes took on a panicked shade. "That God will punish you for my past mistakes."

"Our God isn't like that. He is forgiving and loving."

"Your God, but not mine."

He pulled her hands to his chin and took a few moments before he answered.

"You have so much to learn. Won't you please let me help you be set free from whatever you think you've done that is so bad God would punish you?"

She moved her head to the side and whispered, "It would be so easy for me to give in and think we could go on like I didn't have a past. But I can't do it."

He stopped her and tipped her chin back so their eyes met. "No, you can't, but together we can with God's help."

Rebecca pushed him aside and reached for the door. Her throat tightened when he replied, "I'm only asking one more time. Tell me what is so horrible you'd throw your whole life away because of it."

Tension filled the air for a few seconds; then, she slid down the wall and rested her head on her folded knees.

Eli fell to one knee and rested his hand on her shoulder. "It's time. This has gone on long enough."

Her face showed signs of complete and utter defeat. The rims of her eyes were red, and her face turned a ghastly white. With the back of her sleeve, she wiped the moisture from her face. "You talk about how God is loving and forgiving. But my own father can't accept me for who and what I am. How do you expect me to believe my heavenly father will forgive me?"

Eli moved to the wall beside her, leaned back, and rested his elbows on his propped-up knees. "You know we have more in common than you think we do."

"How so?"

"Our earthly fathers could use some work."

Rebecca nodded solemnly and gave a slight snicker. "I suppose so. But not as much as me."

Eli stretched out his legs, and Rebecca followed suit. "Our fathers really don't know any better. They only do what their fathers before them had done. They follow a bunch of man-made traditions and rules and don't know the true meaning of following Jesus. If you read the Old Testament, God got angry more than once when His people used idols in place of Him. In my books, that's exactly what this long list of rules is to me. Nothing but a bunch of false idols."

"Eli? How can you say such things?"

"Because it's the truth. Do you know what a truth seeker is?"

Rebecca thought for a moment and answered, "*Nee*, I don't think I've ever heard that term before."

"It means we seek to discover the truth as it is clearly written in the bible."

"What does that have to do with our fathers?"

"Our fathers come from a generation where rules and traditions mean more than trusting in Jesus as our one and only way to heaven."

"Eli, you're confusing me. The things you speak of will get you excommunicated in a minute. You have to know that."

"Oh, believe me, I do. Half of the reason it's so important I stay in Willow Springs. But I can't do that without your help."

Rebecca pushed herself up to her feet. "Oh no! I have enough problems right now; I don't need to worry about being shunned. The last thing you need is my help with anything."

Eli rolled to his side and flipped his long legs underneath him until he stood beside her. He took her arms in his hands.

"Look, God's plans are rarely meant to heal every pain. His intention is to heal our hearts first by teaching us something, to show us things about ourselves, and to take our human desires away and replace them with His will."

Eli wrapped his fingers around her hands and brought them back up under his chin. "Becca, we are all a work in progress. God takes every one of our fears and insecurities away, so we can be more useful for His future purposes."

He took his finger and tapped her heart. "You are meant to be His ambassador, just like I am, and you can't be that until you seek his forgiveness."

A new set of tears toppled over her dark lashes. "But you don't understand. My own father thinks I'm not worthy enough. How will God ever forgive me for all I've done, let alone you saddle yourself with the likes of me for a lifetime?"

Eli kissed her fingertips. "His provision will only come when you submit yourself to him."

Rebecca closed her eyes against the sudden tears. She wished she had never come. She wished she had never heard what her father honestly thought of her. And most of all, she wished she hadn't let Eli get so close. It only made it harder to tell him no.

"I'm sorry, Eli, it's too much. God will never forgive me, and I cannot let you carry the weight of my burden." She twisted from his grip. And this time, he let her go.

***

The door bounced when she let it go behind her. She didn't dare turn around and look back. The sight of Eli in the doorway would have killed her. He'd fought hard. She'd give him that. But he had no idea what harm would come to him and his family if he brought her into it.

Her feet bounced against the pavement, and her heart took on a new beat. It was like she was running for her life. Far away from Willow Springs with no plans of returning. Her father's plan to send her to Willow Brook was precisely what she needed. Little did he know it was the perfect plan.

Once she made it down Eli's hill, she slowed her pace and stopped to catch her breath. She let her mind drift back to Eli's words. *His intention is to heal our hearts first by teaching us something.* She brushed a hair away that escaped her *kapp* and mumbled, "How on earth am I supposed to learn a thing from all of this? I've learned enough over the years, and that is to keep everyone I care about at arm's length. And besides, haven't I learned enough already? Especially that my own father, couldn't care less about me."

A warm breeze tickled her nose, and she stopped to watch a pair of new lambs romp through the field at the edge of Eli's pasture. A memory as vivid as the day it happened came to mind.

Anguish filled her until she thought her knees would buckle at the weight. It was the day her mother died. The air stood still, and the cries of her *schwesters* echoed off her mother's bedroom walls. The day she realized it was her fault that God took their mother away. Because of her sins, *Mamm* was gone, and no amount of asking forgiveness would change that. She couldn't stay in Willow Springs and pretend that all would be well. With a shuddering sigh, she walked the rest of the way home.

***

Anna twisted a hankie through her fingers. "Emma, I'm worried. Rebecca hasn't gotten out of bed in two days, and she has some silly idea about moving to Willow Brook instead of marrying Eli."

"Marrying Eli?"

Anna laid her fingers over her lips. "*Jah*, she told *Datt* and Wilma that he asked her to marry him. But now, she said that she's changed her mind. Wilma is so set on the whole thing she keeps saying she is just nervous, and she'll come to her senses. Wilma has gone and started her a new wedding dress, and they haven't even been announced at church yet."

Emma sat on the stool at the counter and crossed her legs. "Eli might just be what our *schwester* needs."

Anna walked to the counter and straightened a jar of knitting needles. "You and I know that, but how do we convince Rebecca?"

Emma snickered. "She surely isn't going to take any advice from me. She can barely stand the sight of me. But if anyone can find a way around this, God can."

Anna smiled at Emma. Her *schwester's* faith was strong even though she often wondered if she and Samuel had veered off from their Old Order Amish traditions.

Anna shuffled a stack of patterns and placed them neatly in the holder near the cash register. "I doubt Rebecca puts much faith in God these days. We couldn't even get her to go to church yesterday. Even *Datt's* threats didn't budge her. She claimed she wasn't feeling well, but she doesn't have any signs of being ill."

"Anna, now you can't say that we don't know Rebecca's heart; only God does."

"I suppose, but nothing I say seems to make a mountain of beans. Please, can't you go talk to her? She might listen to you."

Emma slipped from the stool. "I doubt she'll even let me in her room, but I'll try."

Anna wrapped her arms around Emma's middle. "Oh, thank you."

***

Emma opened the kitchen door and snatched a cookie off the tray Wilma held in her hand. "I could smell these cookies clear out in the yarn shop."

"Emma, what a nice surprise. What do I owe this visit to?"

"Anna says Rebecca is feeling under the weather, and I thought I'd come and check on her."

Wilma set the tray on the table and wiped her hands on the towel flipped over her shoulder. "You're braver than I. She's been like a feral cat the last couple of days."

Emma poured a swig of milk in the bottom of a cup and washed down her cookie. "I've had more experience dealing with the likes of Rebecca. Please, don't hold it against her. She hasn't always been like this. Something happened around the time *Mamm* died that tripped her up. Hopefully, we can get to the bottom of it at some point. Until then, all we can do is keep praying for her."

Wilma sunk her hands in dishwater. "You have more patience with her than I do. I would just as soon stay far away. If she's not going to marry Eli, the best thing that girl can do is move to Willow Brook. I've had just about enough of her sour disposition."

"What a cruel thing to say." Emma's lip twitched.

Wilma didn't turn from her dishes. "What do you know? You don't have to live with her anymore."

"*Jah*, but it wouldn't hurt to show her some kindness."

"Kindness? You think that's all it would take?" Wilma gave a brittle laugh.

Emma caught her breath, and heat rose to her cheeks. "Jesus showed kindness even to the Samaritan woman at the well."

"TSK! I wouldn't know about such things. All I know is that girl is a hard one to like. Not sure how your father's kept her in line all these years. Besides, I have no intention to get in the middle of this ridiculous situation. If Eli Bricker is stupid enough to want to marry her, she best take her one and only shot at a husband. Otherwise, she's going to live a long fruitless life. And I'll tell you this. It won't be under this roof."

Quick tears came to Emma's eyes. *How could she speak so unkindly about Rebecca? Yes, her schwester was a bit hard to handle, but there was something much deeper at work with Rebecca. Why couldn't anyone see it? Especially her father.*

Emma knew she wouldn't get anywhere by talking to Wilma. She carried her cup to the sink and left the kitchen without responding to her stepmother's rant.

Her bare feet barely made a sound as she made her way up the hardwood stairs and to her *schwester's* room.

"Rebecca? It's Emma. May I come in?"

Rebecca let her breath out sharply. "If you must."

Emma pushed open the door. "Anna said you're feeling under the weather. Is there anything I can do for you?"

Rebecca pulled the pillow up over her head. "Not unless you can put an end to this day."

"Oh, it can't be that bad."

Emma pulled the pillow from her head. "How about we talk about whatever is bothering you?"

Rebecca pushed herself up and pulled her knees to her chest. "Why do you care?"

Emma sat on the edge of her bed and lifted her chin slightly. "There was a time when you shared everything with Anna and me. Why would this time be any different?"

"That was a long time ago, and much has changed since we were little girls. And besides, you have no idea what's going on in my life."

"*Nee*, I don't. Tell me."

Rebecca looked back at her in despair. "Why should I? So you can look down your nose at me again and prove that you have a perfect life with the perfect husband."

"That's a bit harsh, don't you think? I don't remember ever looking my nose down at you. If that's what you thought, then I owe you an apology because that was never my intention."

Rebecca pulled her nightdress over her knees and hugged them close to her chest. "Why do you bother with me?"

Rebecca's eyes flickered. "Because you're family, and that's what families do. They talk. They help each other through the tough spots in life. And they do as Jesus would do."

With a snip in her tone, Rebecca said, "And what would that be?"

Emma's eyes softened. "He'd love you."

Laying her head on her knees, Rebecca murmured, "First Mary, then Eli, and now you. I'm sick of hearing about God. He doesn't care a bit about me."

Emma laid her hand on her *schwester's* head. "If God has enough forgiveness and patience for me, He certainly has enough for you too."

"And all this talk of Jesus is going to get you into trouble."

Rebecca's eyes sparkled. "If that's what it takes to get His message heard, I'm up for the challenge."

Rebecca turned her face and laid her cheek on her knee as she studied her *schwester*. "Something is different with you and Samuel. What is it?"

Emma shifted and pushed a wrinkle out of her skirt. "If you'll let Him, God's ability to turn today's messes into tomorrow's masterpieces is amazing. But first, you have to forgive yourself for whatever is eating away at you and move on."

In not much more than a whisper, Rebecca responded, "Easy for you to say."

Emma stood. "*Jah, schwester,* it is. And when you're ready to fight your way back into the light, come find me. Then and only then will I show you the way through Jesus."

Rebecca leaned back against the headboard and flipped her legs out straight. "You best not let *Datt* hear you talk like that, or you'll be in more trouble than you're willing to face."

Emma leaned down and whispered, "All things truly do work together for good, no matter how impossible it may seem at first. And the times when I had felt the most alone and unloved were the times when He was developing depths of spiritual maturity I didn't possess yet. So, you see, *schwester* dear, you should be filled with gratitude, not griping during this season."

Face pinched, Rebecca pushed Emma aside and got up and walked to the window. "You have no idea!"

"Then help me understand."

Rebecca's cheeks flushed. "It's too late for me." Moving toward the door, she pushed Emma to the hallway and closed the door in her face.

CHAPTER 15

All the way home, Emma prayed for Rebecca. Her *schwester* was lost and hurting, and she hoped something, anything she might have said, would make a difference. As she walked past her mother-in-law's house, she waved at Ruth as she hung clothes.

From across the yard, she hollered, "Emma, I was just going to pour a glass of tea. Would you like to join me?"

Waving back, she replied, "I'm sure Katie can handle the bakery for a few more minutes."

Ruth dropped the bucket of clothespins in the empty basket at her feet and moved a loose hair off her forehead.

Locking her arm in her daughter-in-law's elbow, she patted her forearm. "It's been weeks since we've had a chance to chat much. This will be nice."

Emma clasped her hand over the older woman's hand. "It has been too long. I stay busy between the bakery and helping Katie and Daniel with Elizabeth. But I'm not complaining. God is good, *jah*?"

Ruth looked down at Emma's middle. "Perhaps soon you and Samuel will give Elizabeth a playmate?"

Emma struggled with what to say. She and Samuel had decided to follow Dr. Smithson's advice and wait two years before trying for another child. That was a decision they kept to themselves since they were going against tradition and preventing a pregnancy that could harm both the child and her.

She gave Ruth a rueful smile. "When God sees fit."

Ruth led Emma up the stairs and pointed to the two rocking chairs. "It's a beautiful day. It's a shame to spend it inside. Sit, I'll go get us a glass of tea."

From where Emma sat, she could see Samuel and Daniel working on a piece of equipment in the barn. Katie was sitting on the porch of the bakery playing with now six-month-old Elizabeth. Life was just about as perfect as things could be, but sitting there enjoying the day while her *schwester* was so troubled left her empty inside. Her mind was spinning with what she could do to help. But then again, it was all in God's hands, and there was nothing she could do but be a messenger.

She was reminded that it wasn't her place to change Rebecca's heart; that was God's job. All she could do was plant the seed. It would be up to Him to see it flourish and take root. Oh, how she prayed Rebecca could be free of whatever was bothering her.

Ruth pushed open the screen door with her hip, walked over, and handed Emma a cool drink. "Did you go visit your *Datt* and Wilma?"

"*Jah*, I hadn't seen my *schwesters* in a few days, so I walked down to check on them."

"All is well with Anna and Rebecca?"

"Rebecca is a little under the weather, but Anna is doing well."

Ruth took a sip of tea before asking, "I noticed Rebecca wasn't at church. I hope everything is okay?"

Emma sat her tea on the stand between them and sighed. "I think my *schwester's* problems are more emotional than health-related."

Both women set their chairs in motion and let the early June breeze fill the silence between them.

"Emma, do you think this would be a good time to give Rebecca your mother's gift?"

Emma brought her hands to her lips. "I'd forgotten about *Mamm's* gift. Oh, Ruth, this would be the perfect time for Rebecca to get a little piece of *Mamm*. It might just be what she needs."

"Do you want me to give it to her, or do you want to?"

"Oh, no, Ruth, it will mean more coming from you. Do you think you'd have time to give it to her today?"

From across the yard, they heard Katie call out. "Emma, can you come to take care of the customers? I need to put Elizabeth down for a nap."

Emma waved in Katie's direction and smiled before saying, "I best be going. Thanks for the tea, but more importantly, thank you for agreeing to see Rebecca. *Mamm's* shawl saw me through some of my roughest days after James died. I'll pray it will comfort Rebecca as well."

Emma picked up her pace toward Katie and Elizabeth. She only stopped for a second to kiss her niece's forehead before heading into the bakery.

***

Rebecca sat on the edge of her bed, brushing the snarls out of her hair from being in bed for two days. Emma's visit left her questioning so many things, so she wanted to take a walk to clear her head from the swirling thoughts. *Gratitude, not griping. I don't see one thing I have to be grateful for.*

Wilma's voice pierced the air. "Rebecca. Ruth Yoder is here to see you. Do you want me to send her up, or will you come down?"

Throwing her brush on the bed, she twisted her hair in a bun and pinned it at the back of her head. "I'll be down in a minute," she bellowed back.

Of all people, the last person she wanted to see was her mother's best friend. All Ruth would do was remind her that her mother was long gone, and she had no one to turn to when life was unbearable. She slipped on a fresh dress, pinned it closed, and headed down the stairs.

Ruth stood in the kitchen holding a white gift box. When she turned to face her, she held the package out in front of her.

Rebecca asked, "What's this?"

Ruth looked over her shoulder. "Wilma, do you mind if I speak to Rebecca in private for a minute?"

"Better you than me!"

Ruth's eyebrows furrowed, and she gave the woman a snarled look. "I won't keep her but a minute. Perhaps we will go sit on the porch; I wouldn't want to bother your bread-making."

"Suit yourself. I don't get much help from the girl anyway. Take as long as you please. Maybe you can talk some sense into her."

Ruth put her hand under Rebecca's elbow and guided her to the front porch. "Let's sit outside. There is a nice breeze to keep us cool."

Ruth pointed to the swing at the far end of the porch. "It's been a long time since I've sat on your mother's swing. How about we settle there?"

Rebecca steadied the box on her lap and asked, "Am I supposed to open this?"

"In a minute. Let me explain." Ruth laid her hand on the package and tapped it ever so gently. "The summer before your mother passed, she made each of you girls a little something to remember her by. She made me promise to present each of you her gift when I felt you needed it the most."

Rebecca's eyes welled with tears. "A gift for me, from *Mamm*?"

"*Jah*, for you. Please don't be upset with Emma, but she mentioned you had some things you were struggling with right now. And I felt this might be a good time for you to have a little piece of your *mamm*."

A sob lodged in the back of Rebecca's throat, and it closed around it, preventing her from speaking clearly. In a broken cry, she replied, "It's the … bes … best … time."

Ruth stood and placed her hand on Rebecca's shoulder. "I'd better be going. I have a list of chores to finish this forenoon. But please know that even though I can never replace your *mamm*, I'm always there to lend a shoulder to cry on if so need be."

Rebecca wiped a tear from her chin and swallowed hard. "I know."

Ruth put her arm around her. "Whatever has you so broken, please remember … joy comes from within. Dig deep into what you want out of life and make it happen. Don't wait for it to come to you. Go after it and hold on tight. Only then will you find relief from what troubles you."

Trembling slightly, Rebecca nodded. "*Denki*, Ruth."

Waiting until Ruth had made it off the porch, she gripped the sides of the box tightly. A small piece of her mother lay inside. It was like a dream playing out in slow motion as she removed the cover.

Folding back the pink tissue paper, she ran her hand along the tightly woven stitches of a crocheted shawl. She picked it up and held the soft fibers to her cheek.

She remembered watching her *mamm* sit on this same swing and work the tiny stitches. Little did she know the cascading shades of cream and white would one day belong to her.

Opening her eyes, she saw a pink envelope in the bottom of the box with her name written neatly across the front. Her mother's perfect penmanship brought a fresh tear to her eye as she retrieved the letter.

Rebecca,

My darling firstborn daughter. You came into this world crying loudly until you heard the whimper of your baby schwester. Always Anna's protector, I knew there would come a day when you, too, needed someone to come to your rescue.

My days are but short on this earth, and I wanted to leave a little something you could find comfort in once I was long gone.

Always my strong-willed child, you often tried to hide your pain. Perhaps you are afraid someone might recognize your weakness. Rebecca, please hear me. It is okay to be real around those who love you. If we can't be vulnerable around the people who mean the most to us, what kind of life is that?

I have no idea what troubles you on this day, but I know one person who can show you the way to true freedom from whatever pain you're running from. Jesus.

If Mary Bricker is still alive when you read this, please go to her. She is the one person in this community who will show you the truth.

I pray you will wrap yourself in this shawl on those days that seem too much to handle and remember me. Find comfort in knowing I left this world knowing my salvation was given freely. Just as it is for you. It doesn't matter what you've done. He loves you and is waiting for you to call His name. All you have to do is call on Him.

You may think you are hiding your pain, but your pain is hiding you. Put your faith in the one who washes all pain away. He will set you free.

All my love,
Mamm

Even though the sun settled on her shoulders, Rebecca wrapped the delicate piece around her. Closing her eyes and pulling herself into a hug, she imagined her mother's arms holding her tight as she thought. *Oh, Mamm, I need you so, it's been so hard without you. Every day seems harder than the next. You're so right. I am running from a pain so deep I'm not sure I'll survive. I don't understand what you're trying to tell me. Please, Mamm, I wish it were more apparent. I can't go to Mary, she's gone too. I miss your face, the sound of your voice. Please tell me what to do.*

When she opened her eyes, two doves had settled on the ground beneath the bird feeder. Her *mamm* told her doves always traveled in pairs. Where you saw one, you'd see another.

Tucking the letter back in its envelope, she placed the empty box on the floor and walked off the porch. Ignoring Wilma's voice from inside, she headed to the bakery. She had to find out if Emma had received a box from *Mamm* as well.

***

The wind blew traces of strawberries and sugar through the air the closer Rebecca got to Katie and Emma's Bakery. Just as she and Anna had dreams of opening a yarn shop, Katie and Emma spent their childhood dreaming of a bakery. Strawberry season was in full swing, and pies and tarts filled the shelves at the popular fruit stand that held the new bakery.

Letting a group of English tourists' step before her, Rebecca slipped behind the counter and pulled Emma aside.

"What is it, Rebecca? I'm right in the middle of helping a customer."

"Please, Emma, I need to talk to you."

"Katie, can you take over for me for a minute?"

The dark-haired young woman set a piping bag down on the counter and wiped her hands on a towel. "Take your time. That was the last pie I needed to make for the day."

Emma pulled Rebecca into the kitchen and picked up a cup of water. "What's so important it couldn't wait ten minutes?"

Rebecca flipped the white shawl from her shoulders and held it out to her *schwester*. "Did you receive one of these too?" Emma sat on the stool at the counter and nodded.

"*Jah*."

"When?"

"After we lost James."

"Has Anna?"

"Not that I'm aware of. I think Ruth was only to give them to us if she saw us struggling with something."

Rebecca pulled a stool close to Emma. "Did she write you a letter?"

"She did, and I can honestly say she helped save my life."

The words startled her. "How so?"

"I'm not sure what *Mamm* said to you, and you don't need to share that with me. But if she told you anything close to what she told me, you're on your way to discover some pretty amazing things."

She sat, looking pale. Leaning forward, she rested her chin in her hand and struggled not to cry. "Did she talk about Jesus?"

Emma's breath relaxed. "*Jah*."

"And?"

"I discovered the truth."

Rebecca closed her eyes. "I'm trying to understand. But I don't see how Jesus can set me free."

Emma took a few moments to compile her thoughts before she answered. But before she did, the conversation with Samuel about how they had convinced Eli she wasn't in love with him rang loudly in her ear. Wrapping her feet around the legs of the stool, Emma braced herself for Rebecca's rebuttal.

"My battle was much different from yours, but *Mamm* pointed me toward the one person who could help me heal."

Rebecca switched elbows and started to tap her fingers on the worktable. "She said I needed to have faith in the one who could set me free." Rebecca sat up straight and asked, "I've been saved. How much more faith do I need?"

Emma watched her struggle to put all the pieces together, took in a deep breath, and let it out slowly before answering.

"Going through the motions of baptism and the traditions set in place by our forefathers means nothing."

Rebecca put her hand over Emma's mouth and whispered, "Shhh… you can't be saying things like that. What if someone hears you? They will excommunicate you!"

Grabbing Rebecca's hand, she leaned in closer. "Listen to me. The Bible doesn't lie. Neither does God. It's in black and white – if you believe in Jesus, you will have eternal life and be free from whatever you are carting around. That's what *Mamm* meant by having faith. You need to believe that your one true counselor, savior, and Messiah is Jesus Christ. It's who you put your faith in that matters in the end. It's not how you follow a set of rules or how good you are."

Emma took her index finger and tapped on Rebecca's chest ever so lightly. "It's not about the outward appearance or rituals this community is so set on. It's what is in here that counts. It will take a change of heart for you to truly grasp what *Mamm* is trying to teach you."

Rebecca pushed her hand away. "I'm scared for you. *Datt* will go to the bishop if he gets word of how you're talking."

"I don't care about that right now. All I care about is showing you that Jesus is the answer." Emma looked at the line of customers building up. "I have to go help Katie, but before I do, you need to think about this... confession will set you free."

Emma rose and looked at her apologetically. "If you get it out in the open, it will lose its power over you."

Rebecca was left sitting alone to ponder her *schwester's* words. A heaviness pushed at her chest, wanting to escape as she thought. *Could Emma be right? Was it time she was honest with herself and with God? Oh, how she wished she understood all the things Mary, Mamm, and now Emma were trying to show her.*

As she walked out of the bakery, she said a prayer that her *datt* and the bishop wouldn't get wind of what Emma was saying. But if what she said was true, then all the lies, secrets, and deception could be forgiven.

Lost deep in thought, she stepped out in front of a car. A sudden beep forced her to jump away from its bumper. As she waved at the woman behind the wheel, she focused on a large sticker pasted to the side of the vehicle. YOUR PAST DOESN'T DEFINE YOUR FUTURE.

CHAPTER 16

Eli caught his breath as he watched Rebecca step out in front of the car, maneuvering its way into the parking lot. He chose to stay hidden in the shadows of the workshed as soon as he saw her walk down the bakery steps. It had been a couple of days since he let her run away. It pained him to think she carried around something so hurtful it would keep her from finding true happiness. After stewing for days, he left the farm in search of the one person who might help him find a way to get through to her.

Samuel wiped his hands on a red shop rag and walked up to stand beside him. Nodding his head in Rebecca's direction, he asked, "She's wound pretty tight. Are you sure you want to untangle that knotted-up mess?"

Eli stepped back to make sure he stayed hidden. "I look at it as making an investment in my future."

"I suppose you're right. Those Byler girls do get under your skin. Ain't so?"

Eli stood up straighter. "I need to convince her there is more to life than the box she's put herself in."

"Well, you best figure it out soon. Emma says she's planning on leaving for the job in Willow Brook next week."

Reaching for the brim of his straw hat, Eli pulled it tighter on his forehead. "She's not going anywhere if I have anything to say about it."

As he started to walk from the shed, Samuel stated, "Don't forget our meeting tomorrow night at eight. Daniel and Katie will be there along with Emma and me. There is a good chance that Henry and Maggie Schrock are joining us. We have to discuss what we will do if word leaks out about our bible studies. Please don't bring your buggy. We don't want to bring any attention to the house. We will be meeting in the basement, so no one driving by will see the lights.

"Henry Schrock? He was just appointed minister. How did that come about?"

"He's been talking with Daniel. Word has it that his community in Elkhart, Indiana, was much different from here. Daniel said he's having a hard time conforming to our Old Order ways, which are so different from how he was raised."

"I bet now that he's a minister and in the middle of everything, he's figuring out what we already know."

"*Jah*, things are going to get a little hairy around here before too long, and we need to be prepared." Samuel slapped Eli and the shoulder. "See you tomorrow?"

"*Jah*."

Samuel stopped and replied in a hushed tone. "Be certain where Rebecca's loyalty lies before you breathe a word about any of this to her."

Clearly, that was a message that didn't sit well with Eli. "I'm fully aware of where we all need to stand on these issues."

Samuel hesitated before answering. "I just know how vindictive Rebecca has been in the past. If she thinks for one minute that she can use something against Emma, she'll use it no questions asked."

Eli knew Samuel was right, but he still couldn't stand to hear any ill words spoken about the woman who had her heart all entangled with his. "We all need to be trusting in God, and that includes Rebecca. You just worry about Emma and let me take care of Becca."

Samuel smiled slightly. "Becca?"

Eli gave a nod and left without another word.

***

Eli set his buggy in the direction of the Feed & Seed. So much of him wanted to follow Rebecca down Mystic Mill Road. Still, the determination in her step left him turning the opposite direction. He needed more time to think and ponder the words he needed to convince her to stay.

***

Rebecca stood at the end of Eli's driveway and looked around the farm. His buggy horse was not in the padlock, and the barn door where he stored his cart was open. As far as she could tell, he was gone. Did she dare go inside the house? She wanted to feel a sense of Mary and wished she could talk to her.

Why had *Mamm* told her to speak to Mary? All this talk of truth and forgiveness and being set free was swirling around in her head. Wrapping her mother's shawl around her shoulders tighter, she headed to the house.

Guilt assaulted her as she pushed the kitchen door open. Shame filled her, but only for a second until her need for peace took over her better judgment. The kitchen sink was stacked with dirty dishes, and she couldn't help but smile as she thought. *Things never change.*

Mary's sweater still hung on the peg by the front door as she walked through the living room. The woman's presence clung to every part of the home, much like the pleats in the blue curtains. From its blue doors to its white clapboard siding, every house in Willow Springs looked the same. However, the secrets hidden behind each door were what kept them separated, even in Mary and Eli's home.

Sinking down in Mary's chair, she laid her head back and looked out into the kitchen. Sitting on the top of the hutch in the corner of the room was the bible she'd seen Eli place out of sight. She closed her eyes and thought. *Don't do it, Rebecca! It's one thing to walk in his house when he's not here. But looking through his private things?*

Opening her eyes, she swallowed hard and moved toward the hutch. She reached up and grasped the black leather Bible with a shaky hand. She had never held an English bible, and her father's German Bible was large and not comfortable in her hand. Let alone she'd never learned to read German. She relied on her father and the ministers to interpret the old language. The smooth cover rested easily in her palm as she fingered the fine paper inside with her other hand. Tucked in between the pages were notes and pages marked with string.

The tiny hairs on her forearms tingled as she read a few notes Eli had written in the margin. An English version was strictly forbidden but holding the book that held Eli's most private thoughts left her wanting more of him.

The cold floor seeped through her bare feet, and a strange feeling overcame her clear to the top of her head. When her thumb met a folded yellow-lined piece of paper tucked tightly between the pages, she stopped when she saw her name.

She fought the urge to open the sheet of paper. Instead, her eyes followed the underlined text. THEN YOU WILL KNOW THE TRUTH, AND THE TRUTH WILL SET YOU FREE.

The book slid from her hands, as did the letter with her name on it. She couldn't run fast enough from the house. Turning the corner, she ran smack dab into Eli's arms. His bold shoulders absorbed her body without even losing his footing.

She swung from his hold, but not before he grabbed her arm and pulled her back into his chest. "Oh, no, you don't. I'm not letting you run away so fast this time."

Rebecca sighed heavily. "Please, Eli, let me go."

"*Nee!* I'm not letting you go. You came here for a reason. What is it?"

"I'm sorry, I shouldn't have come."

"But you did, and I'm not letting you leave until we talk."

He pulled her in close and whispered, "Why are you running from me?"

She placed her hands on his chest. "Because you deserve better."

He lifted her chin until their eyes met. "Better than what? A woman so set in running from what she truly wants because she thinks her sins are worse than anyone else's?"

"They are?"

He rested his forehead on hers. "But you're wrong. We all have secrets and sins that hold us captive."

She tried to push him back. "Not like mine."

He dropped his hold, took her by the hand, and led her into the house. His bible and notes were scattered on the floor when he stepped inside. He didn't say a word but stooped down, picked them up, and placed them on the table. Pointing to the chair nearest his at the head of the table, he said, "Please sit; I want to read you something."

"Eli, please."

"Please, Becca, hear me out. If what I'm about to read doesn't make sense, I promise I'll let you go home."

For the first time in months, she had no more fight left in her. Exhausted, she sat in the chair and folded her hands on her lap. She waited for him to question her about the book on the floor, but he said nothing.

Taking his seat beside her, he turned toward the back of the book. "This comes from John 8, Verse 12. *When Jesus spoke again to the people, he said, "I am the light of the world. Whoever follows me will never walk in darkness, but will have the light of life."*

She held onto his every word as he continued to read through the chapter in the Book of John, until he concluded with: *"If you hold onto my teachings, you are my disciples. Then you will know the truth, and the truth will set you free."*

Rebecca frowned and dropped her head. She couldn't look into his eyes; they held so much hope. More than she had for herself.

Seconds turned into minutes, and the only sound was the constant tick-tock from the clock on the wall. Not until he laid his hand over hers, still clenched together in her lap, did she look up. With a gentle squeeze to her fingers, he said, "If we confess. He forgives."

A small gasp escaped her lips when his words hit such a tender spot. In an instant, a buzzing took place in her ears, and she was afraid she might pass out before she answered, "Not me. Even if God does, you won't."

"*Jah*, Becca, I will."

Eli moved to the floor and knelt beside her. "You don't give me enough credit. Please, let me be the light that shines brightness into your darkness. We all fail at times, but I promise you I will not fail you. Let me show you all the things no one ever explained to you."

Her tears dropped on her hand, and he picked it up and kissed them away. He leaned in and rested his head on hers. She closed her eyes and let his voice carry them away. She had never heard a man pray out loud before. Still, the husky tone of his voice mingled together with a sureness she'd never experienced before; he lifted her up in prayer. Without any hesitation, she knew more than anything else she'd ever known; Eli Bricker knew God, and God knew Eli Bricker.

He finished with: *"Heavenly Father, open Becca's heart and show her that those you want to use are those who are not perfect. In Jesus' name, Amen."*

Listening to him read from the bible to his outward boldness of petitioning God on her behalf left her speechless. At that moment, she knew she needed to take a chance on love and pour her heart out to the one and only man she'd ever loved. If Eli trusted and had faith in what God could do, she wanted the same reassurance.

She didn't budge. She didn't want the connection they had to leave. He had a hold on her heart, and she felt the rough edges fall away. Without opening her eyes, she whispered, "You may not want anything to do with me once you hear what I've done."

He moved his lips to her forehead and whispered back, "Try me."

She moved her head away from his, twisted from his grip, and walked to the window. When he tried to follow, she quickly said, "Please stay. I can't bear to watch the disappointment on your face."

He moved to his chair. Rebecca crossed her arms over her chest and stared out the window. Then began to tell him her darkest secrets.

"I could have saved Billy Gingerich from getting hit by that truck. But I didn't. I ignored his mother's screams and let him run past me because I was so wrapped up in myself."

She waited for Eli to say something, anything, but when he didn't, she continued to look out the window and kept going.

"Samuel knew what I did and didn't tell anyone. He waited for me to confess, and when I didn't, it'd been too long, so I blackmailed him into lying to you."

The air in the room was still. A chill ran down Rebecca's spine right before she felt his calloused hands rest on her shoulders. Her back stiffened at his touch. She wouldn't allow herself to relax until she told it all.

"It was my turn to be with my mother, but I couldn't sit a minute longer, so I went to the barn. She died all by herself because of my own selfish desires."

"Samuel and Emma lost James because of me. God used their baby as a sacrifice to my sin."

Eli took a deep breath but didn't say a word as he blew it out close to her ear.

"Your grandmother died alone. You trusted me to care for her, but again I chose myself over doing what was right."

She turned and faced him. "I'm not worthy of God or anyone else."

Eli pulled her into his chest and rested his chin on the top of her head. "Becca, no one can know when it's someone's time to go. And whether you were there or not, it's not your fault."

She raised her hands to his chest and buried her face in her palms. "I'm certain it was God's way of punishing me."

He pulled her hands away from her face. "You're wrong. God doesn't punish like that. He loves us, and that includes you."

She looked up into his eyes. "But you? Can you love me knowing all this?"

"I've never stopped loving you."

Through a quick blush, she asked, "But all the warnings my *datt* gave you?"

Fighting back the tears, Rebecca looked at him with pleading eyes. "I even came into your house uninvited."

His face filled with compassion. "If I remember correctly, it's your house too."

In a quieter tone she said, "Still, I had no right."

Until that moment, she had no way of knowing how Eli would react to her confession. But his arms engulfed her, and she relaxed under his embrace.

His cheek rested on the side of her head, and he asked, "Is there anything else? Now is the time to get everything out in the open."

Trembling, she knew she had to tell one more secret that wasn't hers to tell. Eli must have sensed her hesitation because he leaned back and lifted her chin. "What is it, Becca?"

"I know *Mommi* Mary's secret."

Her eyes burned with tears in anticipation of revealing the secret that ruined his family's internal relationship. "It's horrible, and I can see why Noah wanted her to take it to the grave."

Eli sank down in the nearest chair. "I hate the thought of you having to carry around such knowledge, but I'm not sure I want to hear what my grandfather felt was so important that he wanted to keep it hidden."

Rebecca nodded. "She loved your father and tried to protect him, much like Noah protected her. Only your father couldn't see it that way. He blamed her, and I'm certain that came once your father moved to Lancaster."

Eli held her gaze. "Why do you think that?"

She sat down in the chair beside him and picked up his hand. "I think your great-grandfather brainwashed your father into believing things that weren't true."

Eli rested his arms on the back of the table and stretched his legs out in front of him. "Will anything good come from knowing the truth?"

She crossed her legs and pondered his question. After a few seconds, she responded, "Not for you, because you loved your grandmother unconditionally. But it might help your father understand why he couldn't see his parents for what they truly were."

"Then maybe I need to know. My father holds a great deal of resentment for them both. Maybe he could get some relief from the bitterness he holds."

"Oh, he's going to hold bitterness, I'm sure, but it won't be for Mary and Noah."

Despair filled him as Rebecca explained how his great-grandfather had taken advantage of Mary, leaving her with child. To prevent her any more embarrassment Noah took the blame and quietly moved her to Willow Springs.

Eli was confident the pain on his face was the same as the agony reflected on Rebecca's as she shared what she knew.

He leaned forward and rested his elbows on his knees. "What am I supposed to do with that?"

Rebecca moved closer. "Maybe take it to God?"

A slight smile escaped his lips. "There's hope for you yet, Becca Byler."

She put a hand on his arm. "Can I change my answer about marrying you?"

"Only after you hear me out. I have a confession to make myself. Only then will I let you make your decision. You may not want anything to do with me after hearing what I have to share. It will change your life forever."

She patted his arm. "I doubt I'll change my mind, but if you can forgive me, then whatever you have to say makes no difference in my world."

She noticed he didn't look at her while he struggled with finding the words that rolled around in his head.

"There's a good chance if you marry me, we will be excommunicated and asked to leave the church."

Rebecca's response was confident. "Eli Bricker, I will follow you anywhere."

"I don't think you fully understand. I have been attending private bible studies with Samuel and Daniel. Even Emma and Katie have been joining in. We have been studying God's word and learning so many truths that have changed the way we look at our eternal salvation and what God has planned for our lives."

"Does this have anything to do with what is going on with Samuel and Emma? If so, I want to be part of it."

His face went white and bleak. "It may mean you won't be able to speak to your father or Anna. You've already been baptized, so we will be shunned for certain."

Eli saw the determination on her face. "Things are going to change, but I can't promise you it will be easy. The elders of our community will not accept us."

"Please, Eli, I want what Emma has. I want to know the God that's shown you so much grace that you can forgive me as well. I want to truly know the God who loves me even more than my own father does."

Eli took her in his arms and brushed a soft kiss on her cheek. "I promise to protect you and cherish you forever, but what I'm asking you to do will affect your life forever."

She laid her hand on his cheek. "I'm tired of facing things alone. I eagerly want to hear all you have to say. If that means I must leave my old life behind, again, I'll follow you anywhere."

CHAPTER 17

The following two weeks were a complete blur of activity. Neither Eli nor Rebecca had another chance to speak about going against the *Ordnung*. After Eli spoke to Jacob, Wilma returned to work on wedding plans with Anna's help.

While it was highly uncommon for a wedding to occur during the summer months, Eli got special permission from Rebecca's father after sharing the stipulation to keep his grandmother's farm.

Until Rebecca overheard a conversation between Wilma and her father, she hadn't thought twice about what lay ahead. Walking in on their private conversation initiated a pretty intense warning from her father. After that, she was more anxious to get out from under her father's roof and away from Wilma and her meddling ways.

Standing in her room on the morning of her wedding, she allowed Anna to help her pin her new royal blue dress together at the waist.

Anna removed a straight pin she held between her lips and asked, "Are you nervous?"

"Excited, I guess."

"How about you? Are you excited to be one of my side sitters with Ben Kauffman?"

Anna curled her lip upward. "I've thought of nothing else the last few days."

"Whatever happened between Ben's *bruder,* Simon, and you?"

"Now, *schwester*, today is not the day to speak of such things. This is your day, not mine."

Rebecca let Anna help her put on her new white apron and replayed her father's warning in her head.

***

Wilma dried her hands on a towel and lowered her voice. "It's best she gets out from under your care before the bishop gets word of what's going on. It wouldn't look good for you if you had to shun not one of your daughters but two. Especially if she still lived under your roof. We can only hope Anna doesn't fall prey to their influence."

Rebecca came up the basement steps unnoticed and stopped in the doorway when her father's eyes met hers.

"What do you know about meetings being held at your *schwester's*?"

Without answering his direct questions, she was quick to respond. "I haven't attended any meetings at Emma's. Why do you ask?"

Wilma pulled a chair out and let out a sharp "TSK."

Rebecca's heart picked up a beat as she waited for her father to probe further.

"Eli's been seen spending a good amount of time at Samuel's and Daniel's lately. Do you know what that might be about?"

Swift with her response, she said, "They're friends. Why would it be strange they spend time together?"

Her father gripped the arms of his chair. "I'd think they'd have better use of their time."

Wilma gave a slight shrug. "You're awful lucky your father could petition for this early wedding. I would hope you wouldn't do anything that might tarnish his position."

Rebecca looked back at her and bit her tongue. No amount of pushing Wilma's buttons the day before her wedding would prove to solve anything. "I've been too busy the last couple of weeks to pay any attention to where Eli's been." While it wasn't a lie, she surely wasn't going to divulge the little she did know.

Her father tipped his mouth in a bitter frown. "It's best to remember that Eli just switched his church membership to this district, and the both of you are now baptized members of this community."

Her mouth flattened, and she swallowed hard at his warning. "*Jah*," was all she could mutter as she walked through the kitchen and up the stairs to her room.

***

That was last night, and she spent a good part of her evening on her knees begging once again for God's forgiveness. There wasn't anything that would keep her from marrying Eli, not even a stern warning from her father.

***

"Rebecca, did you hear me?"

"*Jah* and be careful with those pins!"

Anna could tell something was bothering her *schwester,* and she hoped it was just wedding jitters. "You seem wound tighter than a rabbit caught in a cage. What are you so deep in thought about this morning?"

Rebecca took Anna's hand. "Please promise me no matter what happens, you'll always find a way to see me."

Anna squeezed her hand. "What's that supposed to mean? We run the yarn shop together; why wouldn't we see each other? Do you have plans to start a family right away?"

A nervous giggle escaped Rebecca's lips. "Only God knows that. I was just worried we wouldn't get to spend as much time together."

Anna tipped her chin. "Who are you, and what have you done with my *schwester*?"

"I don't have any idea what you are referring to."

Anna reached up and pulled Rebecca's new starched white *kapp* in place and asked, "Come on now. The *schwester* I know was a bit tattered and torn. This person is softer around the edges, and if that is what marrying Eli did to you, I need to thank him personally."

Rebecca grabbed her hand and pulled her toward the door. "We better get to Ruth and Levi's before the guests start to arrive. Eli might think I changed my mind if he doesn't see me there early."

Anna pulled back. "So, you're not going to answer me? What has gotten into you today?"

Rebecca grinned her way. "I suppose you need to thank Eli for the change you see in me. He helped me see things aren't always as bad as I've made them out to be over the years."

Anna rolled her eyes. “Where has he been my whole life? If I knew all it would take was for you to fall in love, I would have pushed Eli under your nose a lot sooner.”

Anna let Rebecca drag her from the room, and they chatted giddily as they walked next door to the Yoder’s where the wedding would take place.

The day was full of firsts. Every hurdle Rebecca thought she had to climb herself was replaced with Eli taking charge and being by her side. She was touched by his tenderness and attentiveness throughout the day. Even the solemn looks of her father and Wilma did little to dampen her joyful mood. By the time the wedding ended close to eleven that evening, Eli had bent down and whispered in her ear, “I think it’s time to take my wife home. Are you ready?”

A smile filled her face, and a flash of heat rose from her neck and settled on her cheeks. She savored every minute of their twenty-minute walk back to the Bricker Farm. They would return early the next day to help clean up from the day-long activity, but at that moment and for the rest of her life, she would treasure the feel of Eli’s strong, calloused hand in hers.

***

The warm soil felt good beneath Rebecca’s bare feet as she worked the earth in the garden. When her hoe caught a clump of Mary’s Johnny Jump-ups, she fell to her knees and gently buried the roots. She fell back on folded knees and looked around. The July sun beat on her back, and she marveled at how everything looked well and alive under Eli and her care. She had spent weeks working on Mary’s gardens and prayed she was smiling down on her from above.

Only when her father’s buggy stopped alongside the fence where Eli was working did the hairs on the back of her arms stand up. Being too far to hear their conversation, she knew her husband's stance was one of concern.

***

The steady clip-clop of an approaching buggy alerted Eli's attention away from the sheep he tended to in the pasture. When the metal wheels stopped behind him, he released the young lamb from his grip and turned toward the road.

Eli walked to the fence and waited until Jacob stepped down from his brown-topped buggy.

The lines etched on the old man's face deepened. "I fear trouble is at your doorstep."

Eli took his straw hat off and wiped his brow before returning the sweat-laden hat back to his head. "Trouble? What kind of trouble might that be?"

Eli's face burned hot. No doubt he knew what was coming, but Jacob would need to spell it out clearly before he yielded to his comment.

Stiffening his shoulders, Jacob asked, "Did you not promise to obey the teaching of our forefathers?"

Balancing his foot on the bottom rung of the picket fence, Eli leaned on his knee. "And didn't you agree to teach your church the ways of the Lord?"

Eli watched Jacob's neck turn red, and the vein that ran alongside his temple twitched. He stared at him for a moment, unsure if he should interfere with Jacob's thoughts. Who could blame the older man's confusion at Eli's rebuttal? But Eli wasn't about to let Jacob Byler intimidate him, even if he was Rebecca's father.

"I would hope and pray you would adhere to the traditions of our community when you married my daughter. We are a unified people, and change comes with a price. *Jah*?"

Eli stood up straight and didn't take his eyes from his father-in-law's. "And what would that price be?"

Jacob clenched his jaw and then let out an exasperated sigh. After coughing, he wiped his hand on his trouser leg and continued, "I'd prefer Rebecca not work at the yarn shop."

Silence pressed between them until Eli replied. "That is Rebecca's business. How can you forbid her to work?"

"My word is final. Until we clear up these rumors that are landing on your doorstep, I forbid Rebecca to work with Anna."

Eli was quick to stand his ground. “Then I’ll move the shop here to the farm.”

“You’ll do no such thing unless you’re prepared to buy me out. I footed the bill for that shop and its contents. Are you in a position to do so?”

The muscle in Eli’s jaw flexed as he clenched his teeth. Jacob knew he sunk every penny he had into fixing up his farm. “Not at the moment, but I’ll find a way.”

Jacob turned and climbed back inside his waiting buggy. Before he pulled away, he added, “There is one quick and easy way to settle this matter.”

“What’s that?”

“Put a stop to these rumors and step into obedience to the *Ordnung*.”

There was no way Eli didn’t understand what Jacob was referring to. The man had just given him an ultimatum. He could succumb to their Old Order ways, or he would be forced to forbid Rebecca from running the yarn shop. Both seemed impossible compromises.

Jacob snapped the reins and looked back at Eli one last time before pulling back out in the road. “You’re destined to hell if you choose to turn your back on your promises.”

Without replying to the old man’s threat, he thought. *God has a purpose for my life, and a few wordy threats won’t deter me from the path God’s put me on.*

***

Rebecca placed the hoe and rake in the wheelbarrow and moved it to the back of the house. From the open window, the chime on the kitchen clock rang five. A hollow void filled her stomach as she watched the two men from afar. Something was amiss, and she was dying to know why her husband's stance took on a protective guard.

After moving to the kitchen, she washed her hands and kept a steady eye on the road. If the conversation had been meant for her, she would have been invited, but rarely did such things happen. The man of the house would be held responsible for all household members.

Her father pulled away and instantly encouraged his buggy horse to pick up his trot. It was unusual for her *datt* to push the old mare so quickly. Hoping Eli would return to the house, she promptly went to work, pulling out the potato salad and ham slices she had prepared earlier. With no breeze flowing through the house's open windows, she gathered things to carry out to the picnic table under the maple tree in the front yard.

Keeping an eye on the barn for Eli, she snapped the checkered tablecloth on the table and neatly set supper out. Returning to the house only once to pour two glasses with water, she returned to find Eli straddling a bench at the table.

Nodding her head in the direction of the road, she asked. "What did my father want?"

Eli glanced at the road. "He came with a warning."

"Oh, no, that doesn't sound good."

Eli patted the bench beside him. "Please sit. We need to talk." He proceeded to tell her everything, along with his refusal to permit her to work at the yarn shop.

"But how can he forbid me to work? That is my shop, not his."

Eli reached for her hand. "Did you pay for the construction cost?"

"*Nee.*"

"Did you pay for any of the inventory to get it opened?"

"Nee."

"Have you contributed anything to the overall maintenance of the building other than preparing the fiber for sale?"

"Nee."

"Then I'm sorry, my love. You don't own that shop. He does."

Her mouth trembled. "Can he really do this?"

"I'm afraid he can. But I don't want you to worry. I'll figure out a way for you to keep the shop, or you'll open a new one here."

"But what about the rumors he hinted at. Did he tell you exactly what he'd heard?"

"*Nee*, he didn't. But I have to assume the way he warned me of hell, he's caught wind of our bible studies. Or he at least suspects we are pushing the lines of our baptismal promises."

Rebecca's lips quivered. "This is just the beginning, isn't it?"

He pulled her close and rested his head near her ear. "I've been seeking answers long before your father came into my life. Not one of the ministers or even the bishop could confidently answer my questions. Only Henry Schrock gave me the time of day when I pointed out some scripture for clarity." He paused and turned her head, so he could look into her eyes. "God never promised it would be easy to follow Him. But I have faith that we are on a path that will glorify Him the most. I'm not giving up my bible in exchange for a list of man-made rules and traditions. Even if that means you'll lose the yarn shop, and we are asked to leave the church."

She took in a small gasp and reached for his hand. "Even if it means I lose the yarn shop, I promised to follow you, and I trust you will do what is best for our family."

Eli bowed his head and prayed over their meal, including a short prayer for Jacob. When he lifted his head, he stated, "Your father is only following what he's been taught his whole life. Please don't hold anything against him. He was given a great responsibility to this district that he must abide by. Which includes keeping us in line."

Rebecca put a scoop of salad on his plate, handed him two bread slices for his ham, and asked, "Have you read the German Bible?"

Holding his sandwich to his mouth, he answered, "I don't understand a word of it, and my guess is most of the ministers don't either. We're encouraged to read from a bible we don't understand. And the bishop doesn't understand why so many of our youth have questions."

Rebecca took a sip of water and thought about his response. "*Datt* always said to read too much was giving the devil a way to eat away at our soul."

Eli snickered and shook his head. "That comes from fear of the unknown. Maybe I need to show your *datt* a thing or two about what scripture really says."

The bite of salad Rebecca held in her mouth went down wrong, and she coughed. When she finally was able to wash it down with another sip of water, she said, "Good luck with that."

Rebecca played with a fork of salad on her plate and tipped her head in his direction. "He's also been known to say, 'Unified people hide their knowledge for the sake of the community. It's what keeps our kind separated from the world. When too much learning seeps in, the community is sure to divide'."

"Well, he might be onto something there."

"Ya know what, Eli?"

"What's that?"

"I think it's about time this community gets stirred up some."

He snickered at her sureness. "That's good; because it's going to take a whole lot of God to change the hearts of our people."

She leaned into his arm. "If God can change this woman, he can certainly change the hearts and minds of the surrounding people."

He elbowed her, forcing her to drop her fork. "Let's see if you still feel the same way when Bishop Weaver shows up on our front porch."

She sat up straight and held her sandwich a few inches from her mouth. "I can honestly say I'm not worried. Sure, I might be forbidden to see Anna for a short while, but I still have Emma and Katie. And by the sounds of it, perhaps Henry Schrock's wife, Maggie."

He leaned in kissed her cheek. "Who is this girl? Look at you being content with spending time with Emma."

Compliments came few and far between; hence they were considered prideful. But she couldn't help but blush at her husband's kind words. "I suppose when Samuel re-baptized me in Willow Creek four weeks ago, more of my old thoughts washed down the stream than I realized."

They let her words mix together with the evening nesting of birds in the tree overhead before she added, "I know I'm far from perfect, and at times I still have ugly thoughts I have to push away. But when they get close to landing on my tongue, all I have to do is envision Jesus hanging on the cross."

Jake, their sheepdog, barked at the three buggies, one after the other, as they pulled in their driveway.

Eli stood, wiped his mouth on a napkin and stepped over the bench. "So, it begins."

CHAPTER 18

Rebecca hung back, gathering up their supper dishes as Eli met their visitors. Samuel and Emma were the first to secure their horse to the hitching post and stepped down from their enclosed buggy. Daniel and Katie, followed by Henry and Maggie.

Each face was stricken with an eternal struggle. Emma headed to the picnic table and helped her carry the remnants of the meal to the house. No words were needed as both *schwester's* worked in silence.

Rebecca let Emma step in front of her and followed her to the house. Stopping in the middle of the driveway, Rebecca looked from the porch to the road. An overwhelming feeling of life as she knew it was slipping from her fingers. Remarkably, she wasn't worried. In the distance, a storm ripped away at the landscape, and a crack of lightning hit a lone pine tree in the pasture. The quick flash of light, followed by a blast of fire, tumbled the tree to the ground.

The sound alerted Eli, and he and the men worked quickly to shelter the horses in the barn. The ground shook under the tree's weight, and Emma and Rebecca ran to the house.

Katie held open the kitchen door, and Emma's face convulsed briefly. "Did you feel that?"

Katie's eyes flashed. "Please tell me that wasn't a warning sign of what's to come." Maggie took dishes from Rebecca and replied. "A freak act of nature, ain't so?"

Katie worked on lighting the kerosene lamp over the table and asked Rebecca. "So, did your *datt* pay a visit to you and Eli today?"

"*Jah*. You too?"

Katie looked troubled. Rebecca heard it in her voice and saw it in her hands. All eyes switched back to her when she asked Emma. "I couldn't hear exactly what *Datt* said to Eli, but I could tell it wasn't good."

"*Jah*, me either, but Samuel told me everything he said. Samuel is certain we will be called in front of the church."

Katie moved her hand to her mouth to hide a moan, and Maggie added, "Jacob asked Henry to meet with him and Bishop Weaver in the morning."

Maggie added a pot of water to the stove. "If they do, I'm confident they'll question us about our baptismal oath."

Katie sank down in a chair, opened a tea bag, and draped it in a cup. "I didn't even understand those promises. They were all in German, and who could understand a word of it anyway?"

Emma leaned over the sink and watched the men run across the yard. "Here they come now. Rebecca, you better get a couple of towels."

Taking a seat beside Katie, Maggie added, "For sure and certain we'll be reminded we'll go in the fire for eternity."

Katie sucked in a long breath and covered her eyes with the palms of her hands. "I knew this day would come. I just didn't think it would happen so fast."

Eli was the first in the door and took the towel Rebecca handed him before she stepped behind him to give one to Samuel, Daniel, and Henry.

Eli dried his head. "That came up quick." Draping the towel over Rebecca's arm, he asked, "So I assume we all got a visit from Jacob today?"

After handing the wet towel back to Rebecca, Samuel took a seat at the table. "*Jah*. He gave me little room to speak, but his warning was straightforward. We were not to search for the truth, other than what is taught on Sunday morning."

Daniel pulled a chair out beside Katie and flipped it around to straddle it. Leaning his elbows on the chair back, he added, "My warning was much the same. I was not to lead my family in any way that would go against the *Ordnung*. If I did, there would be no hope for our salvation. And we were destined to do the devil's work."

Maggie pulled a chair out and patted its seat for Henry to sit beside her. Wrapping his arm around the back of Maggie's chair, Henry stated, "My warnings were more intense. It hasn't even been a year since I've been appointed minister. I'm sure my meeting with the bishop tomorrow will come at a price."

Maggie rested her hand on her husband's knee. "God always has a purpose. And all you did was ask questions that neither Bishop Weaver nor the other ministers could answer."

Daniel piped in. "Precisely why we started to seek for our own answers. You all know I'll be blamed for all of this. I'm certain the bishop is regretting ever granting me church membership. I'm the reason you all have questions in the first place."

Samuel leaned back in his chair. "God wanted us to see the truth that they have the salvation message wrong. The church members can no faster get to heaven by their works than I can bring that burned tree back to life. And besides, there's not one person in this district that can claim they will ever be good enough to go to heaven."

Katie wilted against the back of her chair. "Will they bring us all in front of the church to repent?"

Daniel tipped his chin in her direction. "What do we have to confess about? We've done nothing wrong."

Even Maggie's stomach was in turmoil with the possibility. "You know to the members of our church, it's a sin to study an English bible, especially in a group setting. And sin is only forgiven by a public confession."

Henry reached for a cookie off the plate in the middle of the table. "I've been studying the oath we took, and I believe an oath should be based on the truth."

Maggie passed the box of tea bags around the table. "We looked long and hard at the words of our promises and translated them the best we could from German to English."

Henry waited until his wife had finished before adding, "We promised to adhere to the standards of the church and to help administer them according to God's Word. What we promised was to follow a list of man-made rules and traditions that can't be found in the bible."

Emma agreed. "When our Mennonite friends explained that to us, Samuel and I were shocked. When I joined the church and agreed to those things, I didn't understand them. Now that I know my hope comes only from Jesus, those promises I made to the Amish church mean nothing."

Katie crossed her legs and bounced her tea bag up and down in her mug. "I believe everything Daniel has shared with me. I know our future is uncertain, and I trust God's plan. Still, I'm struggling with breaking my promises to God and the church."

Emma moved to sit next to Katie and took her hand. "So did I. Until I repented and asked God to forgive me, I was surrounded by guilt. But once I did, I was released from that heavy burden."

Rebecca stood and poured more cream into the pitcher on the table. "The last couple of months have been freeing for me. Eli's taught me so much in such a short time that I don't ever want to go back to a way of life where I need to be controlled to stay in God's good graces."

Katie followed Rebecca with her eyes and asked, "But what about Anna and the yarn shop? Jacob warned Daniel that the community won't shop at the bakery. I assume that will be the same for the yarn shop. You won't be able to work with your *schwester*."

Emma responded to Katie's question. "I'm not giving up on Anna just yet."

Samuel snickered and nodded his head in Rebecca's direction. "I didn't think I'd ever see a day when you stood among us. If God can work on your heart, I'm certain Anna won't be far behind."

Emma patted Katie's hand. "Stop worrying. All we need to do is keep pointing people to Jesus through God's word. He will do the rest."

Daniel added, "And that means He will direct our path to whatever is to come. Even if that means being put in the *bann*."

Henry took a sip from his mug before responding. "Look, we're in this together and we'll never be alone." He sat his cup on the table. "*Jah*, I know we won't be able to eat a meal with our families or do business with them. But this is bigger than us. And besides, who says no to God?"

Eli threw his hands up in the air and walked to the window. "Not me."

Samuel added, "We can't turn back now. We know too much truth."

In the distance, Eli noticed lights flickering in the driveway from an incoming buggy. "What now?"

Rebecca moved to the window next to Eli. "Who could be out visiting in this weather?"

They watched as the enclosed buggy pulled into the barn. Eli headed to the front door and stepped out on the porch. Two figures moved across the yard, covered with a large black umbrella. The woman held a bundle close to her chest. Eli hollered over his shoulder. "Katie, it's your parents. It looks like they have Elizabeth with them."

Katie ran to the door. "Something must be wrong with the baby. Why else would they come out in this weather?"

Levi ushered Ruth and Elizabeth up the stairs and only stopped once they were out of the rain. Shaking the umbrella off, he leaned it up against the side of the house and followed Eli and Ruth inside.

Katie took Elizabeth from her mother's arms. "What's the matter?" She held the baby up to her cheek. "She doesn't feel warm."

Ruth wiped the rain from her hands and reached down to remove the blanket wrapped around the child. "Nothing is wrong with Elizabeth. But everything is wrong with this family."

Levi cleared his throat. "Ruth, take the girls in the kitchen. I'd like to talk to the boys for a few minutes."

Katie and Ruth headed to the kitchen, passing Henry and Samuel on their way.

Levi took off his hat and sat it on the bench near the door. "I think it's about time one of you explain to me the visit I had from Jacob just now."

Samuel pointed to the far end of the room and the rest of the men found a seat. Samuel followed and took a seat beside him. "What did Jacob say?"

"Word has it, you boys are holding secret meetings and evangelizing to the young folk in the community. Is that so?"

Samuel glanced around the room, looking for support. Henry spoke up. "It's true. Everything Jacob said and the rumors he heard are true."

Levi looked toward his son. Samuel grimaced. "I'm sure we've caused you concern. But it's what we've been called to do."

Levi raised his voice an octave. "You realize what this means, don't you?"

"*Jah.*"

"*Nee,* I don't think you do. You won't be able to work with me. It means your *mamm* won't get to watch after Elizabeth. And your *schwester* and Emma won't be able to work at the bakery. You will be cut off from your family." Without barely taking a breath, Levi looked at Henry. "And you! You're a minister, a leader in our community. God entrusted you. How could you even consider being a part of this?"

Henry took his hands and moved them up and down, hoping Levi would take the cue to lower his voice. The last thing they needed was for the womenfolk to get all worked up. "I think we should take this to the barn."

Daniel looked out the window. "The rain is coming down in sheets. How about the basement?"

Samuel didn't wait for an answer and stood and moved toward the basement door in the kitchen. Each man took his place behind Samuel and followed him downstairs. As they passed through the kitchen, each man found their wife's eyes and nodded reassurance in their direction.

Katie let out a deep sigh as the men's heavy feet met the wooden steps; Elizabeth started to fuss with her tension. Ruth moved to her daughter's side and took the child from her arms. "Now, don't be getting yourself all worked up. They will find a solution, I'm certain of it." She lifted the baby over her shoulder. "God's ways are always better than our own."

Katie glared at her mother's comment. "Do you know what Jacob said to *Datt*?"

In a sureness that had a way of calming Katie's fears, she replied, "I do. And it's an answer to my prayers."

Emma stepped up behind Ruth, brushed a wisp of hair from Elizabeth's forehead, and kissed it softly. "Answered prayer? How so?"

Ruth turned and patted Emma's arm. "It wasn't just you and Rebecca your *mamm* shared her truth with."

Rebecca stepped forward and asked, "You too?"

Ruth sat and balanced Elizabeth on her knee. "Your *mamm* and I were close. We got to spend a good bit of time alone near the end."

Emma leaned in and whispered, "So you know about the truth in Jesus?"

Ruth looked toward the open door of the basement and quietly replied, "I do, and so much more. I've been praying God would find a way to share the truth with Levi."

Katie's eyes misted over. "That would be a great answer. To know you and *Datt* could still be in Elizabeth's life is truly the perfect solution."

Ruth smiled and then answered, "God has a new agenda for all of us. That I'm sure of."

Maggie stood and walked to Ruth and laid her hand on her shoulder. "How long have you been waiting for God to answer this prayer?"

Ruth looked up at Maggie. "Five years."

Elizabeth rooted at her grandmother. Katie leaned over and took the baby from her arms. "You don't seem worried."

"Worrying only tells God we aren't trusting Him."

Rebecca shut the basement door softly and pulled a chair up next to Ruth, folded her arms on the table, and leaned in close. "But you've followed the *Ordnung* for all these years. You seem so satisfied with being an active member of this district."

Ruth crossed her legs and folded her hands around her knee. "On the outside, I may have looked comfortable, but on the inside, I was confused and scared. After your *mamm* shared what she learned from Mary, I started to question my own salvation. I needed to know the truth, so I went to Mary. She showed me where in the bible I could find my answers."

Emma took a seat across the table next to Maggie and asked, "Where did you find your truth?"

"The same place I assume you all found yours. In God's word."

Katie's eyes lightened and glowed. "You've read an English Bible?"

"Several times."

Maggie let her breath out slowly. "You've waited on God for five years. How have you not given up hope?"

Ruth's mind drifted for a few seconds before she answered. "I suppose God was preparing me. If He answered me right away, I might not have had time to study and be ready to serve Him properly."

Emma smiled and asked, "So Levi doesn't know?"

Ruth shook her head from side to side as her lips turned upward. "It's not my place to change his heart. That's God's job. All I could do was pray He would find a way to show him the truth. And look, here we are. I'm assuming the men are showing my Levi what you ladies already know."

Rebecca walked to the basement door and leaned her ear up close. "What if Levi chooses to ignore what Samuel might share with him?"

Ruth leaned back in her chair and replied with a sureness in her voice without hesitation. "Then I'll keep on praying."

Emma tapped on the table and looked at Ruth. "Do you think Mary shared the bible with any other women in the community?"

Ruth rested her elbow on the table and propped her chin up in her palm. "I wouldn't put it past her. She had more visitors than anyone else in the community. It wasn't uncommon to see two or three women a day stop by for a quick chat. As she put it, her kitchen was always open, and coffee was always warm."

Rebecca jumped away from the door as soon as she heard feet shuffle at the bottom of the stairs.

Levi opened the door and didn't stop as he headed toward the front door. "Ruth, come, we're leaving."

Katie reached up and took her mother's hand, feeling torn. Ruth leaned down and whispered in her ear. "I'm not worried, and neither should you be. God is bigger than all of this, I promise you."

Katie leaned her head against her mother's cheek and took in the warm embrace as she repeated her mother's words in her head. Holding onto her mother's hand until the distance between their fingers made it impossible. Her throat went hot and dry as she suppressed an internal sob.

Emma walked over to her best friend and wrapped her arm around her shoulders. The air in the kitchen left with Levi and Ruth, leaving all four couples struggling with Levi's abrupt departure.

Troubled, Katie looked across the room at her *bruder*. "So?"

Samuel shrugged his shoulders. "All we could do was pave the way. It's up to God to take it from here."

Katie was afraid of what life might look like if her parents couldn't be part of it. She looked around the room and started to cry. "Elizabeth won't know her grandparents. Isn't that upsetting to any of you?"

Daniel stooped down to her level and rested his hand on her knee. "Of course, it is. But you must understand that if we are asked to leave the church, it's because we're pursuing Christ. And He will never reject us."

Emma sat down beside Katie and ran her hand over the back of Elizabeth's head. "Don't you want Elizabeth to grow up knowing the true promises of God?"

"*Jah*."

Samuel picked up his now cold cup of tea. "You know *Datt*. He has to think about things. He's not one to make any decision lightly."

Henry stepped beside Maggie. "We hit a nerve with him. I've seen that look before."

Maggie's eyes widened. "How so?"

"When years of instruction collide with God's Word, it doesn't line up and it leaves people questioning what they believe."

Rebecca started to clear the table. "So now what?"

Henry answered, "We're going to go help Ruth and Levi prepare for church tomorrow like we planned. Then we'll show up at church on Sunday like always and leave our fate in God's hands."

Eli carried a couple of cups to the sink. "Jesus never said it would be easy to follow Him."

***

Eli pulled his buggy up to the house and let Rebecca off before he pulled it up to the hitching line set in Levi's pasture. His starched black trousers, white shirt, and black vest clung to his skin. It was barely daybreak, and the humidity was already heavy in the air.

He unhitched his buggy horse and led him to the corral. Henry held the gate open and nodded. "Are you ready for this?"

"How did your meeting go with Bishop Weaver last night?"

"You'll soon find out. Here he comes now with Samuel and Daniel." Stopping short of the gate, Bishop Weaver motioned for Henry and Eli to join him at the side of the barn.

The bishop took his black hat off and held it by its brim, wasting no time getting to the point. "I suspect you all have thought hard and long about the consequences you face with going against the *Ordnung*?"

All four men shook their heads in unison.

"Then you leave me no choice other than to call you before the membership today."

Sweat trickled down Eli's brow and he let it fall to his chest.

"I suggest each of you let today's sermon settle in deep before you subject your family to the shame of ex-communication." He nodded and left without letting any of them answer.

Only then did Eli take off his hat and wipe the moisture from his brow, following the bishop across the yard with his eyes. "We can't change the past. All we can do is move forward." He turned back toward his friends. "Who's in?"

All four men marched across the yard without a word and found their place in line behind the other men.

***

The warm sun did little to heat the chill Rebecca sensed when Wilma walked by. Her stepmother's lips formed a straight line as she tilted her head to the air as she passed. Rebecca whispered over her shoulder toward Emma. "I certainly won't miss her."

Emma pinched her side and whispered back. "Jesus instructs us to love all people, and that includes Wilma."

In a hushed tone, she replied, "But she grates on my every nerve."

"More reason to search your heart and fight against those kinds of thoughts. Remember we're to pray for our enemies."

Rebecca pulled her *schwester* close. "It's going to be a lifelong process for me."

Emma smiled then replied, "As it is with all of us."

Anna pushed herself between them. "What are you all whispering about?"

Emma hushed her. "Shhh … not now. We need to get inside; it's almost nine."

Anna's lip turned downward. "You two never include me in anything anymore."

Emma squeezed Anna's hand. "Soon, *schwester*, soon."

Anna grabbed Emma's arm and pulled her out of line. "What's going on?"

"I promise I'll explain later. But we have to get inside. We're in enough trouble today. I don't want being late added to our problems."

Anna reached out and pulled Rebecca close. "Please tell me what's going on. You're scaring me. *Datt* and Wilma whispered all morning, and I heard Samuel's name. Is he in trouble?"

Emma stepped out of line and moved to the side of the barn, letting the line of women file by. Emma tipped her head in closer to Anna and Rebecca stood guard if anyone got within earshot. "We don't have time to explain everything right now, but please know whatever happens today, we will find a way to see you and tell you everything we know."

Anna frowned. "I don't like this one bit."

Rebecca piped in. "We don't like keeping things from you, but there wasn't time. We promise we'll find a way to explain when the time is right."

The rueful look on Anna's face tugged at Emma's heart. How could she leave her *schwester* behind? She glanced over her shoulder and asked, "Do you trust us?"

Anna sighed softly. "Of course, I do."

"Then follow us today."

"What do you mean, follow you?"

Rebecca pulled them both back into line and whispered, "You'll see soon enough. Just step out in faith. Ignore everything you've been taught and follow us."

Anna's hand trembled under Rebecca's touch, and she brought her *schwester's* hand to cover her heart. "Do you see a change in me?"

"*Jah,* I do. I assumed it was because of Eli."

Rebecca's face changed to a pink hue. "Perhaps he had a little to do with it. But this heart change is God's doing and no one else's."

Rebecca ran her hand over her forehead just as they stepped back in line. "Please, Anna, trust us."

After adopting the solemn tone from the room, they found their place inside. Wilma turned in her seat two rows ahead and gave the girls a disapproving glare. It was uncommon to file in out of order of age, and the girl's tardiness showed heavily on their stepmother's face.

No matter how hard she tried, defensive anger welled up inside of Rebecca. She closed her eyes and asked God to remove the bitterness as she recalled Eli's words. *We can't store hostility in our hearts if we want to be one of God's messengers.*

She looked across the room until she found her husband. He, too, was seeking her. When their eyes met, the lines around his eyes softened. Little air was moving in the barn. But the thought of sitting still in the stifling heat left her more anxious as to what was to come.

The song leader sang the first word of the first song, and everyone joined in. The rhyming slow German song echoed off the barn rafters and made a wonderful noise.

The second song, the *Lob Lied,* also sang in German, would have prepared her heart for the upcoming sermon. But today, it did anything but settle her. The twenty-minute song lasted an eternity in Rebecca's mind, and it took all she had to concentrate on the words.

Thoughts raced through her mind as the habitual words flowed from her lips. *I don't even know what these words mean. For years, I've sung a song that has no meaning to me. Is this how God would want us to worship? Not knowing the meaning behind the songs that we throw up to the Lord each week.*

She took a few minutes to look down the row of young women all about her age. Their dark dresses matched the ceremonial expressions on their faces. Everything about Sunday morning had to be perfect, from the starch in their identical dresses to how many pleats were in their *kapps*. What did God care about starch or pleats?

Why hadn't she noticed it before? She followed the Old Order tradition for years because she was taught to do so. To value a work-based religion over God's actual word. But Eli showed her that her salvation was secure, all she had to do is believe in Jesus and no number of good deeds would pave her way to heaven. Let alone being discouraged from reading any bible but the German one. And that she didn't understand.

Never before had she wanted to scream from the rafters that they had it all wrong. She ached to tell the bench full of women that the only thing that mattered for their salvation was not how hard they worked and served, but by asking in faith for God to forgive them for their sins and ask Him to give them a new life in Jesus who died for them on the cross.

Her mind wandered while their lips moved along with the song. Did they see the change in her since she gave her life to Jesus?

She had to admit that she was even shocked at the radical change. Every passing day left her with a burning desire to share what she had learned. She was far from perfect, and she struggled with sinful thoughts each and every day. But now, she knew for sure her faith in Jesus would secure her eternity.

Oh, how she yearned to tell them that no matter how hard they tried, they would never be good enough to get to heaven without complete faith in Jesus Christ. But more importantly, she died to tell them that if God could forgive her for all she had done, He certainly would forgive them too. Who wouldn't want that kind of everlasting assurance?

Letting out a long sigh, she settled her eyes on the bishop and ministers who were coming into the room. Taking their seats at the front of the room, she silently prayed that the message would be something she could understand.

Her father was the first to speak, and he read scripture from a German Bible and took his seat. Next, Bishop Weaver preached on sin, and more than once, his words lingered on Samuel, Eli, Daniel, and

Henry. She couldn't help but watch Eli's expression as the lines in his jaw struggled to stay still.

After the last minister stood to give his testimony and a recap of Bishop Weaver's sermon, the bishop stood and dismissed all non-baptized congregation members.

Rebecca sat between Emma and Anna. Quickly, she reached out and took their hands. Anna raised her eyebrows, looking for an explanation.

Bishop Weaver cleared his throat and stood silent for an alarming amount of time. Not a sound could be heard as he called all of them to the front of the room.

"I call the Samuel Yoders, Daniel Millers, Eli Brickers, and Henry Schrock's to the front of the room."

Anna let out a small gasp, covered her mouth with her other hand, and held tightly to Rebecca's fingers. Emma and Rebecca stood, and Rebecca bent down and whispered, "I promise you; it will work out perfectly." Reluctantly, Anna let go.

Rebecca, Emma, Katie, and Maggie moved to the front of the women's side while their husbands stood on the other.

Bishop Weaver waited until everyone was in place before asking them to drop to their knees. Rebecca looked toward Eli and waited for his lead. When he nodded his head in her direction, she complied and knelt, and everyone followed suit.

Rebecca held her breath. Not even a sparrow could be heard in the rafters above. It was as if the world stood still while they awaited their punishment.

Heads down and backs toward their community, Bishop Weaver spoke. "Our fellow brothers and sisters have gone against the rules of the *Ordnung*. Their sins are evangelizing and studying the English bible. Both require repentance before the church to stay in good standing with this district."

From behind, Rebecca heard a rustle of whispers. Bishop Weaver quickly quieted the room and continued.

"According to the rules set forth by our forefathers, any outward advances toward public evangelism are highly discouraged. All bible interpretation is through the Lord's appointed ministers and bishops only."

Walking in front of Henry, the bishop stopped and asked, "Henry Schrock, do you repent and promise to abide by the rules of this community, as well as forgoing participating in any public display of bible studies?"

In a show of disobedience according to the Amish church, Henry stood and confidently said, "*Nee.*"

Bishop Weaver continued down the line until he stood in front of Rebecca. All her friends answered the bishop's question in the same manner as she did.

The bishop asked the members to turn away. "As of this day forward, these eight members of our church will fall under the *bann.*"

The room shuffled. Each side of the church turned away from the center of the room toward the wall, and he continued, "To stay in fellowship with this district, from this day forward until a public confession is made, no one will share a table, do business with, or speak to these eight members. If there should come a time when they request proper repentance, they will be accepted back into the church."

Rebecca lifted her head and steadied her eyes on her father. Only momentarily did he catch her eye and she noticed his chin quiver. She tore her gaze away and settled on Eli. His face, while under strain, brightened when she grabbed his eye. She saw nothing but complete assurance in his decision.

Samuel was the first to file down the center of the room. Each followed. Still, in total submission to Bishop Weaver's request to turn their back on the eight of them, Rebecca was shocked to hear Henry proclaim, "Jesus said, He who is not with Me is against Me."

Eli was next, as he added, "A house divided against itself will not stand."

Samuel stopped short of stepping outside and shouted. "If you want to know the promise of God. Follow us."

And as if on cue, Daniel added, "The Word of God is the truth to live by. We are leaving to pursue Jesus Christ."

As Rebecca and Emma reached the door, they heard Anna call their names. When they turned, Anna ran into their arms. "Please show me the truth."

Emma yelled in Samuel's direction. "God heard our prayers."

A line of their family and friends followed them out the door one after another; Levi and Ruth Yoder, Adam and Amanda Weaver, Teena and Lizzie Fisher, Joseph and Barbara Wagler, Ruben and Allie Miller, Bella Schrock, Edna Graber, and the Kauffman boys.

In awe of the scene unfolding, both Rebecca and Emma let out a joyous sigh and proclaimed, "Praise the Lord!"

Anna followed their voices and praised herself as their older *bruder,* Matthew and his wife Sarah, stepped outside into the light.

Rebecca walked toward Eli and let him wrap his arm around her shoulders. She leaned in and asked, "Now what?"

Henry overheard her question and was quick to answer. "Looks like we have the start of a new church. One where we can point people to Jesus through His word and let Him do the rest."

EPILOGUE

Rebecca took a seat on the ground between her mother's and Mary's small white wooden grave markers. Positioned under a large maple tree, Rebecca stretched her legs out in front and played with a pile of red and yellow leaves at her side.

Directing her words toward the small crosses, she began. "What a year it's been. I wish you both were here to see all the wonderful things happening in Willow Springs. Henry Schrock has taken the community by storm and led so many youths to Christ. God has definitely laid a hand on his leadership.

Datt and Wilma still want nothing to do with us, but that's okay. We're doing God's work, and we won't stop praying for them. Anna, on the other hand, is struggling with the separation. I, for one, love that she is living with us, especially since I'll need her help this winter when this little one comes along. Her heart is in the right place, but I fear her anxiety is getting worse with all the conflict with us leaving the church has caused.

Mamm, I wish you could tell me what I should do. *Datt* always said I sheltered her and didn't let her be herself because she always stayed in my shadow. I'm trying to get her to stand on her own, but she's becoming more of a recluse as the days go by. She attends church and bible studies with us regularly, but her mind is elsewhere. I just don't know what to do.

Mary, I can't thank you enough for showing me the way to God's forgiveness. And *Mamm,* your letter came at the perfect moment when I needed you the most.

I'm excited to tell you both I was finally able to track down the toddler's mother at the market and ask for her forgiveness.

God sure does have a way of turning evil into good. Little did I know at the time, but that small boy would go on to save three children at Pittsburgh's Children's Hospital who needed transplants.

Emma and Samuel still have not conceived another child. Still, in their wait, they're planning to serve as missionaries in Canada with Alvin and Lynette Miller from Ohio next spring. Again, God stepped in and filled their days with purpose while he prepares the perfect time for them to grow their family.

Mary, you would be so proud. Emma's been teaching me all about gardening, and with her help, we've turned every bare spot in the yard back into the glory you once had. We even saved the patch of Johnny Jump-ups you were so fond of.

How can I thank you both enough for all you've done to etch away at my cold and lifeless heart? I'm confident I've tested God's patience more than once, but he's a loving God, and I know he forgives all. Even those times, I still struggle with what rolls off my tongue."

Stopping to rub her hand over the small bump across her middle, she continued, "I can only hope I'm half the woman the both of you have been. *Mamm,* I certainly didn't make your job easy. And Mary, you knew what I needed long before I knew myself. Thank you both for showing me the way to Christ."

Anna's

Amish Fears Revealed

THE AMISH WOMEN OF
LAWRENCE COUNTY SERIES - BOOK 3

PROLOGUE

September - Willow Springs, Pennsylvania

A heaviness pressed down on Anna Byler's chest, and she reached out to catch herself from falling. Her heart raced in anticipation all morning of having to go to Shetler's Grocery. Her *schwester*, Rebecca, continued to push her out of the house. But in all reality, she felt the safest tending to the chickens or helping with chores.

The grocery shelf shook under her weight. Before she had a chance to slip to the floor gracefully, her arm caught a stack of cans, making a commotion clamored throughout the store.

A fuzziness floated before her eyes, and she squeezed them tight, praying it would pass quickly. An awful buzz echoed in her ears, and she leaned forward to put her head between her knees and prayed. *Please, Lord, make it go away.*

A tender voice and a warm hand on her back made her tip her head toward the calming call.

"What is it, Anna? Are you ill?"

Even if she wanted to answer Naomi Kauffman, she couldn't form two audible words. The old woman called out. "Simon, where are you?"

Did she hear correctly? Had Naomi called for Simon? *Oh, please, Lord, not Simon. He can't see me like this.*

She tried to stand up with a shuddering sigh, only to fall to her knees.

Mrs. Kauffman supported her arm. "No child, stay put. Simon is here. Let him help you."

The aroma of pine shavings and diesel fuel swirled under her nose, revealing Simon's closeness. After all their years apart, his job at Mast Lumber Mill did little but remind her of the plans they once had.

Their paths rarely crossed since he'd returned to Willow Springs. When he followed his dream instead of his heart three years ago, she'd all but written that part of her life off. But his touch only added to the panic creeping through her skin.

Anguish filled her until the weight crushed her lungs, preventing her from taking an easy breath. Try as she might, she pulled her arm from his grip, but it only caused her knees to buckle further. Simon placed his arms under her legs and around her waist and picked her up quickly.

The sudden rush forced her head to drop into his chest. She stopped fighting and let his strong arms cradle her body without any option but to allow him to carry her.

"Relax, Anna, I've got you."

She didn't have the strength to argue and thought, *Relax? How dare he think I can relax in his arms after all he's done?*

Simon stopped near the cash register and put Anna in the chair Mr. Shetler had pulled out. Simon snapped his head toward the direction of the people who had hovered around them. "Someone! A glass of water."

Simon fell to one knee, rested his hand under her arm, and leaned closer. "Did you have another panic attack?"

There weren't many people outside her immediate family who knew she suffered from spells of anxiety. She'd hoped to keep it that way. When she lifted her face toward the crowd, her heart sank. She leaned onto Simon's shoulder and begged, "Please make them go away."

Simon stood and guided her toward the door. "She's fine. Just a little overheated. A glass of water and she'll be good as new."

Naomi followed them outside and opened the passenger side door of Simon's truck. After helping Anna to the leather seat, he thanked his mother.

Mrs. Kauffman leaned inside and handed Anna a cup of water. "Here, dear, drink this and let Simon turn on the air conditioner to cool you down."

Naomi let her hand come to rest on her son's forearm. "I won't be but a few more minutes. Perhaps we should take her home?"

Tears blurred Anna's vision. "I've made a scene. I'm so sorry."

The older woman patted her arm. "Now, don't think another thing of it. These things happen."

Anna looked worried. "Naomi, if the *People* catch you speaking to me, you'll get in trouble. You know I'm shunned, and you're not allowed to talk to me."

Mrs. Kauffman's tender tone calmed her fears. "You let me worry about that. No one will tell me I can't help someone who needs assistance. It will take more than this to ruffle my feathers."

Simon shut the door and Anna closed her eyes against the sudden tears, leaned her head back on the seat and thought, *Why does this continue to happen to me? And of all people, why did it have to be Simon?* That part of her heart had long closed, and every time she was around him, all it did was stir up memories she had tried to bury.

She opened her eyes when Simon slid into the driver's seat. If fear alone didn't paralyze her, the picture hanging from his rearview mirror and the fishing lure she'd bought him made her gasp for air.

Bile settled in the back of her throat, forcing her to flee the truck. The hue of color from the changing seasons gave her no comfort as she ran across the road and through the field that led back to her *schwester* Rebecca's house. Even the pounding of her heart couldn't block out his cry.

"Anna…please! Let me explain."

CHAPTER 1

Anna fell to her knees, pulse thrashing in her chest. Simon's voice long faded, but his eyes the color of the pebbles along Willow Creek, and his dark turned-up curls beneath his baseball cap were stamped behind her eyelids.

Kneeling at the foot of her mother's grave, she cried. "Oh *Mamm*, how will I ever get over Simon? Ever since he returned to Willow Springs, my heart is all twisted, and all I want to do is run away. But where would I go? *Datt* has disowned me since I decided to leave the church and join the New Order Fellowship, and all I have left of you is this place you share with hundreds of wooden crosses. I feel so lost and alone. Why did you have to go so soon?

I've spent time reading my Bible like our new bishop, Henry Schrock, suggested, but I'm still paralyzed by fear. I'm comforted by the Word, but I'm having trouble applying it to my life. How can Jesus, who knows all my thoughts, deliver me from this constant dread? It's like a chain around my heart, with no key to set me free. When I asked Bishop Schrock, he said, "*Christ holds the key, and he can unlock and banish you from all your fears if you lay them down at his feet.*"

I try *Mamm*, really, I do, but whenever I think I've finally rid myself of worry and fear and hand it over to Him in my heart, something happens. I go and pick up the same concern all over again. How can I say I'm a Christian if I keep reverting to my old ways? Oh, *Mamm*, will God ever forgive me of unfaithfulness?

There are days I'm not even sure what I'm fearful about. But I know since Simon's return, the fear of allowing my heart to be broken again is stronger than ever. I've lost so many things in the last few years that I'm always anticipating the next trial.

First your death, then *Datt's* refusal to accept my choice to follow Jesus, and Simon's broken promises. How will I ever trust again? When I gave myself to Jesus, I thought all my worries would disappear.

That somehow, His voice would be stronger, and I'd overcome the hold anxiety has on me. I've learned God has worked powerfully in people's lives throughout the ages. Why isn't he doing the same for me?

Mamm, how often do I come to your gravesite and pour out my cares? It's the one place in all of Willow Springs I feel you, even though I know nothing is left of you here but a distant memory.

The panic attacks are coming on stronger these days. Before, I could take a few deep breaths and stop them, but now they have taken control of my life. I agonize over them daily. My heart beats so loud I swear it will explode without warning, and my breath escapes, leaving me so weak I can barely stand. It's terrifying, especially when it happens in public, like today at Shetler's.

I've done everything I can think of to stop them. I spend time praying, asking God to help me, not thinking about them. But I don't know what triggers an episode. I'd surely find a way to avoid those situations if I did. I've even written my worries down and burned them, but nothing. They suffocate me to the point I'm finding it hard to leave the house.

Church is about all I can handle these days, and that is getting more challenging since Simon has taken to attending.

This past Sunday, Samuel preached how God solicited Moses to deliver His people. Moses argued with God, telling him he wasn't equipped to carry out His plan to meet with Pharaoh. That's how I feel. I'm not worthy to carry out God's plans. I promise to stop worrying, but I fail repeatedly. How can God trust me with His promises if I can't keep mine?

Oh, *Mamm*, why did Simon come back after all these years? Can't he see his presence upsets me? Leaving the Amish to follow his dream is one thing but breaking his promises to me is another. I see how he looks at me.

I want to trust again. But what happens if…I'm not strong enough to go through that again, especially after all he's done? God may have forgiven him, but can I?"

A flock of birds perched high in a maple tree averted Anna's attention away from her one-sided conversation with her deceased mother. She pulled herself to her feet and brushed the crushed crimson leaves from her wool stockings.

In the quiet of the cool September morning, Anna stared at the host of sparrows finding shelter in the fall foliage. Minister Samuel Yoder's message from Sunday played over in her head.

We're doomed to fail when we try to convince ourselves that we know more than God. God's plan doesn't include us growing in our own self-confidence. He wants us to put all our trust in Him. After all, isn't it only God who is powerful enough to overcome all the pharaohs in our lives?

Anna shielded her eyes and tried to focus on the flight of birds through the sunshine filtering on her face and thought, *I'm nowhere as faithful as Moses. I certainly can't do all you ask of me. Why can't I just be like the birds in the sky and not have a care in the world?*

With a shuddering sigh, she mumbled, "I best go face Rebecca and tell her I can't even be trusted to pick up a few groceries without crumbling to pieces."

***

Simon followed the sway of Anna's green dress as she ran across the road and into the field, running perpendicular to South Main Street Extension. All the families living on Mystic Mill Road used the well-worn shortcut.

It was high time Anna stopped ignoring him and let him clarify his return. Everyone, including his own family, welcomed him home. But the one person who had a pull on his heart greater than anyone else in Willow Springs turned gray every time she saw him.

There was so much riding on his ability to win Anna back that there was little else he could concentrate on. Even his part-time job at Mast Lumber Mill did little to divert his attention from the one woman who held him captive.

He would have chased her down if it weren't for his mother's voice. "Where's Anna?"

Simon moved around the truck and placed his mother's groceries in the back seat. "She decided to walk home."

"Walk? She could barely stand a few minutes ago. I can't believe you didn't stop her."

Simon let his mother rattle on while stacking the bags of bulk food items neatly on the bench seat.

"Mr. Shetler charged Anna's items to Eli and Rebecca's account and inquired if we could drop them off on our way home."

The box contained an array of pantry items, but the jar of Karo syrup and bag of Spanish peanuts caught his eye. The two generic items brought back a muckle of memories, so fresh that his mouth watered at the mere thought of Anna's famous peanut brittle. On more than one occasion, he thought of asking his mother to make it, but it wouldn't be the same if he enjoyed it on his own. Instead, he often stopped at Yoder's Bakery, knowing Anna sold it there.

For two years, as they planned and plotted their life together, a jar of the crunchy candy always made its way to the top of his tackle box. As the creek bubbled over the rocks, he fell in love with Anna Byler. Her chestnut hair and hazel-gray eyes lured him as much as the fluke bait he used to entice the fish in the creek.

But much like the taste of the salty-sweet brittle, their love faded as he picked the world over her. For years he hid his pain in the glory of prestige, traveling the country fishing professionally. His dream came true, but he lost his future in the process. Now, looking back, he wasn't sure it was worth the cost. The girl he loved, whose once beautiful eyes turned cold and sulky under his gaze.

After returning to Willow Springs, his mother filled him in on all that Anna had lost. Her mother, a stillborn nephew, and now her father at the cost of a shunning.

The Old Order Community he left was nothing like he remembered it. Neighbors against neighbors, families against families, all split down the middle. Some adhered to past traditions, while others embraced a more open relationship with Jesus by following the New Order Fellowship.

Even his own family was feeling the strain. His *datt*, set in his ways, was finding it challenging to leave Bishop Weaver's District. At the same time, he and his younger *bruder*, Benjamin, felt encouraged by the younger group of ministers sharing the Word in Bishop Schrock's District.

Stepping away from his Old Order upbringing for a time opened his eyes to a world of believers he never thought possible. He only recently contemplated joining the new Amish church to give his life to Jesus.

But before he could do that, he had to know Anna could accept his past mistakes. God had forgiven him and led him back to Willow Springs, but could he settle here without Anna?

The seatbelt warning chime brought him out of his head and back to the task. "I'll drop you off and then deliver Anna's groceries to her sisters."

Naomi ran a hand over the polished leather seats. "When is Pete coming to pick up the truck?"

"He's bringing a check out to me later this evening. I need to clear my stuff before I sign the title over to him."

"Don't tell your *datt,* but I've enjoyed our grocery runs. He cringes every time you take me somewhere. If you don't miss it, I sure will."

Simon snickered at his mother's fondness for his shiny black Ford 250. "It served its purpose when I was on the fishing circuit, but now that I'm committing myself back to the Amish church, it does nothing but reminds me of my past mistakes."

"Son, I'm thankful you've found your way home every day. I can see a change in you. The peace that you walk with these days overflows me with joy."

Simon sighed, "I wish *Datt* could see the change."

"Give him time. Everything is so raw right now. He has a lot of pressure being an elder in the church. There is much division in our community. He loves his church, but he also loves his boys. He's torn, and realizes if he sides with Bishop Weaver, he'll lose access to many of his friends, his older children, and their families. It's such a heavy burden to bear."

"That's just it, *Mamm*. There is no other way than to follow Jesus. Why can't *Datt* see that?"

Naomi folded her hands on her lap. "He'll follow, I'm sure of it, but we must let that be his decision."

"How can you be so sure?"

"By the long hours he's been spending in his Bible. His strength has always come from his confidence in the Lord and what the Word teaches him. I have no doubt God will speak to him in His own time." Naomi paused and smiled. "Besides, He answered my prayers. Didn't he bring you back to me?"

"*Jah*, He did. But I came back with more than just me. I returned with a pile of problems I need help sorting out."

Naomi tucked her black purse under her arm. "Like I said, we have enough to worry about today; we aren't going to stress over something that tomorrow might or might not bring. We will trust the Lord, and He will show us the way."

Simon tapped his thumbs on the steering wheel. "But I only have a few months before the hearing. I'll lose everything if I can't convince Anna to help me before then."

"Son, when we give God all the praise and glory He deserves, we often discover we can walk peacefully through circumstances that terrify us. This is no different. Let Him change your overwhelmed heart into one overshadowed by His power to change all things for His good."

Simon let out a long breath. "I wish I had your assurance and faith."

"It will come. You haven't walked through enough of your own hardships to put all your faith in His promises yet."

"Enough of my own trials? What do you call the last few months?"

"A test?"

"A test in what?"

"Replacing your fear with God's sovereignty. There is nothing in your life that God allows to happen that He can't work out if you are only willing to trust in His plan."

***

After dropping his mother off at home and heading to Eli and Rebecca Bricker's, his mother's words weighed heavily on his mind. He had to believe God had a hand in everything he'd been through.

Especially by placing him back in Willow Springs, surrounded by the people he needed most.

In the few short weeks he'd been home, he discovered a part of himself he thought he'd lost forever. Now, if he could only convince Anna that God had a purpose for sending him away and bringing him back.

Over breakfast that morning, his father examined one of his favorite questions. *How will you spend this most precious day? The choice is yours. Will you spend it living for the Lord or living for yourself?*

In the past, he would let his father's words roll by him, but today, they dug a hole in his heart as big as the void he had since he left Willow Springs.

For years, Simon had supported a biting spirit due to his disobedience. During those years, he made enough money to buy his heart's desires. But his willfulness poisoned his entire outlook until he found himself in the pits of despair, desperate for a way to claw his way back to the life he once knew.

How could the sins of one man affect so many? His resources should have been used for good; instead, they were devoured by sinful wants and desires. And so, a twinge of remorse crept back into Simon's life as clear as Anna's broken spirit.

A flash of blue and black waved him in as he parked his truck alongside the row of full clotheslines in Eli and Rebecca's side yard. Retrieving the box of groceries from the back seat, Simon carried them up the steps and sat them on the floor near the door.

Eli and Rebecca sat side by side on the swing near the end of the covered porch. Eli set the double chair in motion with his foot and questioned, "What brings you out our way?"

"I told Mr. Shetler I'd deliver Anna's groceries."

Rebecca pressed her hand on the side of her protruding middle. "Without Anna?"

Simon furrowed his eyebrows. "She's not here?"

Eli stopped the swing. "*Nee.* The last we saw her, she was heading to the dry goods store."

Rebecca stood and made her way to the box on the floor. "Why on earth would she need these delivered? It certainly wasn't too much to carry."

Simon lifted his hip and balanced himself on the porch railing. "I suppose I'm to blame. She had a spell at Shetler's, and I tried to help. I planned on bringing her home, but she ran off before I could stop her."

Rebecca pulled her shawl tighter. "Oh, my! Not another one. She's been having more of them lately, and we aren't sure what to do about them." Rebecca exhaled. "This is my fault. I pushed her to step out of the house this morning, hoping a little fresh air and a change of scenery might do her some good."

Eli moved to Rebecca's side and said, "I'm sure she will be home shortly. She probably went for a walk by the creek like she always does."

The mention of their favorite spot along Willow Creek made Simon excuse himself without as much as a goodbye. "I know where she is!"

Gravel flew as Simon backed his truck out of the driveway and headed toward Willow Bridge Road. The only place in Lawrence County where Anna could be is the one place where they confided all their hopes and dreams for the future. He knew it well since he was prone to retreat to the same spot when life became too much to bear, much like every night for the past three weeks.

CHAPTER 2

Anna stayed hidden in the barn's shadow until Simon's truck pulled away. Her heart pounded as she recited Psalm 23. There weren't many things that would calm her racing pulse, but *The Shepherd's Psalm* at least helped put her mind back in line with where she wanted her heart.

As the black truck disappeared over Eli's hill, Anna pondered the weighty question that kept her awake nightly. *Why now?* A heaviness in her chest retold of a bitterness still wedged tight to the point of suffocation. *Oh, Lord, please lay forgiveness in my heart.* Anna turned away with a heavy heart and walked to the yarn shop.

The mailman had left an order on the porch of *Stitch n' Time*, and Anna carried it inside. Her sister Rebecca's husband, Eli, had finished building their new shop across the yard from the main house last year.

The burden of moving the store away from her father's furniture shop had been a stressful project. If it hadn't been for Eli's persistence, their little yarn shop would cease to exist. Since their church district split, her family endured so much division, but Eli and Rebecca stayed hopeful in God's plan. If only she could have such faith.

No sooner had she unpacked the order of needles and patterns then Rebecca waddled in the door.

"I've been worried sick about you. Simon delivered the groceries I sent you after."

"*Jah*, I saw."

Rebecca pressed her hand on her lower back and settled on the stool at the work table. "*Schwester*, we need to find a solution to your episodes. I will need your help with little Mary Ellen and the new *bobbli*. What are we to do if you can't even handle the shopping? Let alone running the shop by yourself for a few weeks."

Anna lifted her head. "I'll do my best." Bending back over her task, Anna remained silent for a few moments. Then she spoke with some hesitation. "I won't let you down, I promise."

Rebecca tied a price tag onto a set of knitting needles. "Eli and I think you need to get out more. Perhaps face some of your fears of being out in public."

Anna snapped, "I get out plenty."

"I hardly count church every other week as getting out."

"But where else do you expect me to go?"

"To start, you can go back to Shetler's."

Anna's voice was quiet. "Please, not there. I made such a scene this morning."

Rebecca reached out and took her hand. "Anna, you're never going to move past this if you don't push yourself. Remember what Eli said about worry and unrest being rooted in unbelief?"

"But I believe," Anna muttered.

"I'm sure you do, but you've allowed it to become a controlling factor in your life. I think your episodes have become a habit for you."

Anna drew a quivering breath but said nothing. After a moment, Rebecca probed, "Did this morning have anything to do with seeing Simon?"

"*Nee*, I didn't even know he and his mother were in the store until Naomi laid her hand on my shoulder."

"Then what was it? What triggered it this time?"

In a broken voice, Anna replied, "I don't know what's wrong with me. I have no rhyme or reason for what causes them or when I'll have one."

Rebecca walked to Anna's side and wrapped her arm around her shoulder. "I believe that worry, stress, and fear are closely related. If you can figure out what is going on in your head, you might be able to find some peace and confidence in this season of life."

Anna said nothing and left her sister's embrace. "I best put this order away, and I have two buckets of fiber soaking in red cabbage I need to rinse out."

Rebecca headed to the door. "Perhaps a cup of peppermint tea would help, *jah*?"

Anna nodded and smiled at her *schwester's* suggestion. "Might be just what I need to soothe my unsettled nerves."

"If Mary Ellen isn't up from her nap yet, I'll bring you a cup."

After she was sure Rebecca had made it off the porch, Anna fell to a stool and rested her chin in her propped-up palms. She tried to push Simon from her mind by covering her eyes with her fingertips. Strangely enough, she was sure her heightened anxiety attacks had everything to do with Simon's return.

***

Simon pulled his truck alongside the covered bridge in the same spot he and Anna had met every Sunday night for two years straight. A vague resentment began to take root in his heart, taking him back to the night he told Cora he didn't love her. How did he let the *Englisch* girl fall in love with him? He chastised himself for allowing it to happen on more than one occasion. Cora's tear-stained face tugged at his better judgment when he allowed his defenses down and gave in to her desire.

In all the time he'd been toying with the *Englisch* life, there was no doubt he wouldn't return to Anna, the one girl who held his affection, even at the cost of hurting Cora.

The thought of traveling the long road ahead without Anna never crossed his mind until that morning. The look of disappointment etched on her face was a disturbing element.

He wandered to the creek bank and skipped a rock across the rippling water. As the flat stone sank to the bottom, he cried out. God, where are you? I've hurt many people and have not done well with everything you've provided. Please help me make things right. And if it's your will, please soften Anna's heart toward me.

After an hour, he stepped back into his truck and headed home. Catching a glimpse of himself in the rearview mirror, his ball cap and blue t-shirt reminded him it was time to leave the life where money and fame meant more to him than securing his future with Anna.

In a few hours, the last remnant of his old life would pull out of his parent's driveway, leaving him no other option but to embrace his future, with or without the girl he loved. And soon, there would be no hiding his past mistakes. His only prayer was to be able to persuade Anna to help him carry the responsibility together.

Simon drew a long breath as he parked his truck beside his best friend Pete's old pickup truck in front of his mother's kitchen garden.

Both Pete and his younger brother stood next to the dusty Dodge. Pete nodded in his direction as he stepped out of his truck. "You're early. I haven't had a chance to clean my stuff out yet."

"No hurry. My kid brother was headed out this way to pick up a load of grain from the Feed & Seed, so I hitched a ride with him." Pete bounced a closed fist on the bed of his truck. "I convinced Jr. that this old girl had plenty of life left in her, and I'd sell it to him cheap."

Simon threw back his head and laughed. "I sure hope you don't expect me to do the same for you."

"Easy," retorted Pete promptly. "A truck as fine as that one comes at a hefty price; one I'm prepared to pay. You have nothing to worry about there. I'm grateful you gave me first dibs."

Pete's younger brother walked around the glossy fiberglass and ran his hand over the hood. "I'm not sure I'd be able to give something like this up in exchange for a smelly horse and buggy."

Simon took his hat off and ran his hand through his hair. "I've had my fun with it. It's time to let it go. Besides, my brothers have shouldered my share long enough. It's only fair I take back some of the responsibility of running this farm."

Pete rested his foot on the hitch. "What about the boat? Found a buyer yet?"

"Yep, already sold. Along with the house on Lake Erie. The new owner was happy to make it part of the deal."

Pete slapped Simon on the shoulder. "Dang, brother, you must be raking in the dough about now."

Simon was surprised at Pete's outburst. "Means nothing to me now."

"How can you say that? You worked hard for every penny. There are guys on the fishing tour dreaming of earning what you did."

After a second of silence, during which Simon contemplated his response, he justified. "It all came at too high of a cost."

"Come on, buddy, you can't tell me you didn't enjoy everything that came from winning two consecutive Bass Master Classics. You had sponsors eating out of your hand, and every chick this side of the Mississippi pined for your attention."

The muscles in Simon's jaw twitched at the mention of how he basked in the afterglow of stardom. He'd trade every ounce of it if it meant he could regain Anna's trust.

Pete turned toward his younger brother. "You should have seen it. The red carpet was rolled out for bass fishing's wonder boy everywhere we went. The news media ate him up. He was all over the papers and on every fishing channel with…*Amish Boy Wins Professional Bass Tour."*

Simon opened the tailgate and pulled labeled plastic totes and rods from the bed. "Do either of you have any use for these?"

"You're not going to sell all your fishing gear, are you?" Pete inquired.

Simon handed Pete his favorite drop-shot rod. "I won't have much time to spend on the lake and I'll be lucky to make it to the creek between chores and my job at the lumber mill."

Pete balanced the rod against the truck and picked up a crankbait pole. "You won your last tournament with this rod. Man, are you sure you want to sell these?"

Simon removed the hook from the eye at the tip of a rod and turned away from the truck. After quickly releasing the bail, he sent the spinner bait across the grass. With a quick adjustment to the drag, he reeled it back in, securing the lure back in place. "Like I said, I have no use for them, and I'm done with that part of my life. Besides, most of this tackle was given to me as part of my sponsorship."

Jr. picked up a couple of the rods and carried them to his truck. "If Pete doesn't want them, I'll take 'em."

"Now hold on there; I didn't say I didn't want them; I just said it was a waste that he's giving them away. What if he wants to get back into bass fishing again?"

"That's not going to happen, so take what you want. Perhaps you can donate the stuff you can't use to the kid's fishing program."

Pete pushed the stuff back into the bed of the truck. "I'll do that. I'm sure the kids would love this stuff."

"But what about me? I'm a kid at heart." Jr. grabbed a tackle box full of plastic worms.

"We'll go through everything later. You best get that load of grain before Dad has my tail for keeping you so long. I'll be home as soon as Simon and I take care of some business."

***

Once Pete pulled away from the house, Simon only allowed himself a split second of pain before he pushed the truck from his mind. Heading to the barn, he was genuinely glad to be home. He hadn't realized how badly he had missed his family and the camaraderie he enjoyed with his *bruders*. It was good to expel his energy working the farm.

However, along with the contentment, Simon felt a restlessness about the state of his relationship with Anna. So many things about the farm reminded him of all the plans he and Anna had made. The dream of building a house in the north pasture to opening an herb farm reminded him of all he had lost.

His brother, Ben, handed him a pitchfork the minute he walked through the barn door and went to work cleaning a stall. Simon pondered his father's statement as he piled wet straw in a wheelbarrow…*A man isn't fit to be a husband until he learns to put the Lord first in all he does. You can't raise a family until you foster yourself in God's image.*

"I'm no sooner fit to be a husband than a father," Simon whispered. "What would *Datt* do in my shoes?" There wasn't a doubt he knew precisely what he would do, and that evening, Simon bowed his head over his Bible.

***

The bell above the door jingled, and Anna followed the sound to the front of the shop.

"Naomi, you shouldn't be here. You know we're not allowed to do business together. You'll be under the *bann* yourself if Bishop Weaver gets word."

Mrs. Kauffman walked to the counter. "The way I see it, I have no other place to buy yarn, so I have no other option. And like I said the other day, you let me worry about the bishop. I'm the least of his worries."

Anna lifted her chin and posed a question. "How so?"

Naomi leaned in close. "The Lord is working his way through the community and my husband. Our boys have raised serious questions that have him looking for some biblical answers. You mark my word; this nonsense of separating families will be a thing of the past. I'm praying that your father and the other ministers will see the light soon."

"Okay," replied Anna with a show of assurance she didn't feel. Her father took his position as minister seriously, and she doubted he'd change his stance on their ex-communication. It had been two years since they walked away from their Old Order Community to join the New Order Fellowship. Anna highly doubted her *datt* and the other ministers would ever consider anything else.

Anna hung a new supply of pink wool yarn on a hook and asked, "What can I do for you today?"

Mrs. Kauffman pulled a magazine from her purse. "I found this pattern in my knitting magazine and want to try it. It calls for two skeins of high-quality wool yarn."

"Do you have a color in mind?"

Naomi pulled her glasses from her bag and pushed them up on her nose while examining the rows of muted colors. "Something different, maybe a color no one else has seen."

Waving Mrs. Kauffman to follow her to the back room, she said, "I rinsed out a batch of yarn this morning that I had soaked in salt and red cabbage."

Naomi admired the roving hanging on the rungs of the wooden rack. "How long before the fiber is ready to spin?"

Anna felt the fiber. "It will take twenty-four hours to fully dry and a day to spin. I could have it ready in a couple days. Do you like this color?"

"*Jah*, it reminds me of the lavender I once grew in my garden." The older woman folded her glasses and tucked them back into her bag. "Not sure what happened to it. It won't bloom anymore."

Anna's eyes twinkled while she considered what the problem might be. "Was it English Lavender? That lavender is the only kind that does well here in our hard winters and is hardier than the others."

"*Jah*, I think so."

"Did you trim it back as soon as it stopped flowering?"

"*Nee*, I didn't know it needed that."

"Typically, it blooms in June and July. After that, you need to cut it back, but don't go too far into the wood. Just clip off the dead blooms."

Anna paused. "Where did you have it planted?"

"I planted it under the window in hopes of being able to smell it all summer long."

Anna picked up a pencil and drew the outline of Simon's mother's house on a pad near the register. "Remind me where your gardens are planted."

"I had Ben till up a new garden bed between the barn and the house in the spring."

"If you had it under the living room window where it gets the most sun in the morning, that is northeast. If you moved it to your new area, it would receive more sun in the afternoon since it faces southwest."

Mrs. Kauffman patted Anna's hand. "I'd forgotten how much you loved gardening. Do you think if we move it, it will come back?"

"Have you noticed any green on it? You might be able to save it if you move it right away."

"I haven't looked at it lately. Perhaps you could come to help me?"

She looked out the window, hoping Naomi wouldn't catch the spasm of pain fluttering across her face with the mention of visiting the Kauffman farm. Stuttering, she uttered, "I, I…don…don't think I could get away. Rebecca's baby is due anytime now, and I'm busy here."

Anna resumed her work diligently, trying to ignore the disappointment fixed on Mrs. Kauffman's face. The older woman evidently hoped her answer would have been different, since she had no daughters of her own. No matter, there wasn't an ounce of her that would agree to help. Just the thought of running into Simon made her chest constrict.

Naomi must have sensed her reluctance and said, "On your own, you'll never be able to face your fears. But if He calls you to face what frightens you, He'll give you the strength to live through it."

As the woman headed to the door, another message Minister Yoder mentioned came to mind. *Fear imagined can be put to death by the Spirit and faith.*

Naomi called over her shoulder. "I'll be back for that lavender yarn in a few days."

The woman's sweet voice carried a memory she had long forgotten. Naomi provided wise words to get her through her grief when her mother died, and Anna replayed them in her head. *Anna, our heavenly Father knows exactly what we need when we need it. We can't run ahead of him, hoping to lead the way. Some things are too hard to comprehend, and He knows this. He will only give us what we need for the day. Beyond that, we tell Him we don't have faith if we question our future.*

Anna sunk to the floor, rested her head on her knees, and prayed. *Lord, I want to put all my faith in you. I don't want to be fearful, and I want to face my fears. If only I could figure out what those might be. Please show me how to quit living in the past and fearing the future. Amen.*

Before she lifted her head off her knees, a vision of Shetler's Grocery came to mind. The image played over in her head as she saw herself facing her first fear.

CHAPTER 3

Rebecca sat at the table peeling potatoes when Anna came in to help with dinner. A cup sat at Anna's place with a tea infuser seeping dried peppermint leaves in hot water. She smiled at her sister and added a spoonful of sugar, stirring it slowly while she took in the calming aroma.

"I had Eli stop at Yoder's Bakery this morning to check on the peanut brittle inventory. Emma asked if we would like to join her and Katie for a *schwester's* day tomorrow afternoon. I thought Mary Ellen and Katie's daughter Elizabeth could play while we visit. Would you like to join us?"

Rebecca went on. "Now, before you say a word, I don't think closing the yarn shop early is a problem. Everyone is busy cleaning out their gardens and has little time for yarn shopping."

Anna grabbed her mug with two hands and blew over the hot liquid. "Not sure I'll have much to add to the conversation since you and Katie will be comparing notes on your growing middles."

"Isn't it amazing how we're all with child simultaneously?" Rebecca mused. "Besides, I'm certain it won't be long before you and Emma start your own families."

"Hmm, I highly doubt that."

Rebecca snickered. "Those who protest too loudly."

"The only thing to protest is there isn't anyone I'd even consider marrying in this county."

Rebecca carried the pan of potatoes to the sink. "By the way Simon came here looking for you the other day; I'd beg to differ."

For the first time, Anna began questioning her reasoning behind ignoring his persistence in speaking to her. What she needed to do was set him straight. Perhaps facing him would stop some of the anxiety associated with his return and end any hope he might have about their future.

Drawing in a long breath, Anna looked up and met Rebecca's grin. "Whatever you thought you saw in his visit is nothing, I promise you."

"Well, I'd say fate has intervened in your plans."

Anna moved to the stove to check on the roasting chicken. "Fate has nothing to do with it. He practically left me at the altar; I'm not allowing myself to relive that pain ever again."

Rebecca pulled a stack of plates from the cupboard and said, "You need to stop focusing on the past. You've already conjured up the worst-case scenario before giving God a chance to show you what He has in store." Her eyes flashed as she continued, "Remember *Mamm* telling us perfect peace comes to those whose mind is fixed on trusting God?"

Anna plopped down in a chair and sighed. "I trust God; I don't trust Simon."

Rebecca added, "Look, I'm probably not the right person to tell you about trusting the Lord. But I'm not as stressed when I concentrate on just the day in front of me instead of the days before me. Eli told me that trust in God grows as we become more familiar with Him. Maybe He is using your nervousness to draw you closer to Him."

"Maybe. All I know is I've been struggling with controlling my circumstances. With Simon around, I feel vulnerable, which is terrifying."

"I'd say you might need to face that challenge head-on."

"Easier said than done by one who doesn't break out in a cold sweat at the thought of leaving the house," Anna muttered.

"Allowing yourself time away from this farm is exactly what you need. And you can start right after dinner by going back to Shetler's and getting the rest of the groceries I sent you for the other day."

Anna didn't dare argue with her *schwester*. Especially since the store's image weighed heavy on her mind since her earlier cry to God.

***

The forenoon sun beat through the kitchen window as Anna finished the last of the dinner dishes. With their lunchtime meal finished, Mary Ellen tucked in for a nap, and Rebecca resting from the morning chores, Anna was free to go back to the dry goods store. Playing Eli's words in her head, she took a moment to take a cleansing breath before stepping off the porch.

Anna, God doesn't want you to put your trust in your own abilities; he wants you to trust Him. Fear is the devil's playground. Satan wants you to be anxious because you're telling God you don't have confidence in Him when you give in to those emotions.

She respected Eli and was encouraged by his wisdom. He had become her voice of reason as of late, and she used his words to get the courage to return to Shetler's.

She took the shortcut through her father's farm and prayed he was busy in his shop and wouldn't notice. Since leaving her father's church, she was forbidden to see or speak to him or her stepmother, Wilma.

She didn't regret stepping away from her Old Order upbringing. Still, when missing her father became too much to bear, she had to remember what Jesus gave up by saving her. Her daily prayer was that God would touch her father's heart and open his eyes to find salvation in Christ, not a set of rules and traditions.

A shower of yellow and gold leaves fluttered before her as she made her way along the row of maple trees that separated the Yoder and Byler farms. The path weaved its way past her brother Matthew's farm, around the dormant strawberry fields, and landed at the banks of Willow Creek.

The flock of Jenny Wrens perched high in the willow tree released a chatter as she passed. Their bubbly song made her smile as she spotted the feast awaiting them at the creek's edge. Slowing her steps, she rounded the corner and stopped at the covered bridge.

Many memories clouded her vision, forcing her to find comfort on a nearby log. Slipping off her shoes, she dipped her toes in the cool water and reminisced about a day much like today but a few years earlier.

Falling in step with Simon, she walked at his side along the winding path that led to Willow Creek. Simon sat his fishing vest and pole at his feet and pulled her down to join him on a fallen log. Reaching for the small plastic box from the vest pocket, he tied a new hook to the end of the line.

Holding up a jar of chartreuse trout bait, he bid, "So do you think they'll bite on this? Or should I give this yellow and brown rooster tail a try?"

She considered the two, then said, "I like that shiny gold thing on the back, so go with the rooster tail. Maybe the sun will reflect off it, and you'll get a good reaction bite."

He tied on the rooster tail and bumped her shoulder with his. "Listen to you, with all that fishing talk. A girl after my heart, for sure and certain."

"That's a start if you're still calling me your girl."

"Why wouldn't I? You're still my girl, right?"

"I wasn't sure since I said some hateful things a couple of weeks ago. And you haven't written to me to let me know otherwise."

Simon released his hold on the lure. "I had a lot of things to think about, and I wanted to give you some time to cool off."

Simon stood and walked over to the edge of the creek. Clicking the bail open, he flipped his rod back and then forward. They watched his lure sail through the air and to the other side of the creek. Letting the line sink for a few seconds, he slowly reeled the lure back, repeating the process over and over for fifteen minutes. His broad shoulders stood firm as he concentrated on watching the line.

"How does your hand feel?" Anna asked from her spot on the log.

Simon twisted his wrist. "I seem to be able to grip the reel tight, but it will take some time to regain my strength. I'm not sure I'll be up for any fluke fishing soon, but it's a good start."

Leaving the log, she moved to his side. "Fluke fishing, what's that again? You've explained it to me once."

A smile encased his face before he eagerly described the technique. "Remember when we went out on Conneaut Lake last year? I used that soft, white plastic minnow with silver specks on it. I swam the lure with a twitch, twitch...paaaauuuussssseeee...twitch...twitch, twitch motion. It takes a lot of wrist action. I'm not sure my hand is up for that yet."

"Oh, now I remember; that was a fun day. We went out for frozen custard on our way home. That was so nice of Pete to come to Willow Springs to get us so you could take me out on your boat."

Simon rubbed his earlobe. "If I remember right, I still have the scar on my ear to show for that little fishing adventure."

"I'm so sorry; I still can't believe I sliced the end of your earlobe with a hook. I told you I had never fished before, so teaching me to cast came with a price."

"Believe me, it was so worthwhile when you caught that four-pound bass. You showed me up that day, even if I got hooked in the process. Let's say that was the day you caught me."

Reeling in his line, he hooked the lure behind an eye on the rod, grabbed her hand, and led her back to the log.

He took off his straw hat, hooked it on his knee, and ran his fingers through his hair. The way he sucked in a deep breath told her he was about to say something important. Turning to face her, he picked up her hands and looked into her eyes. "You understand how much I love you, right?"

Nodding her head, Anna turned her palms over so he could fully grasp her hands. She waited for him to continue.

"I'm sorry I didn't stop by and see you so we could talk this out. You've been so patient with me, and I promised we would get married this fall. Everything didn't go as planned because of my hand, and I didn't know what to do. I had hoped I would get all this fishing out of my blood and be ready to settle down by now. I'm way past Rumspringa age and should be considering raising a family."

He paused, pulled her hands to his lips, and then kissed the back of her fingers. "You're my everything. But once I become baptized, I won't be able to fish as much, and definitely not in tournaments that will pull me away from home." He hesitated before continuing. "I feel like I'm giving up on my dream before seeing it through."

She felt a heaviness in her chest and watched the color drain from his face. Without a word, she pulled her hands from his, stood, and walked away. Tripping over his pole and vest, she scrambled to catch herself just as he scooped her up and kept her from falling.

"Wait, don't go; let's talk," he begged, pulling her close. Allowing her head to relax on his shoulder, he rested his chin on her kapp and whispered, "I can't bear the look of disappointment on your face. I've

made you wait long enough. Fishing or not, I must choose us, or I'm afraid I'll lose you."

Pushing herself far enough away to put both hands on his chest, she summoned her courage to ask, "Does that mean you'll talk to the bishop and start your baptism instruction? When do you think we can start planning the wedding? Who should we get to be our side sitters?"

"Whoa there, I can only answer one question at a time. I'll talk to the bishop next week. Let me take care of that, and then we can go from there. Is that okay?"

"I'm more than okay with your plan; it's perfect."

The day would be etched in her memory for as long as she lived. His broken promises and leaving in the middle of the night set a series of events that shaped her future…much to her dismay.

The sun glistened on the water cascading over a small waterfall in the swell of the pebble-lined creek. Sifting through the rocks near her feet, she found a flat rock and skipped it across the water. Everything she did these days reminded her of Simon.

Pulling herself off the bank, she slipped on her shoes and stockings and pushed Simon and his broken promises from her mind. Climbing the bank leading to South Main Street Extension, Anna savored the peaceful stroll by the gentle stream. However, the closer she got to Shetler's Grocery, the journey resembled a wild sled ride down Eli's Hill. Her heart thumped as if her sled ride was on a collision course with a tree with every step.

A lump settled in her throat as she approached the door. An *Englisch* couple with loaded arms pushed their way through the door, forcing her to the corner of the building. The beat in her ears drowned out her shallow breaths as she forced herself to the door again. Overcome with nausea, she retreated to the shadows muttering, "*I will never leave you nor forsake you; I will never leave you nor forsake you; I will never leave you nor forsake you.*"

Her feet moved without any regard for her wish to stay hidden. A row of brightly colored birdhouses and small wooden wheelbarrows used for planters lined the store's porch and helped her make a slow approach. Frozen to the ground at the entrance, a voice uttered, "Don't let your imagination feed your fear."

Wood dust and hard work filled her nose as Simon's hand reached around and opened the waiting door. An irresistible wave of anxiety engulfed her when she stepped through the threshold. His breath tickled the back of her neck as he followed her inside. A stack of wooden baskets prohibited her from making a quick escape when their handles twisted together in the folds of her dress, tipping the pack to the floor.

Simon stepped in front of her, knelt to align the stack, and handed her a single basket. A fine mist of wood shavings covered his arms, which she tried to focus on rather than his face. Their knuckles met, and the lump in the back of Anna's throat dislodged, letting a small sigh escape.

Simon stood, blocking her way. "It's good to see you out and about."

She tried to step around him. "I must go."

"Anna, there'll come a time when you'll have to give me a few minutes."

"*Nee*. We have nothing to talk about." His hand landed on her elbow. "Please, Anna, let me explain."

Her quiet voice broke with a few ending words as if his presence brought a new grasp of all she'd lost. "Time for defending your actions has long passed."

Simon lifted his heart in prayer for direction before he spoke again. "I've been lonely without you in my life."

Anna pulled away. "Whose fault is that but your own?"

Simon was ashamed as she walked away. Turning in the opposite direction, he headed to find the blackstrap molasses his *mamm* needed for shoofly pie, swallowing hard against her statement. While he knew she only spoke the truth, it was still hard to hear.

Anna waited until she turned to the end of the row before putting her hand to her neck and taking a few cleansing breaths. Her palm, moist from their closeness, felt warm to her skin. His mere presence rattled her, and there was no denying their hearts were still intertwined no matter how she wished otherwise.

She peered over a row of cereal boxes, waiting for Simon to leave the store. With all the worry of another anxiety attack behind her, she reached for Rebecca's list in her purse. Peanuts and corn syrup were clearly marked off; she scanned the items while keeping a close eye on the top of Simon's hat…only releasing her breath after he paid Barbara, the cashier, and left.

***

Simon stopped at his horse's head, pulling the brim of his hat down to block the early afternoon sun. Gazing at the storefront, he waited and tightened the bridle before running a hand over the horse's dark mane. One last look before he headed back to work. He hoped to etch her small frame behind his eyes long enough to carry him through another day.

***

Later that afternoon, Simon settled back into his job at Mast Lumber Mill. The hard work did little to clear Anna from his mind as sweat roosted between his shoulder blades. His triceps, still tense from catching slabs of wood at the bottom of the conveyor belt, flexed when he closed his hands around the rough lumber. Even the never-ending pile of boards lurching at him did little to tire his troubled soul. The only thing that kept him going was knowing the extra money he made as a sawyer would come in handy when it came time to prove to Anna that he wasn't leaving again.

When the conveyor belt finally rolled to a stop, he took off his straw hat, brushed aside damp hair from his forehead, and thought, *No matter how long it takes, I'll continue to whittle away at her heart until all my bad choices and shattered dreams break away, making room for a future. No sense in upsetting her further. I'll keep finding ways to see her, even if it means going out of my way to be in her path. One of these days, I'll wear her down enough; she'll have no choice but to listen.*

CHAPTER 4

Simon carried a cup of coffee to the front porch and sat in a willow-bent rocker next to his mother. With the evening meal and evening chores complete, he could rest. Holding the cup in one hand, he laid the other work-worn hand on his knee and sat silently.

With her bare foot, his mother pushed her chair into motion and said, "I've been watching you, and you're troubled. What is it, son?"

"What makes you think so?" Simon took a sip of his sweet cream coffee and lingered at the rim of his cup.

"Mothers are tuned in to the turmoil of their children."

He answered slowly as he set his cup on the stand between them. "I didn't think getting Anna's attention would be so hard."

An evening breeze blew past them, and Naomi pulled her sweater tighter. "You broke her heart. You can't expect her to step back into your life at your beck and call."

"But *Mamm*," he said, "I don't have much time."

Mrs. Kauffman had to smile at his boyish impatience.

"Surrender."

Simon thought it over, then continued, "How much more do I have to surrender? I've sold everything I had, met with Bishop Schrock about starting instruction classes, and asked God to forgive me more times than I thought possible."

His mother stood and rested her hand on his shoulder. "Could be you're putting something before Him." Raising an eyebrow, she continued, "Or perhaps you're trying to pry a door open He's not ready for you to walk through yet."

She walked to the door and stopped. "Have you been seeking guidance from above? Or have you been relying on your own understanding of what troubles you?"

Simon gripped the chair arms and stared out at his father's dairy farm. Finally, he reacted, unsure if he could express what troubled him most.

"As Christians, we are to forgive, correct?"

"*Jah*. Why?" His mother requested.

"I don't think Anna can get over my betrayal." Simon stayed quiet until his mother spoke. "You are underestimating the power of prayer."

His voice broke as he answered, "*Jah*."

Simon walked to the barn, hoping to find a spot he could have a quiet word with the Lord. Above, the September sky came to life with tiny lights, and as he looked at them, they seemed closer than Anna was. Folding his arms across the top rail of the corral, he closed his eyes and buried his head in his joined arms.

Later in his room he rose from his knees, the Bible still open on the bed. His eyes stung as thoughts of Anna still swirled around. But now, a new warmth of peace surrounded him as He felt God's hand in his life. His mother was right; he had put God's plan above his desires, and just admitting it and asking for forgiveness helped calm his restless mind.

Shutting his Bible, Simon crawled into bed and prayed one last prayer. *"Lord, whatever the cost, I lay this at your feet. Bless Anna and bring us closer if that is your will. Amen."*

***

The following day was full and busy for Anna. She worked from early morning until it was time to help Rebecca with dinner. She hoped all thoughts of Simon would be lost to occupied hands.

After taking a yarn inventory, she set a pot on the propane heater to boil a batch of avocado pits. The all-natural vegetable colorant would turn the white alpaca hair a lovely shade of peach. While the dye simmered, Anna soaked the fiber in a vinegar and water solution that would help set the color of the fiber.

With Naomi's lavender yarn complete, she placed it on the worktable and wrote up a receipt before moving to the spinning wheel on the front porch. While the weather was pleasant, she loved to spin yarn outside, allowing remnants of the fine fiber to float away with the wind.

The clean fiber was silky as she twisted it while pumping the pedal with her foot. After adjusting the tension, she set her foot back steadily as she drew the rope roving back and forth, feeding it on the bobbin. She enjoyed working with alpaca fiber the most, unlike the prickly sheep's wool.

Her back to the driveway she continued to work to fill the bobbin. Typically, it would take her five hours to work through a basket of roving, but today, she only had a short time.

An orange-top buggy pulled up to the hitching post, but she didn't take her eyes off the twisted fiber flowing from her fingers. When she finally slowed the wheel with her hand, Anna looked up, a little frown puckering her brow.

Simon tipped his hat. "Anna."

Her gut twisted, and she snapped, "What do you want now?"

With a grin of determination, he declared, "We live in the same community, so you best get used to me being around."

Anna set the wheel in motion and continued to wind the thin fibers through her fingers. "Why are you here?"

"*Mamm* asked me to stop and check on her yarn order."

The wheel slowed, and she folded the loose roving in her lap apron and set it aside. "I'll get it for you."

She longed for him over the years, which sometimes seemed unbearable. Now he was so close, and all she wanted was for him to disappear. But at every turn, he kept showing up. She would need to stop it, and quickly if she was going to get any peace.

Anna stepped behind the worktable, trying to formulate a plan. "Next time, tell your mother she can call the phone shanty and leave a message. I can easily drop an order in the mail."

Anna held her breath as Simon sighed. "The mail? I'd say that's a tad ridiculous. Why would you waste good money on postage when we live so close?"

"It would save you a trip."

"Did you happen to think I might enjoy seeing you?"

Her lips set in tight. "Did you think I'd much rather not see…*you*?" With shaky hands, Anna tore the receipt from the pad and stuffed it with Naomi's order in the bag. The words stung as soon as they left her lips. When she handed him the brown sack, he took her hand and said, "You can continue to push me away, but you won't be able to stop my prayers."

He dropped her hand before she had a chance to pull away. Leaving her to study his troubled face, she couldn't help but wonder what exactly he was praying for. His eyes didn't hold anger at her harsh treatment, but the softness in his voice spoke of hope.

After he left, she glanced at the time, gathered her supplies from the porch, and locked the shop. Emma and Katie were expecting them for their *schwester* day.

***

Rebecca handed Mary Ellen to Anna before stepping out of the buggy carrying a covered casserole dish. As soon as Anna followed Rebecca, the toddler squirmed out of Anna's arms and ran toward Elizabeth playing in the sandbox in the sideyard. Emma and Katie waved them to the picnic table under the autumn-filled maple tree.

Emma rushed to her waddling *schwester's* side and emptied her arms. "By the way it looks, Mary Ellen will have a new playmate any day now."

Rebecca pushed a kick from her ribcage and lowered herself to the bench. "I'm much bigger than I was with Mary Ellen; I'm sure Eli is getting a new little farm hand with this one."

Anna stood next to Katie and asked, "Who is minding the bakery?"

"My *mamm* and Barbara Wagler."

"How is Barbara doing?" Anna asked. "It was such a shame her John was taken at such a young age. It breaks my heart that she has to raise those boys without their *datt*."

Emma opened her picnic basket and snapped open a red-checkered tablecloth. "I hear John's older *bruder*, Joseph, found his way back to the fold and is helping her with the farm."

Walking around the table, Emma laid out plates and silverware. She continued, "God has a way of stepping in and laying out a plan in the most mysterious ways. We haven't seen the hide or hair of Joseph Wagler in five years, and out of the blue, he comes back ready to join the church."

Katie took the cover off a bowl of seven-layer salad, laid a spoon across the top, and turned toward Anna. "Much like Simon, *jah*?" Katie gave her arm a squeeze.

Anna stuttered, "I wouldn't know his plans, and I…I don't care."

All three women giggled simultaneously, but it was Rebecca who spoke up. "You can deny you don't care with your lips, but your eyes paint a different picture."

Anna busied herself with folding napkins and securing them under each plate as she drew a deep breath. "I'd prefer not to be the topic of conversation this afternoon if you all don't mind."

Katie sat and rested her arm across her widened middle. "But you're the only one with something exciting to talk about besides dirty diapers and sticky fingers."

"What about Emma? Her life has to be more exciting than mine even if she's not with child."

Emma's face illuminated. "Well, there is something I've been intending to tell you all." She didn't need to say another word as her two *schwesters* and her best friend Katie engulfed her in a hug.

Katie was the first to push back. "I thought you had filled out some, but I figured you'd been tasting too many sweets at the bakery."

Emma slapped her arm and laughed. "Are you trying to tell me I'm getting fat?"

Katie blushed. "You have to admit we do a lot of sampling."

Rebecca asked without thinking, "Have you told *Datt* and Wilma?"

Emma's face dropped. "I thought of sending a note off to him, but I'm sure he'll throw it away without opening it."

"But what if…" Anna's voice trailed off doubtfully.

Emma sighed. "There's no use; Samuel and I have gone round and round trying to figure out a way to tell him he'll have another grandchild." Emma turned toward Rebecca. "I suppose if Mary Ellen or Matthew's girls didn't force him to reconsider his stand on our excommunication, I can't think our child will have much pull either."

Rebecca struggled to swing her leg under the table. "I have to believe if *Mamm* were still alive, she would do everything to be a part of her grandchildren's lives. It sickens me that *Datt* is so fixed on the past he won't even consider doing away with this split."

Anna folded her knee under her hip, rested her chin on her propped-up palm, and asked, "Do you think he misses us?"

Emma took a seat beside her. "I think now that his new minister position has worn off some, he may be second-guessing siding with Bishop Weaver and the old ways.

Samuel has talked to many of our neighbors, and most agree the old ways no longer serve our community. Many believe if the ministers and bishop taught more about Jesus, the way the Bible says, we wouldn't lose so many to the *Englisch*."

Katie reached for a ginger snap. "Daniel mentioned both Joseph and Simon have met with Bishop Schrock about instructional classes."

Emma faced Anna. "That's good news, *jah*?"

"I might as well save you all the trouble of jumping to conclusions," Anna said wearily. "That ship has long sailed."

"Why else would he have come back?" Rebecca's lips turned up.

"Quit! I don't care why he returned, and I'm tired of everyone asking me about him. If you want to know, ask him."

Anna twisted her hands in her lap. "I'm sorry, I didn't mean to sound so sharp. I've had a hard time seeing him. I admit running into him so much has gotten me quite worked up."

Emma wrapped her arm around her shoulder. "Could it be you still have feelings for him?"

"I didn't think I did, but my heart races every time I see him. I can't tell if it's anger or anxiety. I thought I'd forgiven him for leaving two days before our wedding, but the way my stomach lurches every time I see him, I don't think I have."

Rebecca added a scoop of salad to her plate. She waited until they all bowed their heads and looked back up before adding, "He was pretty concerned with your whereabouts last week. The look on his face told me more than anything."

Anna stayed silent as the three girls talked about their upcoming births. While she was happy for Emma and Samuel, especially since they had to wait so long before trying again, a deep sorrow was mulling around her heart. If she looked back on how she thought her life would be by now, children were definitely in the picture.

From across the yard, Katie's mother, Ruth, walked their way carrying Anna's peanut brittle basket. "Anna, I hoped I'd see you today. We can't keep your candy in stock. As soon as we fill your basket, we've sold it all before we notice."

Anna took the straw basket from her hands. "What on earth? I made three batches last week. Who's buying it all?"

"We did have a couple of bus tours stop by this week, but the Kauffman boys are gobbling up most of it. Mainly Simon. When I asked him about it, he said it was one of the things he missed most about Willow Springs."

Anna took a drink of meadow tea and coughed out a mouthful at Ruth's statement. After wiping her chin, she fought back the mental and spiritual battle forging inside.

Ruth bent down and muttered close to Anna's ear. "Before you go home today, come over to the house. I have something I've been meaning to give you."

With a quizzical tilt, she answered, "Sure."

Rebecca and Emma exchanged a glance, and Ruth winked at them most peculiarly.

As Ruth returned to the bakery, Anna asked, "What's that all about?"

Rebecca put a forkful of food in her mouth and talked through the bite. "We can't be sure, but I think we both know what Ruth is up to. Trust me, you'll benefit from doing as she asks."

The girls enjoyed catching up and watching Mary Ellen and Elizabeth play in the yard for the next couple of hours. Emma raked a pile of leaves and taught the girls how to jump and hide in fall glory. While Katie and Rebecca were past frolicking in the grass, Anna and Emma chased the toddlers so much that a nap would come easy for them.

Mary Ellen climbed into Rebecca's lap. "Anna, I'm about ready to head home soon. Do you want to go to Ruth's before we leave?"

"Today is a beautiful day. How about you and Mary Ellen head home? I'll see what Ruth needs, and then I'll just walk."

Anna helped Emma clean the picnic table before heading to Ruth's house. She stopped when she noticed Barbara locking the bakery door and waited for her to walk her way.

Anna looked at her friend's face as she walked to the side of the road. Barbara looked weary. "How are you?"

"*Gut,* I suppose. I'm struggling with working both at Shetler's and the bakery. The bishop does not like it one bit. He keeps saying my place is with the boys, but without John farming, we need to eat and pay the taxes. I don't have much choice."

Anna trod lightly. "I hear Joseph is back and is helping you with the farm."

Barbara dropped her eyes. "I have mixed feelings about his return. I'm trying not to overthink it, but I admit his presence rattles me. He wants to help with the farm, but I haven't given in to his pleas yet."

Anna gasped. "I sympathize with you."

Barbara reached out and rested her hand on her arm. "I heard Simon was back."

The lump in Anna's throat began to break up, and for a moment, she could be honest with someone who understood. "I was just getting used to the fact I needed to move on, and lo and behold, he's back. My anxiety level skyrocketed, and all those old feelings came rushing to the surface. To be quite honest, I wish he'd never come back."

Barbara moved in closer and said, "I feel the same way," with a sob in her voice. "Joseph and I had our future planned, and when he jumped the fence to the *Englisch,* I didn't think I'd ever love again. But then John took his place, and now I must deal with all those old feelings again with John gone and Joseph back."

Anna drew in a long shuddering breath. "Oh, Barbara, what are we to do?"

Her friend seemed to struggle for the right words. "John's *mamm* told me I need to trust in the Lord. She also said the trials we face are not the result of God's inability to see what we need, but a sign of his loving care."

Anna snarled, "But look what they did to us, and we're supposed to be happy with their return?"

"Believe me, I'm trying to work through it as much as you. But relying on God and not my feelings is proving to be a challenge. John's parents have been wonderful and gave me some good advice."

Anna wanted to hear more. "May I ask what advice they gave you?"

Barbara smiled and nodded her head. "Andy is wise, and his words often comfort me. Last night, he reminded me that God is always in control. We play God instead of being godlike whenever we try to sway our circumstances."

Anna swallowed hard. "I keep hearing stuff like that. But boy, is it hard to give up all that control."

"I agree! Well, I best be getting home to the boys. I'm sure my mother-in-law has had enough of those rambunctious grandsons."

Left alone on the side of the road, Anna fought back another wave of anxiousness and struggled to gain a sense of peace in her mind before visiting with Ruth.

CHAPTER 5

Ruth peered out the kitchen window, and her heart pained as she watched the two young women at the end of her driveway. Both girls shared similar struggles, but it was her best friend, Stella's daughter, Anna, who consumed her thoughts. She and Stella made many precious memories during their thirty-year friendship, but the one they shared on her death bed tugged at her the most.

The promise to deliver a special gift to each of Stella's daughters was the one thing that kept her dearest friend's memory alive. Ruth poured two tea glasses and sat at the table, a hand resting on the white dress box she'd carried to the kitchen.

***

Anna continued to steady herself before knocking on Ruth's door. With only the screen between them, Ruth called her in, pulled out a chair, and patted the polished oak seat as she entered the kitchen.

"Sit, child. I have a little something I've wanted to share with you." Ruth pulled the box closer and slid it in front of Anna.

"Your mother asked me to share this with you when I felt you needed her the most. I've been watching you the last few weeks and thought this might help bring her closer."

The corner of Anna's lip quivered with the mention of her mother. She lifted the cover off the box and pushed aside pink tissue paper. A light gray crocheted shawl lined the box. Pulling the soft yarn to her cheek, she closed her eyes, hoping a vision of her mother would appear.

Ruth stood and laid a hand on her shoulder. "Take as much time as you need. I'll be out in the garden if you want to talk."

Anna placed the garment across her lap and ran her fingertip over her mother's perfect penmanship on the envelope left for her. A ripple of emotion landed on her nose as she opened her mother's letter.

My Dearest Anna,

From the time you came into this world, on Rebecca's heels, your quiet spirit brought a sense of peace to our family. To that, I will always be grateful for your gentle ways.

If you're reading this letter, Ruth has followed my wishes and presented you with this small gift. She will have only shared this with you when you needed some of my guidance. Please take my words to heart and apply them to the challenges you face today.

Accept this present and wrap it tightly around your shoulders whenever you need to feel me close. With every stitch, I prayed for you and your future. And even though I cannot walk through life with you, I've poured my heart out to the one who can.

Rest assured, God holds today and all of your tomorrows in the palm of His hand. The peace He offers you is beyond your understanding and is better than ever imagined. I promise that if you turn to Him, He will guard you against falling into the depths of despair.

Having to face the end of my life, I've learned much about trusting God. Not only did I have to surrender the care of my children, but I had to admit I couldn't control the outcome of my tomorrow.

Anna, you tend to worry first and trust second. I know these things because I've struggled with the same. It wasn't until I started to go to God in prayer that I truly understood how important it was to pray with gratitude.

When God instructed us not to worry, He didn't say we wouldn't face challenges. Instead, He wants us to focus all our energy on being thankful. When those troubling thoughts make their way into our minds, we can say: "I'm not going to think about that because I've already prayed about it."

Are you going to God in prayer, Anna? Are your thoughts causing you to be fearful? Go to Him in prayer and ask for all things. Then walk away and let Him do what He does best…filling your heart with courage and a solid commitment to follow Jesus. Find your happiness in Him; He will guide your path if you let Him.

One last thing.

Your datt will need you all when I'm gone, for one, you'll need to do everything in your power to keep the family close. Give him lots of grandbabies and keep him involved in your life. I pray he will be surrounded with love and family until he comes to meet me at heaven's pearly gate.

Until we meet again,

Mamm

Anna cried for a few moments before she folded the letter and tucked it beneath the layers of tissue paper. It was like a knife thrust through her heart at her mother's request about her father.

The life her mother wished for would never be with their lovely community split between old and new. Her father on one side, and she and her siblings on the other. As it stood, he had never held Rebecca and Eli's daughter Mary Ellen. He had only seen her brother Matthew's two girls as infants.

She cried, "My Lord, what am I to do?"

Tucking the dress box under her arm, she headed to the garden where Ruth filled a wheelbarrow with the last of the ripe tomatoes. Anna sat at the garden's edge and balanced her gift on folded knees.

Anna looked over the garden long before saying, "I've failed *Mamm,* and I'm sure I've disappointed God."

Ruth emptied her hands and moved to Anna's side, kneeling beside her as she put an arm around her trembling shoulders. Anna drew in a long breath at the loving tenderness of her mother's best friend and let herself relax momentarily. Then, remembering her mother's final request, she stiffened again. Ruth let go and picked up Anna's chin with a single finger.

"Whatever it is, it can't be that bad. And besides, God would never be disappointed in you."

"Oh, Ruth, I'm not sure what I should do. *Mamm* asked me to keep the family together and look at us. *Datt's* never held his granddaughter. It's been almost two years since he has seen any of his children. It would break her heart if she knew the state of her family." With difficulty, Anna suppressed the tightness in her throat.

"Anna, I'm sure your mother would be upset, but you must remember we split from a church that didn't allow us to follow Jesus openly. Without a doubt, she would want her children to know Jesus above everything else."

A look of pain settled on Anna's pale face, and she asked, "Did she know Jesus?"

Ruth's eyes smiled, and she patted Anna's folded hands. "Oh, child. It was your mother who showed me the truth. She not only knew, but she shared her new-found love of Jesus with whoever came to visit her in those last few weeks."

"But why didn't she share it with *Datt*? Maybe if she had, he would have walked away from the Old Order with his children."

"She did. But your father wasn't so quick to accept the truth. He begged her not to sway her children. But she's sent all of you a message of her belief in salvation."

"Matthew, Emma, and Rebecca have all received a letter too?"

"Jah."

Anna admired Ruth and loved her dearly when she saw the compassion in her eyes. "You helped her reach us, didn't you?"

Ruth smoothed out her apron. "She would have done the same for me, for sure and certain."

Anna paused, before asking. "How did you get Levi to leave the church so easily?"

"I had nothing to do with it."

"But how so? You're his wife."

"I prayed. God did the rest."

Ruth walked back to the row of tomatoes, but not before adding, "Anna, you need to get out of your head. Once you realize you have no control other than the prayers you petition God for, you'll be happier. Quit trying to line your life up on a tidy little path, and let God lead your way. Even if it means you must step in a mud puddle a time or two along the way."

Anna stood, brushed dried leaves from her apron, and picked up the dress box. “It’s been hard to see past what keeps showing up in front of my face.”

Ruth peered over the filled wheelbarrow. “Would that happen to be Simon Kauffman?”

After a few seconds of silence, Ruth spoke again. “What are you afraid of?”

Anna’s eyes misted over. “I’m trying to trust when it comes to Simon, but the thought of opening my heart again terrifies me.”

Ruth stood and balanced her hands on her hips. “So, you’ll give up on love in fear of what might happen?”

“The thought of allowing him to become part of my life again is a hard cross to bear.”

“Anna, I can’t imagine how hurt you were when he left you a few days before your wedding, but you must forgive and move on. If you harbor this pain, you’ll never find the peace God offers you. What would have happened if Jesus had walked away from us because it was too hard to do what God asked him to do?”

A peaceful expression flooded Ruth’s concerned face when Anna answered. “I think God sent you to remind me of such things.”

Anna and her *schwester’s* treasured Ruth’s motherly influence and love. And they found consolation in her wise words, which always came when needed.

***

As Anna lay in her room listening to an array of nighttime chatter through the open window, she longed to find a way to reach out to her father. Mixed in the pain of her family’s separation, she struggled to push Simon's face from her mind. A late-season warmth blew past the curtain and settled on her face as she drifted off to sleep.

***

Simon sat on the edge of his bed, holding a small photo up to the light. The dark-haired baby tugged at his heart as he ran his thumb over the tattered picture and whispered, "I'm working hard to get back to you; please don't grow too fast, my son."

He slipped the photo into his Bible and stretched his feet out on the bed. Clasping his hands under his head, he watched shadows from the oil lamp dance on the ceiling and thought of Anna. Remembering the letter from Cora's parents' lawyer, he swung his feet over the bed and re-read its contents.

The letter contained several things he needed to take care of. A letter of character recommendation from the bishop, a financial statement, proof of employment, and the one thing he prayed for daily, evidence of a stable home life. His son's maternal grandparents required all those things before releasing custody of their only grandchild.

After Cora was killed in a car accident, her parents hesitated to hand over the baby to a man whose reputation followed him through the tabloids.

Six months was such a short time to turn his life around and prove to Cora's parents he could be trusted with the only thing they had left of their daughter…*Marcus*. Anna was the key to showing them the child would be well cared for. Somehow, he had to prove to Anna he was on his way back to her long before Cora stepped into the picture.

On those days when he struggled to forgive himself, Bishop Schrock's words reminded him he was present for every wrong decision. Still, those bad choices didn't define his future if he used them to draw closer to God.

Setting the letter aside, he laid back down and talked to the only one who would listen, His Heavenly Father, who saw all, knew all, and forgave him for his free will.

He prayed and longed to raise Marcus in a home that put God first in all they did. And it never crossed his mind Anna wouldn't love his son. However, the barrier would be, could she love him as she once did?

***

A ray of sunshine warmed Anna's face as she greeted the morning. A small child's face invaded her dreams, and she kept her eyes closed, hoping to focus on the fading memory. Suddenly, she sat up and pushed the image away, chalking it up to spending the day with her *schwesters*.

Mary Ellen's cries called to her through the adjoining wall. She met Rebecca in the hallway, shuffling toward her niece's room.

"Oh, thank goodness you're up." Rebecca had become pale as she steadied herself on the wall.

Calmly, Anna took her by the elbow and led her back to her room. "Go back to bed; I'll take care of Mary Ellen."

Rebecca's voice rose. "I'm nauseous this morning and all crampy."

"You're only at eight months. I think it's too early to be in labor, *jah*?"

Rebecca doubled over and moaned. "I'd say this little one has other plans."

Anna helped Rebecca sit on the edge of the bed. "I'll send Eli to fetch Dr. Smithson. Will you be all right for a few minutes?"

"*Jah*."

Anna scooped Mary Ellen up from her crib and headed to the barn. She found Eli huddled over the workbench. "Eli, I think your little one wants to come a few weeks early."

Eli wiped his hand on a red shop rag. "So soon?"

"*Jah*, I'd say so."

Anna followed Eli to the house, put Mary Ellen in her highchair, and placed a handful of cereal on her tray before checking on Rebecca.

Another long sigh met Anna as Eli helped Rebecca move to the chair under the window. Eli pointed to the wet spot in the center of the mattress. Anna pulled the linens from the bed and said, "I don't think we have time to wait for the doctor; go fetch Ruth."

Eli became white and disappeared without another word. Rebecca snickered between contractions. "He can deliver lambs all day long, but this is too much for him."

"Me too; I'd much prefer the doctor to be here," Anna said slowly as the magnitude of the situation dawned on her.

As another wave moved across Rebecca's middle, she groaned, "Not…you too!"

Anna added a layer of towels over the mattress cover before snapping clean sheets over the bed and heading to her *schwester's* side. "Let's get you back to bed before the next round starts."

Rebecca squeezed Anna's hand. "Oh my, this one's going to be quick."

After Anna got Rebecca settled, she checked on Mary Ellen, filled a sippy cup with milk, and added another handful of round oats to her tray. "You be a good girl. I'll be right back, *jah*?"

Mary Ellen held up a single oat to Anna; she took it and kissed her on the top of her head before returning to Rebecca.

Rebecca cried, "The *bobbli* is coming. Eli needs to hurry with Ruth."

The screen door barely stopped bouncing off its frame before Eli and Ruth arrived in the bedroom. Ruth looked in Anna's direction. "How far apart?"

"One right on top of another."

Ruth shooed Eli out of the room. "Go tend to Mary Ellen; we'll holler if we need you."

Eli bent forward and laid his hand on Rebecca's cheek. "Do you want me to stay?"

Rebecca faltered, then glanced at Ruth, her eyes finally resting on her husband. "No, go. I'm in excellent hands."

After Ruth gave Anna a list of instructions, Anna and Eli moved to the kitchen, leaving Ruth to care for Rebecca.

Eli had taken Mary Ellen from her highchair and had set her on the counter washing her hands.

Anna spoke quietly, taking the warm cloth from his hands. "Ruth thinks it best you go for Dr. Smithson. The *bobbli* might need more than she can handle."

Pausing to steady himself before leaving, Eli took a long look toward the bedroom. "I'll hurry. Pray Anna…pray."

The sounds coming from her *schwester's* bedroom caused her to take Mary Ellen outside as soon as they both dressed. The child threw her arms around Anna's neck with the promise of a piggyback ride.

Setting Mary Ellen in the sandbox, Anna dug her bare feet into the cool sand. She couldn't help but marvel at the look of love she witnessed on her brother-in-law's face. Eli loved Rebecca; there was no doubt about it.

Her mother's letter came to mind about how she had prayed over every stitch, and she assumed she did the same for Rebecca and Emma. The reminder about praying to God and then stepping aside and letting him do what he did best floated through the air. All worry left Anna's mind after she stopped to pray, remembering her mother's words…

He wants us to focus all our energy on being thankful. When those troubling thoughts make their way into our minds, we can say: "I'm not going to think about that because I've already prayed about it."

Ruth's voice rang out from the porch. "Anna, come!"

Anna moved to the house, brushing sand off Mary Ellen's dress, and balanced her on her hip.

Mary Ellen ran toward Rebecca's room when Anna set her down. Running after her, she stopped in the doorway at the sight of the newborn snuggled to Rebecca's chest.

Ruth rolled a stack of towels and picked up a basin. "That little guy must weigh eight pounds and is as healthy as a full-term *bobbli*."

Anna sat on the edge of the bed and pulled Mary Ellen up onto her lap. "A new *bobbli bruder* for you."

Mary Ellen reached for his tiny head, and Anna pulled back her small fingers. "Careful now."

Eli stepped into the room and knelt beside his family. "You just couldn't wait, could you, little guy?"

Anna handed Mary Ellen to her father and stepped out of the room with Ruth and Dr. Smithson. As Ruth and the doctor spoke in the hallway, Anna walked outside.

CHAPTER 6

Hours turned into days as Anna spent every minute caring for her *schwester's* family. Little John Paul found his place in the Bricker family. Even Mary Ellen fell in love with her new *bruder* and woke each morning asking for him.

While Anna enjoyed being an active member of the Bricker household, a void had worked its way into her life. She yearned for a family of her own. In those moments when John Paul slept in Rebecca's arms, the realization she may never have a child of her own left her thinking of Simon and what could have been.

Rebecca stopped her as Anna carried a laundry basket through the living room. "I think I can handle the *kinner* for the afternoon. Why don't you go open the shop for a few hours?"

She saw signs of Rebecca and Eli's happy family in every direction. There was an open Bible, Mary Ellen's toys, John Paul's baby quilt, and Rebecca's growing happiness. Oh, how she wished she was content.

"Perhaps I shall if you're sure you'll be okay without me."

"Women have been having babies for years, and most don't have their *schwester* living with them. I'm sure I'll be capable."

Anna was lost, not knowing for sure what was bothering her. When she unlocked the door to the yarn shop, she left the screen door open to let the crisp September air fill the room. After opening a window, she sunk down on the stool near the worktable and laid her head on her folded arms.

As soon as she closed her eyes, the small boy from her dream came to mind. Trying to remember the vision that woke her that morning, she brought the child's dark hair and eyes to life. A warmth filled her, and she squeezed her eyes tighter, hoping to keep the scene alive. Behind her eyes, she knelt, welcoming the boy into her embrace as they tumbled back in a field of lavender. His child-like giggles stopped when the door slammed against its hinges. Lifting her head and rubbing the spots from her eyes, she said, "I'll be with you in a minute."

When her eyes cleared, Simon stood twirling his hat in his fingers looking concerned, then he asked, "Did I interrupt a nap?"

"Hardly; I was just thinking, that's all."

"May I inquire as to what has you so perplexed?"

When she lifted her head to meet his eyes, his matted hair left a curled-up ring around his head, and she couldn't help but laugh.

"What's so funny?"

She straightened a stack of patterns. "You look like you have a tire swing around your head."

He ran his hand through his hair. "If that's all it takes to get you to smile, I'll sport an old tire on my head daily."

The light in her eyes faded. "What do you need, Simon?"

He took a note from his pants pocket. "*Mamm* asked me to deliver this to you. I'm to wait for an answer."

After reading its contents, Anna unfolded the flower-lined paper and dropped it in the trash.

Anna,

Help! My lavender plants are dying.

Naomi

"Tell her I'll stop by tomorrow morning."

He didn't say a word, and as if time stood still, they both stared at one another, waiting for the other to break the spell. It was Simon who spoke first. "Can we sit for a minute?"

She pointed to the stool, feeling relatively small next to his towering frame. Her pulse quickened when he laid his hat on the table and pulled the chair closer to her. The emotional struggle her heart and head were having forced beads of sweat to form on the back of her neck.

She pushed her stool away and tucked her hands under her thighs. When he took longer than she felt necessary, she hurried him along. "I have work to do. What is it you want to say?"

He waved her quiet. "Please give me a minute. I want to make sure what I say comes out perfect."

Her knee bounced, and he stopped it with his large hand. She pulled away, allowing his hand to fall. "There was a time when I didn't revolt you."

Her mouth dropped open. "And whose fault is that?"

"Anna, please, you must forgive me. I've made many mistakes and want to make things right."

"I'm not sure that's possible."

He looked up and smiled wearily, making her chest tighten, with his reply, "All things are possible with God."

The once confident young man she fell in love with was looking at her with eyes begging her to hear him out. The edginess she felt when he first sat down melted away with his hopeful tone. She countered, "I'm not sure I have anything else to give. I gave you my heart, and you trampled on it until it barely beat."

He reached for her hands, but she clasped them on her lap, ignoring his desire. "I've forgiven you. That's not the problem."

"Then why won't you let me make it up to you?"

For a second, there was silence, and she was taken back to the letter she had received from his wife over a year ago. The day all hope of his return washed away with her tears. Disappointment lodged in her throat, and she gurgled, "I don't trust you."

Simon's distress hardened his glare, and he dropped his head.

With a gulp of deep emotion, she added, "I'm not sure why you've come back, Simon. Go home to your family. You've made your choice; now live up to your responsibilities."

She left him sitting in the shop and walked back to the house. He made his choice long ago, and no amount of begging or pleading eyes changed that fact. He had broken her heart and walked out on his wife and child. He had no right even talking to Bishop Schrock. With a long sigh, she pushed open the kitchen door, blocking his *Englisch* family from her thoughts. Anna never shared Cora's letter with anyone and buried the hurt under layers of lost hopes and dreams.

***

Simon waited until he heard the house door close before moving to the porch. He thought he could handle anything she confronted him with, but losing her trust was worse than losing her love. What did she mean by demanding he go home to his family? That is what he had done. He came back to Willow Springs to live up to his obligations.

After a thoughtful pause, Simon stepped up in the buggy and clicked his tongue to direct his horse to the road. A new sense of determination entered the canvas-covered carriage. He vowed to depend entirely on the Lord's lead.

***

Simon found his mother in the basement when he returned home. "Anna said she'd be over in the morning."

"Oh, perfect. If anyone can figure out what is wrong with those plants, she can."

Simon moved a stack of canning jars as his mother swept. The two stayed in thoughtful silence as they cleaned around the jar-lined shelves, which took up one whole side of the basement. Naomi emptied a full dustpan into the trash and spoke slowly. "Give her time. She'll come around, I'm sure of it."

Simon sat on the step and rested his elbows on his knees. "I'm not so sure. She doesn't trust me."

Naomi turned over an old milk crate and took a seat. "I'm sure the Lord is using this healing time to help the both of you shape your future."

"I'm not sure we have much of one, but I am leaving it up to Him to figure it out."

"You wouldn't have found your way back to us unless there was a reason you were meant to be here. Have patience in God's timing."

"But Cora's parents won't give me Marcus unless I can prove he'll be raised properly. In my books that means both a *mamm* and *datt*."

"Simon, you must remember his grandparents are in their sixties and in no position to raise a child. I am confident he'll be reunited with you when God sees fit and not one moment before."

He reached for his mother's aging hand and helped her up. "Thank you," he said warmly.

***

A mix of clouds and sun met Anna as she walked through the covered bridge and onto Willow Creek Road. The three-mile walk to the Kauffman farm gave her ample time to contemplate her life, or the lack thereof, as her mood indicated.

Pushing through an overwhelming heaviness, the closer she got to Naomi's house, the more she begged God to help her trust Him instead of her own feelings. *Lord, I want to obey you and follow your path for me, whatever it might be. Please help me see you in every part of my life and help me understand why you've placed Simon back in my path. No matter how fearful I feel, I want to be strong in you. I'm nothing without you. I want to grow in my faith and not be foolish in understanding your plan. Help me rise above my past and live solely in your present. Amen.*

A light rain speckled the road as Simon pulled up beside her.

"That dark cloud is about to let loose. Best let me take you to the house."

Anna looked to the sky and back to Simon. "I'm fine."

"Dag gone-it, Anna. Quit being so stubborn and get in."

The rise of Simon's chest forced her to walk in front of the buggy and climb inside. He had both sides of the canvas rolled up, allowing the rain to find its way to her face. Pulling off to the side of the road, he handed Anna the reins and hopped down to snap the orange canvas closed.

No sooner had he let down the driver's side covering than the sky opened, and a steady shower bounced off the road as he guided the buggy back to the blacktop. Simon's black standardbred horse threw his head and sidestepped, lurching the cart off the pavement. He led the carriage back to the side of the road and turned on the battery-operated safety lights.

"We best sit tight for a few minutes."

Anna looked at the house less than a quarter of a mile away. "I suppose."

Simon secured the foot brake and relaxed his shoulders against the blue-lined seat. "Thanks for helping *Mamm.* I'm sure you'd much rather be anywhere but here today."

"I like your *mamm*; she was always polite to me."

The only sound in the carriage was the music of the late autumn rain. Showers of colored leaves blew around, leaving a few stuck to the front window. Rex, Simon's horse, dropped his head and let the rain cover his back as Simon and Anna searched for words to fill the void.

Simon wiped his forehead with the back of his hand. "Can I ask you something?"

Anna's eyes fell to the floor. "Do I have a choice?"

"Why did you tell me to go home and live up to my responsibilities?"

Anna articulated, "How hard is it to understand? You have obligations you need to live up to."

"But that's what I'm trying to do."

Anna said, "What makes you think you can do it here in Willow Springs?"

Simon leaned forward and rested his elbows on his knees for a few seconds before responding, "Home is the one place where I have caused the most pain. It was only fitting I return and do my fair share."

Anna tried to think of something to calm the frustration creeping up her neck, but in the end, she spat out, "Whose pain are you talking about? Your pain, my pain, or perhaps your wife's?"

Simon sat up straight. "What on earth are you talking about?"

Anna expressed her frustration with a long sigh and a shake of her head. "I know all about Cora. Last year, she wrote me and clearly told me you wouldn't be coming back to me or your Amish family."

Emptying his lungs of air, he groaned. "Anna, I didn't marry Cora or anyone else for that matter."

Anna stayed quiet for some moments, then spoke hesitantly. "But I thought…"

"You've been misled." Simon turned to face her and continued, "Anna, you must believe me when I say my heart has always belonged to you and no one else." His face flushed, then paled. "I let my guard down with her in a weak moment, and I regret every minute I led her on."

An array of emotions surrounded Anna making it hard for her to speak as she swallowed down her emotions at Simon's statement.

"Anna, I've hurt you, and it will take time to earn your trust back, but won't you please let me try? Don't let the devil have a stronghold of your heart."

Simon saw a spasm of pain cross her face as a single tear trickled down her cheek. He pleaded, "You don't need to answer me now, but promise me you'll think about it." He picked back up the reins.

They rode silently until they pulled into the driveway, and Anna's eyes fixed on the garden. Rain still hung in the air at the passing shower, but the last colorful blooms held their heads to the sky, basking in the last few days of warmth. Fumbling for a handkerchief, Anna wiped her nose, drew a long breath, and said, "I need to pray over it, then leave it in God's hands."

Simon glanced her way and tried to think of something to say that was comforting. "I'll pray that it's His will as well."

***

For the rest of the afternoon, Naomi watched Anna trim back the lavender plants and tie oregano and thyme sprigs to dry over the stove for winter.

"It's a shame you're not somehow putting all your plant knowledge to work for you. Whatever happened to your dream of owning an herb farm?"

"Those dreams are long gone," Anna said wearily.

The older woman bent over to dig the root of an old thistle plant out and threw it in the wheelbarrow. "I would say that's a matter for us to pray over and see where the Spirit leads."

Anna shrugged. "Seems like I'll need the Spirit's direction for many things."

Naomi sat down on a bench at the side of the garden and lifted her chin in the direction of Simon across the yard. "You're not the only one."

Anna followed her gaze for only a second before she busied her hands. She swallowed hard, wondering if she could confide in her old friend. After a long silence, she dropped to her knees and studied the lines around Naomi's eyes.

"What is it, child?"

Finally, she gulped and said, "I thought he was married."

"Who?"

Looking past her to where Simon was splitting wood, Anna said, "Simon."

Naomi's laugh was bigger than life, and when she found her voice, she asked, "What on earth would make you think that?"

"Cora sent me a letter last year telling me so."

Naomi shook her head. "That girl couldn't be trusted. Twisted my boy's better judgment every which way."

Anna tilted her head and flipped her eyes in his direction. "When I received her letter, it was like I had to relive him leaving again."

"Did he set you straight?"

"*Jah*."

Naomi brushed the dirt off her hands. "Thank the Lord. Maybe now you both can work your way through this misunderstanding."

Anna stood and wiped the mud off the front of her dress. "I'm not so sure it will be that easy."

Simon's mother made a sympathetic clucking noise. She remarked, "Sometimes, we let our head overrule our heart, which will only cause trouble. Don't think too hard about what was but look to the Lord for all answers. He'll never let you down."

The two women sat in thoughtful silence, then Naomi changed the subject.

"Word has it your *datt* is under the weather. Hasn't been to church in over a month."

Anna stopped digging through a deep-rooted weed and leaned on the hoe. "Do you know what the problem is?"

Naomi crumpled her eyebrows together. "*Nee*, can't say I do, but I wanted to mention it."

"I'll tell Matthew and my *schwesters.*" Anna resumed loosening the soil with her hoe and added, "Not too sure what we can do about it. It's not like Wilma would let us help even if *Datt* let us in."

"You could at least try," returned Naomi with loving concern.

"It's been almost two years. I'm certain he won't budge."

Naomi stood. "End of life softens even the most hardened souls. And don't give up on this community yet. I think things are about to change."

Anna gasped, "End of life? Is he that bad? And what do you mean about the community?"

"It must be serious for Jacob Byler to miss two church services. As far as this community goes, you all have stirred things up, and many older ones are starting to question the *Ordnung*."

The old woman didn't say anything but left Anna alone in the garden. Her chest suddenly heavy with worry, she turned her face to the parting sun and prayed for her father's health.

***

Simon eyed Anna as she held her face to the sun. His biceps tightened as he swung the ax over his head and let it land, splitting the dried oak log in two. He wanted to run to her but set up another log on its end and swung again to keep his desire under control. In the back of his head, a small voice whispered, *Patience, my son.*

As he conversed with his Heavenly Father, he realized all his cares and burdens concerning Anna became just a small part of God's plan. The old Simon, consumed with his own pleasures, would have bolted over to Anna and demanded that she give him an answer. But the new Simon was trying hard to be patient and wait on God to point the way.

CHAPTER 7

It was still dark when the clock made Wilma Byler aware that life still went on in the quiet farmhouse regardless of how long she'd been awake. She took a long look around the kitchen, wishing there was something she could do to take her mind off how worried she was about Jacob.

Climbing the stairs slowly, she stood in the doorway and studied the rise and fall of her husband, Jacob's, chest. The glow from the kerosene lamp on the dresser bounced shadows off the wall in unison with his labored breaths. Laying the back of her hand on his damp forehead, she sighed at the warmth.

Another day with no change, Wilma headed back downstairs with misty eyes. Jacob's stubbornness forbade her to send for the doctor, but she had an unsettled concern about his progress. They needed help, but who could she turn to? Guilt consumed her at the part she played in encouraging Jacob to side with the community and not his children. Was this God's punishment for her selfishness in wanting to keep Jacob all to herself?

Never having children of her own, she was jealous of her new husband's desire to stay connected to his adult children. She understood the last few years had not been easy on any of them but forcing his hand in their ex-communication changed Jacob. He missed his children and mourned the loss of his grandchildren to the point of depression.

The news made him despair as soon as he heard Rebecca was about to have her second child. On more times than she could count, she found him standing on the porch, straining to hear Matthew's young twin daughter's laughter through the trees that separated their farms.

Wilma drew on her hat and coat, picked up the egg basket, and headed to the barn. An early morning wind swirled around her skirt, reminding her winter was close at her heels. How would she ever take care of the animals, the furniture business, and the house all by herself?

Trouble and sorrow rolled over Wilma in such a tidal wave she clutched the barn door and cried out, "Oh, Lord, what have I done? If you can hear me, Lord, please forgive me for all the wrong I've done to this family."

***

"Rebecca, what should we do? If *Datt* is sick, shouldn't we at least try to see if Wilma needs our help?"

"I can't see either one going against Bishop Weaver's ruling," admitted Rebecca.

Anna refilled their coffee cups and wiped the milk off Mary Ellen's tray before sitting back at the table. "I think I will talk to Emma and Matthew after I tidy up the kitchen. Maybe they've heard something with living so close."

Rebecca balanced John Paul over her shoulder and patted his bottom until his whimpers surpassed. "I'm not sure how much help I'll be, but I'll agree to anything you decide."

Anna stirred cream in her cup. "*Mamm* would expect us to be there for him, especially if he's under the weather."

"But Anna, that was before Wilma came into the picture; that woman is…."

Anna interrupted, "Rebecca, don't go there. Get those ugly thoughts out of your head. Like it or not, the woman is our stepmother and deserves our respect, regardless of how she's treated us."

Rebecca jerked her head to the side and let an unladylike, "Tsk, ugh!" spill from her lips.

"Come on now, I thought we'd seen the last of that snippy attitude from you."

"You have; that woman just gets under my skin!" John Paul stirred with Rebecca's tone. She continued softly, "If it weren't for her, I'm certain *Datt* wouldn't have pushed so hard to have us excommunicated."

"Now, we know nothing for sure. *Datt* was only following the rules of the *g'may*. It was our choice to walk away from the Old Order."

Rebecca stood and swayed, rubbing small circles on her son's back. "I wouldn't change a thing, but it would have been nice for *Datt* to know his grandchildren."

Anna washed Mary Ellen's face and placed her on the floor. "Maybe God already has a plan we don't understand. Naomi seems to think we have cause to hope for this community."

"How so?"

"People are starting to ask questions about the *Ordnung*. Has Eli mentioned anything about that?"

"*Nee*."

Rebecca laid the baby in the cradle and pulled Mary Ellen onto her lap. "Go ahead and go now. You've been doing so much for me; it's about time I get back to caring for my children and this house myself."

Anna tied her blue headscarf around her chin and slipped into her coat. "I hope to catch Emma at the bakery; maybe she'll go to Matthew's with me."

***

Anna pulled her coat tighter and ducked her chin against the wind. The bitter fall morning left swirls of wood smoke floating along Mystic Mill Road. She would swear it was winter if it weren't for the crimson maple trees. Her nose burned both from the cold and an array of emotions that edged on closing her throat.

Too many things were muddling around in her head; she had trouble deciding which one to pray about first.

Lord, I'm so consumed with everything I'm facing that I don't even know where to start. Please fill me with the Holy Spirit today and give me the wisdom to do the right thing.

Just like I've turned over whatever you have planned for Simon, I also want to turn over this separation from Datt. There are so many hurt feelings, and our family is broken. I can't believe it's what you have in store for us. Please help us find a way to see each other again.

And that goes for Simon as well. Is this your will? If so, please make it perfectly clear, and give me the strength to leave it at your feet. Amen.

When Anna stepped off the side of the road to let a truck pass, the black Ford reminded her of Simon and the picture hanging from his rearview mirror. The image of the woman and the child struck her so hard that day at the dry goods store that it took twenty minutes of running before she could think straight.

She thought he was married all this time, and the picture only confirmed it. Getting her emotions back in line would take more than a few days. But even so, it didn't explain the child. If he wasn't married, whose child was Cora holding and why would he carry their picture?

At one time, having children, but more importantly, Simon's children, was all she could think about. Did she dare even let her mind wander about such things? She shook her head, hoping her heart would follow.

A mixture of wood, sugar, and spice wafted through the air as she stepped into Yoder's Bakery.

Katie stood at the counter. "Good morning, Anna. What has you out and about so early?"

"I'm hoping I could speak with Emma if she's not too busy."

"I'm certain she'd enjoy the break. She's been making donuts for hours."

Anna took a cinnamon roll off the tray Katie held out and made her way to the kitchen.

Emma added kindling to the deep fryer wood box and latched the door before turning her way. "Well, hello there, *schwester*. How did you get away from Rebecca's little ones this morning?"

"I had a disturbing talk with Naomi Kauffman yesterday. I needed to see you and Matthew."

"Matthew went to pick up a load of horses from Sugarcreek. He won't be back for a few days. So, all you got is me. What's on your mind?"

"Naomi said *Datt's* been sick. Says he hasn't been to church in three weeks."

Emma dropped a piece of dough in the fryer and watched it sizzle. "Does she say what's the matter?"

"*Nee*. I'm concerned. It's not like *Datt* to miss church."

"I'm not sure what we can do. Wilma will never let us see him."

Emma dropped a few donut rings into the hot oil. "Perhaps we need to put it in God's hands."

Anna sat on a stool near the stainless-steel worktable and picked at her roll. "I think we should at least try. Don't you think *Mamm* would want us to check on him?"

"What did Rebecca say?"

Anna's heart grew anxious. "She left it up to us."

"Anna. I tried to see him about a month ago, and Wilma stopped me at the gate. She didn't say a word but turned her back to me. That pretty much told me all I needed. They are both dead set on abiding by the ruling. Samuel and Matthew have tried talking to him, but nothing."

"What did Matthew and Samuel want to talk to him about?"

"They've been trying to reach out to everyone in the Old Order, especially *Datt*. They're on a mission to spread the Gospel. It's important to them that everyone understands that the way to Jesus doesn't rely on how well they follow the *Ordnung*."

"I can't imagine *Datt* or Wilma ever wanting to leave the old ways."

Emma flipped the donuts. "It's not a matter of leaving the Old Order; it's about following Jesus. All I can do is keep praying for his heart to soften. I can't believe he's content not having his children or grandchildren around. Matthew said he caught him watching the twins through the trees."

Anna's eyes turned sad. "Oh, that breaks my heart. Just the thought of Matthew and Sarah's girls not knowing him hurts. And to think, *Datt* longing for them is so depressing."

"Tell me about it. After everything Samuel and I went through with losing James, not being able to share our news with him is awful. As you said, *Mamm* wouldn't be happy about this."

Anna stood and wiped her sticky fingers on a napkin. "Well, I'm going to try. The worst that can happen is she turns me away. But I will not leave until she tells me what's the matter with him. We have the right to at least know his ailment."

***

Wilma stood in the doorway as Dr. Smithson walked through the gate and up the porch steps. Her eyes were wide with fear as she led the doctor to their room. "I'm afraid for him. I've tried everything, and he's not getting any better."

Dr. Smithson took his coat and hat, laid them over the rocking chair, and opened his bag. "How long has he been like this?"

"He hasn't felt well for weeks, but he's been wheezing like that for three days. Hasn't so much as gotten out of bed in as long."

Using a stethoscope to study Jacob's lungs, he flipped them around his neck and picked up his limp wrist. "Fever and pneumonia," he snorted. "You should have called me earlier."

Wilma pulled a chair up to the side of the bed and watched as he worked on breathing some life back into her husband. After giving her a list of instructions and medicine, he added, "Remember, lots of fluids. And I'd get Anna over here to make some strong herbal tea. She was a big help when her mother was ill, and I'd feel better if she was here to help you."

"It might be better if you tell me what you think he needs; I'm not so sure I can get Anna here."

Dr. Smithson drew on his coat and picked up his bag. "I've been doctoring this Plain community for forty years, and I've never seen anything like it. Fathers against daughters, families being torn apart. This one not talking to that one. Ridiculous! And then Jacob at the head of it. I've always held him in high regard and admired his faith. But this splitting of the community has me baffled."

Wilma shuffled behind him as he headed to the door. After seeing him out, she went back to sit at her husband's side. He still lay breathing hoarsely but sleeping. He stirred slightly but sank back to sleep as the minutes turned into an hour.

After running a pan of water and collecting a few fresh towels, she walked back to his bedside and stared at his flushed face on the pillow. She placed the compresses on his warm forehead and whispered, "Jacob, please forgive me. I'm sorry I forced you to turn your back on your children. This isn't right. I promise I'll find a way to bring your family back together if you fight through this."

Her stomach lurched as his raspy cough forced his chest to heave in labored breaths. His eyes flickered open but shut once the cough subsided, and she cried out to God. "*Please, Lord, show me what I need to do.*"

***

The closer Anna got to her father's house, the more her pulse quickened. She pushed a fresh wave of anxiety away as she asked God to help her love Wilma more than she feared her. More than anything, Anna wanted to help her father just like she had her mother. A calm came about as she realized love was stronger than fear, and there was no reason to be frightened. She didn't need to worry if Wilma wouldn't talk to her; she needed to be more concerned about showing her love, and the rest, God would work out if she trusted him. She pulled her shoulders back and knocked on the door.

To her surprise, Wilma opened it. Without saying a word, the two women stood in silence. Years of separation filled the silence as they struggled to fill the void. Lines etched the older woman's face to the point that Anna wondered if the woman was under the weather herself.

In not more than a raspy whisper, Wilma said, "You shouldn't be here."

"Wilma, I'm not here to cause you grief, but I don't care what the bishop or any other community member might say about me being here. I hear my *datt* is ill, and I'd like to see him."

Wilma stuttered, "He…he…isn't good."

"Naomi Kauffman mentioned he hasn't been to church. It must be bad if he can't get out of the house. May I see him?"

Stepping aside, she let Anna enter, and a sudden weakness forced Wilma to the couch. "Dr. Smithson said he has pneumonia."

Without waiting for her stepmother to answer, she headed to the stairs. "Anna?"

"*Jah*?"

"Watch him carefully, and the doctor said you should make him a strong herbal tea."

"Let me check on him first, and then I'll make a Respiratory Tea."

"What do you need to make it?"

"Peppermint, oregano, coneflower, and comfrey leaf. I'm sure *Mamm* had all those things in her garden once."

"I'm not too good with plants, but I think oregano exists. Do you want me to go get some?"

"It might be easier for me to get all I need at once."

Anna barely made it up the stairs before Wilma laid down and pulled a blanket over her shoulders. The woman's dingy *kapp* and soiled dress tugged at Anna's sympathy. For the first time, she had compassion for the woman who took her mother's place in her father's heart.

As the day continued, her father's fever mounted, and he tossed and turned, thrashing in broken sentences. Sometimes he called out to her mother and shouted to his children for others with a mixture of anguish she couldn't always place. When at last his body tired, he drifted off to a restful slumber. Once he settled, Anna massaged Lung Fever Salve over his chest and on the bottom of his feet. Wiping her hands free of cedar oil and menthol, she watched the rise and fall of his chest and prayed.

The hiss of the kerosene lamp over the kitchen table met Anna as she carried a tray to the sink. After a long nap, Wilma moved to the table. "I should have reached out to someone earlier. I'm having a hard time forgiving myself for not doing more."

"But you did, and that's all that matters."

"I had no idea he was so sick. He seemed a little depressed, and we thought he just had a cold. But he didn't bounce back."

After a few minutes of silence, Anna spoke up. "I'm trying to learn to trust God in all of this, but what he needs is family."

Wilma dropped her head, and a tear moved to the end of her nose. Wiping it away with the back of her hand, she verbalized, "I'm to blame for most of that."

Anna tried to console her. "Maybe we can figure it all out when *Datt* gets better." Her stepmother's tears flowed more freely, and she laid her head across her folded arms and mumbled, "I've made so many mistakes."

Anna moved to her side. "Never too many that God won't forgive us for."

Wilma turned her face to look at Anna and asked, "After all I've done to keep you from your father, how can you sound so forgiving?"

"We all go through different challenges in life. Maybe we've been placed in the middle of this so He can shed some light into our hearts."

The older woman sat up, wiped her face with the hem of her black apron, and said, "Your *datt* believes what you and your siblings stand for."

"What? How is that so? He'd been so against us leaving the church."

"It didn't take long for him to realize you were all on to something. After becoming minister, he started studying more, but it was too late by that time."

Anna sat down at the table and leaned in closer. "But Wilma, it's never too late to trust in Jesus."

Wilma's tired eyes filled with tears, and her lips quivered. "It was when he had me chirping in his ear all day to let it be. I just started making friends here and didn't want to leave the Old Order. And besides, I wanted your *datt* all to myself."

Wilma's shoulders shook with sobs, and Anna pulled her close. With a silent prayer for strength, Anna let the shattered woman lean on her as she whispered calming words in her ear.

Her restless form settled, and Anna silently thanked God for allowing her to love the woman who had caused her family so much pain.

"*Denki,* for coming."

"Really, Wilma, it was no trouble. I need to be here taking care of *datt*…and you."

Wilma pulled away and wiped her nose on the crinkled-up hankie she pulled from her sleeve. "Your *datt* is one thing, but me? I don't deserve your kindness."

"Wilma, please, we understand how hard it must have been to step into a ready-made family. Especially when we refused to follow the old ways."

Anna walked to the stove, took the steaming tea kettle to the metal-lined sink, and poured it into a dishpan. Wilma carried a bucket of cold water from the hand pump in the back room and ran just enough in the dishpan to warm the water.

Plopping down in Jacob's place at the table, Wilma sighed. "So many changes to the way things have always been. I'm not sure any older folk want to embrace everything this New Order Fellowship is about."

Anna stopped working on the stack of dirty dishes, dried her hands on a towel, and sat beside her stepmother. "There is only one thing you need to concern yourself with, and that is following what the Bible tells us."

Anna laid her hand across Wilma's arm and said, "Jesus clearly instructs that the only way to the Father is through Him. So that means we must put our trust in Jesus and not a set of rules created by man."

"But what will happen to our heritage and history?" Wilma pleaded.

"Nothing is going to happen to any of that." Anna assured her. "We still keep ourselves separated from the outside world, and we will live the same way. The only thing changing is following Jesus, which means sharing His love with everyone."

"I don't see how Bishop Weaver or any of the other ministers will go for this."

Anna smiled and walked back to the sink. "I don't either, but God is bigger than any of this, and He will find a way to bring this community back together, I'm sure of it."

Wilma's face was pained. "I'm not one to accept change so quickly, but if your *datt* pulls through this, I'll definitely do my part to being open to hearing you children out."

Anna looked over her shoulder. "How about you go sit with *Datt*? I'll finish up these dishes and be up in a minute."

Jacob slept all day, and Wilma did not leave his side. Once, when Anna came up to check on him, Wilma was on her knees by the bedside. The next time she sat quietly, stroking his hand, speaking in hushed tones. There was no doubt in Anna's mind that her stepmother truly cared for her father. She was wrong about her stepmother and silently asked God to forgive her for all the times she let her mind drift to unpleasant thoughts about the woman who took her beloved *mamm's* place.

CHAPTER 8

Jacob rested and slept for a week as Anna and Wilma took turns helping him regain strength. Anna stayed in her old room and reported to her siblings about his care. Even when her father was less than cooperative in her presence, she came into his room with a cheerful greeting.

When she slid a chair close to his bedside and opened the jar of salve, he quickly took the container from her hand. "I'm done with that stinky stuff. And besides, I'm more than capable of rubbing it on my chest."

Anna tugged it back from her father. "You might as well resign yourself to my care until you're up and out of this bed."

She unscrewed the metal lid and held up the jar. "This ointment had a lot to do with your recovery."

Jacob swung his feet over the side of the bed and growled, "Why are you here?"

"That's a silly question. Why else would I be here but to take care of you? And besides, I was part of Dr. Smithson's order. Well, me and my Respiratory Tea."

Her father stammered and took a labored breath. "I…I…think it's time for you to leave. Any care I need…Wilma can tend to."

A pang of hurt landed deep in Anna's chest, and she gulped hard before responding. "I was hoping we could bury all this behind us and start fresh."

Jacob steadied himself on the nightstand as he stood. "Are you coming back to the Old Order?"

"*Nee*, I'm not."

"Then we have nothing left to say. I will have to go before the bishop with you being here. Wilma should never have allowed you in."

Anna reached out, and he pulled away as a look of pain passed over his pale face. "Anna, please, you need to go."

She set the jar of salve on the stand, looked her father in the eye, and said, "You can continue to push us away, but we will never turn our backs on Jesus."

Jacob lowered himself back to the bed as soon as his daughter left the room. The desperate crack in her voice tugged at his heart. Once keen and analytical, his mind seemed broken and lethargic, much like his body. He knew her care probably pulled him through the worst of his sickness, and she did have a way with herbs and tonics.

He laid in his bed, listening to the friendly chatter between Wilma and Anna for days. He never thought it possible that the woman would ever warm up to his children. But again, it was Anna; her sweet disposition rubbed off on Wilma, eventually winning her over. He longed to regain his strength and get on with life. But he had one uneasiness that continued to haunt him throughout his ordeal. And that was his first wife's, Stella's, dying wish.

***

The November wind snapped at Anna's head scarf as she tied her horse to the hitching rail beside Shetler's Grocery. Barbara Miller greeted her as she stepped inside and out of the wintry air. Several shoppers in dark brown bonnets and black coats mingled around the store and smiled at her as she entered.

It had been a week since her father turned her away, and her mood had spiraled much like the wind through the gray skies. Anna went to the back of the store where colorful bolts of fabric were stacked neatly between the shelves. Rebecca had sent her for a fabric supply in preparation for the winter sewing season.

She picked out blue chambray for Eli's work shirts and a dark purple and blue royal crepe for new dresses for herself, Mary Ellen, and Rebecca. Blue denim was on the list for little pants for John Paul and work trousers for Eli. Finally, she added a white organdy to her pile for new *kapps*.

Barbara moved to her side, laid the fabric bolts on the long worktable, and asked how much she needed of each. After Anna told her the total yardage, she added black winter stockings, thread, and shirt buttons to the table.

Barbara slipped a couple of straight pins between her lips and mentioned. "You just missed Simon."

Just the mention of his name made her stomach flip. "That's good; I'm in no mood to entertain his questions."

"Are you going to give the man another chance?"

Anna let out a long sigh. "I don't know what I want to do. I'm starting to feel like I'm in the way at Rebecca and Eli's, *Datt* refuses to let me help him, and I don't like working in the yarn shop."

"*Stitch n' Time*? I thought that was something you and Rebecca did together."

"*Nee*, that's Rebecca's dream, not mine."

"Do Emma and Katie need help at the bakery?" Barbara asked.

"Even that leaves a sour spot in my stomach. I enjoy making peanut brittle, but do I want to bake every day? I don't think so."

"Sounds like you need a change of scenery."

Anna whined. "As long as that scenery doesn't involve a bunch of people. I'm uncomfortable when I get around lots of faces. I can barely handle waiting on customers at the yarn shop."

Barbara laid her scissors down and walked to the bulletin board at the front of the store, waving Anna to follow her. "An *Englisch* man stopped by this morning and asked if I knew of an Amish woman who would be interested in being a nanny."

She removed the thumbtack and handed Anna the postcard. *NANNY FOR HIRE. Looking for a responsible young woman to care for an eight-month-old baby. Transportation and meals are provided. Lake Erie area. Please call for more information.*

"So, what do you think? It might be just what you need to figure out what you want to do about Simon. Some time away."

"But what do I know about babies?"

Barbara laughed before replying. "Anna don't be silly. You've been taking care of Rebecca's children for months now, and if you can calm colicky John Paul down, you can handle an eight-month-old. Besides, you have a way of calming *kinner* down. Who does everyone go to during church when they need a break? You, of course."

"I suppose. But Erie is an hour and a half away. That's a long trip back and forth every day."

Barbara took the postcard back and looked it over again. "I got the impression they wanted someone to care for the child in the house and stay with them during the week. They asked about church services and wanted to be sure it was a single girl who didn't have a family she needed to return to each night."

"My palms are sweating just thinking about it. A strange house and an *Englisch* one at that."

"Oh, come on, Anna. It would be good for you. It will give you time to ponder the future and get away from this church division for a while. God knows I'd like nothing more than to leave Willow Springs for a short time myself."

"You want to leave Willow Springs?"

Barbara looped her arm in Anna's. "*Nee*, not really. But with Joseph back in the picture and two little boys underfoot, a change of scenery certainly sounds tempting."

Anna tucked the card into her black pocketbook and picked up the stack of fabric. "I'll keep the card for a few days and bring it back if I decide not to call."

"Do it. I think it will be good for you. Nothing like a baby to take your mind off your worries."

Barbara leaned in close and whispered, "And besides, I guarantee you Simon Kauffman needs a taste of his own medicine, if you grasp what I mean."

Anna slapped her friend's arm away. "That's not nice. I know how it feels to be left behind, and that's not something to look forward to."

"I'm just kidding, but it wouldn't hurt for Simon to feel what it's like to be left in limbo."

In a severe tone, Anna asked, "But what if I decide I don't want to give him another chance right now? I can't expect him to wait on me forever."

"I'd say that's a conversation you need to have with him. And as antsy as he is to have you back in his life, he's not going to like it one bit."

Anna tilted her head and furrowed her brow. "I'm not sure why he's in such a hurry all of a sudden. I waited on him for years, and once I finally thought I'd closed that part of my heart, he wants me to open it like a window at the first sign of spring."

A customer walked up behind them, and Barbara leaned in close and said, "Take your time. When the time is right, God will direct your path."

***

The following day, after Rebecca had gotten the children down for an afternoon nap, Anna spread out the denim material and retrieved the homemade brown paper patterns from the drawer. Trying not to waste a bit of fabric, Anna carefully cut out enough pieces for two pairs of trousers.

Rebecca pulled a chair to the treadle sewing machine in front of the window to take advantage of the ready-made sunlight. As she lifted the cabinet's lid, elevating the sewing machine head from a concealed position, she asked, "You've been awfully quiet this morning. What's weighing so heavily on your mind?"

Anna stacked the cutout fabric pieces in a neat pile and pushed them to the side of the table. "I suppose I've been pondering a few things this morning."

Rebecca sifted through the drawer until she found the exact color of the thread needed and proceeded to fill a bobbin. "I'm all ears if you'd like to talk things through."

Smoothing out the wrinkles in the blue chambray material, Anna replied, "What would you say if I was thinking about taking a nanny job in Erie for a short time?"

Rebecca placed a filled bobbin beneath the plate under the pressure foot and turned in her chair. "Why would you want to take on a job? You already have one in the yarn shop."

Anna pinned a paper pattern to the material and replied, "That's just it. *Stitch n' Time* is your passion, not mine, and you understand I'm uncomfortable dealing with customers. And besides, I'm starting to feel like you and Eli could use some time without me underfoot so much."

"Now that's just plain crazy. I wouldn't know what to do without you here. You've been such a help to me, especially with the *kinner*."

"I reckon so, but for what it's worth, I need to figure out what I want in life, and right now, my head is going in a million different directions. I think if I allow myself a change of scenery for a time, things will become clearer."

Rebecca put the first piece of fabric under the needle and lowered the pressure foot to keep them in place. With her right hand, she gave a quick tug to the wheel on the side of the machine, and with her foot, she rocked the treadle beneath the machine, setting the needle in motion. "You've never been content in the yarn shop, but becoming a nanny, what do you know about doing that type of work?"

"I assume it won't be much different from what I've been doing for you, except I'll be living with an *Englisch* couple during the week."

Rebecca carefully guided the needle along the seam of Eli's new pants a quarter of an inch from the edge. "You can't even go to the store without breaking out in a cold sweat. How do you think you'll be able to go live with a strange couple in unfamiliar surroundings?"

Anna sighed as she folded the cut fabric pieces in a neat stack. "Rebecca, please understand, I need to get away from Willow Springs for a time. With Simon back, my emotions are all stirred up, and I can't seem to think straight. I'm hoping if I step away for a little bit, God will make things clearer for me."

Snipping the ends of a loose thread, Rebecca asked, "Are you going to tell Simon?"

Anna slipped into a chair, propped her elbows up on the table, and rested her chin in her hands. "Ohhhh…I don't know. Do you think I should?"

The sewing machine stayed quiet for a moment before Rebecca said, "All I can say is you need to remember how you felt when he took off without any word of his plans or where you stood. I don't think you have it in you to do the same to him."

"Maybe you're right. I sure wish *Mamm* were still around. I could use some of her wise words about now."

Rebecca moved to Anna's side and rested her arm on her shoulder. "Perchance, are you trying to figure everything out on your own? What would *Mamm* say to you right now?"

Anna rested her forehead in her palms and muttered, "She would say I need to get out of God's way and quit trying to pick up his pen. He'll write the words himself and doesn't need my help."

"Precisely. Now, if you feel strongly about this nanny job, I'd say you need to discuss it with God. Perhaps he's laid it in your path for a reason."

Anna reached up and patted her *schwester's* hand. "How have you become so smart about things?"

"Smart, absolutely not, but I've learned from my past mistakes. It never turns out well when I get in God's way or think I know better than him."

"But what if that's not what He has planned for me? Could it be I'm just running away from Simon because I don't like the conflict it's causing me to face?"

Pulling out a chair beside her, Rebecca answered, "Whenever I'm struggling with a decision, I go back to the questions Bishop Weaver explained to us once. First, does what I want to do line up with scripture? Second, have I researched and fully understand the consequences of my decision? And lastly, have I sought wise counsel?"

Anna sat up straight. "I'd forgotten about that sermon. Thanks for reminding me. I'll do those things before I make my final decision."

Rebecca stood and headed toward the back bedroom. "Do you mind finishing that pair of pants while I care for John Paul?"

Anna nodded and took a seat at the sewing machine. The constant motion of the needle and the pedaling with her foot calmed her anxiety. At least she was able to line her thoughts up in order. After supper, she would call the number on the card to ask more questions about the job. Next, she would spend the evening searching scripture for guidance, and then she would think of someone else she could talk to that would give her direction.

Perhaps Bishop Schrock, better yet, maybe she could have a heart-to-heart with Naomi. Even if she was Simon's mother, she could always count on the older woman to speak truth into a situation.

***

As soon as Anna finished helping Rebecca with the supper dishes, she settled down at the kitchen table with a pen and paper. The thought of facing Simon was too much; a letter would have to do.

Eli quietly read Mary Ellen a story, and Rebecca was nursing the baby in the living room. An early November cold front left everyone wanting to stay close to the wood stove that nicely warmed the two rooms separated by a wide doorway.

Anna looked up from her letter and glanced around the room. The cozy scene left her yearning for a family of her own, which only made the words she needed to write even more challenging.

Watching Eli and Rebecca sitting in their matching willow-bent rockers beneath the glow of the gaslight tugged at her heart. The baby cooed softly as Rebecca placed him over her shoulder. Eli winked at her *schwester* in the most endearing manner, making Anna turn away before her brother-in-law caught her staring.

She added a few words to the lined paper, only to tear the sheet from the notebook and wad it up in a ball. Giving up on the letter, she opened her Bible and let the pages fall as they may, leaving James 2:4 before her. '*Ye have not because ye ask not.*'

Re-reading the verse a few times, she asked, "Eli, what do you think this verse from James 2:4 means? '*Ye have not because ye ask not.*'"

Eli set Mary Ellen on the floor and picked up his Bible to turn to the book of James. After reading the scripture for himself, he stopped to think before answering. "I think we need to read verses one through three to get James's entire message. He is trying to get us to see the motives behind what we ask for. Reading it closely reveals that the problem is not really in the asking. The problem is in the reason why you are asking."

"I guess I'm still not understanding it."

Eli carried his Bible to the table and sat down beside her. "What drives many of us is the burning desire to get something we don't have. This is known as coveting. To be jealous of something someone else has, or to possess an eagerness to get something that doesn't belong to us."

Anna traced her finger over the scripture again and asked, "How do I know if I'm doing this?"

Eli looked at her tenderly and asked, "How do you feel when you see others around you being blessed and it seems like God is passing you by? Do you rejoice in their blessing, or do you envy them?"

Anna sat quietly, recalling her yearning when watching her *schwester's* family.

Eli continued, "Look at James 2:3 again. '*When you ask, you do not receive, because you ask with wrong motives, that you may spend what you get on your pleasures.'*"

Reaching for a cookie out of the covered plastic dish in the center of the table, Eli said, "God chooses not to answer prayers pursued with wrong motives. Can you imagine how we would be if God answered our prayers from our selfish motives? We'd all be a big mess."

Eli reached for another cookie and headed back to the living room. Anna studied the verses again and couldn't help but question her own motives. Was she asking for God to set her path straight for selfish reasons? Why was she so eager to run away from Simon?

In her heart, it was easy to answer her own questions. She wanted Simon to suffer as she had. And yes, she wanted to leave Willow Springs because watching Rebecca and Emma and their perfect families made her jealous.

She was even more confused now. She didn't want to pray for clarity if it meant she was hiding behind her own selfish desires. Was the fear of being hurt again forcing her to run away from what her heart truly wanted?

To walk away from anyone or anything that would cause her distress in hopes she could keep her anxiety tied up in a neat little box. Hadn't she done that her whole life? Stay safe, at arm's length, not letting anyone upset the balance of her life.

That was until Simon came along. He was the only one she let in and look what he did. He'd emptied the whole apple cart at her feet, spilling an array of emotions she tried so hard to keep neat and tidy.

Anna rested her folded hands on her closed Bible and prayed.

Lord, please make your desires my desires. I'm not sure what you want me to do, but I have faith you will guide my steps along the way you want me to travel. If it's Simon, show me your will. If you want me to care for that little one, clear the path and make it happen. And please remove the envy from my heart and help me celebrate alongside Rebecca and Emma's blessings. I know my day is coming; I'm sure of it. Just help me be patient while waiting. Most of all, help me remember that asking and faith matter greatly, but my motives matter more. Amen.

She carried her cup to the sink and told Rebecca she was heading to make a call. She wrapped a shawl around her shoulders before heading out the door. Once inside the phone shanty, she turned on the battery-operated lantern and retrieved the postcard from her pocket.

Her heart raced as she dialed the number. On the third ring, a man answered, "Buckhannon residence."

CHAPTER 9

All morning, Anna played her conversation with Mr. Buckhannon in her head. A *bobbli* cried in the background as she asked him to explain what the nanny job consisted of. His major concern was that whoever they hired was able to stay with the child throughout the week. The baby needed a daily companion and caretaker. Mr. Buckhannon declared he and his wife would care for the child over the weekend, leaving her to return home for a couple of days.

He mentioned he'd like to set up a live interview and a chance to meet the child beforehand if she was interested. Her usual uneasiness when making a phone call, especially to a stranger, was gone, replaced with an overwhelming peace.

After she hung up, she couldn't help but notice how confident she felt about accepting the position. But she refused to commit to anything before she had a chance to talk with Naomi or Bishop Schrock.

As she unlocked the door to the yarn shop, she heard the clip-clop of an approaching buggy and stopped to welcome their visitor. God himself had already set her day in motion, and she smiled at His goodness when she bid good morning to Naomi.

Walking back down the steps, she held her hand out to help the older woman down from her enclosed buggy. Without asking, she picked up the lead off the buggy floor, fastened it to Naomi's horse's bridle, and wrapped it around the hitching post.

"What has you out and about on this chilly morning?"

Naomi loosened the ties on her heavy brown bonnet and followed Anna back up the stairs. "I needed a few things at the Mercantile, and for some reason, I felt led to stop by and check on you."

Anna only smiled as she pushed open the door, took the lamp from the center of the worktable, and jiggled it slightly to hear if there was enough fuel in the tank. "I'm glad you did. I would like to talk to you about something."

Naomi held her hands over the small wood stove in the corner of the room. "Jebediah said the cow's neck hair is extra thick this year. That's a sure sign we are in for a hard winter. Even the Farmer's Almanac is predicting it."

Anna nodded in agreement. "I'm thankful Eli came out early and lit the stove for me. This cold spell came early, for sure and certain."

Anna put the lamp on the table, attached a small pump to the valve on the base, and pumped a dozen or so strokes before turning the nob to allow a small amount of fuel in the narrow tube. With a quick light from two matches, the flame ignited, and she adjusted the light and hung it on a hook from the ceiling.

Anna held her hand to the side of the teapot on the stove. "I made a pot of lemon verbena tea this morning. It should have seeped long enough by now. Would you like a cup?"

"Just what I need to warm these old bones."

Anna took two mugs below the counter and a honey pot and set them in front of her.

Naomi held her cup up for Anna to fill. "So, what did you want to talk to me about?"

After stirring a healthy spoon of honey into her cup, Anna turned serious. "You've been a dear friend to me over the years, especially since my mother died."

After a thoughtful pause, Anna went on. "I don't want to put you in the middle of the challenges I'm having with accepting Simon's return."

Naomi looked dubious. "Why do I think there is a but coming?"

"Not really. I just need some sound advice, and I trust your opinion."

Naomi took a long sip of her tea. "What is it, child?"

Anna signed. "I'm thinking of taking a nanny job in Erie."

"Oh, my dear! What brought this on?"

"I'm confused and think I need a change of scenery."

"I understand Simon's return caught you off guard. But are you sure you're not just running away?"

Anna sipped her tea and took a few seconds before replying. "I asked myself that same question. And I keep going back to trusting in

God to lead me where he wants me to go. At this moment, I felt led to answer the ad for a nanny."

"How about you tell me a little about the job?"

"I spoke to the couple last night. Seems the child is quite a handful for the older couple, and they need help tending to his daily needs. It would only be during the week, and I can return home on the weekends. They will send a weekly driver to fetch me late Sunday evening and take me home early Saturday morning."

Naomi tightened her grip on her mug and tried not to let Anna know her concerns. Somehow, she had to convince the girl to stay in Willow Springs. Little did Anna know that Simon was counting on her to help him bring his son home. In the back of Naomi's head, she was contemplating how Simon would still get to see her, and it might be enough time each week to regain her trust.

Pausing long enough to send up a quick prayer for the right words, Naomi stated, "Caring for a baby is hard work, let alone becoming attached to a child whom you may never see again. Are you up for that?"

"I haven't thought of that, but the assignment is only for a few months until the woman gets back on her feet. Seems she's been under the weather and hasn't been able to give the child the care he needs."

"Are you sure you're not taking this job just so you don't have to face what the future might bring?"

"Oh, Naomi, my head is swirling with so many things, and I can't help but think if I leave here for a little bit, I'll see God's plan play out better."

"What is it you want clarity on?"

Anna set her cup down, folded her hands, propped up her elbows on the work counter, and rested her chin on her fingers. "Like why God isn't delivering me from my fears."

Naomi made a little sympathetic clucking noise and remarked, "The main reason we suffer is because God isn't so concerned with our comfort or happiness in this life."

"What do you mean?" Anna asked, surprised.

"His goal is our eternal happiness. When He allows for difficulties in this life, it's because He's more interested in building our faith, changing our character, and freeing us from our fears here on earth."

Releasing a long breath from her lungs, Anna asked, "Are you saying I'll always be fearful of the future and making the wrong decision?"

"Not necessarily; I am saying He may allow it to happen so you will draw closer to Him. If you didn't struggle with fear and anxiety, you wouldn't have any need for Him."

"But Rebecca and Emma, or any other girl my age, doesn't seem to suffer like I do. Why aren't they bothered by such things?"

Naomi looked amazed. Then laughed lightly. "Is your memory so short you don't remember Emma questioning her faith? What about Rebecca? Didn't she struggle with pride and a sharp tongue? Just because they don't struggle the same as you, doesn't mean their challenges weren't meant to draw them closer to the Lord."

Anna let out a long breath. "So, do you think taking this job is good or not?"

After a few seconds of deep thought on how she could advise her young friend, Naomi decided that God was bigger than anything she or Simon could do. She needed to leave it to Him. "I can't tell you that. Only God can point you in that direction. But I think He is interested in seeing a change in you. And who knows? He may have orchestrated this job for a reason. He may be glorified because of it, which is the goal of everything He does."

Anna quietly said, "I feel like God is directing me to take it. I have peace about it like nothing I have ever done before." "Well, I can't argue with that. If you and the Lord agree on something, that is all the reassurance I need."

"*Denki*, Naomi. And I appreciate you taking the time to talk to me, even if you shouldn't be here."

"Like I said before, you let Jebediah and I worry about such things. This whole church split thing is for the birds in my books. The more Jebediah and I learn, the more we think you younger folks have it right. I wouldn't be surprised if you don't see the likes of these old folks showing up to your church before too long."

Anna reached for Naomi's hand and squeezed. "You really think so?"

"I'm sure the situation will right itself in time."

"I wish my *datt* would see things that way. Wilma let me in to help, but he sent me away once he got some of his strength back."

Naomi looked dubious. "Don't let that get you down. I think he's already been thinking long and hard about what those manmade rules have cost him. Change is coming. I feel it in my bones."

"You're such a comfort, Naomi. *Denki* again."

"We must pray that God will deal with our leaders and stir their hearts to a point they want nothing better than to follow Christ. I know my Jebediah's heart has been changin'. And I suspect old Bishop Weaver and your *datt* will be following suit anytime now."

Anna clapped her hands under her chin. "I hope you're right. I would love nothing more than to see my family reunited."

"Tell your *schwesters* and *bruder* not to give up hope and don't stop praying for a change. I'm sure God is using this to help us all. Sometimes He uses sharp tools to shape our lives, and I believe he is using this to prepare us for a special purpose."

Then silence reigned, broken only by a log falling in the woodstove. Naomi tied her bonnet in place and headed to the door. "I must go but promise me one thing first."

"What's that?"

"Talk to Simon before you leave."

Anna didn't answer but nodded in the woman's direction. The mere thought of facing Simon brought a sick feeling to her stomach. A part of her wanted to leave without saying a word, but her heart told her otherwise. There was no denying his return affected her in ways she didn't think were ever possible again. But was she ready to allow him to bury his heart with hers again? She wasn't too sure of that.

Slipping her arms in her coat, she went to the phone shanty to set up a meeting with Mr. Buckhannon.

***

The chilly ride to the Mercantile gave Naomi ample time to petition God on Simon's behalf. She almost felt guilty for encouraging Anna to take the nanny position. She couldn't deny Anna's peace about stepping out of her comfort zone. As long as she knew the girl, not once had she taken the initiative to do something as bold as taking a job so far away from home.

Perhaps God had a reason for putting the opportunity in front of her. Naomi's only concern was how Simon was going to handle the news. His heart was set on marrying only one girl, Anna. And as he acknowledged last night, she was the only choice he would accept as the mother of his child.

She wondered if her son's faith was strong enough to withstand a *"nee"* from God. Some of our best plans didn't always align with God's purpose, no matter how hard we prayed.

Naomi pulled her buggy aside from the hitching post in the back of the Mercantile and took a long breath as Bishop Weaver pulled up beside her. His stern face and demeanor warned her that it wasn't a day for a friendly hello. As close as he was to pulling in behind her gave her the impression it was his buggy she pulled out in front of as she was leaving *Stitch n' Time*.

***

Anna pushed the door open with some apprehension, now that she had put off speaking to Simon until the last minute; Mast Lumber Mill, the black letters on the door said.

Sarah, her *bruder* Matthew's wife, sat at the front desk and held up a finger while she completed taking an order over the phone. Putting the phone back in its cradle, she asked, "Anna, what has you out and about today? Does Eli need us to deliver more fence posts?"

Anna shifted from one foot to the other. "*Nee,* I…I hoped I could catch Simon on his lunch break and speak to him for a few minutes."

Sarah looked up at the clock the minute the lunch whistle blew loud enough the workers could hear it over the debarker. "Just in time. Go ahead and cut through *Datt's* office; he won't mind. You should find them all gathering in the lunchroom."

Anna hesitated and asked, "Do you mind getting him for me? I'd like to talk to him in private."

Her *schwester-in-law* rose and smiled in Anna's direction. "No problem. You can stay right here. I need to discuss an order with my *datt* anyways."

Anna untied her blue scarf and let it drop around her shoulders. The oil stove in the corner kept the small office plenty warm, which added to the already rising heat from her chest. She agonized over talking with Simon all morning. As she turned from the window, a shadow lingered in the doorway, and she grimaced when his eyes met hers. "Anna?"

Her heart pounded against her chest as she drew in a breath. Simon waited as she wrung her hands together, and while she struggled to find her words, he asked, "Is everything all right?"

"*Jah*, I have something I need to tell you."

Simon took off his straw hat, sending curls of wood shavings to the floor. He pointed to the two chairs under the window. Anna sat, folded her hands in her lap, and looked straight ahead, trying not to make eye contact. She couldn't bear to see the disappointment on his face. "I came to tell you I'm taking a job in Erie."

Simon balanced his elbows on his knees and twirled his hat in his fingers, keeping his eyes focused on the floor. "I see."

Dismay spread over Simon's face. "Tell me about it," he said softly.

"It's a nanny job. The couple is having trouble caring for their baby. Seems the woman has been under the weather lately and has not been able to give the child the attention he needs."

"I thought you were helping Rebecca with her *kinner*. And what about the yarn shop? Doesn't Rebecca need your help with that?"

"Rebecca doesn't need my help any longer, and I don't particularly like working there."

At length, he paused. "Why now?"

"I don't feel I have anything holding me back right now."

"I…thought…" he stammered, at a loss for words.

"I know what you thought," Anna said quietly, "but what you want from me right now, I'm not too sure I'm ready to give."

Simon stood and went slowly to the window on the room's other side while Anna waited listlessly. Pain edged its way over her forehead, and her hands were moist. She wished she could alleviate his pain, but there was no way around it. She needed this time away.

Turning back and making his way to her side, he knelt and picked up her hands in his. "I wish you wouldn't leave. I was hoping we could spend some time together to get to know one another again."

Anna lifted her chin and stared into his eyes. "A few years ago, I would have given anything to hear those words. But right now, they mingle together with a slew of broken promises."

"How am I ever going to make this up to you?"

"Time…Simon, I need time."

He pulled her hands up and rested his forehead on their combined fingers. "Time is not one thing I have much of."

Anna pulled her hands away. "What does that mean? We have our whole life ahead of us. All I want is to be sure of things, and right now, my emotions are all mixed up."

Simon lifted his head with wonder. "So, does that mean there might be hope for us at some point?"

"Simon," her fingers gripped the edge of the chair. "I won't promise anything. All I know right this minute is I felt led to take the job. It's only during the week, and I'll be home on the weekends. If God has it in His plan to help us work things out, I will be open to His promptings. However, now I have peace about taking care of this child. I have no idea what may or may not happen."

Calmly, Simon spoke. "I can't stop you, and I agree that it will happen if it's in God's will. I've already put our future in His hands."

She stood and tied her scarf under her chin. "I must go. A driver is due within the hour."

Simon stood anxiously and asked, "Do you know how long the job is supposed to last?"

"I assume just until the woman gets back on her feet. Three or four months, I think."

A lump formed in the back of Simon's throat, and he swallowed hard as she left. He only had a few months to prove to Cora's parents that he could provide a stable home for Marcus. He wasn't sure they would ever agree to give him custody without Anna. He followed her small form disappear down Mystic Mill Road until his eyes couldn't find a trace of her black coat and blue scarf.

CHAPTER 10

The long black car stopped in front of a spacious two-story old Victorian on the banks of Lake Erie. "Here's your stop, miss," said the driver, then went back to open the trunk to retrieve her small black suitcase.

As the car pulled away, Anna took a long look at the house as the wind blew off the lake, swirling under her skirt. Pushing back down the hem of her dress, she tucked her chin and made her way to the porch. Lights from the front window shone brightly across a light layer of snow that had settled on the stone-lined porch.

Setting her suitcase beside the door, she rang the bell. The chime made an incredible noise, and she couldn't help but smile at the welcoming sound. Hearing footsteps approaching, she straightened her dress and tried to calm the nerves that were set on drying her mouth.

When the door opened, Mr. Buckhannon greeted her. "Anna, you made it. We've been expecting you all afternoon. Please come in out of the cold."

Anna stomped the snow from her boots before stepping in on the tile lined entryway. "The driver got stuck in some traffic on 79."

He held his hand to take her suitcase. "The Mrs. and I have been watching the weather. We are due for a nor'easter off the lake. Supposed to drop over a foot of snow. Haven't seen a forecast like that this early in over forty years."

From her interview with Mr. Buckhannon earlier in the week, she already knew he was a friendly kind of fellow, which she didn't mind since she wasn't much of a talker.

Mr. Buckhannon set her suitcase on the stairs' bottom step and waved for her to follow him. He led the way into a warm and comfortable-looking living room. Mrs. Buckhannon was covered with a blanket in front of the fire and pointed to the chair beside her. "Sit there, close to the fire, and get warm."

As she spoke, she slipped her arms out of her coat and removed her heavy brown bonnet.

Mr. Buckhannon spoke up. "We have your room ready right next to Steven's. The little guy just went to sleep, but I guarantee you it won't last long."

Anna laid her winter things over her lap and looked toward the staircase. "Perhaps I should get settled before he wakes?"

"Now, just relax, Anna. You'll have plenty to do with that little one. I'm afraid we spoiled him greatly, and you'll have your hands full."

Anna shyly reacted. "I hardly think a child can be spoiled, especially at eight months old."

Mr. Buckhannon snorted. "Oh, are you in for a surprise. The boy is quite colicky and hasn't grown out of it yet. I've done my best, which isn't much considering I've held and rocked him for the better part of the last eight weeks since Margaret's back has been giving her fits."

Mrs. Buckhannon asserted, "I've not been able to get him on any schedule, and he's prone to throwing tantrums now." The woman's face twisted in pain as she repositioned herself in her chair. "The pediatrician says he's underweight and isn't thriving, which I don't understand; he eats all the time. Well, I take that back; he always takes a bottle, but he spits most of it back up."

Anna was already concocting a baby tummy calm tincture in her head as she listened to them explain Steven's behavior.

The baby bellowed from his upstairs room as if on cue to prove his demanding nature. Anna stood. "I'd say my job begins."

"Here, let me show you the way," Mr. Buckhannon suggested. "No, no, you stay. I won't have any trouble finding him."

Mr. Buckhannon lifted his hands and smiled. "Be my guest, and good luck."

Anna grabbed her suitcase with a bounce in her step and ran up the stairs. After depositing her bag in the room to the left of Steven's, she quietly pushed the door open and followed the dimly lit nightlight to the boy's crib.

"Now, now, little one." She said in hushed tones. "What's all the fuss about?"

The child was howling so hard it just about broke Anna's heart. Mrs. Buckhannon was right. The infant was skinny and sick looking. His little red face shook in unison as he pulled his knees to his chest.

Anna cradled the small child in her arms and rubbed small circles on his tummy. "Are you having tummy issues, little one? We'll take care of that as soon as I can. But let's get to know one another first. How about we start with that wet diaper? Then we can see what we can do about that upset tummy."

After changing and dressing him in a fresh sleeper, she carried him downstairs. His cries settled to a whimper when she brought him to the living room. "Mr. Buckhannon, do you mind showing me to the kitchen where I can find his formula?"

He waved her to follow him, but Anna stopped him to ask Mrs. Buckhannon a few questions. "Do you mind if I try a few things on the little guy?"

"What do you mean?"

"I see he has a bit of diaper rash. Sometimes a little bit of plain yogurt will clear that up. And I see he has some cradle cap. If you have some olive oil, that might do the trick in a few days."

Both Buckhannons smiled, and Margaret answered, "You do whatever you see fit. We've tried so many things, it can't hurt for some good old-fashioned baby remedies to add to the mix."

The vote of confidence encouraged Anna, and she bounced Steven over her shoulder as she followed Mr. Buckhannon to the kitchen.

He opened the pantry and pointed to the shelf where the formula was stored. "We've tried a few different kinds. His doctor suggested we try a goat's milk-based formula yesterday. I picked some up this afternoon. Perhaps you should give that a try."

Anna picked up the can and read the directions. "I think we should. He was pulling his knees to his chest when I picked him up like his tummy was upset."

"Would you like me to take him while you mix it up?"

"I think I can handle both. I'm pretty good at juggling things. I've cared for my sister's children for the last few months, so I've gotten pretty good at doing things with one hand."

"All right then. I'm going to my study to get some work done. Make yourself at home, and you know where to find me if you need anything."

Anna rubbed her chin on the top of Steven's head, trying to calm the child while she hurried to get his bottle made. She learned quickly with John Paul, who had a few bouts of colic, that fussy *bobblis* responded better to a quiet person. Her *schwester*, typically high-strung, often took advantage of Anna's calming personality to tend to John Paul during his moments of distress.

For the rest of the evening, Anna held and rocked Steven in his room, singing in his ear and letting them get to know one another. When he finally drifted off to sleep, she placed him in his crib and made her way to her room.

After unpacking her suitcase and taking advantage of the bright light the lamp on the nightstand gave, she reached for the stack of books she'd brought with her. One on all-natural herb remedies, one on overcoming fear and anxiety, and her leather-bound bible. An overwhelming peace settled somewhere between her heart and her head when she realized, for once in her life, she felt useful.

Steven had taken to her quite nicely, and the way Mr. & Mrs. Buckhannon welcomed her into their home was refreshing. With a sudden urge to write Rebecca, she picked up the flower-lined stationery she'd brought and flicked on the light on the small writing desk under the window.

Dear Rebecca,

My trip to the Buckhannons went as well as expected, considering an accident on 79 delayed us. I was welcomed warmly and given complete control over Master Steven. Mrs. Buckhannon is recovering from back surgery and spent most of the afternoon in the front room in front of a warming fire.

Little Steven has a set of lungs that, even on John Paul's crankiest day, would overpower him. He seems underweight compared to children his age. I think even John Paul will outweigh him within a month or so.

What has me the most concerned is the extent of his temper tantrums when he is not tended to quickly.

Even though this is only my first day here, I am confident this is where God led me. I feel so comfortable here. My room is beautiful and suitable next to Steven's. I even have a door connecting the two, which I have opened just a crack, so I can hear him stir in the middle of the night. I can't wait until morning to see the view from my window. This part of the house overlooks Lake Erie, and I'm sure the scene will be breathtaking.

I'm not so sure I'll be coming home this weekend. A storm is predicted to hit, and I'd hate to have the driver fight the interstate in such weather.

I pretty much wanted to let you know all is well. I should lie down and try to get some sleep if I can. The presence of a sleeping baby in the next room does something to me, but don't worry, I am really enjoying all of this.

More later, all my love,

Anna

Tiptoeing into Steven's room, Anna brushed her fingertip over the boy's cheek and whispered a sweet goodnight. "I'm not sure what God has in store for us, little one, but I'm here to help you thrive. Maybe God sent me here so we can help each other."

***

Jebediah Kauffman was a man of few words, but when he did speak, his wife and boys stopped to take notice. "Naomi, I'd like you to gather the boys this evening for a family meeting."

Naomi moved the cast-iron skillet, sizzling with bacon, off the fire and turned toward her husband. "All of them? It might be hard to corral everyone up in one place. Most of the grandchildren will need to get to bed for school tomorrow. Let alone the boys' other jobs off the farm."

With a glint in his eye, he smiled. "If anyone can, you'll make it happen."

"May I ask what's so important?"

Jebediah laid his hand on his open Bible. "I've made a decision that will affect us all."

Naomi moved the crisp bacon to a plate and set it on the table. She didn't need to ask what he was referring to; it was the one thing she'd been praying for, for nearly two years. With a shimmer of moisture in her eyes, she asked, "It's time?"

"*Jah.*"

For nearly forty years, her husband only decided on something after much thought and prayer. She didn't need for him to discuss things with her in detail because she was sure he had already hashed it out with the only one who mattered, *God.*

Jebediah held his cup up for her to fill with coffee. "After breakfast, I'm going to meet with Mose Weaver and Jacob Byler."

Naomi filled her cup and asked, "You've been friends since you were all youngsters. They'll try to talk you out of it. You know this, right?"

"*Jah*. That's why I want to meet with the boys. This will affect us all."

After drizzling a spoon of bacon grease in a clean pan, Naomi cracked a couple of fresh eggs and quickly lapped the hot fat over the whites. "Won't be any trouble for Simon and Benjamin; not too sure about the other five."

"It will be up to the older boys to decide what's best for their families, but I feel it's my place to take a stand for what is right according to God's Word."

Naomi filled Jebediah's plate and took a seat to his right. As they both bowed in silent prayer, Naomi thanked God for shining His truth on her husband's heart.

***

Simon sat on a fallen log overlooking the allotment of land his father deeded to him. The three hundred acres his father had purchased fifty years ago were divided between him and his six brothers. His older brothers had all claimed their portion, and only he and his younger *bruder* Benjamin had yet to take their share.

Willow Creek weaved its way along the backside of all seven parcels of prime farmland. At one point, Simon could have cared less about the property. Still, now with Marcus in the picture, he couldn't imagine raising his son anywhere else. A twinge of panic twisted his stomach, and he chased it away as quickly as it entered. He wouldn't give into worry, especially since he had already placed it in God's hand.

With a sketch pad on his lap, he traced out the lay of the land, positioning the gardens and greenhouse at the right angle of the rise and fall of the sun. He didn't give up hope for Anna's dream and made concessions for the herb farm in his plans. He prayed expectantly that God would bring them back together, in His time and at His will.

Sprigs of dried wheat swayed in the breeze as Simon studied a pair of yearlings maneuvering their way through the open field. Oblivious to his presence, the deer meandered into the woods. Memories of the first day of deer season came to mind, and he couldn't help but smile at the possibility of sharing the same with his son someday.

A twig broke, and Simon turned toward the sound. "*Mamm,* what are you doing up here?"

"I saw you head this way and figured it would do me good to take a walk. It's been years since I've been back here."

Simon moved over on the log and held his hand out to help his mother take a seat.

"Whatcha' got there?" she asked.

Simon held his plans up for her to see and pointed to the area beside the woods. "I think the house would be best there. The trees would shield the hot afternoon sun but allow the morning light to warm the porch nicely."

Naomi giggled. "If I didn't know better, I'd say you have a woman's comfort in mind."

"Not just any woman."

"There's no mistaking who that might be."

"Anna stopped and saw me the other day at the sawmill."

Naomi took the pad from his hands and examined the plans he sketched. "*Jah*, and how did that go?"

"She came to tell me she was taking a job in Erie for a few months."

"*Jah.*"

Simon furrowed his eyebrows. "You already knew?"

"*Jah.*"

"And you weren't going to tell me?"

"It wasn't my news to tell."

"Why didn't you try to stop her?"

"Again, that's between her and God. She felt led to go."

Simon rested his elbows on his knees. "I'm running out of time. My hearing date is only two months from now, and I'm not one step closer to proving I'm capable of caring for Marcus."

Naomi laid her hand on her son's arm. "Simon, quit trying to rush God. He doesn't expect you to sit back and do nothing. He wants you to actively work toward a goal, but He will line things up in His own time. Continue to work on the house and work hard for your *datt* and Mr. Mast."

Simon interrupted, "But I've wasted so much time chasing dreams…."

"And had you not chased those dreams, there would be no Marcus to worry over."

"But I would have had Anna."

"Did you ever think that perhaps God placed you on that path so there would be a Marcus?"

"Why can't I have both?"

"Nobody said you couldn't, but it might not be how you envision."

Simon took his pad back and sat up straight. "For now, my plans include both."

Naomi stood. "I came up here to tell you *datt* is calling a family meeting. I've sent word to all your *bruders* to come by after supper. Not sure where Benjamin is. But I'll catch him when he comes home for afternoon milking."

Simon knew his younger *bruder* was probably hanging out around the Apple Blossom Inn, hoping to catch Bella Schrock's eye. He'd only recently met the young Amish girl from Indiana that had his brother thinking of nothing else. He wasn't too sure the likes of even his *bruder* could convince the girl to give up her *Englisch* notion and step back into the life of the Amish. But again, who was he to judge? He'd done the exact thing, to the extent of losing the one he valued most for his own selfish desires.

Concentrating back on his drawing, he tucked Anna to the side and did an internal count of how many days before he could see her again at church.

***

Jebediah pulled his buggy alongside Bishop Weaver's, retrieved a lead, and fastened his horse to the hitching post in front of Jacob Byler's furniture shop.

The two men sat on the front porch in matching bentwood rockers. Jacob, much thinner than the last time he'd seen him, and Mose wearing his typical stern expression, greeted him as he made his way up the steps. Tipping his hat in their direction, Jebediah addressed them. "Pleasant weather for the second week in November, *jah*?"

Jacob nodded his head in the direction of the pond across the road. "Ducks and geese are already gone. Sign of a hard winter for sure and certain."

Mose grunted. "Saw two woodpeckers sharing a tree. That's another sign."

After a long silence, Jebediah turned and leaned up against the railing. "We've seen things change in our community over the last fifty years, *jah*?"

Jacob replied, "Some good and some bad, I'd say."

Mose bounced his thumbs on the arms of his rocker. "Been times when I've questioned why the good Lord appointed me to this position. That's for sure."

All three men thought in silence for a few minutes.

Jebediah folded his arms across his chest. "In all the years we've been friends, I can't say we've seen eye to eye on everything."

"Nope, can't say we have," Jacob mumbled.

"But there's one thing we all can agree on."

"What's that?" Mose asked.

"We all want to live by the truth," Jebediah replied.

Jacob looked toward Mose, landed on Jebediah, and asked, "What truth is that?"

"You know as well as I do what truth I'm talking about."

Mose held his hand up. "Not you too!"

Jebediah stood, dropping his hands to his side. "I've been studying, and I believe that the young men of the New Order Fellowship are on to something."

Jacob sat quietly, pondering his misgivings about siding with the older Bishop. Being laid up in bed for the last two months gave him ample time to do his own research and come to his own conclusions. None of them corresponded to his Old Order's rules and regulations. At the heart of it, and after wondering if his days on earth were numbered, he sought the truth himself, hoping it would rectify the state of his family.

After letting Mose settle, Jacob added, "I have to admit, I've been questioning the *Ordnung* myself. Change is bound to happen, no matter how pig-headed and driven by tradition we are. God gave us the New Testament to free us from the bondage of the old ways. Isn't that true, Mose?"

Mose raised his voice an octave. "Regardless, you and I accepted our positions to lead this community. What the New Order Fellowship is preaching goes against everything we stand for."

Jebediah relaxed back on the railing. "Isn't following Jesus and loving our neighbor as we love ourselves the only thing God asked us to do?"

Jacob stopped his chair from rocking and leaned his elbows on his knees. "Now that I know the truth, how can I teach my grandchildren the only way to heaven is by how well they follow the *Ordnung*? Thank God all my children chose to leave the Old Order."

Mose directed Jacob. "Now you too! We need to be in obedience to keep the world out. If not, our culture will fade from existence, and there will be no more separation."

"Mose, I don't know all the answers, but I have to believe God has a new focus for all of us."

"What's that?" Mose asked.

Jebediah replied, “To be followers of Christ, and we can’t do that by holding on to things that don’t matter when it comes to eternity.”

Mose stood and walked to the end of the porch. “I’d like nothing more than our community to be united again. But I don’t see that happening in my lifetime.”

Jebediah moved to his side. “I’ve spent my whole life hoping I’ve been good enough to get to heaven. Over the past year, I’ve seen the light regarding our works-based salvation.”

Jebediah laid his hand on his old friend's shoulder. “We’re never going to be good enough if that is our only hope for heaven.”

Mose jerked his shoulder away. “Do as you like. You’ll go to hell with the rest of them.”

Bishop Weaver turned his back, and Jebediah quietly left the porch and headed home.

CHAPTER 11

Simon counted every minute of every day during the week leading up to Sunday services. Taking time on Saturday to wash and clean his buggy, he hoped Anna would allow him the privilege of driving her home from the youth *singeon* on Sunday night. Anything to earn her trust back was a start. He wasn't sure if she still attended, but it was worth a shot.

Early Sunday morning Simon turned his horse and buggy over to the boys charged in caring for the rigs; Simon made his way to the side of the barn where the men had gathered. All dressed in black vests and starched Sunday best white shirts, the men spoke of weather and crops while waiting to file into the Yoders' home.

As the women walked past the barn and into the bank basement, Simon kept his eyes open for Anna. When he saw Rebecca, but not Anna, he blew a silent breath through his lips. Maybe he had missed her. His current prayer was she would be in attendance.

His *bruder*, Benjamin, elbowed him and nodded his head toward their father's buggy. "True to his word, here come *Datt* and *Mamm*."

"Other than Bishop Schrock's new preaching style, I don't think they'll find the New Order Fellowship service much different from the Old Order."

Benjamin lowered his voice and leaned in closer to Simon. "Ya think any of the older boys will make the switch?"

"I couldn't say. Seems like each one of them needed to give it some serious thought. Many of their wives have families in the Old Order. It would mean more separation, for sure and certain."

Simon followed his *bruder's* eyes as they fell on Bella walking across the yard. Benjamin noted, "All I know is I'm glad we ain't married yet, so we can pick a wife from this church. That way, there's no questioning." There was no denying Benjamin's reasoning, and he hoped to do the same.

Stepping in line according to age had been a tradition Simon didn't mind following, as was sitting with the men on the opposite side of the room. There were several long-lived Amish traditions the New Order Fellowship adopted, and a few they didn't. But he had to agree it was nice seeing the women dressed in brighter colors than the drab, dark blue and burgundy.

However, nothing mattered more than following scripture and spreading the word of Jesus more openly. If their culture was going to survive, it would be changes like the one Bishop Schrock and the newly appointed ministers encouraged that would grow their followers. Just having a church full of the younger members of Willow Springs was encouragement enough in his books.

After Simon shook Daniel Miller's hand, the man to his immediate left, he found his place on the bench and scoured the women's side of the church. He closed his eyes as he picked up the *Ausbund* songbook from his seat to stifle his disappointment.

***

Anna pushed Steven's stroller along the winding sidewalk lined by the cliff overlooking Lake Erie. Bright sun rays broke through the trees and added to the serene landscape. It had been a week since arriving at the Buckhannons', and she could already tell Steven was responding to her care. Just that morning, she'd been able to get him to take a few bites of baby cereal before he finished a whole bottle. And to her surprise, not one ounce was wasted or spit up. An improvement for sure.

While she missed Mary Ellen and John Paul, Steven was also making a way in her heart. His curly dark hair and big brown eyes gave her purpose, something she hadn't felt since her *mamm* died. Perhaps God sent her to take care of him to show her she did have a reason in life, even if it might not be raising a family of her own.

Nearing the back entrance, feathery wisps of snow started falling, and Steven reached up and tried to grab the frozen crystals. His infectious baby-like giggle landed on her, full of joy and peace. At that moment, she wouldn't have wanted to be anywhere else.

She knelt near his stroller and held out her tongue until a dime-shaped snowflake landed and melted just as quickly. Mimicking her actions, he fumbled with his tongue as he reached out to her face. Catching his tiny fingers, she kissed them and said, "Your little mitts are cold. Best get you back inside. There will be plenty of snow for another day, I promise."

Setting the lock on the wheel, Anna picked Steven up and whispered calming words in his ear as she carried him inside. Mr. Buckhannon sat at the bar separating the kitchen from the breakfast nook, reading the paper. Looking over his glasses perched low on his nose, he said, "You're a natural. Not sure how we got so lucky finding you, but I'm glad we did."

Over the last week, the Buckhannons became more like friends than employers. Their friendly mannerisms and giving her free will to care for the child as she saw fit made for a comfortable work environment.

Anna shifted Steven to her hip and wiggled out of one side of her coat and then the other. When she hung it on the hook near the back door, she couldn't help but ask. "I'm sure there are nanny services here in Erie. Why did you look for a nanny so far away?"

Mr. Buckhannon folded his newspaper, laid it aside, and picked up his coffee. "We'd heard great things about Amish nannies, and we only wanted the best for Steven."

Anna shyly smiled. "But why me? I didn't have any formal training or references I could give you."

"I knew from the moment I met you. And besides, you were the answer to our prayers. We had just prayed for God to send us the perfect person to care for him, and twenty minutes later, you called. If that wasn't a sign from God, I don't know what else was."

Steven yawned and rubbed his tiny fingers across his nose. "Looks like all that fresh air did this little guy in. If you'll excuse me, I'll put him down for a nap, and then I'll be back to take care of the stroller."

"I'll put things away. You just tend to the baby."

Anna shook her head and smiled. As she walked through the kitchen and into the hallway, she thanked God for guiding her to the

Buckhannons. They could have picked any other Amish community in the tri-state area but chose Willow Springs; for that, she would ever be grateful.

Mrs. Buckhannon called from her place on the sofa as she passed the living room. "Anna, I haven't seen Steven all morning. Please bring him to me."

Anna whispered in his ear. "Just a few more minutes, little one, and you can take that much-needed nap."

Mrs. Buckhannon held her arms out to Steven, and he leaned into Anna's shoulder. When Anna tried to pass him to Margaret again, the child held tighter and started to cry.

Defeated, Margaret dropped her hands and said, "I suppose that's my fault. I haven't been the most welcoming to him. Neal cared for Steven the most before you came along. He's not comfortable with me."

Anna didn't know what to say to the woman's confession. "I'm sorry. Maybe we should spend more time with you, and he'll get more comfortable. That might be all it takes. Children can sense pain and uneasiness. Steven might have picked up on that if you've been in a lot of agony."

Margaret's face dropped, and a glistening of moisture clouded her eyes. "Oh, I've been in pain, but most has been emotional."

The woman pulled the blanket up under her chin and turned away from Anna. "You can go now. Looks like he needs a nap anyways."

It seemed like the air in the room turned cold at Mrs. Buckhannon's comment. Something was bothering the woman, and if Anna could find a way to ease the woman's emotional pain when it came to Steven, she surely would try.

***

Margaret lay on the sofa, watching the flames bounce around the fire and thought back over the last six months. Such a short time for things in her life to change so dramatically. A quick shopping trip turned into a devastating car wreck, which took her only daughter's life and left her unable to care for her only grandchild. Finally, things had started to get better after almost a year of constant upheaval at her daughter's unplanned pregnancy. Why was God punishing her so? Wasn't it enough that he took her daughter, but he wasn't going to allow Steven to form a lasting bond with her? Why had life gotten so unbearable?

At this point, she was tired of fighting with both God and Neal. Whether Simon could prove he was a fit father or not, maybe Neal was right; Steven belonged with him. Especially since they couldn't keep someone like Anna caring for their grandson indefinitely. Besides, if Anna was any indication of how the Amish raised their children, what harm would come of allowing Steven to be brought up Amish.

All the time she had spent lying around, Margaret started questioning her motives for keeping Steven from his father. Wasn't it her own daughter who confessed to tricking Simon into sleeping with her in the first place? Cora knew Simon didn't handle alcohol well, but she spiked his drink anyways.

Simon wanted to do right by her daughter and the baby. But in the end, Cora refused to allow him to marry her after finding out he had planned to return to his Amish community and marry his childhood sweetheart. Cora wouldn't settle for second best for anything, especially Simon's heart.

The never-ending pain of losing Cora never entirely left her. She had learned to push all memories so deep there was no trace of Cora's face to pull from. After coming home from the hospital, she made Neal take every remembrance of their daughter and lock them away in her room at the end of the hall.

Maybe one day she could open the door and find comfort in the things that reminded her of her only daughter. But for now, she'd hide in pain with forced hellos and fake smiles.

***

Anna was awakened by Steven's early chatter during the break of the horizon that comes right before dawn. She rolled over and stayed as quiet as she could. Initially, she wanted to rush to his side. Still, he needed to learn to occupy himself and not demand her attention at every whim.

Amish children were taught early on that their existence was a gift from God, but that didn't mean the world revolved around them entirely. It took all her better judgment not to follow the pattern the Buckhannon's had already put in place by giving in to his every whim. But it took everything she had to follow through with their line of dealing with the crying child.

Anna made her way to his crib just as his gurgles turned into a full-fledged scream. When he laid his eyes on her, he sat up and reached out; her heart melted. Rebecca's words echoed in her ears. *"What happens if you become too attached to a child that's not yours? I would think that would be harder than you can imagine."*

Anna tried to reason with herself. *Perhaps I have a soft spot for the little one, but maybe that's because my heart is aching and empty for a child of my own. When the time is right, I'm sure I'll be able to leave him and go on with my life. I'm sure I'll be sad, who wouldn't be? But right now, he's filling me with joy. And besides, I believe the Lord wants me here.*

***

After breakfast and a clean change of clothes, Anna carried Steven into the front room and sat him on the floor next to Margaret. "I thought perhaps we could spend some time in here with you for a spell…that is, if you are feeling up to it."

Mrs. Buckhannon gazed off into the fire. "I see no harm in you both enjoying the warmth."

Not the response Anna had hoped for, but she would take the little the woman offered. "He's starting to pull himself up. Look!" Anna let Steven wrap his hands around her fingers and remained firm as he pulled himself up.

A slight upturn of Margret's lip gave Anna hope, and the woman replied, "Well look at that. I'd say he's getting stronger."

"He just needed a little encouragement and some floor time."

"Floor time?"

Anna smiled. "Time to roll around and explore. Before we know it, we won't be able to stop him."

With a gulf of emotion, Margaret added, "We haven't had a little one in the house for a long time. I suppose we forgot a lot."

Steven plopped down, turned to his stomach, and pulled himself up on all fours, rocking back and forth. "See what I mean? It won't be long, and he'll crawl all over the place."

The look on the older woman's face confused Anna, and she asked, "You had other children?"

"Just one," returned Margret thoughtfully. "But we weren't around much when she was little. We had a nanny to take care of most things."

Mrs. Buckhannon grinned and then asked, "What is he doing?"

Anna smiled as Steven fell to his tummy and pulled himself back up on all fours. "He's learning to crawl."

As the two women enjoyed watching the little guy perform his new trick, Margret asked, "Do you plan on having children one day?"

"Lots, I hope."

"How many is that?"

Anna thought for a moment. "Oh…I don't know. I suppose however many God allows."

With a rise in her tone, Mrs. Buckhannon asked, "You don't determine that before marrying?"

Anna giggled, "No, we leave that up to God."

Margaret straightened her lap blanket and picked up a needlepoint project. "I guess that's one of the differences between the Amish and English."

After a thoughtful pause, Anna went on. "One of many, I suspect."

Margaret asked, "Do you mind if I ask a personal question?"

Anna helped Steven sit upright. "Of course not."

"You are so good with him; why aren't you married yet with your own babies?"

A twinge of regret constricted Anna's throat, and she had to swallow hard before answering. "I think God has other plans for my life right now. I'm trying to depend solely on the Lord's guidance and not rush into anything."

"That's quite commendable for such a young girl. I'm impressed."

"Oh, don't be. I have many faults when it comes to trusting in God. For years, I've wanted everything my way, on my timetable. When I didn't get it, I let myself be consumed with worry and anxiety." Anna let out a nervous sigh. "Most times, I have to remind myself I don't know better than Him."

Steven rolled over and picked up a toy to chew on. "Besides, I'm enjoying taking care of your son. He's been good for me. The more I concentrate on him, the less I worry about what's happening at home."

Margaret stopped weaving a needle through the canvas. "My son? Oh, I think you misunderstood; Steven is our grandson."

Anna pulled her knees up to her chest. "I'm sorry. I assumed you were his mother. May I ask where his parents are?"

Margaret spoke slowly. "His mother passed away in a car accident six months ago."

"And his father? Where is he?"

An edge in her voice gave Anna the impression Mrs. Buckhannon wasn't too fond of Steven's father.

"Hopefully, he's getting things in place to step up and take responsibility for his actions."

"I don't understand."

"Steven's biological father had some growing up to do, so we've given him six months to prove to us that he can be responsible."

"That makes sense now why you only need me for a few months."

"With any luck, the boy, while really he's a man, will come through and prove we can trust him to raise Steven right."

Anna crossed her legs and added, "I'm sorry about your daughter. I bet you miss her terribly."

A slight sob escaped Margaret's lips. "I do. We hadn't always seen eye-to-eye, but we were finally making a breakthrough after the baby was born. She had calmed down some and wasn't so wild. I think having Steven changed her."

Anna looked tenderly at Steven. "Does he favor your daughter?"

Mrs. Buckhannon studied the child's face. "He looks a lot like his father. His curly dark hair and face shape, but those brown eyes are all his mother's." Anna smiled as the woman lovingly pondered over her grandson.

"So, how did you end up with Steven and not his father in the first place?"

"It's a long story and one I'm not proud to tell, but in a nutshell, they weren't married."

"Oh, my. I'm sorry."

"Those things happen, especially with my daughter. She was known to do whatever it took to get her way. I suppose that is half my fault. Her father and I didn't do too good of a job raising her. She spent more time in boarding schools than with us. But in the end, she tricked the boy's father. He didn't even know about him until after he was born."

"I hope it works out."

"So do we. The young man comes from a good family, and we think it's just a matter of time before he gets everything in place to care for him. But, enough about that. I want to learn more about you. Tell me a little about yourself."

"Not much to tell. What do you want to know?"

"Let's start with, is there anyone special in Willow Springs waiting for you?"

Anna looked away, busied herself with Steven, and muttered, "Maybe."

"Tell me about Mr. Maybe."

She snickered and said, "It's a long story, and one I'm not proud to tell." Both women laughed.

"Mr. Maybe left for a few years and has just returned home, and he wants to pick up where we left off."

"And you don't want that?"

"It's not that. He…he left me a few days before we were to be married. I'm not so sure I can trust him again."

"What are you afraid of? If he came back to claim you and your heart is still open, why wouldn't you want to at least explore it?"

"He broke my heart, and it took me years to get over him."

Anna let out a small sigh. "He swears he never stopped loving me and always planned to return."

Mrs. Buckhannon raised her eyebrows. "I'd say if it's been a few years and you didn't let anyone else step in and take your heart, you haven't gotten over him."

"Perhaps. That's why I decided to take this job. I hoped that if I got away for a while, I could hear God's voice clearer, and he would guide me to which path he wanted me to take."

"So, what is Mr. Maybe's name?"

"Simon, Simon Kauffman."

Margaret dropped her needlepoint on her lap and let out a small gasp. Anna turned at the sound. "Everything all right?"

"Ohh…oh yes, my dear. Looks like Steven's ready for his morning nap, and I'd also like to rest for a while."

Anna stood and picked up Steven and his toys. "This was nice. Would you like us to visit with you later this afternoon again?"

Margaret nodded and added, "That would be nice. Can you go to Neal's study and let him know I'd like to have a word with him when he gets a break from his work?"

"Yes, ma'am. Anything else you need before I go?"

"No, I don't think so. But Anna."

"Yes?"

"I think God sent you exactly where you need to be."

Mrs. Buckhannon reached out and squeezed Anna's hand lovingly. "You are the answer to our prayers."

Anna headed to the study at the back of the house, balancing Steven over her hip as she went. It was good to see Mrs. Buckhannon at ease with her, especially after her blue mood the day before. Perhaps God did have a purpose in sending her to the Buckhannon's.

CHAPTER 12

Outside, the snow glistened in the morning sunshine. In the distance, Simon waited as Benjamin tried maneuvering the manure spreader out of the barn. It was two weeks before Christmas, and Simon was beside himself. Only three more weeks before his hearing date, and he wasn't even close to proving anything to the Buckhannons.

Benjamin hollered his direction. "I could use some help over here!"

Simon followed his *bruder's* voice and reached out to settle the two Belgian horses struggling to back the full spreader out of the narrow double doors. "Isn't it too early to spread this? I'm not sure the ground is even frozen enough yet."

Benjamin bellowed, "We've managed fine without you for the last three years; now is not the time to tell us how we need to do things."

"Whoa, there! I'm doing no such thing; I just don't want you to get this thing buried in mud."

"And you don't think these guys are strong enough to pull it out if we do?"

Jebediah came around the corner, shovel in hand. "What's all the yelling about?"

Benjamin picked up the reins and guided the horses around Simon. "Mr. Hotshot here thinks he knows it all. Maybe you can convince him otherwise."

Simon jumped back and moved to his father's side. "Sorry about that. I think I might have stepped on his toes."

Jebediah headed back into the barn with Simon on his heels. "I think the boy has girl trouble. He's been in a foul mood all morning."

Simon let the first cow in the row out of its stanchion and led him to the door. Morning milking was complete, and the cows were free to move outside, giving Simon and his older *bruder's* ample room to clean the stalls.

A chill in the air mixed with steam coming off fresh manure allowed Simon time to clear his head. He needed to figure out a way to spend time with Anna. On more than one occasion over the last few weeks, he wanted to ask Eli if he had any word about when Anna planned to come home. Not knowing if Anna had shared things with Rebecca kept him from probing too deep.

As he made his way down the cement-lined barn, he worked at scraping manure into the cow alley. Only stopping when he reached the end of the twenty-stanchion row, he removed his hat and wiped his brow with the back of his hand.

His father came out of the cement block milk house and sat on a hay bale. "Keep that up, and you won't have any need for your *bruders* and me."

Simon pushed his bangs off his forehead and replaced his straw hat. "Some days, I need hard work to sort things out."

Jebediah snorted and pointed to the bucket beside him. "Take a seat, son. There's plenty of work for all of us. No one said you have to do it alone."

Simon looked around the barn and noticed his five older *bruders* working in unison, laughing, and cutting up on each other, oblivious to his sudden burst of energy.

"What's got you all worked up today?"

Kicking a glob of wet straw off his boots, Simon took off his gloves and rested them on his knee. "I'm running out of time."

His father nodded at one of his eldest son's jokes and asked, "I didn't know you were privy to God's timetable."

"*Nee.*"

His *datt* smiled cryptically and stood. "I didn't think so."

His father's wise words were all it took to get Simon's head back in line with God's plan.

***

Anna brushed snow off Steven's snowsuit before setting him down on the rug just inside the back door. "I'm not sure who had more fun just now, you or me." Steven whimpered and held his hands up. "I know, little one; let me get out of my coat first."

Mr. Buckhannon came to her rescue; he picked his grandson up and wiggled him free from the cumbersome layer of warmth. "Did you have fun sitting in the snow with Anna?"

The child rubbed his nose with his tiny fist and leaned back toward Anna. After hanging her coat up and slipping out of her boots, she pulled Steven back into her arms. "I do believe I wore the little guy out."

Mr. Buckhannon asked, "Do you think it's a good idea to have him out in the cold for so long?"

Anna walked to the sink to make a bottle and tipped her head in his direction. "Children need sunshine, and a little cold air never hurt anyone."

Neal shrugged his shoulders and smiled. "I suppose you're right, but our daughter's nanny hated the cold, so she never took her outside to play."

"In my community, we encourage our children to be outside as much as possible. Even at this age."

"I'll take your word for it. I can tell he's thriving under your care, so I trust you."

Steven took the bottle and threw his head back on Anna's shoulder. "I'd say all that fresh air has more than one benefit."

"He'll be out in less than ten minutes," Anna expressed.

Mr. Buckhannon picked up a stack of mail. "After settling him, will you meet with Margaret and me in the living room? We have something we'd like to discuss with you."

Anna moved Steven in her arms to a more comfortable position and replied, "Of course."

***

Once Steven had fallen asleep, Anna went to the front room where Mrs. Buckhannon was waiting.

“That was quick,” Mrs. Buckhannon smiled and pointed to the chair near the sofa.

“Steven had a big breakfast and enjoyed the time outside. I knew it wouldn’t be long, and he’d be fast asleep.” Anna said.

Margaret only smiled, then Neal, who had just stepped in, added, “You’ve been so good for the boy, and we don’t know what we would have done had you not answered our ad. We just want you to know how pleased we are with the progress you’ve made with him over the last month.”

Unaccustomed to praise, Anna shyly added, “You have no idea how much fun I’ve had caring for him. He is such a sweet boy and has brought me such joy.”

Margaret added, “We’ve noticed you thoroughly enjoy him. So different from our daughter’s nanny. That woman acted as if she was a bother. Whereas you’ve put your whole soul into his care. We want you to know how much we appreciate loving him like you do.”

“Really, he’s an easy child to love.”

Mr. Buckhannon took a seat in the wingback chair that mirrored Anna’s. “We asked you to meet with us because we have a little problem we hope you can help us solve.”

Anna didn’t answer but listened intently.

“Margaret’s doctor wants her to consult with a spine specialist in Atlanta in two days. He hopes this new doctor agrees with his prognosis. If he does, she’ll need another surgery in Atlanta.”

“Oh, no. How can I help?”

Mrs. Buckhannon added a bookmark to the book she was reading and laid it aside. “We aren’t comfortable leaving you alone in this big house so far from home. We hope you’ll agree to take Steven back to your sister’s until after the first of the year.”

“You want me to take him to Willow Springs?”

Neal asked, “Do you think your family would mind?”

Anna thought for a moment and smiled. “I think that would be a wonderful idea. My niece, Mary Ellen, would love another playmate. And I’d like nothing more than to introduce Steven to my family. I’m sure they would love it.”

Margaret winked in Neal's direction. "We hate that we'll be gone over Christmas, but I'm sure Steven won't even realize we're gone. He's grown quite attached to you."

Anna flushed. "I hope that doesn't bother you."

"Heaven's no. If it weren't for you, we'd still be doing everything wrong because we thought we knew best. But now we see he is much happier with you in his life."

"Good, I certainly don't want to take your place."

Neal nodded in agreement. "No one can take our place. But someone can certainly do a better job of raising him than us. We are much too old to take on that responsibility full-time. And until his father gets his life together, we're counting on you to see to Master Steven's wellbeing."

Anna crossed her leg, weaved her fingers around her knee, and asked, "When are you leaving?"

The older woman responded, "We leave tomorrow afternoon. And if you agree to take Steven home with you, Neal will call our driver and hire him to take you home this evening."

"Today? I'll need to get things packed and ready to go." Anna stood. "I'm honored you both trust me with your grandson, and I promise to take good care of him while you're away."

Neal smiled and responded, "We know you will, and we wouldn't trust Steven's care to anyone else."

As Anna left the room and up the stairs, Neal turned to Margaret and asked, "Are you sure we shouldn't tell her we know about her connection with Simon? Won't it be awkward when she shows up with his baby?"

"Oh, Neal, you worry too much. Simon's not going to recognize him. The child was only a few weeks old when he saw him last. Steven has a full head of hair now, and I doubt the child even had his eyes open when Simon held him. And other than the picture Cora sent him of the two of them, he'll not recognize Steven Marcus."

Margaret paused for a few seconds while she shifted on the sofa. "I'm certain he won't put two and two together and figure it out. Besides, Cora introduced Steven as Marcus, so I'm certain the boy calls him Marcus, not Steven."

Mr. Buckhannon shook his head. "I feel like we're deceiving the girl, and I'm not sure I like it."

Margaret patted the back of her husband's hand. "When it comes to heart matters, you let me figure that out. And after all we went through with losing Cora, I feel we need to give Steven the best chance at life as we can."

Neal covered his wife's hand and squeezed gently. "You really think Steven's best shot in life is being raised Amish? They live such a backward way of life."

"Backward to who? You and me? I've never met a girl quite like Anna. She's pretty special, and if Simon holds even an ounce of similar values as Anna, how can that be wrong?"

Neal sighed, and Margaret beseeched him. "Look, Neal, I know it will be hard to let him go, but I promised myself months ago that if I had the chance to make things up to Cora for all the wrong I did while she was growing up, I would. I believe God sent Anna here so I could make things right."

"But what about college and a good education? They don't encourage their children to get an education past eighth grade?"

Margaret whispered tenderly, "Let's cross that bridge when we get to it." Gradually, Margaret continued, "What good did all that schooling do for Cora? All it did was expose her to all kinds of things that we wish she wouldn't have explored.

Perhaps we're the ones who have it all wrong. Maybe separating our children from the world isn't bad after all. It certainly hasn't hurt Anna. By talking with her about her family and church, I see a loving community where children prosper. How can that be wrong?"

Neal covered her hand with his other. "I trust your judgment on this one. But I don't understand how keeping all we know from Anna is right."

Margaret assured him. "God is already at work here, and He doesn't need our help. If His plan is for the two of them to work things out, then I trust He'll make it happen. We're just putting the pieces in place; it's His job to line them up perfectly."

***

Two hours later, Anna stood in the hallway while Mr. Buckhannon gave Steven a kiss on his forehead and wished them both well. The driver had already carried their bags to the car and was securing Steven's car seat in the backseat.

"Do you have everything?" Mr. Buckhannon gave her an envelope with money in it. "I want you to take this, and if he needs anything, use this. I wrote my cell phone number on the outside. If you need whatsoever, you call me, and I'll send whatever you need."

"Really you don't need to do that. I'll have everything I require at Rebecca and Eli's."

"I'll not take no for an answer. I don't want you to put your family out in the least."

She laughed. "Put them out? I hardly doubt that. They will be overjoyed we've come to stay, especially with Christmas so close. I wish I had time to let them know we were coming."

In a concerned tone, Neal asked, "Do you think it will be a problem?"

"A problem? No. I just know Rebecca, and she will have wanted to have everything just perfect upon our arrival."

After fastening Steven in his seat and slipping in beside him, Anna leaned around his chair and waved at Mr. Buckhannon. He stood on the front porch until they pulled away.

Anna gave Margaret ample time to visit with Steven before she left and caught the woman wiping away a few tears. The older woman's outlook changed entirely after the day they spent getting to know one another. Anna understood more about Mrs. Buckhannon's guilt and tried to help her work through her pain.

Anna looked back toward the old Victorian one last time before the driver pulled onto the highway. For some odd reason, it was like she was seeing the house for the last time. A twinge of sadness settled quickly but left as fast as it came when Steven reached out and touched her cheek.

She leaned in and kissed his tiny fingers. "You'll have the best time getting to know John Paul and Mary Ellen. And Rebecca and Eli are going to love you as their own. Mary Ellen will try to mother you just like she does John Paul."

Anna leaned back in her seat and took in a deep, cleansing breath. It was good to be going home, but it brought an onslaught of worry about facing Simon. She'd been so busy with Steven that she hardly thought about what was facing her back in Willow Springs. Except for the few times Simon's face and the mysterious dark-haired child made their way back into her dreams.

As she turned back to study Steven, a small gasp made its way to the hollow of Anna's throat. The boy who filled the hours right before she awoke looked much like the child filling her days between dawn and dusk.

***

Just before eight, the driver pulled into Eli and Rebecca's driveway. The warm glow from the single gas lamp in her *schwester's* front window made Anna giddy. She unhooked Steven's seat and stepped out of the car. A swirl of chimney smoke encased her nose, and she followed the light to the front door.

Before she could open it, Eli stepped out onto the porch. "Anna? We wondered who would be calling this late at night."

"I know; I didn't have time to leave a message. But I've come home to spend the holidays with everyone."

"That's *gut* news. Rebecca will be pleased. She's putting the *kinner* to bed. Go in, and I'll help the driver with your bags."

Rebecca's home was welcoming, and the matching rockers were moved closer to the wood stove in the living room. The cookstove's oven door had been left open in the kitchen, and Eli's gloves and hat were hanging on a drying rack above the stove.

Steven hadn't stirred, and she laid him on the daybed in the kitchen corner while she removed her winter clothing. She had missed the coziness of her *schwester's* home and thanked God for allowing her to return safely. Untying Steven's hat and unzipping his snowsuit, she moved him to the side of the daybed. Rebecca loved to have the children close and often used the daybed for quick naps or cuddle time.

Anna rushed to the door to help Eli just as Rebecca came down the stairs. “Anna, you’re home. Why didn’t you tell me? I would have gotten your room ready for you.”

“It happened so quickly I barely had time to pack, let alone get a message to you.” Anna grabbed her *schwester’s* hand. “Come see what I’ve brought with me.”

Anna put her finger to her lip and whispered, “Shhh…he’s sleeping, but Mr. and Mrs. Buckhannon let me bring Steven.”

Rebecca smiled and leaned over the sleeping child. “Look at those curls. He is the cutest thing ever. Oh…Mary Ellen is going to be so excited.”

“*Jah*, I know.”

“How long are you staying?”

Anna pulled Rebecca back into the front room. “Mrs. Buckhannon had to go to Atlanta for her back, so I’m here until she is back home. Most likely a few weeks.” Anna paused. “I hope that’s all right?”

“Of course, it is. Don’t you agree, Eli?”

Eli opened the door to the brown metallic wood box in the living room and raked the coals together before adding a few pieces of wood to the pile. “We’re so glad to have you home, Anna, and I can’t think of anything better than to have another child in the house.”

“I told you.” Rebecca linked her arm to Anna’s. “Come, let’s make some tea, and you can tell me all about the little guy.”

CHAPTER 13

Milking time at the Kauffman farm picked back up as soon as supper was over. Simon and Benjamin followed their *datt* to the barn, where Jebediah pushed the button to the milk house and started the diesel engine. Simon began sanitizing the milkers and Benjamin started to herd the one hundred Holstein into their stanchions. The older boys showed up and found their places throughout the barn.

It didn't take Simon long to become a welcomed addition back on his father's dairy farm, and he worked hard to prove himself to his *bruders* and his *datt*.

Benjamin hollered over the head of a cow in Simon's direction. "I've been meaning to ask if old man Mast needs any help at the lumber mill."

Simon stopped momentarily from washing out the inside of the milk tank to respond. "Who wants to know?"

"I do!"

Simon chuckled. "It's hard work. You think you're up for that?"

Benjamin hollered over the herd of Holsteins, finding their way to their stanchions, one after another. "I suspect if you can handle it, anyone can. Besides, it's good money, and I need to make some extra cash."

Simon hollered back, "I'm ready to give my notice, so I bet you can take my place."

"What? You're quitting?"

Simon lifted his head in his father's direction. "It's time I start building on that piece of land *Datt* gave me, and I don't have time to do all three. Work here, at the mill, and build a house. There's only so much time in a day."

"Why do you need extra cash all of a sudden?" Simon asked.

"The same reason you want to leave. It's time I step up and make something of myself. And that takes money. It's one thing *Datt* giving us land, but it's another if we want to build on it."

Each cow knew exactly where she belonged. Simon's oldest *bruder* chained the cow's metal stanchion around each neck and remarked, "It's about time!"

Jebediah shoveled grain into a long trough that lined the barn. "It's time you both contribute to the next generation of Kauffman boys, *jah*?"

Simon lowered his eyes, and his mind went to Anna. He picked up the sprayer to drown out their voices as he hosed out the milk tank.

After seeing that his sons had everything under control, Jebediah followed Simon into the cement block milk house, closed the door, and sat on an overturned bucket. "*Mamm* saw Rebecca Bricker at the Mercantile this afternoon."

"*Jah?*"

"Anna's back."

Simon snapped his head up. "For good?"

"Don't think so. Seems she's brought a child back with her."

"Ohhh…"

"That's not the worst of it."

"How so?"

"Rebecca mentioned the child's name to your *mamm*."

"*Jah*, so what does that mean to me?"

"She referred to him as eight-month-old Master Steven Buckhannon."

Simon dropped the hose and ran toward the house to speak to his mother.

***

Naomi knew long before she heard the heavy steps on the porch who was about to enter her kitchen. Her after-supper discussion with Jebediah was sure to cause an uproar in the barn, for sure and certain. She dried her hands on a towel and turned toward the door.

"*Datt* just told me you saw Rebecca this afternoon. Tell me it ain't true. Tell me Anna hasn't been caring for Marcus all this time."

"Calm down, Simon. Ain't no use getting yourself all worked up over nothing."

"Nothing? How can you say it's nothing? This just lays another layer of stuff I must dig through to earn her trust. I hadn't told her about Marcus yet."

"I told you she needed to know. I still don't understand your reasoning behind keeping something so important from her."

"I didn't want him to be the reason. I wanted it to be us alone."

Naomi slid down in a chair at the table and wrung the dishtowel in her hands. "I just don't know, son. I think you should have been honest with her from the start."

"Ohhh…*Mamm*, this just complicates things even more."

"*Nee*, what muddied things is you not being forthright with her from the start."

He raised his voice slightly. "How can I do that if the woman won't give me the time of day?"

Naomi crossed her arms.

Simon took a seat next to his mother and lowered his head. "I'm sorry, *Mamm*. I'm so frustrated with the whole situation. I'm trying hard to let God handle things, but all I see are roadblocks."

His mother smiled, and he asked, "What?"

"You see roadblocks; I see the Lord paving a way into Anna's heart."

"How so?"

"Come on, Simon, open your eyes. How did your son end up with Anna despite all the jobs and the young girls who take nanny jobs in this community?"

He leaned back in his chair and bounced his fingers on the table. "*Jah*, I think you're right."

"There's no thinking about it. God has his hands all over this. And if you can't see that, you're just plain crazy."

Simon relaxed a little in his chair and asked, "Now what?"

Naomi stood and walked back to the sink. "Seems like the good Lord didn't need your help thus far; he surely doesn't need it now."

Simon pushed in his chair and headed toward the door. "Best get back out there."

"Son."

"*Jah*?"

"You already gave it over to Him once, don't go picking it back up. He doesn't need your help. Keep praying, be in His Word, and trust His will, His way."

Simon tipped his head and smiled as he went out the door. The temperature continued to drop, and air burned his chest as he returned to the barn. He couldn't help but yearn to hitch up the buggy and pay a visit to the Bricker house. But he would heed his mother's advice and let God show him what to do next.

While the cows were being milked, Simon went to the hayloft and threw bales through the hole in the barn floor. He also threw the corn fodder down they would use for bedding once milking was complete.

When Benjamin removed the milker from the last cow, he helped Simon clear the gutters in the floor of manure. At the same time, the older boys continue to ready the milk for the five o'clock milk tanker arrival.

Now that the cows were ready for the night, the boys could relax and prepare for the whole thing to start over in twelve short hours. Dairy farming was hard, but Simon enjoyed the grueling work. He couldn't think of anything else than how it would provide a steady income for his future family. He prayed that God would soften Anna's heart and she would fall in love with Marcus and agree to make a life with both of them.

While that was his ultimate dream, he could only imagine how she would handle the truth once it was revealed. An empty hole in the pit of his stomach turned as he thought about how easy it had been to keep the truth from her. Was he ever going to learn that honesty was always the best choice?

He heaved a long sigh as he climbed the stairs to his bedroom. Even the hot shower did little to wash the concern from his mind. Anna didn't like to be deceived, and he was afraid he may have made it worse by keeping Marcus a secret from her.

His damp hair stuck to his forehead, and he brushed it aside as he picked up the picture on his nightstand. The only time he met his son was when Cora told him of his existence. She died shortly after, leaving him to independently sort out their son's future. That was almost seven months ago, and he couldn't formulate a clear picture of what he might look like now.

He certainly wouldn't need to wait long since he was sure they both would attend church in the morning. It was like moving boulders to get the Buckhannon's to consider him taking full custody. They didn't like him from the get-go, and he didn't blame them much since he left their daughter to bear the burden of their one-night stand by herself.

He rubbed his thumb over Steven Marcus's tiny figure in the picture and thought, *I promise son, I'll make this up to you and your momma. Anna will make a good mother, I'm sure of it. We just need to be patient and let God do His thing.*

***

Rebecca giggled at the mess Steven had made on his tray. "I think he'd do just as well by himself."

Anna sighed and let him twist the spoon out of her hand. When it hit the floor, he laughed aloud. Both women joined him in his amusement.

"Such a trickster for a nine-month-old," Rebecca commented as she shifted John Paul over her shoulder. "I can tell he will light his own way."

"Most days, I let him get used to a spoon, but I'm anxious this morning."

"Why's that?"

"I think the whole idea of taking him to church has me all flustered. What if I can't keep him quiet and he starts to fuss?"

"Now, Anna, you're getting all worked up about nothing. You've quieted more than one fussy baby in your lifetime, and Steven won't be any different."

"But he's never had to stay quiet for so long. You see how busy he is; he's not happy unless he's exploring."

"Then let him explore. Bishop Schrock and the rest of the ministers are much more laid back than Bishop Weaver. I don't think you have anything to worry about."

Anna wiped the child's face with a towel and looked at the clock. "Oh heavens, I'm not even dressed yet. Eli will have the buggy pulled around any minute."

Rebecca laid John Paul in the center of the daybed and shooed her *schwester* away. "I'll get Steven cleaned up. You go get dressed."

***

Snow fell in great feathery wisps as Anna handed Steven up to Rebecca. After she stepped into the backseat of Eli's family buggy, she pulled Mary Ellen close and balanced Steven on her knee. Eli walked around the horse, making sure the harness was secured. Rebecca turned in her seat and asked, "Do you think your edginess has anything to do with church being at the Kauffman's today?"

"I can't help feeling a little overwhelmed by it all."

Rebecca turned her attention to her husband, who was fastening down the side of the canvas curtain to keep out the December air, leaving Anna to sort out her apprehension alone.

The grinding of the steel wheels and the clopping of the horses' hooves got louder as Eli left the gravel driveway and pulled out onto the blacktopped road. A light layer of snow covered the road and added to the peacefulness of the line of buggies, all with a bright orange triangle on the back, making their way to the Kauffman's.

***

Jebediah stood back and watched all seven of his sons do their part in ensuring there wasn't one thing out of place on the Kauffman farm. This was the first time he had hosted church since switching his membership to the New Order Fellowship.

As he stood on the porch before dawn, Naomi met him with a cup of coffee. Taking the cup in one hand and pulling her in close, he asked, "Did you ever dream in all our years that each of our boys would follow us to this new church?"

Naomi looked up lovingly. "I'm not surprised. You've done a fine job of instilling the love of God in each one of our sons. And besides, I've been praying for each of their families for the last couple of years."

"For two years?"

"*Jah*, I knew the day Henry, Eli, Samuel, and Daniel walked out of the Old Order that we'd follow someday."

"How could have you been so sure?"

"I'm not sure; I just knew. I haven't been married to you for this long, not knowing you live by the truth. That and Eli's grandmother, Mary, shared the truth of salvation with me long before that."

"She did, did she?"

"*Jah*, I knew it was just a matter of time until you got curious enough about what the young men were preaching that you found out for yourself."

He squeezed her tighter. "You're a good woman, Naomi Kauffman."

The soft glow of the battery-powered lights leading the way of a parade of buggies up Jebediah's driveway forced him to take a long sip of his coffee before handing the cup back to his wife.

"I'd say that's my call to the barn. You've got everything under control in the house?"

Naomi grinned. "Now Jebediah, you know me better than that. Moreover, before they went home, our daughters-in-law had everything laid out last night. I suspect they're in there now double-checking things."

***

Simon pulled his black waistcoat tighter and stepped out to meet the first family who had arrived. Bishop Schrock stopped at his side, and Simon reached to steady the horse while bidding each other good morning. Henry walked around, held his arms out to lift down his two children, and then held a hand to his wife, Maggie.

"*Gut* day for the Lord, *jah*?" Henry asked as Simon led the buggy away.

Simon nodded in his direction and countered, "This snow keeps up like this, and we may have to dig our way home in a few hours."

For the next thirty minutes, family after family pulled up to the Kaufmann farm. When Simon noticed Eli's carriage stop at the barn, he was the first to lend a hand in hopes of seeing Anna.

Stepping up to the carriage, Simon watched as Rebecca handed down her black train case diaper bag and John Paul to Eli before reaching back for Mary Ellen.

Waiting for Eli and Rebecca to step aside, Simon held his hand out to help Anna out of the back of the buggy. Struggling to balance Steven and pick up her train case simultaneously, Simon reached up and took Steven from her arms.

His son, smaller than he imagined, smelled of Anna. A hint of lavender and vanilla filled his nose as he balanced the child on his hip. To his surprise, the boy laid his head on his shoulder. The simple act warmed Simon's heart until Anna purposely avoided eye contact.

He pulled the child close before Anna took him from his arms. "*Denki*," she mouthed as she fell into step with Rebecca and Mary Ellen.

Simon followed Anna with his eyes as he led Eli's buggy away, watching as she lined up to enter the house, oldest to youngest, as they had done for centuries.

His stomach churned at the thought of Anna's reaction when she discovered what he'd kept from her. He prayed continually and found his place in line as the men entered the house.

The living room and kitchen of his parent's home were filled with people, all sitting expectantly on wooden benches. After allowing the men in front of him to find their seats, he sat at the end of the row, which happened to be directly across from Anna, who sat straight to his left. He struggled to keep his head forward with only a few feet between them.

After the first hymn ended, there was a pause before the song leader sang the first few words to the *Lob Lied,* the second song sung in every Amish service across the country. As the drawn-out hymn echoed on the bare walls, the ministers prepared for the morning service in an upstairs bedroom.

Few things had changed from the Old Order Service to the New Order Fellowship, except for following the scripture more closely and laying aside some of the rules of the *Ordnung.*

Simon enjoyed Bishop Schrock and the ministers preaching more from the Bible and sharing more about Jesus. Even the prepared message was understood better since it was taught in *Englisch* and not Old German. After the second song ended, he heard the minister's footsteps making their way back downstairs.

Out of the corner of his eye, he noticed Anna bouncing Marcus on her knee as he chewed on a small toy. She had removed his hat, revealing a layer of delicate dark curls. Simon moved his hand to the back of his head and matted the unruly waves, hoping Anna wouldn't notice the resemblance.

As Minister Yoder spoke, Simon struggled to concentrate on the message. However, Samuel stopped and emphasized his point. "Anyone who is born again will live for Christ, but those who are just living the life of a Christian are only living for themselves."

Simon forced his thoughts from the woman on his left and turned an ear to Samuel's final words. "If anyone here finds they are trusting their salvation on their outward Christian appearance, I encourage you to meet with me after service about being re-baptized in Jesus. Baptism should be a change of heart, not a ritual into adulthood."

As Minister Bricker took his place in front of the congregation, Simon noticed Anna struggling to keep Steven Marcus still. In hushed whispers, she relented, allowing the child to sit on the floor. Within seconds, he crawled across the break in the benches and pulled himself up to Simon's knee.

A quick look in Anna's direction met apologetic eyes, and without hesitation, he picked the child up. Letting his son stand on his lap to look over his shoulder, Simon tried to focus on what Eli was saying.

"If we wash only on the outside but never address the inside, we as Christians will never amount to anything but a worldly, sinful people."

Simon thought, *Is that what I've done? Have I cleaned myself up well enough to look like an Amish Christian on the outside but ignored what's going on inside?*

Glancing only momentarily to Anna and then up to his father, who was intently listening to the service, he couldn't help but think about his *datt*. Not once had his father not put his family first, right after God, in everything he did.

Simon hoped that at one point, his son would gaze at him the same way. His father was a man who was clean both on the inside and out. He wanted to be that kind of person. He wanted to raise his son with the same moral values he'd learned as a child.

As Steven Marcus rubbed his nose and chin on Simon's shoulder, the child relaxed in his arms and laid his head in the crook of Simon's neck.

Never in his whole life had he felt so much responsibility for a child he barely knew, but something inside of him snapped to the point that he held the child tighter. Simon closed his eyes as he let Eli's words settle deep in his soul.

"Brothers and sisters, I plead with you to examine yourself. Being a Christian isn't about how we look on the outside. It's not our dress or coverings; it's not neat yards, straight rows, or even a set of rules that don't get us closer to heaven.

It's about how we share God's Word. It's about being honest about the condition of our hearts. Please remember what Jesus's instruction tells us. Love the Lord thy God and love your neighbor as yourself."

As soon as the last prayer was over, Anna stood and took the sleeping child from Simon's arms without uttering a word. Simon didn't move until Benjamin kicked the side of his boot, urging him along.

Anna disappeared into an upstairs bedroom. Simon helped a group of men turn the benches over to convert them to adjoining tables for lunch. Someone had lifted the cover off the large pot of simmering bean soup, filling the air with the pleasant aroma. Lingering as long as he could without getting in the way, Simon headed upstairs to grab a pair of gloves.

***

It was all Anna could do to escape Simon's longing eyes. His fresh scent remained embedded in Steven's hair long after she'd changed his diaper and fed him a bottle. Without realizing it, she had slipped into Simon's bedroom. The picture that had once hung from his rearview mirror was propped up against the gas light on his nightstand.

As she rocked Steven, she studied the picture. The young, dark-haired girl looked oddly familiar, and an edge of bitterness crept up her neck. The letter she had received from Cora over a year ago still played in her mind. For years, she had held onto the hope Simon would return to her, but in an instant and within a few lines on a piece of paper, all of her hopes and dreams washed away. And now, to find out Cora's letter was nothing more than a lie did little to ease her discomfort.

Her brother-in-law's words rang in her head. Perhaps Eli's words were meant for her, she thought. *Have I hidden behind my outward appearances without giving any thought to the actual condition of my heart? Have I been so angry with Simon I've entirely ignored God's teachings? I've forgiven him. Haven't I?*

At that moment, she felt no better than Cora by allowing her bitterness to put a wedge between her and Simon. She buried her nose in Steven's curls and took a deep breath, hoping to absorb more of Simon.

Closing her eyes, she prayed, "*Lord, only you know your plans for my life. Please fill my heart with joy and help me remember that your will is better than anything my human mind can conceive. Show me any area in my life where I'm not honoring you.*"

When she opened her eyes, Simon stood in the doorway of his room. After stepping inside, he said in no more than a whisper, "I need to talk to you."

Anna put her finger to her lips to quiet him and gently laid Steven in the center of the bed. After patting his bottom to be sure he was asleep, she moved to the window, and Simon followed.

Shifting from one foot to another, Simon asked, "How have you been?"

Ignoring his question, she commented, "*Denki,* for helping me with Steven."

"It was nothing."

"It was something, especially since he's never gone so easily to someone else for as long as I've cared for him."

Simon glanced at the bed. "He's taken to you."

"*Jah*, I'm pretty fond of him myself."

Simon turned toward the window and then back toward the door when noise from downstairs seeped upward. "There is so much I need to explain to you, but this isn't the place."

Anna paused to steady her voice, then continued slowly. "Not too certain we have much to say to one another right now. I'm still trying to sort through all we've been through and the path the Lord might have me on."

Simon looked distressed. "And I'm trying to do the same. However, I haven't been quite honest with you about something."

All was quiet as Anna pushed down a wave of anxiety. She trembled to think what it might be and wasn't too sure she could handle another blow against her already raging heart. Simon sighed when she dropped her head, rubbed her eyes, and said, "I'm not ready to hear what you might need to say, Simon. You must remember I waited for three years for you to come back and explain something…anything. But not a word, and now you're all antsy to confess something that you need to get off your chest."

Simon reached out to her, and she recoiled. "It's taken me this long to get over you, and you must realize it might take me just as long to decide if you are right for me again."

Simon dropped his arms to his side and watched as she picked up his son and left. The muscle in his jaw twitched as he let her slip away, unable to say a word to fix what his selfishness had caused.

CHAPTER 14

The following day, Simon received a letter from Mr. Buckhannon and two official papers. Confused, he glared at Mr. and Mrs. Buckhannon's signatures on both documents. Shuffling through the papers, he opened the handwritten note included.

Dear Simon,

With much sadness, I'm writing to inform you that Margaret and I can no longer care for Steven Marcus. After an intense medical examination, it has been determined that Margaret suffers from inoperable tumors on her spine. Her condition will continue to decline rapidly until she can no longer care for herself, much less Steven.

We are too old to continue giving Steven the care and attention he deserves. In place of our upcoming court date, we have instructed our lawyer to draw up the attached documents providing you with two options for Steven's continued care.

As you may have already figured out, we hired Anna Byler to care for Steven. We have come to love the young girl and know he will be safe with her until you decide what is best for your son's future.

Simon, I know we have not always made things easy for you, and we apologize for demanding you prove to us your worthiness. After spending so much time with Anna, we feel raising Steven as Amish would be in his best interest. And we also know Anna was the young lady you intended to marry before our Cora deceived you.

We pray you'll be able to work things out with Anna and trust you will do your best whatever you decide.

Please take time to seriously consider the enclosed two documents and determine what would be best for all concerned.

Sincerely,

Neal and Margaret Buckhannon

Simon carried the papers to his room and sat on the edge of his bed. The official documents bore a hole in his heart. He had been given two options. Accept full custody or put his son up for adoption.

He thought of nothing else but bringing Marcus home for months. But now, after Anna's continued refusal to hear him out, he didn't have much hope of reconciling Anna's heart. In his mind, taking on the responsibility of raising the boy hinged on her being his wife. Would it be in his son's best interests to accept custody if he meant he had to do it alone?

Maybe the Buckhannons gave him the option to sign over his parental right because that would be the child's best chance for everyday life. At least then, the child could be adopted into a loving family where both mother and father could be present.

Simon dropped the papers to the floor, rested his head in his folded hands, and cried out. *Oh, Lord. What should I do? I've made such a mess of things. I should have been honest with Anna from the start, but you know as well as I do that she hasn't given me much chance to explain anything.*

A knock on the door interrupted his prayer, and he picked up the papers and tucked them under his pillow before answering. *"Jah?"*

His mother opened the door. "Is everything all right? *Datt* said you received some official-looking papers."

Simon handed his mother the documents, and after reading the letter, she moaned and sat beside him.

"Oh, dear. I'm certain it was hard for them to relinquish the care of their grandson. But this makes things much easier, *jah*?"

Simon dropped his chin. "I'm not sure."

Confused, Naomi asked, "What are you not sure of?"

"They gave me the option to put him up for adoption."

Naomi straightened her shoulders, took a breath, and breathed out. "You're not considering that?"

Simon stood and walked to the window. Once littered with stars, the night sky started to cloud over, much like his heart. "I'm not sure what's best, but how can I think of raising him alone?"

Naomi stood and rested her hands on her hips. "Simon Kauffman, you best think long and hard about what you deem necessary."

There was no mistaking his mother's disappointment by the way the door rattled as she closed it. Eli's words played over in his head as he watched the frozen ground beneath him take on a fresh layer of snow.

Suppose we wash ourselves only on the outside but never address the inside. In that case, we as Christians will never amount to anything but worldly, sinful people.

He was certain Eli's words were a message from God. Almost like a warning of sorts. For the last four years, he'd put his wants and desire before everything and everyone else in his life. And here again, he contemplated putting his desire to have Anna above his son's needs. He'd done everything right. He came home, put back on his Amish clothes, and sold everything that reminded him of his *Englisch* life. He even started attending an Amish church, praying, and staying in God's Word.

But had he ever addressed the selfishness of his own heart? Had he genuinely repented his past sins? He had given the situation over to God on more than one occasion. When the Lord started to answer his prayers, Simon wasn't sure he liked the answers. Especially if it meant Anna didn't come along as part of the package.

As if the devil gave him permission, the scenarios swirled around in his head like the smoke from his eldest *bruder's* farmhouse across the lane. If he signed the custody papers, he might lose Anna, but if he put him up for adoption, the boy would have two parents instead of one. And if that happened, and without Marcus adding to the problem, he might just have a chance to start over fresh with Anna. She may never find out about what he had done, and besides, they could have plenty of children of their own one day.

Distressed by his thoughts, he put the letters in his top dresser drawer and went to the barn to help with the evening milking.

***

Anna re-read Mr. Buckhannon's letter to be sure she understood it.

Anna,

It's not good news. The doctors have discovered inoperable tumors on Margaret's spine. We thought her back issues resulted from the car accident; we were unprepared for the aggressive cancer diagnosis. We are devastated, to say the least. This changes so many things, especially our ability to care for Steven.

I know this is a shock, but we are praying you will consider helping us with our grandson for a little longer.

We had our lawyer draw up a temporary guardianship for Steven in your name. This gives you complete control over his care until his biological father decides what his next step might be.

Until then, I have enclosed a check to cover his expenses and your payment for the next two months. That should give his father plenty of time to decide if he'll accept full custody or if he'd like us to continue the proceedings to place him up for adoption.

Anna stopped and read the last line over again. A deep ache settled in her chest at the thought of Steven being adopted.

Please pray his father will do what is right and accept responsibility for him. A son should be with his father.

As we discussed, we gave Steven's father a time limit to prove he could care for him. Even though we regret not allowing him the opportunity to have Steven when he asked, there is nothing we can do about it now. All we can do is wait for his reply and hope for the best. We pray he hasn't changed his mind.

Sincerely yours,
Neal Buckhannon

Anna folded the letter, tucked it back inside its envelope, made a little sympathetic clicking noise, and said aloud, "How terrible!"

Rebecca asked, "Problem?"

"Mrs. Buckhannon is not doing well. They want me to continue caring for Steven for a couple more months."

"Is that a problem?"

"I'm not sure, is it?"

"Oh, Anna, don't be silly. We love him being here, and he brings you so much joy. Eli and I were just commenting on how happy you are these days."

Anna reached over and kissed Steven's head as he sat in his highchair, chasing cereal over his tray. "I have taken quite a liking to the little guy."

"I'd say it's more than that. You are downright smitten."

Rebecca turned from the sink and dried her hands on a towel. "So, what now? What happens after two months?"

Anna knelt to pick up wayward cereal from the floor and answered, "Mr. Buckhannon mentioned that they had sent a letter to the boy's father asking him what he wanted them to do. They gave him the option for adoption or to take full custody."

Mary Ellen sat on the floor playing with a stack of plastic bowls, and Anna let Steven join her. "It sickens me to think he might have to go up for adoption. A child needs to be with his family. How will he ever know who he is or where he comes from?"

Anna sat at the table and rested her chin in her propped-up palm. "I can't help but think of Emma. Look how upset she was when she found out *Datt* and *Mamm* kept her identity a secret for so long. To live sixteen years thinking you were someone and then finding out you were not that person at all."

Rebecca sat down beside her and took a long sip of her tea. "*Jah*, it was hard on Emma, and it was hard on us too."

Anna exhaled. "I'm heart sick. Steven means the world to me, and I know you warned me about getting too attached." She paused and smiled at the children playing on the floor. "Just look at him. He's so happy and content. What if his father doesn't want him? I can hardly bear the thought of that."

"Now, Anna, you're putting the cart before the horse? You have no idea what's going on in the boy's father's life. Maybe he's not able to care for him. We have no idea what his life might look like. For all we know, he might not have the means to take care of him properly. Wouldn't it be wiser for him to go to a home with two parents?"

Anna stirred a long dollop of honey in her tea. "I suppose you're right, but it doesn't make it any easier to accept."

"Remember, *schwester*, you're just his nanny; you have no say in what his grandparents or, for that matter, his father decides to do."

Anna thought for a moment and excitedly cried, "I have an idea."

"*Jah?*"

"What if I write Steven's father a letter? Perhaps hearing how well-adjusted he is, how he sleeps through the night, and how he isn't a fussy baby might help him make the right decision."

Rebecca smiled and patted the back of Anna's hand. "I'm sure it wouldn't hurt, but you must realize that God already sees what's going to happen, and he doesn't need your help."

Anna pulled her arm away. "I know He doesn't need my help. But it won't hurt if Steven's father knows what a good baby he is."

A small giggle escaped Rebecca's lips. "If a letter will make you feel better, then there is stationary in the top drawer of the hutch."

***

After chores, Simon hooked up his buggy horse and headed to the Bricker farm for the day. He needed to speak to Eli, and maybe he'd catch a few words with Anna.

Big flakes gathered in his horse's mane as he passed Willow Creek. So many memories were made there with Anna that just driving through the covered bridge made his heart pause.

All night he struggled to understand God's plan. He knew he needed to have faith that God could see things that he couldn't, but when things weren't moving in the direction he planned, he felt himself giving up hope. Perhaps Eli would have some wise words. Maybe he'd help him understand things differently.

Simon pulled up beside the yarn shop and tethered his horse to the hitching post to the right of the porch. Smoke swirled from the small chimney, and without looking for Eli first, he followed the small imprints in the snow to the door.

A bell above the door clanged, and he heard Anna holler from the back room. "I'll be with you in a minute."

Simon brushed snow from his hat's wool brim and stood inside the door. A few tiny giggles made their way behind the curtain separating the workroom from the showroom. Marcus, balanced on Anna's hip, kicked his feet as she stepped from behind the room separator.

"Simon? Has your *mamm* gone through all that yarn already?"

"*Nee*. I'm here to see Eli. I thought I might stop in to talk to you for a few minutes first."

Anna sat Marcus on the floor and pulled a couple of empty yarn spools from the worktable for him to enjoy. Without taking her eyes off her ward, she asked, "What do you want to talk about?"

Simon shifted his weight, knelt to stack the wooden spools, and showed Marcus how to knock them over. Interested, Marcus crawled over closer. "Us?"

Anna sat on the stool and watched Marcus encourage Simon to stack them again. "Why are you in such a hurry? I've already told you I'm going to wait on God. Every time I take things into my own hands, I make a mess of things."

A heaviness in Simon's chest forced him to clench his teeth, and he leveled out his voice before he answered. "Please tell me what I must do to prove to you that I'm sorry and I've changed."

Anna waited and let silence fill the air before answering. "You don't have to prove anything to me. I must prove something to myself."

"What's that?"

"That I can wait on God and have faith He'll direct my steps when the time is right."

"But what if it's too late by then?"

Anna tilted her head in his direction. "Too late for what?"

Simon stood and squared his shoulders. "I don't know. Maybe us."

Anna shuffled a stack of pattern books. "Simon, you're not rushing me into anything. And besides, I'm not sure how I feel about you…or about us for that matter."

Letting out a breath, Simon asked, "How much time do you need?"

Anna shook her head. "Oh, Simon, you don't get it, do you?" Her voice cracked as she continued, "I was devastated when you left; I crumbled into a pitiful mess for years. It's only been the last few months since I've finally felt like I had a purpose in life other than waiting for you to make up your mind and return home. Now that the shoes are on the other foot, you aren't liking it much, are you?"

Simon dropped his shoulders and let her continue.

Anna paused before she affirmed. "There is no doubt that I still care for you, but I've been unable to figure out if I'm still romanticizing our courtship or truly have enough feelings left to build a future."

His eyes lifted, and he asked, "So there might be a future?"

"I didn't say that. All I'm saying is that a little part of my heart still has a place for you. Is that more than friendship? I don't know. Only God can see that through."

Simon put on his hat. "I suppose I understand that. Do I like it? *Nee*, but I understand. But I came back for one reason: to prove I could be trusted and still love you."

"Is that the only reason you returned?"

Simon struggled with telling her the truth, and he veered from being honest at the last moment. "You were the foremost reason."

She shook her head. "Then I'm afraid you came back for all the wrong reasons. I assumed you returned to find your way back to God, and if I was your only draw, then you need to go home and think about the condition of your heart."

Anna shook as she picked up Steven and pulled him close. "I have way too much to do caring for this child right now, and I don't have the time for this. Perhaps we can talk again when my nanny job is finished, but until then, I think we both have some healing to do."

Simon reached for the doorknob and started to say something but stopped before letting himself out.

Anna rested her chin on Steven's head and patted his back. "It's okay; Simon and I have some things to work out, that's all."

***

Simon took a deep breath and tipped his head against the heavy snowfall as he stepped off the porch. He was in no mood to seek Eli out. All he wanted to do was go home and find a place he could sulk in private.

In less than ten minutes, Anna shot down every hope he had about their future. Thoughts came racing through his head so fast he couldn't distinguish one from the next.

What did she know about the condition of his heart anyways? Was she any better by holding on to all his past mistakes? What did the Bible say about forgiveness? Maybe he needed to point that out to her.

She had no idea about his plans for their future home or the herb farm he wanted to build for her. And what would she think if she knew she cared for Cora's baby? I bet her holier than thou heart wouldn't be so kind, now would it? Life was easier when he didn't have to worry about caring for a child he had never planned.

CHAPTER 15

Jacob sat with his head bowed. For weeks, an uneasiness surrounded him, almost like a warning he was about to face something much worse than his illness. At night, he would wake up, and the familiar feeling would return. What was God trying to show him? Was there something in his life He was trying to bring to his attention?

Wilma slid a plate of pancakes under his chin. "Please, Jacob, you need to eat. You've barely touched your food in weeks. You need your strength. Should I fix you a cup of Anna's tea again?"

"*Nee*, I'll eat." He picked up his fork and pushed the cold food around his plate. How could he explain the turmoil of feelings rushing through his head to his wife? Would she understand the pull he felt from God?

Wilma warmed his coffee. "What is it, Jacob? I wish you'd talk to me. I know something is eating away at you, and you've shut me out. Perhaps I can help you sort things out. Or we could take whatever it is to God and let him deal with it."

Jacob lifted his chin and sneered, "You don't think I've already done that?"

Wilma sunk into her chair. "How am I to know what you've done? You've barely said two words to me in weeks."

Jacob took a bite and thought. *She has no idea how hard it has been for me to walk away from my children. To shun them and turn them away. To give up my will and accept whatever I've been called to do. And now to hear promptings to go another direction entirely. How could that be from God? It must be my own will taking over my better judgment. It couldn't possibly be from Him. He certainly wouldn't assign me to one church and then put it on my heart to join another. It just wasn't right. It just couldn't be.*

While sipping his coffee, he remembered Bishop Weaver's words from the day he accepted the minister position for their Old Order Community. His friend, Mose Weaver, uttered a sentence that would be forever embedded in his memory. *It's a heavy burden that God has placed upon you this day, however, you can choose to make it one of your greatest job assignments. It's up to you. God has appointed you, but the responsibility lays in your hands, not God's alone. What you choose to make of it is yours alone. Will you decide to make it a joy or a burden?*

Chosen by lot, appointed by God, he promised to visit the fatherless and widows, help the sick and needy, and admonish sinners. But more than anything, to be a shining example of the gospel. Had he been that to his children and to the members of his *g'may*?

He pushed his plate away. "I'm just not hungry. I'm sorry you went through all this trouble. Keep my plate on the stove to warm. I may come back for it."

A cloud of mist filled his wife's eyes. "Sure. I'll do whatever you wish."

Jacob reached for her hand. "Wilma, I'm sorry. I know these last couple of months haven't been easy on you. I have a lot on my mind these days, and I just need some time to figure a few things out."

He slid his chair back and stood as if trying to find his words. "Stella had an *Englisch* Bible on her nightstand when she died. I looked for it this morning, and it wasn't where I thought it might be. Have you seen it?"

Wilma went to the cupboard near the back door, pulled a small step stool over to the counter, and removed the book from the top shelf.

Before handing it to him, she reached for his hand. "I pray you find the answers you're searching for."

Jacob nodded and retreated to the living room. Something happened during his illness that he couldn't quite explain. It was like a longing overtook him, and he couldn't stop living in the past. At every turn, he heard Stella's voice as loud as if she was still living.

In the dark of the night, with Wilma lying beside him, Stella visited him in his dreams. Their last few moments were so vivid in the hours right before dawn that the pain of losing her was heavy on his chest when he awoke.

Her last plea was for him to seek Jesus and to make sure all their children and grandchildren knew the truth of the Bible. She begged him to read the *Englisch* Bible and understand what Jesus taught about salvation. At the time, he didn't know why she felt it necessary, but he granted her the last wish, at least in words. And then life happened, and he'd forgotten his promise.

Only after Anna had nursed him back to life did Stella's words become louder. Not even after all four of his children left the church was her voice as clear. She cried out to him in the dark, reminding him of his promise.

Just that morning, he woke with tears on his pillow as Stella's last words hovered in the darkness. *Promise me, Jacob, I'll see you in heaven.* After coming close to death himself, her words haunted him to a point he'd been questioning everything he'd ever stood for.

Wilma stood over his chair with a fresh cup of coffee. "I warmed it back up for you."

"Denki," he muttered and pointed to the side table.

Wilma turned to leave, and Jacob asked, "Why did you allow Anna in when I was sick?"

His once surefooted wife lowered her head. "I prayed for help, and Anna knocked on the door within minutes."

He mumbled, "Coincidence."

Wilma stood in silence and let his word sink in before responding. "*Nee*, an answered prayer."

She slipped in her boots near the front door and wrapped a shawl around her shoulders. "I'm getting the mail."

A gust of wind blew around his chair with the opened door, and he watched Wilma, out the window, shuffle toward the mailbox.

Wilma had changed over the last couple of months. Maybe it was his brush with death, or perhaps she was tired after all they had been through. Whatever it was, she was quieter and more reserved than ever before. He found himself comparing her to Stella and half enjoyed the change.

Regret and guilt covered him, like the scarf Wilma tied around her chin. When he married Stella, it was for love and nothing else but to serve the Lord the best way he knew.

He never dreamed he would marry again. However, when it came time for the ordination of new ministers, he knew his only chance to be considered would be to take a wife. Jacob would be the first to admit those first few months with Wilma were difficult.

Never having children of her own, she didn't understand the family dynamics, especially regarding adult children. Let alone the challenges they faced when their community split.

When she opened the door, a whirl of snow followed her, and she assured, "No doubt about having a white Christmas this year." She handed Jacob the stack of mail and slipped out of her boots.

Jacob sifted through the stack of seed catalogs. He unfolded the Budget newspaper, releasing a letter to the floor. Wilma bent to pick it up and read the name neatly printed in the upper left-hand corner. "Emma Yoder?"

Jacob scoffed. "She could have left it on the porch. What a waste of a stamp." Wilma hung her coat and scarf on the peg by the door and headed to the kitchen.

Before releasing the flap, Jacob held his daughter's letter in his hand. For over twenty years of Emma's life, Jacob and she had been inseparable. A pang of remorse lodged in his throat at all he missed with his youngest child. Emma and Samuel lived less than half a mile down the road. But as far as their two communities split, she might as well live in Willow Brook, ten miles away. Pushing regret from his mind, he read her letter.

Dear Datt,

This letter is long overdue, but I must try once more to plead with you on behalf of your children and the grandchildren you barely know. Too much time has passed, and I have missed you so much during our separation.

Like every day in the past two years, life has gone on without much regard for the Byler family. We work, bake, take care of animals, and raise our families like our ancestors have done for centuries without regard for the hardships laid before us. I never dreamed of facing the future without you in it.

But I've wept instead when I've needed to talk to you. Even to sit in your presence, but again I'm unable to express the yearnings of my heart.

I know God has a plan and a purpose for all He does. A master plan I can't even begin to comprehend. And I know He doesn't ask me to understand, only to believe, trust, and submit to His will. I'm sure in His own time, He will explain, perhaps more importantly, when I'm truly ready.

However, in the meantime, He laid it on my heart to reach out to you one last time. I wanted to come to visit with you in person, but after you chased Anna away, I didn't want to upset you more. And to do so would have been wrong according to the shunning.

Lately, I am reminded of something you once told me while going through the challenges of my teenage years. You said to me that God does not want to make our problems smaller to make them bearable. But He wants us to let his grace become greater to make the task possible. That's where I find myself today. Praying that I will accept the job he has put before me. The mission of living so close but still so far away from you.

Datt, I beg you to reconsider this separation. I know Mamm shared her newfound love for Jesus before she died. I also know she made sure each of us children knew the truth regarding trusting our salvation through Christ and not through a set of rules and regulations meant to scare us into obedience.

I understand you've been put in a tough spot to follow the ruling of the Old Order, but please, Datt, open the Bible and read for yourself. The men of the New Order Fellowship are not wrong in their interpretation. Jesus gives us two things to follow. Love your neighbor as you love yourself, and no one comes to the Lord except through Him.

I don't know about you, but I want to be with Mamm and James in heaven one day, and the only way I will do that is through Christ. Not by how well I followed the rules of the Ordnung.

I'll leave you with this last thought...

The ties in a family are often formed by the challenges they face together. Please, Datt, I know we have not always agreed on everything, but I hope we agree that we need to share the burden of life together as one.

God gives us only one family and precisely puts us exactly where we need to be to bring him the most glory.

Your loving daughter, Emma

P.S. The Lord has granted Samuel and I a second chance at parenthood come this spring.

Jacob folded the letter on his lap and stared out the window. He relied on a living hope for his salvation all his life. One that was orchestrated by how well he followed the rules and what kind of person he was, believing his deeds would favor him with God.

Now, what his children and his deceased wife proposed was something he couldn't fathom. How can one trust in Jesus to secure salvation? This notion was the same thing that forced the excommunication on his children. To accept this as truth would lead him down the same path.

As he closed his eyes to lift a heartfelt prayer, Jacob heard Stella's voice whispering, "*Just say, 'Jesus.'*"

***

Emma donned a wrap and slipped out the side door into the clear, cold winter air. Carrying a plastic container full of peanut butter cookies, she braced herself for the mile walk to Rebecca's. According to Samuel, a surprise visit with her *schwester's* is precisely what she needed.

She still prayed the letter she'd sent to her *datt* three days earlier would make a difference. Agonizing over the words for hours, she hoped they would convey her heartfelt plea. She told Samuel she would never stop trying, even if the letter said it was her last try.

The scraping of metal wheels on the snow-packed road made Emma move off to the side. The buggy slowed as it passed and stopped a few yards ahead. When she made her way to its side, the canvas covering had been unsnapped, and Wilma sat waiting.

Emma struggled against the resentment rising up in her, the hurt and betrayal at her stepmother's hand laid heavy on her chest. If it wasn't for Anna's reassuring words about how Wilma treated her during their father's illness, Emma might have turned away.

"I want to explain a few things…" Wilma's voice cracked.

The expression on Emma's face must have unleashed a warning because Wilma pleaded. "Please hear me out."

Wilma blinked and stared into the mounting snow. "Are you headed to Rebecca's?"

"*Jah.*"

"Please get in out of the snow."

Emma pulled her coat tighter, but the cold still seeped in. Not so much from the temperature, but from the icy reception Wilma had always given her.

Shame filled Emma as she tried to find a way to graciously decline her invitation. *Honor thy father and mother…*rang loudly in her head, so she climbed into Wilma's buggy. *Oh, Jesus, forgive me. What sort of witness am I of your love if all I can think of is all the wrong, she has caused this family?* Folding her hands on her lap, she prayed, *Let me be your light.*

Suddenly calm inside, Emma knew what to do…*listen.*

Wilma snapped the reins and pulled back out to the center of the road. "Emma, I know we didn't have the time to get to know one another like we should have. And that is no fault of yours. I take full responsibility for my shortcomings."

Wilma let out a shuddering breath. "I waited so long to marry. When it finally happened, I was jealous of your *datt's* relationship with his children, especially you."

Her face was white, her expression concerning. "I wanted him all to myself." The steady clip-clop hung in the air as Wilma continued. "I poisoned your father against you all."

Emma filled with sorrow at her confession. "Wilma, you didn't poison him against us. We know *Datt* loves us. He turned his back on us because we left the church, which had nothing to do with you. That was our decision."

Shame etched Wilma's face. "But you don't know how hard I've worked to keep you separated and this community divided."

"I find it hard to believe your one voice had anything to do with it."

"Oh, Emma, you underestimate me. I've had a lifetime to hone my craft of stirring up trouble. If I want something bad enough, I'll do almost anything to make it happen."

Emma stopped and began to realize things through Wilma's eyes and asked, "But why?"

"If I encouraged Jacob to uphold his position, I didn't have to fear he'd push me out of his life in exchange for his children. As long as he was a minister, I was accepted. Even though I knew it was wrong to live a lie."

"Wilma, this doesn't have anything to do with his position. It has to do with the condition of his heart. We want you and *Datt* to know the truth and live by it. As followers of Jesus, it's not our job to save you. Only God can do that. But it's our job to show you the way."

Wilma started to cry as she pulled into Rebecca's driveway. "But you don't understand. If I kept him focused on the behavior-oriented path toward pleasing God, he wouldn't want to look into the inward transformation he was seeing in his children."

Emma let out a small gasp. "You know!"

Wilma pulled the buggy to a stop. "Oh, Emma, I know more than you think, and I fully understand what your church stands for."

"I'm so confused."

Wilma took a few seconds to respond and kept her eyes straight ahead when she spoke. "I'm ashamed to confess, but I can't hide behind a curtain of lies any longer. Emma, please understand, that when your father asked me to be his wife, it was my answer to a lifelong dream. I said yes before I realized his church still followed the rules and expectations that promised God's acceptance in return for their human effort."

"But you married him anyway?"

"I had reservations. I felt I could follow him even though I knew I was encouraging your father to be pridefully focused on his good works even though I knew it to be wrong."

Emma shook her head. "Do you believe Jesus is your answer to salvation?"

Wilma wrapped the reins around the knob and folded her hands on her lap. After waiting a few seconds, she replied, "I do, but I've come to realize I'm no better than the Pharisees in the Old Testament. They would honor God with their lips, but their heart was far from Him." Wilma paused and continued with a crack in her voice. "I know God hates the outward show, and I've lied to Jacob and myself in thinking I could continue this way."

Emma turned in her seat. "Admitting the wrong is half the battle. You know all you have to do is repent, and you can make it right?"

"I know, and I have. Confessing the part I played in all of this is part of that repentance."

Emma took off her glove and rubbed her forehead. "It's so much to take in."

"That's not all." Wilma paused. "In the beginning, I thought I could save him, and I prayed that God would open his eyes to see the truth. I believed that if I continued to petition God on his behalf and be a supportive wife, there would come a time I could speak to him about the truth. I…I knew we weren't equally yoked…but I wanted to be married so badly."

Wilma pulled her coat tighter. "After a while, I came to enjoy the status of being a minister's wife. The women in the community looked up to me. I didn't have that in my old *g'may*. And…and then I became jealous of you children."

"Oh, Wilma, you need to tell *Datt* all this."

"I'm certain your father is already figuring much of this out himself. God is already working on his heart; I can feel it."

Emma laid her hand across Wilma's arm. "You think so?"

"I do. He asked for your mother's Bible this morning, so I've decided to wait to see what happens. I want him to come to this on his own, without prompting and prodding from me. If he asks, I will certainly tell him that the gospel offers life-giving, life-transformation through the gift of salvation. But he has to realize that for himself."

"Oh, Wilma, I pray you're right. Wouldn't it be wonderful if our families could be restored?"

"Emma, I don't want you to get your hopes up too much. It's going to take a lot for him to leave a rule-following group where they believe that their behavior and beliefs are right and everyone else is wrong. He doesn't know any other way."

Emma smiled. "But he does know; I'm sure *Mamm* shared it with him, just like she did all of us."

Emma reached out and squeezed her stepmother's gloved hand. "Please come inside. It's time you got to know your grandchildren, and Anna and Rebecca need to hear all this."

***

Jacob waited until Wilma pulled away from the barn before opening Stella's Bible. A wave of emotion stung his nose as he ran his thumb over the thin pages. During the last few days of Stella's life, she insisted the *Englisch* Bible stayed tucked at her side.

As he sifted through the chapters, a small slip of pink paper stopped his thumb. A single verse in Stella's dainty handwriting, and his name stared back at him.

Luke 23:43 – Jacob

Jacob turned to the Gospel of Luke and read the verse aloud. *"Truly, I tell you, today you will be with me in paradise."*

Stella's dying words came to his mind again, and he tried to make sense of her message and the scripture. Re-reading the entire scripture about the crucifixion of Jesus, he laid back in the chair and asked, "Lord, what are you trying to show me?"

He closed his eyes, played the scene in his head, and thought. *The men who hung on either side of Jesus that day were thieves. Naked and alone, doomed to suffer for their sins on the cross without any hope for the future.*

One man hurled insults at Jesus, and the other rebuked him. The first thief asked Jesus to remember him when he entered his kingdom, and Jesus replied, "Truly, I tell you, today you will be with me in paradise."

Jacob opened his eyes and closed the Bible. As he wandered to the window, he thought. *That sinner didn't follow any rules. He wasn't even dressed in fine clothes; he was naked. What did he have to offer Jesus? He had no proof of his good works. He had nothing to give him but his belief.*

A letter he received from Matthew came to mind. A frantic search through a stack of papers on his desk revealed Matthew's plea.

Datt,

I know you struggle with understanding my decision to leave the Old Order, and I pray it will become clear one day. Until then, I wanted to share a few truths I've discovered.

First, we cannot earn God's acceptance by observing a set of rules and traditions. Not even the most religious, hardworking, and faithful person will be good enough to get to heaven without going through Jesus first.

Second, the purpose of the Old Testament's law was to show us we needed a savior. Not one of us can say we haven't broken one of the Ten Commandments. The law shows us we aren't good enough and need help.

And lastly, righteousness from God comes from faith in Christ alone to all those who believe in him.

Sarah and I will continue to pray for you.

Matthew

When Jacob received the letter more than a year ago, he tucked it away, giving it no more than a passing thought. But as he re-read the words, the thief on the cross came to mind. That sinner had nothing to prove to Jesus but his faith.

Jacob sunk down in a chair, buried his face in his hands and prayed. Oh, Jesus, help me have faith like that thief. *Lord, here I am. I have nothing good to offer, other than from this moment forward, I believe you are who you say you are. Please forgive me for all the years I've trusted in my own flesh to enter the kingdom of heaven. I can't believe*

I've wasted all these years. Please take me as a sinner of false hope and make me whole. Amen.

CHAPTER 16

It had been three weeks since Anna had heard from the Buckhannon's. Christmas had come and gone, and any hope of Steven's father coming to claim him vanished.

"You look tired, Anna," said Rebecca, as she passed. "You look like you're bearing the world's weight on your shoulders."

"*Jah*, I haven't slept well the last few nights," Anna admitted.

"I would think you would be as happy as me after *Datt* and Wilma showed up to church on Sunday."

"I'm pleased about that, don't get me wrong." Her eyes brimmed with tears and her voice trembled. "It's just that I fear for Steven. I hoped his father would have come for him by now. I'm afraid he's decided to put him up for adoption."

Steven toddled out from under the table and pulled himself up on Anna's lap. "If only he'd come to meet the little guy before he decided."

"Now, don't go and get yourself all worked up. You don't know anything for sure." Rebecca wiped John Paul's nose and asked, "Did you ever write that letter you mentioned?"

Anna picked Steven up and checked his diaper. "I started to, but then I got pulled away for some reason and never finished it."

"Perhaps it would help. His father doesn't even know him. At first, I didn't think it a good idea, but it might be your letter will show him what he's missing."

***

Simon kept his head hung low as he made his way to a seat on the wooden bench in the Yoder's living room, where church was being held that day. For weeks, he'd thrown himself into work in hopes of it drowning out the turmoil his conscience experienced. Even the sympathetic silence he'd received from his parents the last few days was deafening.

As he waited for the rest of the younger men to file in, he lifted his head high enough to locate Anna. Her starched white *kapp,* which laid slightly askew from Marcus pulling on her strings, swayed when she pushed the child's hand away. Propping him over her shoulder, Marcus caught Simon's form and muttered something in words only another baby would understand.

Anna turned in her seat and followed the child's outstretched hand. With little more than a recollection nod, Anna pulled the child to her lap and faced the front of the room.

Simon struggled to understand how his heart could be so wound up in things he obviously couldn't have. Was it punishment for all the pain he caused both Anna and his family over the years? Perhaps it was God's punishment for walking away from his faith and leaving Anna. He even asked his father if he felt the Lord would withhold the longings of his heart for past mistakes.

His father's words were little comfort as he explained God doesn't punish us because Jesus took that for us on the cross. But the Bible did say bad things can happen due to God's discipline. They are not a punishment for sin; instead, they are a correction, much like a parent would correct a child.

His mind and heart constantly battled over wanting Anna and doing the right thing for Steven Marcus. To have one meant giving up the other. What should he choose? He'd kept his secret too long for Anna to trust him again.

Simon mouthed the words to the chant-like songs that his friends and family sang around him, giving little thought to the meanings. He couldn't help but feel like a failure in everything he'd tried to do.

Surrounded by men who had taken a stand against their Old Order's teachings, he felt inferior to their strong faith. He was nothing but a liar. He said all the right things, dressed in the right clothes, and faithfully attended church every other Sunday. But was his heart right with God? Did he really understand his character?

The more he sat and tried to listen to Minister Yoder's teachings, the more he felt suffocated by his conflicted yearnings. Had all his prayers and confessions fallen on deaf ears? If his God was all he said He was, wouldn't He answer his prayers? Distressed by his doubts, he quietly slipped out the back door.

A burst of cold air burned Simon's lungs as he followed the path alongside Yoder's Strawberry acres to Willow Creek. The sun glistened through the frozen trees, and he pulled his waistcoat tighter and buried his hands in his pockets.

He sauntered to the spot where he and Anna had discovered their love for each other so many years earlier. He longed to roam through the woods, to sit on a log, and listen to the ripples swishing over the rocks. Life was so much simpler then.

He sat on a frozen overturned log, exhausted and quiet, waiting patiently for some form of reassurance. A sudden peace overcame him where a storm had been raging for weeks, and he prayed, *Forgive me. I keep stumbling, and I seem to keep losing my way. I want to do what is right, even though it means pain and sacrifice. Lord, make your will, my will, and help me accept it without question.*

After a while, he arose, opened his eyes against the bitter wind, and felt peace. He knew what he must do.

***

Naomi sifted through the stack of mail, and her heart leaped at the letter addressed to Simon. The familiar return address of Buckhannons' lawyer set off an array of emotions she tried to settle before returning to the house. She knew Simon struggled with accepting what he must do, and she prayed he would make the right choice for the sake of her grandson.

No matter how old her sons were, their challenges seemed to grow greater the older they became. As children, it was easy to put a band-aid on things and send them on their way with a cookie in hand.

However, now their struggles sent her to her knees more than ever. Her chest ached in the hollow of her heart for them to choose the Lord over their human desires. Her constant prayer was that they would humbly accept their path.

It was harder now than ever to be a parent of adult children. Their wise counsel fell on deaf ears most times, and she and Jebediah both had to stand back and silently watch. Jebediah often reminded her the best thing they could do was petition God on their behalf.

As she entered the warmth of her kitchen, Simon sat at his place at the table, sipping a cup of coffee. Naomi hung her coat, unwrapped the blue headscarf she had tied under her chin, and said, "There is a letter from the Buckhannon's."

Simon pulled the official-looking envelope from the stack and slid his finger under the sealed flap.

After a quick note from the lawyer, he laid the message aside and unfolded the handwritten letter.

To Steven's father,

I know you don't know me, but I am Anna Byler, the nanny Mr. and Mrs. Buckhannon hired to care for your son. It has come to my attention that you may consider putting your son up for adoption. I pray that you will prayerfully take heed to my words.

Your son, Steven, is an energetic and thriving eleven-month-old. His dark curly hair and brown eyes sparkle as he meets each new day. Once prone to tantrums, your son has become a joyful child.

As he grows, I see more and more of his determination to figure things out on his own. He is curious and loves exploring his surroundings, but don't all boys? He has a zeal for life and plays peacefully with my sister's children.

You may not be aware of my Amish upbringing, but I was raised in a culture where God, family, and community are at the core of our being. I pray that whatever your background may be; you have a strong faith and will dig deep into your understanding and do what is best for Steven.

Considering that, I beg you to ponder how Steven needs to know where he comes from and who his family is. I am so afraid that he'll never understand those things if you put him up for adoption. Children need to be surrounded by family, and I am heartbroken to think he won't know you.

I am confident the Buckhannons' will interview and choose a family best suited for Master Steven, should you decide on that path. Still, I wouldn't be able to forgive myself if I didn't at least try to help you see who your son is and how badly he needs you. A strong-willed child needs a strong father; from how his grandparents described you, you carry those qualities.

I understand you may feel you can't raise a child on your own, but I must believe one father's love can be sufficient if it comes from the heart.

I must trust in the judgment of Mr. and Mrs. Buckhannon, and they tell me you come from a strong family who will support you in all things. In times like these, we must put our desires aside and do what is right in the eyes of God...even if it goes against our hearts.

I will continue to pray for both you and Steven.

Sincerely,

Anna Byler

Simon's heart pounded so hard he could scarcely place the letter back in the tight envelope. Without a word, he carried the letter to his room and put it in the spot where his signed document once lay just that morning. Before dawn, he placed his decision in the mailbox, leaving his son's fate in the recipient's hands.

***

Naomi held her breath until Simon's footsteps made their way back to the kitchen and watched as he carried his empty cup to the sink. Hesitant to break the silence, she declared, "Whatever it is, don't let it still your peace. You've made your decision, and you must live with it."

Simon stood and stared out over the frozen landscape of his family's home and mumbled, "This is the hardest thing I've ever had to do."

Her son's pain, so clearly etched on his young face, spoke of great sacrifice in doing what he felt was best for Steven Marcus. She lifted a silent prayer on his behalf that God would show him Grace and understanding in accepting his choices. Shifting her weight to accommodate her aging knees, she said, "This is surely a matter to be prayed about. God will prevail; he always does."

Without turning his gaze, he retorted, "Please pray I don't wallow in this season long."

CHAPTER 17

The days flew by that week in anticipation of Mr. Buckhannon's planned visit. A letter had come earlier in the week stating that he would be driving through Willow Springs on his way back to Atlanta and wanted to stop by and see Steven.

She hoped Neal would notice how much Steven had grown and how he seemed happy and content in his surroundings. There was no doubt he had grown so much that she had to sew him a dark pair of trousers and a small light blue shirt to match the style of the other children in the community.

On the outside, he blended into his surroundings and had become a constant member of the Bricker household. She wondered if Neal would reject her choice of clothes for the child.

The sound of tires on the frozen driveway alerted her attention to his arrival. Wiping a smudge of leftover oatmeal off Steven's face, Anna headed to the door, balancing the child on her hip.

When she opened the door, Mr. Buckhannon had already made it up the front steps. "Welcome, please come in out of the cold," Anna said as she stood aside, letting Neal step into the warmth of the living room.

A genuine smile encased the older man's face as he reached out and held Steven's tiny fingers. "Look at you! You've grown so much in just a few months. I hardly recognize you." Neal poked Steven's belly. "Miss Anna hasn't had trouble getting you to eat."

Anna pushed his shirt into the waistband of his little pants. "Eating is no longer an issue for sure and certain."

Mr. Buckhannon wiped his feet on the blue and yellow braided rug at the door and took off his jacket. "I had some business to take care of in the area and had to stop and visit with you both."

Anna pointed to the pair of rockers under the front window. "Do you want to sit for a spell? I made fresh coffee and baked a batch of cinnamon rolls this morning."

Neal found a seat. "That sounds wonderful. I've missed your baking. The hospital food is anything but appealing these days."

Anna stopped and asked, "How is Margaret?"

Neal's tone turned serious. "As well as expected, I guess. She's in a lot of pain, and they keep her heavily medicated most days. I had to come home long enough to take care of some business, but when I get back, I'll need to start the process of moving her to a care facility. The hospital's done all they can do for her now."

"I'm so sorry. I know she was hoping to get back on her feet again."

Neal handed Steven a toy. "I'm afraid all we can do now is keep her comfortable. I've realized it's only a matter of time now. The cancer continues to spread, and at the rate it's growing, it's just a matter of time."

Anna shook her head and moved toward the kitchen. As she made a tray to carry in the front room, her thoughts made her chest heavy. Thinking about how Steven wouldn't remember his grandmother weighed on her and reminded her that her mother never had the chance to meet any of her grandchildren.

After setting the tray on the stand between the two rockers, Mr. Buckhannon took one of the filled cups and sat back in his chair. "Anna, I can't thank you enough for taking such good care of our grandson. It was refreshing to know he was well cared for, and I didn't need to worry."

Anna crossed her legs and took a sip of her sweetened coffee. "It's what you hired me for, and it was more of a joy for me than a job. Honestly, I'm not sure what I'll do when the little guy leaves."

Mr. Buckhannon's face turned solemn. "I'm afraid that will happen soon. I met with our lawyer the other day, and he drew up the final paperwork, and I delivered it to his father this morning."

"What did the father decide?"

"That is good news. His father has asked to have full custody."

Anna relaxed in her chair. "Oh, thank goodness. I've been praying he would make that decision. Steven needs to know his father and where he comes from."

Her stomach flipped slightly when she realized she would no longer be needed to care for the child she so fondly fell for. "When...when will he come for him?"

"That is what I came to tell you. If it suits you, he'd like to come this afternoon."

"Today?" Anna's voice cracked.

"Two o'clock, to be exact."

Neal watched as the young girl processed the timing. After visiting with Simon that morning, he figured out she and Simon had not reconciled, and Simon would be raising the boy on his own. He wished he could persuade Anna to give the young man another chance. However, after learning Simon had yet to confess to being his father, he felt it best to let it rest. He trusted things would work themselves out if it was in God's plan. Besides, everything would come out in the open soon enough.

Neal raised an eyebrow and asked, "What will you do next?"

Anna sat her cup down and leaned back in her chair. "I guess I really don't know. I suppose I'll return to helping my *schwester* in the yarn shop."

"By your tone, it doesn't sound like something you'll enjoy."

"*Jah*."

"You're so good with Steven; perhaps I could help you secure another nanny position."

"I've thought of that. But I'm not sure I can do that again. I'm going to miss him so."

A slight upward grin settled on Neal's lips. "Perhaps you'll not miss him as much as you think?"

"Ohhh...I'm certain of it. I've grown quite attached to him."

"I can see that, and I'm sure he'll miss you too. I'm just saying you might be able to set something up with his father where you could still be part of his life. He is a single father, so he might need an extra set of hands. Especially in the beginning when he needs to get accustomed to his schedule and all."

Anna wrapped her arms across her chest and pondered Mr. Buckhannon's suggestion. "You mentioned he comes from a close family, so I'm certain they won't need my help."

Neal smiled. "I wouldn't be so sure of that."

"We'll see. I'll offer my help and let his father decide."

Mr. Buckhannon stood. "Anna, I can't thank you enough for all you've done to help us out, and if I can do anything to help you find another assignment, call me."

Neal knelt and kissed Steven on the top of his head. "You, my little guy, I'll see soon. Your father knows how much it will mean to me to stay in your life and has agreed to keep me involved."

Anna's eyes lit up. "That's wonderful news. Steven needs to know his grandfather."

Anna walked the older gentleman to the door and let him engulf her in a hug. While the endearment was mostly an *Englisch* tradition, she felt comfortable in the grandfatherly affection. As Steven crawled to her side, she picked him up and waited until Mr. Buckhannon pulled away before shutting the door.

Only after she was alone with Steven did she allow a set of tears to release to her cheeks. She never dreamed it would be so hard to let him go. To abruptly stop caring for him and release him to the unknown. Would his father know how to calm him in the night? Would he be aware of his tendency to put every little thing he found on the floor in his mouth? What about his tender tummy resistance to cow's milk?

Placing the child on the floor, she retrieved a pad and pen out of the drawer and started writing down Steven's likes and dislikes and his sleep and nap schedule. The thought of him waking up in a strange room made her anxious, and she wondered if she should suggest she come help him adjust to his new surroundings.

At every hour, the clock rang, and Anna cringed at the finality of it all. Eli and Rebecca took the children to her father's so Eli could help her *datt* with a project in the woodshop. She couldn't help but be joyful at the door that had been opened concerning her father but devastated at another closing before her eyes.

Anna gathered all of Steven's things and placed them in two boxes near the front door. After a short nap and a fresh set of clothes, they sat on the floor playing with wooden blocks shortly before two.

The knock on the door alarmed her, and she peered out the window, surprised at the horse and buggy tethered to the post near the front of Eli's porch.

She couldn't see the visitor from where she sat and was instantly annoyed at the impromptu visitor. It wasn't a good time, with Steven's father due any minute.

Patting the top of Steven's head, she moved toward the door. A burst of cold entered the room as soon as her eyes fell on Simon's form. Looking around him, she said, "Simon, this isn't a good time. I'm expecting someone."

Tucking his chin to the wind swirling around the house, he asked, "May I come in?"

Again, Anna looked down the driveway and back toward Steven. He was playing on the floor, oblivious to the change about to take place. "For a minute, I suppose. At least to keep the cold out."

Simon stepped inside and removed his hat. Without moving off the rug, he stepped out of his boots.

Her mouth became dry, and she found it hard to speak when she took notice of his intended stay, Anna stiffened. "Simon, this really isn't a good time."

Simon's chest beat so hard, he was sure Anna could hear it from where she settled back on the floor next to his son. The muscle in his jaw tensed, and he swallowed hard. "Anna, I'm the visitor you're expecting."

"How can that be? I didn't even know you were coming."

"You did. I know Mr. Buckhannon was here this morning and told you of my arrival."

As if in slow motion, Anna looked to Simon and back to Steven. The curls that had flipped up at the back of Simon's head mimicked the tight curls covering Steven's head. The shape of his chin and bridge of his nose matched the man staring back at her.

A wave of nausea and pain at Simon's confession left her speechless. Steven crawled to Simon's side and held his hands up to him. Accommodating his son's request, Simon pulled him close and waited for her response. The uncanny way the child felt at ease with Simon left her knowing what he said was true.

"I…I tried to tell you multiple times, but I never could quite find the words." He paused long enough to let her absorb it all. "Please, Anna, say…something…anything."

She handed him Steven's jacket. "I wrote out his schedule along with his likes and dislikes. I tucked it in the side of that box."

Simon nodded and sat down in the rocker to balance Steven Marcus on his knee to put on his coat.

An eerie quiet surrounded them as they both struggled to make sense of the unfamiliar territory. "Anna, he's going to miss you. Please tell me you will help us make this transition easy."

Anna walked to the door, held it open, and took the child from his arms as he carried the boxes to the buggy. When all of Steven's belongings were tucked safely in the back of the carriage, Simon held his hands out to accept his son.

Anna released her hold on Steven and fought to control the tears teetering her bottom lashes. "You won't need my help. Your *mamm* is plenty capable of helping you navigate through parenthood."

The sting of her words took on a new level of discouragement. "Perhaps so, but I was hoping you'd agree to let me turn to you."

Anna remained still, trying to comprehend all he was asking. The pain of knowing he failed to be honest sent her spiraling into the depths of despair. In just a few minutes, all the progress she'd made to control her anxiety and offer Simon forgiveness resurfaced in an ugly place of bitterness.

When Steven wiggled and turned toward Anna with outstretched arms, she stepped back into the house and closed the door. Only after hearing Simon's footsteps descend the porch did she allow herself to breathe. Leaning back against the door, she slid to the floor, burying her head in her hands.

***

For the rest of the afternoon, Anna tried to busy herself with meaningless tasks until Eli, Rebecca, and the *kinner* returned home. As soon as Mary Ellen had removed her winter wear, she ran to the front room, calling Steven's name. The emptiness returned as her *schwester* explained things to her daughter. As resilient as children were, Mary Ellen accepted the change and went on about her play.

Rebecca laid her hand on Anna's shoulder. "It must have been harder on you than you imagined."

Anna wiped her nose on the wrinkled-up hankie she held in her hands. "You have no idea. It was far worse than I ever dreamed."

"Oh, Anna, what can I do for you? I was afraid you were getting way too attached to him."

Anna couldn't control the long hiccup sob as she tried to speak. Tenderly Rebecca pulled her close and let her rest her head on her shoulder. "It…it's…not…that. It's…Si…mon.

"Simon? I'm confused. Did Simon visit today?" Rebecca hugged her tighter. "Oh, you poor child. Of all days for Simon to stop by."

A shudder of deep-throated cries shook Anna's tiny frame, which Rebecca tried to soothe by whispering comforting words in her ear. When the last of the moans subsided, Anna pulled away and wiped her face, and blew her nose. Allowing time for Rebecca to question her. "What did Simon say that has upset you so?"

"He's Steven's father."

"What? How can that be?"

Anna rubbed her eyes with the palm of her hands. "All this time, he let me care for Steven and never told me he was his?"

In shock at Anna's explanation, Rebecca stayed quiet and let her continue. "I should have put two and two together. Steven took to him easily, and they favored each other. Why didn't I see it? I feel like such a fool."

"Oh, Anna, why do you feel foolish?"

Anna raised her voice slightly. "Don't you see? I gave my heart to two Kaufmann boys, and I can't have either."

Rebecca reached for the box of tissues and handed them to her *schwester*. "Who says you can't have them?"

Anna didn't answer but blew her nose and glared at Rebecca.

"Now, don't give me that look. I think you're too upset to see the big picture. I see God's hands all over this. How on earth did you, just by coincidence, answer an ad to care for Simon's child?"

"Oh, Rebecca, I miss him so!" she exclaimed suddenly. "The pain almost tears my heart in two. How will I ever live knowing that my little Steven is so close but still so far away?"

"I'm not entirely sure, but I know where you can find comfort."

"*Jah.*"

"And I can't help but think this is all in God's plan. Maybe once the shock of it wears off, you can stand back and see what the Lord is trying to teach you."

"I know you're right, and please remind me I need to concentrate on the blessing He gave me by allowing me to care for Steven, if only for a short while. But I'm still inclined to want my own way. And my inner will wants to be mad at Simon for letting me down again. It's like he left me all over again."

"Anna, you just need to get over that. You've been carrying around this resentment toward Simon for too long. I can't help but think it's half the reason why you struggled with anxiety for so many years."

Anna stood to set the table as Rebecca started supper. "Caring for Steven helped me through much of that. I honestly haven't felt that underlying edge of worry in the last few months. Maybe being busy helped me through the worst of it."

Rebecca added hamburger to a hot skillet and added, "I think the power of love is stronger than fear. When you were busy loving and caring for Steven, there was no room for your fear or anxiety to take root."

Anna pulled a stack of plates from the cupboard. "I must admit, I'm afraid of what will happen now. I don't want to lose myself in that self-pity again; to be quite honest, it's exactly what I've done all afternoon. The thought of being around Simon and Steven makes my pulse race."

Rebecca turned from the stove and said, "God didn't promise to keep us from trials; rather, He promised to use our trials for our good and His glory."

Anna filled Mary Ellen's sippy cup with water. "I trust in God's promises, really I do."

"Then you have nothing to worry about, *jah*?" Rebecca asked as she stirred in leftover potatoes, carrots, and a quart of stewed tomatoes into the cast iron pan.

Before Anna could answer, Eli walked in the back door. "Anna, there was a message for you on the answering machine. Neal Buckhannon called to say they are allowing him to bring his wife home and wanted to know if you would be free to come and help him care for her. You are to call him back at this number."

Anna took the slip of paper from Eli's hand and replied, "This is not good."

Rebecca asked, "How so?"

"Neal mentioned that there was nothing the doctors could do, and they were just going to keep her comfortable."

Rebecca shook her head and added a concern, "Tsk, tsk, such a shame. Perhaps you need to help. Besides, it will keep you busy, and remind you the power of love is stronger than fear."

Eli raised his eyebrows questioningly, and Rebecca mouthed, "I'll explain later."

***

Two days later, Anna carried out her small suitcase down the stairs and handed it to the Buckhannons' driver to secure it in the trunk before settling in the backseat. When she returned Neal's phone call, he explained how Margaret wanted to live at home for the last few weeks of her life. While he was grateful for Anna's help, he agonized over her returning without Steven in tow.

Anna wanted to question him about Simon, but knew it wasn't the time or place to satisfy her curiosity about how much he knew about the past she shared with Simon.

The drive to the Buckhannon home left her plenty of time to process what she might do next. While she could continue to work in the yarn shop, it didn't give her pleasure like caring for Steven had. She considered asking Mr. Buckhannon for a reference to apply for another nanny position.

Over the past few days, she had learned to leave her troubles in the quiet moments of God's presence. However, somehow, there was still an emptiness with the memory of Steven's giggle or the way his chin quivered when he didn't get his way.

A change of scenery is exactly what she needed to take the focus off herself and concentrate on helping her dying friend live out the last few weeks of her life.

As she got out of the car, Neal stood on the front porch. His eyes revealed a deep sadness, while a forced smile welcomed her with only a few words of thanks.

CHAPTER 18

Simon pulled Marcus onto his lap and laid his lips on his warm brow. "*Mamm,* are you sure this is normal? Perhaps I should go get Anna. She'll know what to do to bring his fever down."

Naomi laid the back of her hand on her grandson's forehead and chuckled. "Oh, Simon, you worry too much. The lad is just teething. Haven't you noticed the puddles of drool on his chin?"

"But maybe Anna will have an herbal remedy that will help."

The older woman returned to washing dishes and said, "You need to leave the girl alone. All you're doing is muddying the waters by your constant badgering."

Simon stiffened his shoulders. "I'm not pestering her."

"*Nee*? What do you call it then?"

A deafening silence filled the kitchen, and after a few minutes, Naomi added, "Exactly. God will find a way to soften her heart if it's meant to be."

Simon put Marcus in his highchair and pushed his arms into his coat sleeve. "And what if He doesn't?"

"Then you'll move on. But until then, I'm plenty capable of helping you with the child. So, get out of my kitchen and leave us be. Your father needs you more in the barn than I need you in here. I didn't raise all you boys to not know what to do with a teething baby." She shooed him away. "Now, out!"

Simon gave his mother a puzzled glance and headed to the barn. His mind, filled with thoughts of Anna, circled back to the disappointed expression on her face the day he'd picked up Marcus. The need to see her, mixed with a heavy breakfast, stirred in his stomach, making his mouth water.

Going against his mother's advice, he planned to swing around to the Bricker farm on his way to pick up lumber that afternoon. He prayed she'd give him a few minutes of her time.

He picked up a pitchfork with a faraway look and helped his *bruder* lay fresh bedding under the row of dairy cows. The familiar barn bantering did little to pull him from his mission to prove to Anna that he was worthy of her attention.

***

Anna pulled the blanket over Margaret's body and sat down next to her head. "What else can I do for you this morning? Are you up for a cup of tea yet?"

Margaret's weakened state left her little energy to even communicate. Still, Anna knew what the woman wanted most was her company. "Please…ju…just sit with…me."

"I'll sit right here for as long as you want." Anna stood and walked to the window. "How about I open the drapes? The sun is so pretty glistening off the frozen lake."

Margaret barely opened her eyes, but her lips turned slightly upward. Anna sat and asked, "Would you like me to read to you some more?"

"No…tell me ab…about Steven."

A sudden rush of remorse settled in Anna's chest. How could she admit to her friend that she had shut both Steven and Simon out of her life? Instead of answering, she smiled at her friend, hoping some comforting words would come.

Margaret opened her eyes. "Remember the day you told me about your friend?"

Anna tilted her head, trying to recall the conversation.

Margaret uttered, "Mr. Maybe."

"*Jah*."

In the two weeks Anna had been caring for Mrs. Buckhannon, the woman barely had enough strength to formulate a complete sentence, but Margaret took in a ragged breath and said, "I knew your Mr. Maybe was Simon. You coming to care for Steven was an answer to a prayer. God sent you here to fall in love with your future child, and you didn't even know it."

Anna started denying God's plan, but Margaret held up a shaky finger. "The Lord doesn't make mistakes. I've come to learn how much God loves us; even in the middle of our denial and sinful nature, he provides answers to our deepest desires."

Margaret pointed to a glass of water, and Anna helped her take a drink before the woman continued, "That afternoon, it dawned on me that our little boy was enjoying time with his future mother: you just didn't know it yet. I wanted to shout for joy because I had lain here for months agonizing over my inability to care for Cora's child. I prayed God would send us the answer. And he sent you."

Margaret struggled to clear her lungs, and Anna helped her sit up to dislodge a cough before the woman fell back to her pillow. After a few calming breaths, she continued, "It became clear to me that day that I'd be leaving this world soon, and once I realized you were the woman Simon's heart was wrapped around, I was at peace."

Anna asked, "But how did you know that?"

"Oh, Anna. Cora tried everything she could to entice Simon, but he never faltered from his love for you. He didn't even know Steven was his until after he was born. His plans were always to go back to you. Take the money he had made fishing and build you the house and herb farm of your dreams."

A small gasp escaped Anna's lips as she tried to say, "But…I thought…"

"I can see in your face what you thought, but the man loves you. How can you not see that? I had prayed for a woman to take Cora's place, and here you are."

Anna turned her face to the window, and silence reigned. When she returned her glance to Margaret, the woman had closed her eyes and slipped into a deep sleep. Later that evening, Margaret joined Cora by taking her last breath with Neal knelt beside her, with his words of endearment still heavy on Margaret's lips.

***

One week later to the day, Anna returned to Willow Springs. Pushing a snow drift away from the door with her foot, she stepped into the loving warmth of her *schwester's* kitchen.

The house was quiet, and she wandered into her room, threw herself across the bed, and then despite all reasoning, gave way to tears. She wasn't even sure what she was crying about, but she lay exhausted and quiet. A warm sensation surrounded her, bringing reassurance in place of where sorrow once reigned. "Oh, Jesus, please forgive me for not trusting in your plan," she murmured.

For the next few weeks, she hovered in a silent ache and remorse that hadn't left her since the day she closed the door on Simon.

Each morning, she woke with a prayer of thanksgiving and a plea to God to help her find a way to open her heart back up. Trusting in His ultimate timing, she busied herself and waited.

Spring had arrived early in Northwestern Pennsylvania, and new life could be seen everywhere. The trees were budding, the crocus was making its way through the thawing ground, and Eli's sheep were lambing. As she gathered eggs, her attention was drawn to the buggy making its way up the Bricker driveway. After locking the gate to the hen house, she saw Simon balancing Steven between his legs, pulling up beside her.

Simon looked anxiously at her, then said softly, "I'm taking the boy on his first fishing trip. I figured I'd start him out early." Simon paused and smiled at Steven Marcus's excitement at seeing Anna. "I'm sure he'd enjoy your company. He's…well I'm, hoping you'll come along."

Anna set her egg basket on the ground and walked to Steven's waiting arms. Simon handed the child to her, and she melted her lips against the child's cheek. Just as a barn cat wandered by, Steven kicked and wiggled out of her arms. His chubby little legs carried him away, and she marveled at his newfound freedom.

Left alone with Simon, Anna quietly gazed at Steven. After a brief silence, Simon spoke hesitantly. "What do you think? Can we pull you away from your chores?"

Simon looked straight into Anna's eyes, and she flushed under his steady gaze. Her voice shook, and she dropped her head as her answer surprised her. "*Jah.*"

She dared not look up as Simon stepped out of the buggy, fearing her eyes would reveal the longing in her heart.

Simon was speechless at her reply, and it took a few moments before he said, "I know I don't deserve to see you again. And I came here knowing your answer might have been *nee.*"

Simon puckered his lips and gave a clear whistle, which Steven responded to and followed his call. As they stood watching the child waddle his way back, Simon added, "If we let Him, God will heal what is broken between us."

With her eyes fixed on Steven's confident shuffle, Anna responded with a faltering voice. She recounted how God had given her peace about being still in the waiting and was satisfied in His perfect timing. As she talked, she expressed gratitude to God for shaping the path He had put them on. Simon picked up Steven and pulled Anna in close.

"Anna," he said tenderly.

"*Jah*?"

"The good Lord led us down two completely different paths and gave us both the time to navigate them alone—but don't you think His will for us is that we go the rest of the way together?"

"Do you truly believe that is what He wants for us?" she bade.

"Oh, Anna, I want that so much, I can't even begin to explain the yearning in my heart for us to be a family." His arm tightened around her waist.

She drew a long breath, then lifted her eyes to meet his. She brushed a wayward curl from Steven Marcus's eye and spoke quietly. "I love you both dearly, and if we can go forward together, it will make me happier than I ever expected."

He smiled at her confession and said, "Then it's a plan. And God willing, we will travel together for the rest of our lives."

With their son wiggling between them, Simon led them to the buggy to pick up where their love had ended so many years earlier. Simon drove them to their favorite fishing spot along Willow Creek with two fishing rods extended out the back side of the buggy, a jar of her famous peanut brittle, and a tackle box full of love. With all confidence that God would lead the way.

EPILOGUE

"*Mamm,* I admit I'm finding my need to come to sit at your gravesite less and less with each passing day. While I will miss our chats, I'm getting stronger in trusting the Lord, which is an accomplishment for me.

Over the past year, I have questioned my faith more than once. You taught us to put our trust in the Lord, but I haven't always done that quickly. It was much easier for me to trust in my own feelings. It was a continual struggle to tell myself that just because I feel a certain way doesn't make it true.

Ever since Ruth gave me your special gift and letter of encouragement, I've struggled to make sense of it all.

Life has been a challenge over the last year, that's for sure and certain. I have had to ask myself on more than one occasion if I was relying on my feelings or fears. I was so consumed with what might happen that I didn't allow myself to love. At times, I didn't feel I deserved God's love, let alone Simon's. The fear of what might happen kept me frozen in anxiety.

Now I'm not saying I still don't struggle with bouts of worry, but now I know where to turn when that little uneasy feeling creeps up. It's incredible how just whispering "*Jesus*" will calm me in those times of turmoil.

You would be so proud of Rebecca's husband, Eli, and Emma's husband, Samuel. They both have become such truth-speaking and faithful followers of Jesus. They, along with Bishop Schrock, have grown the new church to a point where we may have to split into two churches.

Even *Datt* and Wilma joined the New Order Fellowship. That was an answer to so many of our prayers. I'm sure you are smiling down on him and the changes he's made.

Mamm, you touched so many lives those last few weeks of your life, and your memory lives on. And you can rest assured that your grandchildren will continue what you started.

As I think over the last year, I can see how many prayers He has answered. God provided Emma with two little farm hands to replace the one they lost two years ago. Rebecca is with child again and is quickly filling her home with laughter. And Matthew and Sarah have been a blessing to Sarah's father at the sawmill during his illness.

And then there is how God opened my eyes through my dying friend to show me the path He had planned. In that, I prayed and patiently waited for God to soften my heart to the point that I had no other option than to trust in Him and Simon. And because of His every loving provision, Simon and I will be married in a few short weeks, giving Steven Marcus two loving parents.

Life sure has a way…let me take that back. God has a way of turning a fearful believer into a trusted daughter of the one and only true king. It took a long time to get here, but I can genuinely say, *The Lord is my helper; I will not be afraid.*"

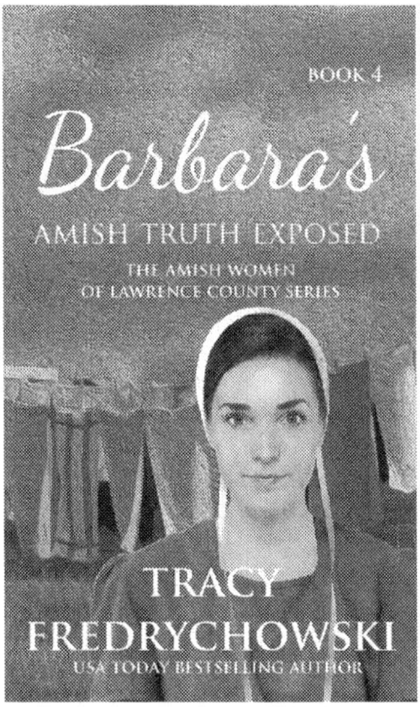

Read the next book in the
The Amish Women of Lawrence County Series
Barbara's Amish Truth Exposed

Barbara Wagler carries a heavy burden of shame after concealing a secret that dishonored her late husband's memory. Devastated by his sudden death, she faces the daunting task of raising their sons alone. When Joseph Wagler, her first love, returns to Willow Springs, Barbara wrestles with buried emotions and the threat posed by Roy Mullet, a widower from Sugarcreek. As she faces unresolved guilt and the fear of history repeating itself, Barbara embarks on a journey of truth-seeking, challenging her faith in *Gott's* promises and confronting her father's troubled past. Will she find the strength to confront her own lies and allow *Gott* to heal her shattered heart, or will fear and shame continue to dictate her path?

BOOKS BY TRACY

AMISH OF LAWRENCE COUNTY SERIES

Secrets of Willow Springs – Book 1
Secrets of Willow Springs – Book 2
Secrets of Willow Springs – Book 3

APPLE BLOSSOM INN SERIES

Love Blooms at the Apple Blossom Inn
An Amish Christmas at the Apple Blossom Inn

NOVELLAS

The Amish Women of Lawrence County
An Amish Gift Worth Waiting For
The Orphan's Amish Christmas

THE AMISH WOMEN OF LAWRENCE COUNTY

Emma's Amish Faith Tested – Book 1
Rebecca's Amish Heart Restored – Book 2
Anna's Amish Fears Revealed – Book 3
Barbara's Amish Truth Exposed – Book 4
Allie's Amish Family Miracle – Book 5
Savannah's Amish Ties That Bind – Book 6

WILLOW SPRINGS AMISH MYSTERY SERIES

The Amish Book Cellar – Book 1

www.tracyfredrychowski.com

ABOUT THE AUTHOR

Tracy Fredrychowski's life closely mirrors the gentle, simple stories she crafts in her writing. With a passion for the simpler side of life, Tracy regularly shares tips on her website and blog at tracyfredrychowski.com

In northwestern Pennsylvania, Tracy grew up steeping in the virtues of country living. A pivotal moment in her life was the tragic murder of a young Amish woman in her community. This event profoundly influenced her, compelling her to dedicate her writing to the peaceful lives of the Amish people. Tracy aims to inspire her readers through her stories to embrace a life centered around faith, family, and community.

For those intrigued by the Amish way of life, Tracy extends an invitation to connect with her on Facebook. On her page and group, she shares captivating Amish photography by her friend Jim Fisher and recipes, short stories, and glimpses into her cherished Amish community nestled deep in the heart of northwestern Pennsylvania's Amish County.

Follow her at:
Instagram - instagram.com/tracyfredrychowski/
Facebook - facebook.com/tracyfredrychowskiauthor
Private Group - facebook.com/groups/tracyfredrychowski/

Printed in Great Britain
by Amazon

55143405R00308